Kafka's Travels

D1127406

Kafka's Travels

Exoticism, Colonialism, and the Traffic of Writing

John Zilcosky

KAFKA'S TRAVELS
Copyright © John Zilcosky, 2003.
All rights reserved. No part of this book may be used or reproduced in
any manner whatsoever without written permission except in the case of
brief quotations embodied in critical articles or reviews.

First paperback edition 2004.
First published 2003 by
PALGRAVE MACMILLAN™
175 Fifth Avenue, New York, N.Y. 10010 and
Houndmills, Basingstoke, Hampshire, England RG21 6XS.
Companies and representatives throughout the world.

PALGRAVE MACMILLAN is the global academic imprint of the
Palgrave Macmillan division of St. Martin's Press, LLC and of Palgrave
Macmillan Ltd. Macmillan® is a registered trademark in the United States,
United Kingdom and other countries. Palgrave is a registered trademark in
the European Union and other countries.

ISBN 1-4039-6767-9

Library of Congress Cataloging-in-Publication Data
Zilcosky, John.
Kafka's travels : exoticism, colonialism, and the traffic of writing / John
Zilcosky.
    p.   cm.
  Includes bibliographical references and index.
  ISBN 0–312–23281–0 cl., 1-4039-6767-9 pb.
  1. Kafka, Franz, 1883–1924—Criticism and interpretation.   2. Kafka,
Franz, 1883–1924—Journeys.   I. Title.

PT2621.A26 Z36   2002
833'.912—dc21

                                                                2002029082

A catalogue record for this book is available from the British Library.

Design by Letra Libre, Inc.

First paperback edition: October 2004
10 9 8 7 6 5 4 3 2 1

Printed in the United States of America

*To my parents
and the memory of Charles Bernheimer*

Contents

Plates follow Chapter Four

Acknowledgements

It gives me great pleasure to acknowledge all the people who helped me over the years of researching and writing this book. First and most importantly, I remember the late Charles Bernhéimer, who helped me to conceive this project eight years ago and offered me an enduring model of intellectual generosity. I also thank Mark Anderson, who read through the entire manuscript with great care and first encouraged me to publish it, and Frank Trommler, who gave me important historical advice and stood by my side when I really needed him. Others who have read all or part of this manuscript (in its various drafts), presenting often lively criticism, include: David Clark, Rebecca Comay, Stanley Corngold, Ned Fox, Gerald Gillespie, Rolf Goebel, John Noyes, Jean-Michel Rabaté, Jim Retallack, Charity Scribner, Fred Seliger, Peter Stallybrass, Klaus Wagenbach, Silke Weineck, Liliane Weissberg, and David Wellbery. I also thank Steve Statler for the mellow pleasures of an old friendship, and for offering—after he read through the penultimate draft—the invaluable perspective of a non-academic Kafka aficionado. For research grants in Germany, I am grateful to the Fulbright Commission, the DAAD, the Comparative Literature and Literary Theory Program at the University of Pennsylvania (especially its benevolent and savvy administrator, Joanne Dubil), the Canadian Social Sciences and Humanities Research Council, and the Connaught Fund at the University of Toronto. The librarians at the Deutsches Literaturarchiv, the Berlin Staatsbibliothek (especially Dr. Gisela Herdt), and the University of Toronto (especially Perry Hall) greatly facilitated my research. Gabi Gottwald and Sólveig Arnarsdóttir provided homes away from home in Berlin. For the opportunity to present drafts of my work as public lectures, I thank the Humanities Center and the German Department at Williams College (Helga Druxes, Bruce Kieffer, and Gail Newman), and the University of Toronto's Joint Initiative in German and European Studies. My "mentor" at the University of Toronto, Janet Paterson, generously helped me find my way in a new university. My research assistants Hang-Sun Kim and Christine Koch assisted in preparing the manuscript for publication; they devoted long hours and extraordinary care and diligence to rendering the book presentable and bibliographically accurate. Finally, I am grateful to my father, who offered me, at a crucial moment, his wisdom on completing long and ostensibly unfinishable projects, and to my mother, who taught me how to tell stories (and listen to them). And I thank Rebecca Wittmann, whose critical yet kind eye accompanied me through the final phases of writing and re-writing, and who always seemed to know exactly how much to help. She even promised to go traveling with me when it was all over.

Earlier versions of chapters five, six, and the epilogue appeared, respectively, in *A Companion to the Works of Franz Kafka,* ed. James Rolleston (Rochester, NY, 2002), *German Life and Letters* 52 (July 1999), and *Alphabet City* 8 (2002). Permission to reprint is here gratefully acknowledged.

List of Illustrations

brief childhood'" (Walter Benjamin).
Archiv Klaus Wagenbach, Berlin.

11. A map of central Europe, from the 1910 Baedeker's
    Austria-Hungary: Handbook for Travelers owned by Kafka.
    Karl Baedeker, *Österreich-Ungarn (nebst Cetinje
    Belgrad Bukarest): Handbuch für Reisende* (Leipzig, 1910).

12. The Métro station Père Lachaise.
    Archiv Hartmut Binder, Ditzingen.

13. View of Broadway from above;
    originally printed in Arthur Holitscher's
    Amerika: Today and Tomorrow.
    Arthur Holitscher, *Amerika: heute und morgen* (Berlin, 1912).

14. Parisian prostitutes.
    Bibliothéque nationale de France, Paris.

15. Photograph of lynching—ironically subtitled
    "An Idyll in Oklahoma [*sic*]" by Arthur Holitscher
    in his critical travelogue about America.
    Holitscher, *Amerika: heute und morgen.*

16. Title page of the 1910 Baedeker's *Austria-Hungary:
    A Handbook for Travelers,* which Kafka owned;
    it announces 143 maps and plans, as well
    as two panoramas and six floor plans.
    Baedeker, *Österreich-Ungarn.*

17. Cover of *The Sugar Baron* (volume 54 of
    Schaffstein's *Little Green Books*), the book that,
    according to Kafka, "affects me so deeply that
    I feel it is about myself."
    Oskar Weber, *Der Zuckerbaron* (Cologne, 1914).

18. Sketch from *The Sugar Baron,* accompanying
    the narrator's description of shooting an ape,
    who, after falling, "sat exactly like a man with
    his back against the trunk" and "looked at me
    almost reproachfully with big, dark eyes."
    Weber, *Der Zuckerbaron.*

19. Cover of *In the Hinterlands of German East Africa*
    (volume 3 of Schaffstein's *Little Green Books*).
    Adolf Friedrich zu Mecklenburg, *Im Hinterlande
    von Deutsch-Ostafrika* (Cologne, 1910).

20. Sketch from *In the Hinterlands of German East Africa*
    accompanying the narrator's description of a lion

Note on Abbreviations and Translations

I use the following abbreviations to refer to Kafka's works. Whenever I have found it necessary to emend the standard translations, I note this parenthetically. I refer to Kafka's original German only when the nuance of analysis requires this, but I do cite the German page numbers throughout (or, in the case of some letters and diary entries, the pertinent dates), so that readers can easily locate citations in the original.

At any point in the text where no translation is cited, the translation is my own.

A   *Amerika.* Trans. Edwin and Willa Muir. New York: Schocken, 1974. See *V.*

B   *Briefe, 1902–1924.* Ed. Max Brod. Frankfurt a. M.: Fischer, 1958. See *L.*

BO   *Briefe an Ottla und die Familie.* Ed. Hartmut Binder and Klaus Wagenbach. Frankfurt a. M: Fischer, 1974. See *LO.*

BF   *Briefe an Felice.* Ed. Erich Heller and Jürgen Born. Frankfurt a. M.: Fischer, 1967. See *LF.*

BM   *Briefe an Milena.* Ed. Jürgen Born and Michael Müller. Frankfurt a. M.: Fischer, 1986. See *LM.*

BV   *Letter to His Father/Brief an den Vater* (bilingual edition). Trans. Ernst Kaiser and Eithne Wilkins. New York: Schocken, 1966.

C   *The Castle.* Trans. Mark Harman. New York: Schocken, 1998. See *S.*

D   *The Diaries, 1910–1923.* Trans. Joseph Kresh and Martin Greenberg. New York: Schocken, 1976. See *Ta* and *EFI.*

DL   *Drucke zu Lebzeiten.* Ed. Wolf Kittler, Hans-Gerd Koch, Gerhard Neumann. Frankfurt a. M.: Fischer, 1994. See *MO.*

DS   *Description of a Struggle.* Trans. Tania and James Stern. New York: Schocken, 1958. See *NSI* and *NSII.*

EFI   Max Brod/Franz Kafka. *Eine Freundschaft.* Vol. 1 (Reiseaufzeichnungen). Ed. Malcolm Pasley. Frankfurt a. M.: Fischer, 1987. See *D* and *M.*

EFII   Max Brod/Franz Kafka. *Eine Freundschaft*. Vol. 2 (Briefwechsel). Ed. Malcolm Pasley. Frankfurt a. M.: Fischer, 1989. See *B*.

GW   *The Great Wall of China and Other Short Works*. Trans. Malcolm Pasley. London: Penguin, 1991. See *NSI* and *NSII*.

L   *Letters to Friends, Family, and Editors*. Trans. Richard and Clara Winston. New York: Schocken, 1977. See *B*.

LF   *Letters to Felice*. Trans. James Stern and Elisabeth Duckworth. New York: Schocken, 1973. See *BF*.

LM   *Letters to Milena*. Trans. Philip Boehm. New York: Schocken, 1990. See *BM*.

LO   *Letters to Ottla and the Family*. Trans. Richard and Clara Winston. New York: Schocken, 1982. See *BO*.

M   *The Metamorphosis, the Penal Colony, and Other Stories*. Trans. Willa and Edwin Muir. New York: Schocken, 1975. See *EFI* and *DL*.

MO   *Metamorphosis and Other Stories*. Trans. Malcolm Pasley. New York: Penguin, 2000. See *DL*.

NSI   *Nachgelassene Schriften und Fragmente*. Vol. 1. Text. Ed. Malcolm Pasley. Frankfurt a. M.: Fischer, 1993. See *DS, GW, WP*.

NSI¹   *Nachgelassene Schriften und Fragmente*. Vol. 1. Apparatband. Ed. Malcolm Pasley. Frankfurt a. M.: Fischer, 1993.

NSII   *Nachgelassene Schriften und Fragmente*. Vol. 2. Text. Ed. Jost Schillemeit. Frankfurt a. M.: Fischer, 1992. See *DS, GW, WP*.

P   *Der Proceß*. Ed. Malcolm Pasley. Frankfurt a. M.: Fischer, 1990. See *T*.

S   *Das Schloß*. Ed. Malcolm Pasley. Frankfurt a. M.: Fischer, 1982. See *C*.

T   *The Trial*. Trans. Breon Mitchell. New York: Schocken, 1998. See *P*.

Ta   *Tagebücher*. Ed. Hans-Gerd Koch, Michael Müller, Malcolm Pasley. Text. Frankfurt a. M.: Fischer, 1990. See *D*.

Ta¹   *Tagebücher*. Ed. Hans-Gerd Koch, Michael Müller, Malcolm Pasley. Apparatband. Frankfurt a. M.: Fischer, 1990.

V   *Der Verschollene*. Ed. Jost Schillemeit. Frankfurt a. M.: Fischer, 1983. See *A*.

WP   *Wedding Preparations in the Country*. Trans. Ernst Kaiser and Eithne Wilkins. London: Secker and Warburg, 1973. See *NSI* and *NSII*.

Become a traveler

—diary, July 31, 1917

Introduction

Kafka's Travels?

"Kafka's travels?" "Did he travel?," people ask me. "Didn't he always stay in Prague?" Kafka indeed never moved from Prague until the final year of his life, and, yes, his travels were limited to short trips through Europe. But Kafka was an avid *textual traveler,* a voyager who traveled as a reader and a writer despite (or because of) his personal stasis.[1] I discovered this in one of Kafka's letters to his first fiancée, Felice Bauer, where I came across one of the eccentric biographical details that, according to Roland Barthes, force us to reassess an author's entire oeuvre.[2] The creator of the claustrophobic narratives *The Metamorphosis* and *The Trial,* it turned out, was also an enthusiastic reader, throughout his life, of popular utopian colonial travel stories written mostly for boys. According to Kafka, who was thirty-three years old when he wrote this 1916 missive, the exotic dime-store adventure series known as Schaffstein's *Little Green Books* (*Grüne Bändchen*) included his "favorite" books. He tells Felice with great solemnity that one of these volumes "affects me so deeply that I feel it is about myself, or as if it were the book of rules for my life, rules I elude, or have eluded" (*LF* 532; *BF* 738, trans. rev.). Spurred on by this vision of the otherworldly poet of alienation being so moved by juvenile adventure stories, I began my own adventure, my own detectival quest.

I searched Kafka's letters and diaries for further references and, later, examined these pulp chronicles themselves. They generally tell the simple stories of down-on-their-luck Germans gaining wealth, satisfaction, and a "*zweite Heimat*" (second home) abroad.[3] Kafka claimed to "especially love" three of these volumes and was moved to tears in 1913 by a fourth one (*EFI* 300n30; *D* 248; *Ta* 615). Even on his deathbed, no longer able to speak, Kafka refers to popular travel literature—scribbling a request, "*Library of Travel and Adventure,* Brockhaus Verlag, Leipzig," onto a slip of paper

(*L* 416; *B* 484). Kafka's lifetime ardor extended to travel writing in general. He avidly read Goethe's, Hebbel's, Fontane's, and Flaubert's travel diaries and, as a look at his library reveals, various other travel memoirs: about South America, Palestine, the United States, Africa, Mexico, the South Seas, and the North Pole. While working my way through these books, I realized that Kafka's own writings are also shot through with stories about journeys—to America, to China, to Africa, to a penal colony, and to an unnamed village at the foot of a castle hill. Moreover, Kafka's work includes the infamous traveling salesman who turns into a bug, as well as a rigorous detailing of travel clothing and the means of travel: by foot, bicycle, tram, train, automobile, ship, airplane. Kafka, it turned out, was a travel writer of sorts. Hidden within his telltale narratives of desperate claustrophobia were also the hopes and promises of the journey.

Kafka's interest in travel began in his youth and led to his own limited travels. Probably incited by postcards from his "interesting cousin from Paraguay" and his maternal uncles (who became popular heroes of a sort when, to the family's great pride, they left home and made careers in Spain, Panama, and Africa),[4] Kafka began to imagine that travel could liberate him from Prague; that is, from the strictures of home, school, and office that, to this day, stereotypically define his character. If Prague was the "*Mütterchen,*" the little mother with claws who does not let go, as Kafka remarked in one of his first extant writings, then only travel beyond her borders could liberate him (*L* 5; *B* 14). After graduating from the Gymnasium in 1901, he made his first trip abroad, voyaging by himself to the North Sea islands of Norderney and Heligoland. Later, in his early twenties, Kafka traveled several times to the Bohemian countryside, and his feelings about these trips are recorded in letters that reveal a surprisingly jovial and virile young man—a version of Kafka generally obscured in biographies (see figure 1). As Kafka writes from Zuckmantel in 1905, he mingles happily with "people and womenfolk" and has become "rather lively" (*L* 20; *B* 32). He then flirtatiously sends Max Brod—Kafka's best friend, travel companion, and eventual editor—a postcard addressed in Kafka's handwriting but inscribed (beneath the picture of a forest) with a woman's hand, "This *is* a forest, in this forest one can be happy. So come along here, then!"[5] According to Brod, this playful card issues from Kafka's first sexual liaison.

In 1907 in Triesch, following a mind-numbing law internship in Prague, Kafka reports to Brod a similar *joie de vivre:* "I ride around a lot on the motorbike, swim a lot, lie nude in the grass by the pond for hours, stay in the park until midnight with a bothersomely infatuated girl." All of this, Kafka claims, after having already "set up a merry-go-round, [. . .] played a lot of billiards, taken long walks, drunk a lot of beer" and, on top of everything, "fall[en] in love" (L 25–6; B 37–8, trans. rev.). Travel was, for Kafka, as it still is for many, equivalent with vibrant living, material pleasure, and sexuality. It marked his entrance into what he, following Flaubert, repeatedly referred to as "le vrai."[6] Kafka views the foreign ambiences with a sensual delight almost completely absent in Prague. In 1908, after returning from Spitzberg in the Bohemian Forest, he writes: "After the happy eight days in the Bohemian Forest—the butterflies there fly as high as the swallows do at home—I have now been in Prague for four days, and so helpless" (L 45; B 59, trans. rev.). Many years later, he remembers having his only satisfying sexual experiences while traveling: having "never yet been intimate with a woman apart from the time in Zuckmantel. And then again with the Swiss girl in Riva" (D 365; Ta 795). Finally, less than a year before his death, he ends one of his last letters to Brod with an unabashedly nostalgic reference to their 1911 journey to Switzerland: "Farewell, and may the Lugano sun shine upon us—innocent or guilty—once again" (L 394; B 461, trans. rev.).

These letters from the countryside (as well as Kafka's later, 1909–12 diaries from Switzerland, Italy, and Paris) present a man who has found, in traveling, the pleasures that eluded him in the confines of Prague (see figures 2–5). Brod remarks on the joys of traveling with Kafka: "Never in my life have I been so equably cheerful as during weeks of holiday spent with Kafka. We turned into happy children, we hit upon the queerest, loveliest jokes [. . .] even his hypochondria was still entertaining and full of ideas." And, later, "We used to swim, we used to sun ourselves, we got hardened."[7] Brod correctly remarks that Kafka's 1909–12 travel notes, taken during the friends' brief summer holidays in Europe, are uncharacteristically "pleasant." A distinctly "brighter mood" prevails in comparison with the better-known Prague diaries (D 489). Moreover, as Brod writes in his 1927 afterword to Kafka's novel about America, Kafka's fantasies about travel were almost always benevolent, if not utopian: he loved to read travel books, longed for "free space and distant lands,"[8] and even had one of his protagonists imagine that Americans wore an "unchanging smile of happiness" (A 45; V 62–63).

Brod's comments help to explain Kafka's fantasies in his early letters from the Bohemian countryside—when he first began to imagine that more travel and, finally, emigration could lead to a new and better life. The possible destinations mentioned by Kafka, already before he turns thirty years old, boggle the mind with their apparent randomness: Paris, Vienna, Spain, South America, the Azores, Madeira, Palestine, and a generic island in the south. In the end, the place itself is not as important as is the fact that it is elsewhere—beyond Prague, beyond the family, beyond the office. In the words of Charles Baudelaire in "N'import où hors du monde," this place is anywhere "où je ne suis pas." Two more letters from 1907 will serve to exemplify Kafka's typically utopian, unspecific understanding of travel. In August, from rural Triesch, he asks Max Brod to learn Spanish with him so that the two of them can procure a position in Spain through Kafka's uncle. If this does not work, Kafka writes, "we would go to South America or the Azores, to Madeira." Just two months later, South America and the Azores seem to be forgotten, and they are replaced with another remarkably vague, exotic space: "I am in the Assicurazioni-Generali [Kafka's first employer in Prague] and nonetheless have hope of someday sitting in chairs in very faraway countries, looking out of the office windows at fields of sugar cane or Mohammedan cemeteries"(*L* 25, 35; *B* 37, 49, trans. rev.).

Travel and Writing

Why do these utopian fantasies matter? On the surface, nothing could be more banal: a young man has a boring bureaucratic job and dreams of a wondrous elsewhere. But this fantasy, it turns out, is integral to Kafka's writing. Laurence Rickels has already pointed out how travelers permeate Kafka's work. But neither Rickels nor anyone else has examined this in a methodical way: it is indeed "striking and curious," as Rickels claims, that scholars have paid so much attention to "the bachelor figure, the artist figure, the student figure and so on," while "none has dealt, with equal rigor, with the traveler figure."[9] Traveler figures extend through Kafka's texts: from the apparently static, claustrophobic ones (*The Metamorphosis* and *The Trial*) to the more obviously foreign ones (*Amerika,* "A Report to an Academy," "In the Penal Colony," *The Castle,* "The Hunter Gracchus"). In the former, Kafka employs travel to indicate abrupt upheavals and transformations in his characters' lives: Gregor Samsa, a "traveler" (*Reisender*) by trade, and Josef K., whose guard wears something resembling a "traveler's outfit" (*Reiseanzug*), will both witness their internal and external landscapes begin to "travel" extraordinarily. In Kafka's texts about foreign lands, travel likewise denotes disruption—here, of an often-utopian journey: The foreign world's strangeness is so magnified in *Amerika* and *The Castle,* for example, that the main character will never be able to be at home in it. Karl Rossmann does not make it to the exotic "Nature Theater of Oklahoma [*sic*]," and K. fails to be accepted by the Castle. Neither will ever transform the foreign world into, in the words of one of Kafka's favorite adventure heroes, a "second *Heimat.*"[10] If, as one contemporary travel writer claimed in 1916, fin de siècle exoticism could be summarized as a "*Heimweh nach der Fremde*" (homesickness for a foreign country), then Kafka's characters suffer from this paradoxical nostalgia as well.[11] Unlike the heroes of the contemporary adventure stories, however, they never cure what ails them, no matter how far they travel.

I argue that travel is, for Kafka, an overlooked theme promising utopia and, what is more, a metaphor for the internal processes of writing itself.[12] As Gilles Deleuze and Félix Guattari argue in their *Kafka: Toward a Minor Literature,* writing is an "immobile voyage that stays in one place," and, in the words of Charles Grivel, "writing means *not keeping still, going where one isn't.*"[13] Writing is traveling without going anywhere: a peculiarly static journey that is a magical supplement for the stay-at-home. Like travel, writing promises the possibility of utopia. Writing can take one, Kafka insists, to the "holiest" spaces visited by pilgrims—even to the realm of "the pure, the true, and the immutable" (*WP* 99; *D* 387; *NSII* 77; *Ta* 838). And writing proposes the same tension within utopia that travel does: it promises a utopia yet can always only present this in an incomplete form. Both writing and travel consist in continual processes of deferral.

In Kafka's personal experience, however, an important distinction between travel and writing pertains: Whereas the writer (who never finishes his novels) does *not* arrive, the traveler *does* arrive (and never in utopia, rather only in Paris, Berlin, Vienna). Writing thus seems to possess an endless promise that supersedes—and even opposes—actual travel's necessary disappointments. Writing clings to utopia in a way that travel, which eventually leads *some*where, cannot.

To cite one important example: Kafka's initial "love" letter to Felice Bauer opens with an invitation to travel together to Palestine. This same letter ends with the postponement of that journey, a journey Kafka pointedly replaces with the promise of more writing: "if doubts were raised, practical doubts I mean, about choosing me as a traveling companion, [. . .] there shouldn't be any prior objections to me as a correspondent—and for the time being this is the only thing at issue" (*LF* 5; *BF* 44). In the end, writing remains the only thing at issue—for five years and hundreds of letters—and the trip is never taken. Kafka uses travel as a ploy: a promise of sexual intercourse, marriage, and the Promised Land lures Felice into a game of writing.[14] Kafka fears actual travel (which hints at unwanted arrivals) but notes travel's value as a promise-to-be-broken: travel becomes the writer's most formidable foe (a guarantor of arrival, an agreement that someday one must stop traveling) and his greatest ally (an unfulfillable promise, a catalyst for writing's deferrals). Kafka thus masterfully abstains from his pledged journey, as well as from additional trips to Felice's home in Berlin, and finally from the planned marriage itself. Fearing that a successful utopian journey—to Palestine, to Berlin, toward marriage—would strip writing of its capacity for deferral, Kafka deliberately transforms from Felice's prospective travel companion into her loyal, but scheming stay-at-home correspondent. Like Moses, Kafka is on "the track of Canaan" for much of his life (planning to go to Palestine again, a year before his death, with Dora Diamant) (*D* 394; *Ta* 867). But unlike the ancient prophet, the modern writer needs to abstain from the journey. Kafka finally turns Felice and the promise of Palestine into the enemies of his writing, to be destroyed through the postal network. As I will demonstrate in Kafka's similar dynamic with his second epistolary lover, Milena Jesenská, Kafka's weapon is a relentless flow of letters, telegrams, and postcards.[15]

Real travel thus threatens the immobile voyage of writing. In Grivel's words, writing becomes a form of non-traveling travel: travel that denotes "getting out of traffic."[16] This opposition becomes painfully clear in Kafka's later years, when his tuberculosis reaches an advanced state. In 1922, Kafka suspects that he may be suffering from "*Reiseangst*" (travel anxiety) and equates this, first, with his "fear of death" (*L* 333–34; *B* 384). He is afraid of traveling (to a writers' conference in Georgental) because he fears that, by leaving the house, he will attract the "attention of the gods" and (as contemporary psychoanalysis would have it) initiate his own final voyage unto death (*L* 333).[17] But Kafka insists that he does not fear death only for death's sake. More concretely, he fears that death will bring about the end of his writing. The main etiology of his travel anxiety, he insists, is "*schriftstellerisch*" (writerly) (*L* 335; *B* 386). Travel might indeed signify *le grand voyage,* but it also, first and foremost, tears him away from the stability of his writing desk and thus toward madness: "This ridiculous thought [that I will be kept away from the desk for at least several days] is really the only legitimate one, since the existence of the writer is truly dependent upon his desk and if he wants to keep madness at bay he must never go far from his desk, he must hold onto it with his teeth" (*L* 335).

Kafka's determination to abstain from traveling and instead to hold firm to his writing desk "with his teeth" has become indicative of the "Kafkaesque."[18] Correspondingly, literary pilgrims still return to Prague's constricted passages, miniature houses, and tiny doorways (as in Kafka's temporary Alchemistengasse residence) as if to the logical birthplace of his cramped fictional heroes.[19] Even Kafka's harshest critics refer to him in terms of this peculiar immobility: in the words of Georg Lukács, Kafka is the poet of personal and political "stasis" (*Stehenbleiben*).[20] But, as I will demonstrate here, this metaphor of inertia is in need of revision. Kafka's famously hermetic works—*The Trial* and *The Castle*—equally depend on the *opposite* of spatial paralysis, on a Promised Land of sorts, for their powerful effect: Josef K. longs for the mythical Highest Court; K. dreams of reaching the Castle. Most of Kafka's protagonists are driven toward similarly sublime spaces, which promise at least a release from claustrophobia and, at the best, wide-open spaces and a new, better *Heimat.* Karl Rossmann yearns for the open-air Nature Theater, where everyone is accepted; the ape, Red Peter, nostalgically imagines his jungles in Africa; the hunter Gracchus crosses the world's oceans searching for a suitable spot for dying. What is peculiarly powerful in Kafka's writing, then, is not just the crushing sense of claustrophobic immobility. Rather, he also insists on the effervescent fantasy of spatial freedom and escape. The narrator of one of Kafka's very last stories, "The Departure," finds himself at precisely this breakpoint when, asked where he is going, he seems to be at once desperately trapped *and* hopeful of new horizons:"just away from here, just away from here. On and on away from here, that's the only way I can reach my goal" (*GW* 137; *NSII* 374).

Travel Culture

Looking at such writings in historical terms, we see that Kafka's vehement personal resistance to travel would be insignificant were it not for the passion with which his era—and, at times, Kafka himself—embraced it. Kafka was born into the era of unprecedented middle-class tourism,[21] and, before Kafka the writer began holding fast to his desk with his teeth, Kafka the traveler welcomed the new culture of tourism with all the energy of his day. And with good reason. Tourism made promises much grander than merely a vacation in the sun. It proffered a cure, however temporary, for modernity's *Heimweh nach der Fremde*. If modern man was ill, alienated from his labor, his gods, his home, and himself, then he could regain his health by boarding a train or steamship and traveling elsewhere. It is no coincidence that the earliest extra-European Baedeker guides and Cook tours were to the Promised Land itself.[22] The average man could repeat Moses' failed journey to Canaan, but this time with success. Baedeker promised what God withheld. Be it Palestine or South America, the *Fremde* paradoxically offered the traveler a cure. As we shall see in the opening chapter, this cure entailed locating an "authentic" sense of both self and home, which could be granted only through traveling.[23]

Kafka accepted travel's promise with both utter solemnity and dark humor, and this mixed reception extends from his early travel diaries through to his most famous fictions. An example is Kafka's use of travel guides: first, during his own travels and, later, within the text of *The Trial*. While touring Central and Western Europe in the summers of 1909–12, Kafka sees his Baedeker guide as something of a traveler's Bible, and so identifies himself as a "tourist." He and Brod seem to carry it everywhere, mentioning it a combined total of seven times during their 1911 journey alone, loyally checking off the most important cultural treasures of Milan and Paris.[24] Later, Kafka even convinces Brod to begin drawing up a new series of travel guides with him. Called "Billig" (On the Cheap)—"On the Cheap through Switzerland," "On the Cheap in Paris," etc.—they were meant to rival Baedeker.[25]

Kafka's early faith in travel guides heralds Josef K.'s eventual use of one in the famous, penultimate "Cathedral" chapter from *The Trial*. In the midst of K.'s greatest existential despair (symbolized by his entry into the Cathedral), he carries along a guide that lists the city's most important cultural sights. The priest, upon seeing K. in the Cathedral, wants to know the nature of the book that K. has brought along to this sacrosanct space:

> "What's that in your hand? Is it a prayer book?"
> "No," replied K., "it's an album of city sights." (*T* 212; *P* 288)

This typically comic juxtaposition of the mundane and the sacred leads to a recurring effect in Kafka's fiction: the admixture of absurd joke and whispered transcendence. The tour guide seems to be the last, most frivolous accoutrement K. would need at this precarious moment in his trial. But it also echoes K.'s uncle's earlier suggestion that, in K.'s desperate scenario, a journey might be the only thing that could save him.[26] K.'s album thus takes on—as does Baedeker's *Palestine* (already in its seventh printing by 1910)—the aura of possible redemption. As Kafka suggests ironically *and* in grave seriousness, the tour guide might be proper reading in a church. It might be our only remaining sacred text.

Kafka's fantasy of holding onto his writing desk with his teeth (and avoiding travel at all costs) thus cannot be considered separately from his desire to release his jaws from this desk and travel. When invited to the above mentioned writers' conference, for example, Kafka typically claims that his travel anxiety is exacerbated by his private desire for hyper-stasis: "I may not go out of Bohemia, next I will be confined to Prague, then to my room, then to my bed, then to a certain position in bed, then to nothing more" (*L* 335; *B* 386). But this "nothing more" is Kafka's response to a widespread cultural desire to move. Kafka's reaction stands in opposition to the ubiquitous promises of vacations, pilgrimages, and writers' conferences: to a travel culture suddenly supported by an unprecedented expansion of the rail system, the invention of the automobile and the airplane, and the "opening" of Africa, Asia, and the Middle East through colonialism. Instead of going to Georgental with his fellow writers, Kafka will remain at home and tenaciously write his way into nothingness. This offers him a utopia, too, in the strictest sense: he goes to a place that is the absence of place.

Kafka's desire to protect himself from travel's sensual appeals and its utopian promises gains further importance through the fact that he forged his literary identity during the era of high modernism: a moment characterized by its debt to travel.[27] As Malcolm Bradbury argues in his landmark volume on European modernism (*Modernism: 1890–1930*), the experience of travel—either voluntary or involuntary—is constitutive of the work of

Joyce, Hemingway, Lawrence, Mann, Brecht, Auden, and Nabokov (we might add Stein, Eliot, Barnes, Pound, H.D., Conrad). Bradbury claims that the modernist writer "becomes a member of a wandering, culturally inquisitive group—by enforced exile (like Nabokov's after the Russian Revolution) or by design and desire. The place of art's very making can become an ideal distant city, where the creator counts or the chaos is fruitful."[28] Paul Fussell, citing many of the same figures, argues that travel is "one of the signals of literary modernism, as we can infer from virtually no modern writer's remaining where he's 'supposed' to be."[29]

Kafka, who (like Proust) exceptionally did remain mostly in his hometown, may not have known of the "ideal distant" emigré cities of his traveling European and American contemporaries. But he certainly knew of the many Austro-German literati of his era who defined their work more or less through their globetrotting: Hermann Hesse, Kasimir Edschmid, Alfred Kerr, Waldemar Bonsels, Bernhard Kellermann. Moreover, one year before his self-proclaimed artistic breakthrough in 1912, Kafka showed that he, once again, was tempted by travel's promises. He imagined that travel was the magical ingredient missing from his stalled progression as a writer, remarking admiringly that George Bernard Shaw had simply given up his job in Dublin in 1876, and then "traveled to London and became a writer" (*D* 90; *Ta* 199). Kafka enthusiastically conjures such a trajectory for himself: "How this possible life [Shaw's] flashes before my eyes in colors of steel, with spanning rods of steel and airy darkness between!" (*D* 91).

Travel Diaries

But Kafka remains at home, with the important exception of his annual (or semi-annual) 1909–12 holiday journeys.[30] These short, inner-European voyages further emphasize Kafka's connection to travel culture, and, moreover, specifically tie that culture to his self-schooling as a writer. According to Brod, Kafka would never have become the writer we know today if it had not been for the almost 200 diary pages resulting from these journeys (available in unexpurgated form only since 1987, and only in German).[31] Brod relates the narrative of Kafka's travel-writing apprenticeship as follows: Kafka's writing had come to a standstill in 1909, before the friends departed on the first of their four annual trips through central and western Europe. At the train station in Prague, Brod surprised Kafka with two brown notebooks, one for himself and one for Kafka, and announced: "We will keep parallel travel diaries"[32] (see figure 6). Once in Brescia, Brod challenged Kafka to a writing contest, in which each was to write an essay about the airplane show they were about to witness. The friends agreed that they would later publish only the one version that they deemed best.

"The Aeroplanes in Brescia," one of Kafka's first publications and one of the earliest essays about an air show issued in German, later appeared in *Bohemia* (see figure 7).[33]

Each of the following two years, the friends traveled to their artistic Mecca—Paris—and in 1911 they began writing the extensive travel diaries that led to their never-finished, co-authored travel novel, *Richard and Samuel: A Short Journey through Central European Regions.*[34] Brod argues that this early series of travel writings—beginning in 1909—unclogged Kafka's creative channels. Without travel writing, Brod maintains, Kafka would never have begun the Prague diaries out of which many of his most famous works spring: "I claim that it is thanks to me that this diary [the one Kafka kept in Prague] ever came into being; even Franz's quartos grew directly out of *our little notes on our journeyings,* were in fact in a certain sense sequels to them."[35] Later, in *Der Prager Kreis,* Brod writes, "it is well-known that the short pieces in *Meditation* [Kafka's first published book] developed out of Franz's diaries; then came 'The Judgment.' The little brown [travel] notebooks, the predecessors of his momentous quartos, decisively ended the stagnation of his poetic creativity."[36] Kafka's voluminous Prague diaries indeed do not begin until 1909.[37] The early pieces in *Meditation* (*Betrachtung*) as well as Kafka's September 1912 breakthrough piece, "The Judgment" ("Das Urteil"), all start out as diary entries. For Brod, the travel writings are an irreplaceable impetus for the "sequel"-like later work. Without them, there is no diary, no fiction, no "Kafka."

Even if we view Brod's midwifery account with some suspicion, the narrative's chronology remains telling.[38] After Kafka experiences his literary revolution with "The Judgment" in 1912, he seems to lose his interest in traveling. He still travels after this, but the later journeys (with the exception of his temporary 1923 move to Berlin) are generally related to his profession or his failing health; that is, they are not touristic in nature and, more importantly, do not result in significant travel notes. Following the writing of "The Judgment," then, it seems that Kafka no longer had any particular use for travel. Traveling appears to have served its purpose.[39]

Entries from Kafka's 1911 Prague diaries (just preceding both his remarks on Shaw and his final journey to Paris) support this theory. We see here that the notorious stay-at-home—generally so wary of travel—sensed, like his fellow modernists, a possible symbiotic connection between travel and writing. Shortly before departing for Italy and Paris, during a painful stall in his work, Kafka claims that good writing and good travel might be interdependent: "I don't have time for the least bit of good work, [. . .] time to stretch myself out in every direction in the world, as I would have to do. But then again I believe that my trip will turn out better, that I will apprehend better if I am relaxed by a little writing, and so try it again" (*D* 50; *Ta* 37, trans. rev.). Writing, Kafka imagines, will help traveling, but not in the sense of helping him to have a more enjoyable vacation. Rather, writing will specifically allow him to "apprehend" or "perceive" (*auffassen*) better while traveling. Here, we see that Kafka understands his writing as a way of improving his traveling and vice-versa: traveling will allow him to improve his skills of perception and—when converting these perceptions to travel notes—literary description. If Kafka perceives the foreign world better, his travel writing will improve; this, in turn, should lead to better fiction writing.[40] Kafka implies as much just after returning from his trip. Attempting to transform his travel notes into fiction, Kafka remarks: "Wrote badly, without truly [*eigentlich*] arriving in that freedom of true description which releases one's foot from the experienced" (*D* 80; *Ta* 87, trans. rev.). The "experienced," here, are Kafka's travel notes. If he is successful as a writer, Kafka claims, he will leave the fragmentary quagmire of these notes behind and move on toward a more flowing "freedom of true description": toward the seamless unrolling of "my dreamlike inner life" (*D* 302; *Ta* 546).[41]

Before Kafka achieves this release toward his mature—smooth, "dreamlike," hallucinatory—style, he focuses, in his travel diaries, on jotting down his disconnected, non-narrative "experience[s]." On the model of his beloved Flaubert (who underwent his own travel-writing apprenticeship sixty years earlier), Kafka concentrates on discrete objects, most likely, as Malcolm Pasley argues, in order to hone his skills of objective description.[42] Kafka thus writes predominantly what he calls, just after returning from Paris in 1911, "*Augenblicksbeobachtungen*" (observations of the moment) (*D* 56; *Ta* 43). He zooms in on details (the foot of the Borghese Gladiator in the Louvre, the teeth of a prostitute in Paris, the belly of a prostitute in Milan, and the individual panes of the Milan Cathedral's huge stained-glass windows), granting each object only an *Augen-blick,* a glance of the eye (*D* 460, 459, 444, 445; see figure 8). The result is a distinctly paratactic style, as these observations from a steamboat on the Lake of Lucerne in 1911 demonstrate:

> Man in high boots breakfasting against the wall. 2nd-class steamer. Lucerne in the morning. Poorer appearance of the hotels. Married couple reading letters from home with newspaper clipping about cholera in Italy. The beautiful residences only visible from the lake; you're on the same level here. Changing shapes of the mountains. Vitznau Rigi-railway. Lake seen through leaves, feeling of the south. Surprised by the sudden broad plain of the Lake of Zug. Bouquet with Rigi, what is it waiting for? Woods like at home. Railway built in '75, look it up in an old *Über Land und Meer*. Historically Engl. turf; here they still wore checks and sideburns. Telescope. Jungfrau far away, rotunda of the Monk, shimmering hot air lends motion to the picture. Outstretched palm of the Titli. (*D* 437–38; *Ta* 954, trans. rev.)[43]

Pasley, one of the few critics to pay attention to Kafka's travel diaries,[44] correctly argues that this jagged, collage style is typical of Kafka's travel notes, and that Kafka eventually exchanges this style (and travel writing in general) for his telltale "filmic" idiom: after 1912 images roll out of Kafka smoothly, as if connected on "film" (as opposed to as a series of photographs, placed down abruptly and juxtaposed before the eyes of the viewer).[45] Such a shift is dramatized, in concentrated form, in Kafka's last Parisian diary entry in 1911: a five-page account of a traffic accident he witnessed in front of the Opéra. Instead of describing the accident paratactically, as might seem fitting for an event so determined by speed (and apparently appropriate for the Lucerne steam-boat ride and other occasions in Italy and Paris), Kafka utilizes the smooth, laconic style that had already begun to appear in some of his fictions and, in 1912, surfaces finally and irrevocably: "a motor-car, on the point of turning off onto a side-street and while yet on the large square, runs into a tricycle, but nevertheless comes gracefully to a halt, doing little damage to the tricycle, only stepping on its toe, as it were" (*D* 462; *Ta* 1012, trans. rev.). This passage's fluidity distinguishes it from the paratactical seventy pages that precede it and demonstrates Kafka's attempt to move from his *Augenblicksbeobachtungen* toward flowing narration.[46] Supporting this claim is the fact that Kafka resembles the note-taking policeman who, through his writing about the accident, achieves a final "calm" or "peace" (*Ruhe*) (*D* 465; *Ta* 1017). Proleptically for Kafka, this *Ruhe* issues from the act of writing.

Pasley sees in this writing policeman—correctly, I think—Kafka's self-depiction at the brink of his own literary career. However, Pasley limits his remarks to Kafka's literary biography. In so doing, he sees travel only as a means to an end, and he implies that Kafka felt the same way. Pasley thus represses the enduring symbolic importance of travel in Kafka's oeuvre and, moreover, fails to understand Kafka's mature style as a "traveling" style. Mark Anderson has pointed out the "traveling" aspects of *Der Verschollene,* where he compares Kafka's style to the cinema: the "moving images" that Kafka lets run before Karl Rossmann's eyes "like a ribbon of celluloid images passing before the eye of the projector."[47] Here, we see how Walter Benjamin's 1936 theoretical connection of travel to film applied for Kafka already in 1912: the experience of watching a film mimics the sensation of traveling, allowing us, without leaving our seats, to "calmly and adventurously go traveling."[48]

Brod, without mentioning this connection to film, had already remarked on Kafka's traveling style in 1954: it is "perfection on the move, on the road. [. . .] Hence calm, perspective, freedom, as if above the clouds."[49] Kafka's remarks just after returning from Paris in 1911 point toward his desire for precisely such a sublime motion. Referring enviously to the "calm" style of Goethe's travel diaries, Kafka claims that, when travel was less mechanized, it was still possible to write smoothly and without "violence." The Goethean mail-coach allowed for an apparently more natural form of writing, as yet undisturbed by train-induced parataxis:

> Goethe's observations on his travels different from today's because made from a mail-coach, and with the slow changes of the region, develop more simply and can be followed much more easily even by one who does not know those parts of the country. A calm [*ruhiges*], so-to-speak pastoral form of thinking sets in. [. . .] the onlooker need do no violence to the landscape and he can see systematically without great effort. Therefore there are few observations of the moment [*Augenblicksbeobachtungen*] [. . .]. (D 56; *Ta* 43, trans. rev.)

At this crucial point in his development, then, Kafka envies Goethe a style that is calm and apparently non-violent but nonetheless remains steadily in motion.[50] Goethe's writing is not "driven by unrest [*Unruhe*]," as Kafka feared of himself (D 156; *Ta* 329). Rather, it "travels" seamlessly, as one does on a mail-coach or, as Kafka discovered later, in a dream.[51]

Kafka ruminates earlier that same year on precisely this form of travel— and its relation to visual techonologies—while visiting the Emperor's Panorama in Friedland (see figure 9). This panorama, like travel, offers Kafka visions of faraway places—"Brescia, Cremona, Verona"—but in the calm form reminiscent of Goethe's mail-coach. This form, Kafka insists, is anathema to the cinema: "The pictures more alive than in the cinema [*im Kinematographen*] because they offer the eye all the repose of reality. The cinema communicates the restlessness of its motion to the things pictured in it; the eye's repose would seem to be more important" (D 430; *Ta* 937). As does Goethe's travel writing, the panorama offers the viewer the promise of travel without the modern technological disruptions of train and *Kinematograph*. Kafka's desired "traveling" writing style, then, does not always correspond, in Anderson's words, to a "cinematic apprehension of reality."[52] Rather, Kafka desires a new technology that, unlike the *Kinematograph,* could create sublime motion and, at the same time, the longed-for peace of the photographic still: "Why can't they combine the cinema and the stereoscope in this way?" (D 430).

This technological fantasy presages Kafka's own new writing technique, which masterfully creates the doubled effect of cinematic speed and photographic motionlessness. I think here of the "Flogger" scene from *The Trial,* where Kafka punctuates an otherwise flowing narrative with the unforgettable snapshot that remains unchanged even when the protagonist revisits the scene the following day. Kafka first achieved this amalgamation in September 1912, with "The Judgment." This story rolls out of him fully formed, "like a real birth" or, better, like the film of a real birth (*D* 214; *Ta* 491). But this is a peculiar film because it is not *unruhig*. It has a Goethean smoothness: Kafka only needs to watch as the "story developed before me, as if I were advancing over water" (*D* 212; *Ta* 460). The story's even inevitability, however, is punctuated by an elaborate, photographic gesture (the father standing, half-naked, on his bed above Georg, and sentencing him to death). Kafka's literary breakthrough, then, also might signify the invention of a modern "traveling" technique that unprecedentedly combines film and stereoscope: cinematic fluidity merges with the calm power of the still.

Travel and Reading Strategy

I maintain that Kafka's telltale "traveling" style emerges out of his typically fin de siècle interest in travel culture and technology and, moreover, that travel materializes as a repressed theme in Kafka's works at the precise moment when Kafka ends his actual travels. Throughout this book, I contend that travel developed, for Kafka, from a private fascination (in his travel diaries) into a prominent metaphorical system. Because travel's allures necessarily meander, for Kafka, between "real" and "imaginative" travel, it is essential for us, as readers, to move between formalist/metaphorical and biographical/historical methodologies. Many Kafka critics have tended to position themselves on one side or the other of this "text/context" divide. This rift is nowhere more apparent than in the scant existing work on Kafka and travel, which focuses primarily on his 1914 story about a "traveler's" journey to the tropics: "In the Penal Colony." Here, historicist critics—primarily Klaus Wagenbach and Walter Müller-Seidel—have accurately uncovered this story's relations to actual penal colonies and World War I.[53] These critics valuably expose the text's heretofore overlooked interwovenness in culture. But historicist criticism sometimes obscures the fact that Kafka's story is *also* highly self-reflexive and hermetic, concerned with its own rhetorical structures. For Laurence Rickels, correspondingly, "travel" is "In the Penal Colony's" governing *metaphor;* that is, it is Kafka's vehicle for the tenors of writing and death, especially for their collision on the site of the dead officer's illegible body.[54] Despite Rickels' elegant elucidation of particular passages from "In the Penal Colony," however, his essay suffers from a lack of historical particularity. "Travel" loses its specific frictions within the Austro-German fin de siècle and transforms into a free-floating signifier.

More recent critics, influenced by the "New Historicism" and the critical discourses of Orientalism and postcolonialism, productively turn "In the Penal Colony" and other Kafka texts back against the historical grain.[55] Again, however, because of the mass of historical material they introduce, these interpretations do not always adequately register what Rainer Nägele has called the "stubborn presence of the text."[56] Moreover, these readings again generally focus on "In the Penal Colony." Or, as in the case of Rolf Goebel's more expansive *Constructing China,* they do not adequately address Kafka's major works—especially the novels.[57] An important exception is Anderson's essay on *"Verkehr"* (denoting traffic, intercourse [social and sexual], circulation, commerce) in *The Man Who Disappeared/Amerika (Der Verschollene),* which combines attention to Kafka's rhetoric and style with rich cultural detail concerning modern "traffic."[58] My own approach to Kafka, similarly, seeks to connect cultural history with close readings, but not simply because such a mixture, if successful, brings out the strengths of two competing interpretive models. Rather, this approach is determined by the subject matter itself: When writing about travel in Kafka, we cannot stand still. More exaggeratedly than most of us, Kafka experienced travel as both the possibility of the real exotic journey (to America, Africa, Palestine) and an imaginative compensation for desperate, physical stasis. The former gives rise to the fictional journeys to a tropical island, America, and Riva del Garda (drawing us to the historical markers of exoticism, colonialism, and tourism), whereas the latter manifests itself in the internal journey into the text, as in Kafka's desire to devolve into "nothing but a single word" (calling us to remember, like Kafka's contemporary Robert Müller, that the tropics themselves are a series of tropes) (*LM* 25; *BM* 33).[59]

Because I want to set the historical and theoretical stage for Kafka's textual journeys, I begin by delineating fin de siècle travel discourse—which remarkably prefigures present-day theories of travel. Turn-of-the-century travel culture, both "high" and "low," was dominated by a convergence of alienation and melancholia that sent European travelers to the far reaches of the globe in search of a utopian *zweite Heimat.* At once attracted and repelled by this fantasy, Kafka (with Brod) began a travel novel, *Richard and Samuel: A Short Journey through Central European Regions,* that overtly engages this popular, and according to Kafka and Brod, "superficial" brand of exoticism. Kafka and Brod, like today's cultural anthropologists, turn popular exoticism on its head when they discover the exotic within the *Heimat.*[60] Although aborted after one chapter was published (and generally ignored by scholars), the *Richard and Samuel* fragment is an indispensable clue to our understanding of the stakes that travel writing held for Kafka on the verge of his literary breakthrough. Kafka's decision to write a travel novel about quotidian "central Europe" (and not, in the manner of so many contemporaries, about India or Japan) is not unrelated to his later decisions, in 1912 and 1914, respectively, to use an ordinary European bedroom for the site of Gregor's metamorphosis and Josef K.'s arrest.

With fin de siècle travelers' melancholic utopianism in mind, I argue that travel shifts from an overt interest (in travel writing) to a dominant repressed theme at the precise moment of Kafka's literary self-realization. Drawing on travel diaries, train schedules, tour guides, and exotic adventure books, I then undertake new close readings of this submerged metaphor in Kafka's major works. I group my observations throughout around Kafka's repeated use of the prefix *"ver-,"* which denotes "digressing from the course," "rendering false," and "turning something around into its opposite" (as in the English "mis-"), but also "amplifying" and "intensifying" (as in, in some cases, the English "hyper-"). *"Ver-"* thus sends readers on at least two possible paths: one promising a reversal or falsification of the stem's meaning (as in *vermessen*) and the other an intensification of it (as in *verirren*). In chapter two, I read Kafka's 1911–14 travel novel, *The Man Who Disappeared (Der* Ver*schollene)*, as a narration of the "disappearance" of the exotic self. While Kafka's contemporaries sent their heroes off to faraway lands to discover themselves, Kafka dispatched Karl Rossmann with the specific task of becoming *"verschollen"* and *"verirrt"* (lost) in America. By narrating Rossmann's *Verschollen-Sein* and *Verirrung,* Kafka at once disorients Rossmann and derails the expectations of the travel-literature reader. In chapter three, I argue that *The Metamorphosis (Die* Ver*wandlung)* and *The Trial* grew out of this earlier attempt to render the traveler exotic to himself. We can view this progression in terms of four concentric circles: from Richard and Samuel's central Europe to Josef K.'s European hometown, to Josef K.'s and Gregor Samsa's bedrooms, to, finally, K.'s and Samsa's structures of mind. The operative term for my interpretation of *The Trial* is *"Verfahren,"* denoting both legal "proceedings" and, in its reflexive form *(sich verfahren)*, "losing one's way."

In my examinations of "In the Penal Colony" and *The Castle,* I turn toward the dominant political narrative of turn-of-the-century travel culture: European colonialism. Kafka could well have drawn his Penal Colony torture apparatus and his *Castle* protagonist from the popular colonial adventure series that, as he claimed, supplied him with the "book of rules for my life, rules I elude, or have eluded." But my essays move beyond debates on sources and toward the turn-of-the-century *discourses* of colonial sado-masochism and land-surveying (in German, "ver*messen,"* which denotes "surveying," K.'s profession in *The Castle,* but also being "presumptuous" and, in its reflexive verb form, "making a mistake while measuring"). In both narratives, I ask how much Kafka resists, or eludes, these discourses of domination and how much he, like the officer in the Penal Colony, is simultaneously "verführt" (seduced) by their narrative "enthusiasm" (*D* 248; *Ta* 615). This critical double bind of self-indictment, entrapment, and duplicity informs all of Kafka's writings and is perhaps constitutive of the

"Kafkaesque"—but nowhere is this more evident than in Kafka's colonial narratives.

Kafka's self-consciously literary *Letters to Milena* turn us, as did his *Letters to Felice,* toward travel's modern technologies and Kafka's fear of their concomitant "Ver*kehr*"; that is, their networks of desire, motion, and exchange (enhanced by the train and automobile) that threaten to engulf him and his writing. Shot through with remarks about railway strikes, timetables, telegrams, and stamps, *Letters to Milena* demonstrates how fin de siècle technologies of intercourse helped to determine his attachments and detachments—and how he attempts to fend off physical *Verkehr* through technologized (postal) writing. As I point out in the final chapter, Kafka senses that his writing is powerful enough to forestall more than just *Verkehr.* It might also create a space between living and dying that delays— triumphantly *and* painfully—our final voyage to death. Kafka represents this middle space in "The Hunter Gracchus," whose protagonist, although apparently dead, is unable to really die: his death ship "ver*fehlte die Fahrt*" (went off course), and he can never get to the beyond. "The Hunter Gracchus" thus displays succinctly Kafka's critical twist on the popular *Heimweh nach der Fremde:* Gracchus yearns for a peaceful second home in the other world but in the end only discovers the exotic within himself.

I hope that these analyses expand our horizons for reading Kafka and, in so doing, offer a reading experience that is not unlike traveling. As Walker Percy writes, reading and traveling sometimes converge to suspend alienation in the form of a "quest for the new as the new, the reposing of all hope in what may lie around the bend, a mode of experiencing which is much the same in the reading as in the experiencing."[61] I attempt to supply this newness (in Percy's words, "rotation") through fresh interpretations of Kafka's texts, but at the same time to perform what Percy calls a "repetition" or a "return"; in this case, to the home base of fin de siècle travel culture. This book, then, does not attempt to rise above the tensions of Kafka's era but rather to repeat the opposed reactions to alienation that still punctuate our lives today: the open-ended, imaginative "rotation" versus the "return" to our historically particular constructs of home. The latter refers to real, exotic destinations (Africa, South America, Palestine) that might, if the traveler is lucky (or properly deluded), become a utopian *zweite Heimat;* the former is the fantastic nowhere of creative writing, a place that is unnamable and may not require an actual journey but rather only what Xavier de Maistre called a "voyage autour de ma chambre."[62] Literary history has already taught us which path Kafka chose. But this decision was by no means an obvious one. It emerged out of the pressures of its opposite: Kafka's final writerly journey meant denying the real, exotic one and, in the end, sublimating it in the form of a governing fictional metaphor. Kafka encapsulates this friction between writing and the utopian journey when, in 1913, he abruptly withdraws his offer to Felice to travel together with her to the "south":

> The best plan would probably be [. . .] to go south with you forever to some island or lake. In the south I feel everything is possible. And there lead a life of seclusion, feeding on grass and fruit. But I don't need to look into myself very deeply to see that I don't even want to go south. *Simply to race through the nights with my pen, that's what I want. And to perish by it or lose my reason* [*irrsinnig werden*]. (*LF* 289; *BF* 427).

As Kafka's rare underlining emphasizes, the breaking point of this decision between real travel and writing is at once the limit of reason and the starting line for art. It is the place where all travel begins, the place where I too will start, as I attempt to "travel" with Kafka.

Chapter One

Transcending the Exotic:
Nostalgia, Exoticism, and Kafka's Early
Travel Novel, *Richard and Samuel*

The purpose of this work is [. . .] to let [the countries traveled through] be seen with a freshness and significance too often unjustly reserved for exotic regions only.

> —*Franz Kafka and Max Brod,*
> *foreword to "The First Long Train Journey"*
> *(the first, and only completed chapter of* Richard and Samuel—
> A Short Journey through Central European Regions*)*

The narrative of Kafka's travels opens in the writer's earliest childhood, with the famous photograph described by Walter Benjamin (see figure 10). This photograph, taken in a tropically upholstered studio, plush with draperies, easels, tapestries, and palm trees, features the young Kafka at approximately age six. The claustrophobic studio is congested, as Benjamin writes, with the typical accoutrements of exotic travel:

There is a childhood photograph of Kafka, a rarely touching portrayal of the "poor, brief childhood." It was probably made in one of those nineteenth-century studios whose draperies and palm trees, tapestries and easels placed them somewhere between a torture chamber and a throne room. At the age of approximately six the boy is presented in a sort of greenhouse setting, wearing a tight, heavily lace-trimmed, almost embarrassing child's suit. Palm branches loom in the background. And as if to make these upholstered tropics still more sultry and sticky, the model holds in his left hand an oversized,

wide-brimmed hat of the type worn by Spaniards. Immensely sad eyes dominate the landscape prearranged for them, and the auricle of a big ear seems
to be listening for its sounds.[1]

We could add to Benjamin's palm trees and hat the boy's riding crop, his
sailor's collar, and the boatman emblazoned boldly across his chest—a fore-
runner, perhaps, of Kafka's 1917 eternal sailor unto death, the hunter Gracchus. Like the fin de siècle "*Reiseanzug*" (traveler's outfit) later worn by the
guard in Kafka's *Trial,* the boy's suit is too tight and is bedecked with
pleats, pockets, buttons, and a belt (*T* 3, 14; *P* 7, 22).

For Benjamin, this sultry, exotic setting calls to mind a "torture chamber." A close look at the boy reveals, in fact, that he seems to be in some
pain. The suit is uncomfortably snug, and the hat is comically bulky, too
large for a six-year-old; the young Kafka awkwardly crooks his elbow to
keep the lower brim from extending to the floor. Typical of nineteenth-
century photographs, the boy's right arm mimics the stiffness of a suit
dusted off only for such occasions, and his hand tensely grips the riding
crop. The boy is thus made rigid and heavy, overburdened by the accessories of imaginary journeys. Not surprisingly, according to Benjamin's
trademark melancholia, the boy's eyes dominate the picture with their
"immense sad[ness]."[2]

But these same eyes veer off to the right, and in so doing, according to
Benjamin, dream of an antidote to claustrophobic melancholia: utopia. As
Benjamin writes later, the young Kafka's gaze into the distance suggests his
yearning to be elsewhere, to break out of this humid, stifling frame and into
a new realm of freedom and adventure. This is the boy's desire to "become
a Red Indian," Benjamin claims, to travel, in the spirit of Karl Rossmann, to
foreign lands—toward the mythical racetrack at Clayton, the Nature Theater
in Oklahoma (119). Benjamin thus offers the boy a typically fin de siècle
cure for unhappiness. He claims that the young Kafka's best mode of freeing
himself from the restrictive exotic frame would be, paradoxically, to embark
on an exotic journey. The fulfillment of the boy's private wish, Benjamin
claims, is "America" (a premonition of Benjamin's own final, unfulfilled
wish). Only in that promised land of wealth and felicity could a Kafkan alter-
ego, otherwise mired in central European despondency, achieve happiness.
As Benjamin writes, the "K."'s of *The Trial* and *The Castle* degenerate into
anonymity (the "mumbled initial"), whereas Karl Rossmann, in *Amerika,*
achieves a "full name" and a "rebirth on a new continent" (119). For Benjamin, the exotic journey liberates Karl Rossmann just as, after the fact, it
should free the six-year-old Kafka from his suffocating frame.[3]

Benjamin wants to liberate the boy retroactively by sending him to a
utopian America, but Benjamin also achieves the opposite effect. Within

the symbolics of the photograph, Benjamin's dream of America precisely does *not* free the boy (just as Rossmann's eventual journey only earns him the right to be called "Negro"). Rather, it adds another exotic ornament to an already overburdened body. Benjamin encumbers the Kafka-image further by attaching to it another adult-sized fantasy. Writing within the exotic discourse that informs the photograph, Benjamin inadvertently repeats the original discursive gesture of "trapping": thereby adding to the boy's burdens of too-tight travel suit, too-heavy hat, useless riding crop. He does not consider that the exotic fantasy—and its promise of utopia— might be the source of the boy's melancholy and *not* the solution to it. This chapter attempts to reverse Benjamin's gesture by illustrating how the young Kafka, although "trapped" in some of his exotic fantasies, still attempts to travel away from travel; that is, against the grain of dominant utopian travel fantasies. Specifically, his early, never-completed travel novel, *Richard and Samuel—A Short Journey through Central European Regions (Richard und Samuel—Eine kleine Reise durch mitteleuropäische Gegenden)*, begins to undermine the dialectic between "home" and "away" that is so central to exotic desire. *Richard and Samuel* does this not by denying exoticism but rather by *furthering* its impulses—by locating the "exotic" in regions imagined to be free of it.

Exoticism: The Taste for Difference

Critical attempts to define "exoticism" are manifold,[4] but for my purposes I will focus on the straightforward explanation offered by the term's etymology. Stemming from the Greek root *éxō,* exoticism is, in its simplest definition, the representation of that which is "outside." In more specifically aesthetic terms, exoticism is, as the *Encyclopaedia of World Art* claims, a "taste" for "cultures that are experienced as distant and different."[5] Exoticism, then, in both its etymological and art-historical senses, is an interest in or taste for that which is perceived to be outside, distant, and "different."

This fondness for difference was especially strong in Kafka's fin de siècle, partially because exotic fantasies were encouraged by imperial governments attempting to populate colonies as well as by a burgeoning tourist industry. Moreover, travel was made easier by advances in railway technology and because "outside" territories once deemed inaccessible, such as Japan or China, were suddenly "opened" to the West. Writers and artists who had been limited to their own fantasies now had the opportunity for first-hand experience. Although in this most obvious sense imperialism and rail expansion rendered the exotic project simpler, these same developments also made it more difficult. Empire-building brought with it relative homogenization and the Europeanization of what were once foreign worlds.

Therefore, the fantasy of an authentic, un–Europeanized Other drew further and further away. Because of colonialism, the exotic writer needed to travel greater distances, both actual and psychological, to uncover difference.[6] Conrad left for the Congo, Kipling was in Asia, and, more important for this investigation, Hermann Hesse and a new generation of German writers visited faraway sites in India, Japan, and South America. The returns on these exotic investments were often, as we shall see, the profitable—if worn-out—signs of a fetishized Other.

Modern German-language exoticism, like German imperialism, lagged far behind its British and French counterparts. When it did develop around 1910, though, it did so with compensatory energy. German publishing houses paid large sums for well-known literati, such as Max Dauthendey, Norbert Jacques, and Bernhard Kellermann,[7] to tour South America (Dauthendey) and Japan (Jacques, Kellermann)—to bring back travelogues that would satisfy the domestic appetite for difference. One example of this German-language exoticist burst is Kellermann's *A Stroll through Japan* (*Ein Spaziergang in Japan,* 1910). Here, Kellermann (a critically acclaimed novelist whose 1910 Prague reading Kafka attended) plays on clichés of an authentically foreign Japan, repeating the impressionist tropes of tea houses, geishas, and rock gardens: in so doing, he offers bourgeois Germany its commodified fantasy of the "Japanese."[8] Waldemar Bonsels, another celebrated writer, used a different methodology but shared Kellermann's goal of representing the apparently genuinely foreign. In his fabulously popular documentation of his 1900 travels, *Indian Journey* (*Indienfahrt,* 1916) (the best-selling German travelogue of the twentieth century), Bonsels searches for the true India, but he avoids the clichés borrowed by Kellermann. Bonsels traveled off the beaten track in order to discover what Dean MacCannell has termed "authentic" touristic "back spaces."[9] Bonsels' journey toward the exotic, then, takes him even further from Europe's psychological "home" than does Kellermann's. But Bonsels' back-space journeys to plague-ridden alleys and incense-filled brothels do not wholly differentiate him from Kellermann.[10] Both writers—Kellermann with his tea houses, Bonsels with his back spaces—are interested, as we will see with Hesse in 1911 India, in capturing some "authentic" form of foreignness.[11]

If these popular quests for the strange represent a trend in German-language modernism, then Franz Kafka's contemporaneous travel writings offer us an instructive counter-example. As discussed in the introduction, Kafka was mostly a "textual traveler" who never left Europe—and thus his notion of travel writing was significantly more local than that of his contemporaries.[12] The year 1911 is a case in point. While Hesse tramped through Asia, Jacques published the popular *Hot Cities: A Journey to Brazil* (*Heiße Städte: Eine Reise nach Brasilien*), and Gustave Flaubert's *Voyage en Orient* was first translated, to great outrage and celebration, into German,[13] Kafka and Max Brod—likely avid followers of the Flaubert debate as well as of Hesse's and Jacques' writings[14]—spent four weeks at the end of that same summer traveling, albeit to nowhere exotic. They toured decidedly prosaic central and western Europe: Germany, Switzerland, Northern Italy, and Paris. It was here that they began an autobiographical travel novel that, as I will delineate, attempted to transcend fin de siècle exoticism by turning it inward—toward the structures of home and self.

Richard and Samuel:
The Exoticization of Europe

On Kafka's suggestion, the young friends used their journey to start the critically neglected novel *Richard and Samuel—A Short Journey through Central European Regions.*[15] This was to be more than just a novel; it was also, as Brod claimed years later, meant to be an aesthetic statement challenging contemporary exoticism. According to Brod, Kafka proposed paradoxically to write a travel novel about places with which he was already familiar. In so doing, he and Brod could critique what Brod called the "superficially" or "externally" (*äußerliche*) "exotic"—presumably, the writings of Kellermann, Bonsels, Jacques, and perhaps even Kafka's esteemed Flaubert.[16] The first and only completed chapter of the planned novel appeared in the May 1912 volume of the *Herder-Blätter* as "Die erste lange Eisenbahnfahrt (Prag—Zürich)" ("The First Long Train Journey [Prague—Zurich]").[17] Deliberately monotonous, this early experiment has partially earned its subsequent critical neglect. But *Richard and Samuel's* dullness is part and parcel of a calculated challenge to fin de siècle exoticism, and it defines a crucial, overlooked juncture in Kafka's literary development.

The plot of *Richard and Samuel* is simple and, as Brod claimed later, intentionally tedious: consisting mainly of two young men taking an uneventful train ride from Prague to Switzerland. "Richard" (who sometimes resembles Kafka) and "Samuel" (who sometimes resembles Brod) leave Prague early in the afternoon, headed toward Munich. In their compartment, they meet a young woman, with whom they eventually disembark in Munich and take a short and speedy automobile tour. The two friends then reboard the train and travel farther, through the night, to Switzerland. The chapter ends with Richard and Samuel looking through a train window at the Swiss countryside. The authors' promise at the end of this chapter—that "a sequel will follow"—is never kept (*EFI* 206).

Most interesting for our purposes is the authorial introduction, which explains the authors' aesthetic intent. I quote from the introduction's final

sentence (to which I will return later): "The purpose of this work is [. . .]
to turn a double light, from two contradictory angles [*eine widerspruchsvolle
Doppelbeleuchtung*] upon the countries traveled through, and by this means
to let them be seen with a freshness and significance [*in einer Frische und
Bedeutung sehn zu lassen*] too often unjustly reserved for exotic regions
only" (*M* 280; *EFI* 193). In contradistinction to their contemporaries,
then, Kafka and Brod claim to not need to travel to "exotic regions" in
order to find meaning ("*Bedeutung*"). Rather, they will describe familiar
countries with the "freshness and significance" too often unjustly reserved
for faraway lands. The goal of their book, we could rephrase, is to challenge
exoticism precisely by *transcending* it. "Transcending" is the apt word here
because Kafka and Brod do not attempt to criticize exoticism by discred-
iting the term and then distancing themselves from it. Rather, they subvert
traditional exoticism precisely by extending it beyond its ordinary limits:
by climbing (*scandere*) over or beyond (*trāns*) it.

Kafka and Brod endeavor to locate exotic significance—semiotic
difference—within their familiar world. They are, like the exoticists to
whom they refer, on the lookout for alterity. But their "exotic" world is not
a place always already deemed different by cultural stereotype and national
boundary. Rather, it corresponds to a moment in which the traveler, to return to the *Encyclopaedia* definition, "experience[s]" his world as "distant and
different." *Richard and Samuel* thus attempts to transform foreignness from a
mappable geographical space into a structure of mind. Dependent as it is
only on a mode of seeing ("*sehn*"), *Richard and Samuel's* perspectival exoticism is portable. It can conceivably produce the exotic anywhere.

Many years after this chapter of *Richard and Samuel* was published, Brod
argued for the importance of this project in the young Kafka's aesthetic development. Brod refers to the authors' choice of a provocatively prosaic
and ironic subtitle: "We [Kafka and Brod] were already at that time the
avant-garde [*Vorkämpfer*] for the novel without plot and without superficial exoticism. We thus selected as the subtitle for our opusculum 'A Short
Journey through Central European Regions.'"[18] According to Brod, he
and Kafka were ultramodern writers who had discovered a new form of
the novel that, in its deliberate banality, would resist traditional plottings as
well as the exigencies of exotic intrigue. This new novel, in Brod's reading,
would undermine the superficial exotic binary of home and away, as well
as the novel's narrative tradition of *Bildung*. It would produce its significance, its semiotic force, precisely out of apparent insignificance: for example, the story of two friends traveling through central Europe (see figure
11). The co-authors' aesthetic mission was to trace meaning within meaninglessness, freshness within cliché, the unusual within the mundane, the
exotic within the domestic.

Considering this resistance to "superficial" fin de siècle exoticism, Kafka's 1911 idea to write a travel novel about central Europe instead of, say, India is not unrelated to his later decisions, in 1912 and 1914, respectively, to use an ordinary bedroom for the scenes of Gregor Samsa's metamorphosis and Josef K.'s arrest. The "outside," in these stories, invades the heart of an apparent "inside." In *The Metamorphosis,* the family's familiar Gregor—a traveling salesman (*"Reisender"*) by profession—suddenly becomes a tropically gigantic "monstrous vermin" in his bed (*MO* 76; *DL* 115). In *The Trial,* a guard dressed in a *Reiseanzug* appears uncannily at Josef K.'s bedside—a startling replacement for the homier landlady with her breakfast tray. As these famous openings suggest, Kafka's mature aesthetic pushes the envelope of the exotic; that is, they realize Kafka's earlier attempt to subvert the exotic by transcending it. While Kellermann, Bonsels, and Jacques traveled across the world to locate the strange, Kafka—the voracious reader of travel narratives—discovered it in his bedroom, in the imagined core of the central European *Heimat.* From this viewpoint, Kafka's famous *Metamorphosis* extends exoticism beyond its conventional limits. The bedroom, this prototypical space of privacy and intimacy,[19] proves *not* to be domestic. Rather, it is merely another crease in an all-encompassing exotic exterior, an inward fold (*"Falte"*) not unlike those that Josef K. eventually notices on his intruding jailer's travel garments (*T* 3; *P* 7).

In the light of Kafka's later development, this early challenge to exoticism in *Richard and Samuel* deserves our further attention. As Brod writes on the first day of the friends' 1911 journey, the complex nature of Kafka's idea for the novel was not immediately evident: "Kafka's suggestion of a communal travelogue. Incompletely explained. Simultaneous description of the journey, in which each person describes the other's perspective toward objects" (*EFI* 73). On the same day, Kafka seems to want to recant his own plan, calling it "bad": "the bad idea: simultaneous description of the journey and our inward attitude [*innerlichen Stellungnahme*] toward each other concerning the journey" (*D* 433; *Ta* 943, trans. rev.). But the problem with Kafka's idea is not, I maintain, its inherent badness; that is, not a theoretical shortcoming. Rather, the obstacle was that the project's radical experiments proved to be practically unrealizable.

The authors offer information about the revolutionary promise of their project in the final sentence of the introduction, already quoted above. Here, they reveal their aesthetic means for pushing contemporary travel writing beyond its traditional limits: "*widerspruchsvolle Doppelbeleuchtung,*" which literally means "contradictory double-illumination" and, in the terms of Kafka's and Brod's project, suggests something like "contradictory stereoscopy" (*M* 280; *EFI* 193). What is this "contradictory stereoscopy" and how does it relate to the authors' challenge to exoticist writing? According to Kafka, this term designates two different people describing the same object at the same time (thus, the double illumination necessary for "stereoscopy") but also from the *other person's* perspective (thus, "contradictory"). This technique moves beyond the double-vision that forms the basis for depth-perception (i.e., two slightly divergent views of the same thing overlaid to produce the illusion of three dimensions): by forcing Kafka to see the world as would Brod (who is trying to see the world as would Kafka, who is trying to see the world as would Brod, etc.), contradictory stereoscopy destabilizes the individual perspectives necessary for successful stereoscopic vision. The two discrete images will not combine to produce the effect of a single picture, as they did at the Kaiser's Panorama in Friedland (see figure 9). Rather, the result will more resemble an endless series of photographic double-exposures (*Doppelbelichtungen* instead of *Doppelbeleuchtungen*) that, like Kafka's childhood photograph, conjures contradictory images when viewed through the different lenses of exotic discourse.

This avant-garde technique was, according to Brod, one of the first major interventions of the so-called Prague School (thus, its publication in *Herder-Blätter,* the first organ of the Prague School).[20] Its triumph was to allow the voices of "Kafka" and "Brod" to mix to the point of virtual indistinguishability. The final product was to be a masterpiece of simultaneous double-impersonation. All "original" sources would have been, ideally, always unlocatable. If a manuscript scholar would attempt to establish who wrote what (a strategy against which the authors defended themselves, as we shall see), this scholar would always only find the "what" in the author's impersonation of the other.

The friends attempted to commit the theoretical force of Kafka's plan to practice: they wrote the chapter together—not separately, in their own homes—on several Sundays in the fall and winter of 1911. They worked in concert, doing everything in their power to cover the traces of their individual voices. As Brod writes, person "A" or person "B" did not independently compose separate sections that were later worked together in editorial sessions. Rather, "A and B," on these Sundays, were "indistinguishably involved" in the composition of "the *whole.*"[21] Even the obvious question of who held the pen cannot be solved. The writers composed their fair copy for the *Herder-Blätter* alternately, literally passing the pen back and forth, and thereby disguising authorship even from *Herder-Blätter*'s editor, Willy Haas, whom both Kafka and Brod knew personally. The practice of *Richard and Samuel* thus mirrored its theory. The writers effaced individual authorship in conceptual *and* practical terms. They truly conceived the text together: first, by thinking the other's thoughts and, later, by taking turns writing these down.

The few scholars to deal with *Richard and Samuel* have failed to appreciate the radical aesthetics of contradictory stereoscopy. Mark Anderson, otherwise sensitive to the text's double vision, makes a telling slip when he claims that Kafka and Brod wrote "alternate chapters"—as did Flaubert and Maxime DuCamp in *Richard and Samuel*'s pretext, *Par les champs et par les grèves*.[22] If Anderson's claim were true, then individual authorship, as in *Par les champs et par les grèves,* could easily be established. Hanns Zischler makes a more egregious error when he blankly attributes all of the "Richard" texts to Kafka even though some fragments of Richard's dialogue are clearly culled directly from *Brod*'s travel notebook.[23] Hartmut Binder claims that scholars could perhaps locate individual authorship and thereby stabilize the text's stereoscopy if one would only painstakingly compare Brod's and Kafka's travel notes with the text of *Richard and Samuel*.[24] But such a project is at best only partially realizable (some of *Richard and Samuel* does not appear in *either* writer's travel notebook) and, moreover, would contradict the spirit of the work. Truth-seeking critics would be rewarded for their labors only with a dismembered text and a smattering of "Kafka's" words—words they already knew to be "Kafka's" from the travel diaries. Such a critical strategy is precisely the one the authors work against.

According to the authors' introduction, contradictory stereoscopy should assist them in their effort to find the exotic within the domestic. Their strategy does not therefore have to do so much with *what* one sees (here, prosaic central Europe) but rather with *how* one sees it. This de-emphasizing of place distinguishes Kafka and Brod from their exoticist contemporaries, who were always interested in specific non-Western sites. In many traditional exotic narratives, the narrator climbs to the top of a faraway church tower, minaret, or mountain and looks down on the foreign landscape, in order to better survey, demarcate, and map South America, Africa, or Asia. Such a strategy provides the traveler with what Mary Louise Pratt has termed the "monarch-of-all-I-survey" view.[25] This view—recurring in travel texts from Goethe to Flaubert to Hesse—affirms the traveler's power over the foreign world in two ways: it allows him to delineate the exotic lands' borders and, more important for a discussion of literary innovation, to bolster the singularity of his perspective.[26] Through this view from above, the traveler can gain a better sense of the land's specificities, his own point-of-view, and, finally, his "self": "Here 'I' am in (Asia) (Latin America) (Africa), looking out over a relatively untrodden landscape and discovering a new perspective on the world and on myself." Contradictory stereoscopy assaults precisely such a narrative structure of exotic self-location. Kafka and Brod use perspectival dispersion to estrange the traveler from his own subjectivity.

One of many possible counter-examples to *Richard and Samuel*'s contradictory stereoscopy is the typical "monarch-of-all-I-survey" scene appearing in Hesse's *Out of India* (*Aus Indien*). Writing in the same autumn
weeks of 1911 that Kafka and Brod worked on *Richard and Samuel,* Hesse
describes climbing the Pedrotagalla, the highest mountain peak on Ceylon
(now Sri Lanka). This ascent establishes Hesse's perspective in three distinct
yet related senses: his perspective on the landscape below him; on the foreign world in general; and on himself as a German. The climb is marked,
at the onset, by Hesse's inability to adequately see the landscape. He is surrounded by a "dense, withered thicket of bushes"; his "view" of the valley
is rarely clear.[27] As Hesse nears the peak, this loss of sight increasingly frus-
trates him. He is surrounded by thick vegetation and even claims that the
forest seems to be "staring" back at him—a reverse view that transforms
Hesse into the (uncomfortable) *object* of the forest's gaze. But the traditional exotic struggle between man and nature—here, between staring forest and staring human—eventually turns Hesse's way. Hesse finally finds a
path out into the open that allows him to stand above the forest that once
fixed him in its sights. He obtains a singular impression of it from above
and, moreover, in a concentrated form that he can bring back home with
him. Like a landscape postcard, Hesse's vista purports to capture the entire
Ceylonese world. Hesse's view from above, thus, is the "purest" thing he
"took back with [him] from all of Ceylon" (106). It represents his writerly
booty—in the form of a packageable landscape perspective.

Perhaps most importantly, Hesse's view relieves him of the sense of
alienation that had accompanied him at home in Europe and, until this
moment, throughout his journey in Asia. Up until this point, everything in
Asia had seemed "foreign" (*fremd*) and "strange" to him (106). But his view
from above reverses this situation. "India" is suddenly "entirely close" and,
moreover, "entirely my own" ("*ganz nah und ganz zu eigen*"). As suggested
by the word "*eigen*," Hesse has gained a sense of property. He can take this
personalized Ceylon back to Germany with him, along with a new sense
of uncanny homeyness—a "dark and grateful sense of home [*Heimatsahnung*]" (107). India satisfies his exotic longings, he claims, by paradoxically
transforming itself into his (and "our") long-lost Germanic home. If Kafka
and Brod render the domestic world exotic, then, Hesse, in the end, does
the exact opposite: he makes the foreign world seem like "home." Hesse
writes: "It was first here [. . .] that it became absolutely clear to me how
completely our essence and our northern culture are rooted in wilder,
poorer lands. We come to the South and the East full of longing, driven by
a dark and grateful sense of home, and here we find paradise" (106–7).
Hesse continues by claiming that his ancient German-Indian *Ur*-home
persists beneath the surface of modern India, and can be recaptured by

him. The alienated modern German, then, was never permanently lost: he only needed to re-locate his roots. In this way, Hesse (and other Germans) can magically transport a newfound "sense of home" back to Germany, where "we" will use this *Heimatsahnung* to construct a new, paradisiacal "northerly future" (107).

There's No Place Like "Home":
Heimweh nach der Fremde

Before returning to Kafka's travel novel, it is important to note that *Out of India*—which Kafka likely read—adds a typical twist to the definition of exoticism I cited above. Hesse's exoticism expresses the traditional "taste for difference" (the desire to travel to distant worlds and locate what Hesse terms the "primitively authentic" Other),[28] but *Out of India* also features an enduring longing for the familiar, for what Hesse calls *Heimat*. In the course of *Out of India,* in fact, Hesse begins to see "home" everywhere: in Penang, he notices a "deep fog like at home," and on the Pedrotagalla, he sees "alp roses," something that looks like "edelweiss," and many other of "our native [*heimatlichen*] wildflowers" (138, 105). Similarly, when viewing half-naked Singalese youths in Kandy, Hesse is overcome by an "atavistic contentment and feeling of home [*Heimatgefühl*]" (101). Hesse seems to suffer from what Waldemar Bonsels called in 1916 "*Heimweh nach der Fremde*" (homesickness for a foreign country): Hesse obsessively turns foreign sites into domestic ones such that India becomes his long-lost home.[29] His 1911 poem "River in a Primeval Forest" ("Fluß im Urwald") is a case in point. One evening, on the banks of an ancient river, Hesse's narrator notes that the Indian fishermen's songs sound completely "foreign" to him. But he then notices that these songs resemble none other than the ones sung by "fishermen and maidens" along his native Neckar and Rhein:

> The song is strange [*fremd*] and no word is familiar,
> But does not sound any different, than at home [*daheim*]
> Sounds like the evening song on the Neckar and Rhein
> Of fishermen and maidens: I breathe fear
> And breathe longing, and the wild jungle
> And foreign [*fremde*] dark stream is like home [*Heimat*] to me.[30]

Hesse, here, deftly transforms the *Fremde* into the *Heimatliche,* thus enacting Bonsels' *Heimweh nach der Fremde*.

This *Heimweh nach der Fremde* was not particular to Hesse. Rather, Bonsels' concept offers a theoretical frame for the entire era. As Caren Kaplan

recently pointed out—in her critique of traditional, literary-historical accounts celebrating modernist "exile" (in the lives of Joyce, Pound, Eliot,
Hemingway, Fitzgerald, etc.)—modernist writing is generally more concerned with re-locating "homes" than it is with exploring displacement.[31]
Kaplan sees the literary historical construct of "modernism," despite its traditional alliance with displacement, as deeply nostalgic. "Nostalgia" is, after
all, a distinctly modern lexical amalgation (combining, first in the late sev-
enteenth century, the Greek *nostos,* a return home, with *algos,* a painful
condition).[32] And, as Kaplan argues, our concept of nostalgia depends on
two very questionable assumptions relating to "home": first, that we know
where "home" is and, second, that it is "natural" for us to return there (thus
curing us of our modern pathology of nostalgia, which was in fact first
viewed as an *illness*).[33] Nostalgia, Kaplan claims, becomes "melancholic"
precisely because it depends on a return "home" for its cure. In the light
of Freud's differentiation between mourning and melancholia, Kaplan
maintains that modernism is melancholic because the modern subject cannot accept the fact that "home" is irredeemably unattainable. Thus, he (for
Kaplan, a male subject) resembles the melancholic refusing to acknowledge
the loss of an idealized Other. What is lost in this modernist, melancholic
nostalgia is the idealized and, in Freudian terms, "introjected" fantasy of
Heimat.[34]

Modernity creates this problem of melancholic nostalgia, but it also
promises a cure. As Renato Rosaldo points out in his description of "imperialist nostalgia," modernity disrupts the fantasy of home through industrial
progress but then tempts the exiled nostalgic with the promise of a return
to a pre-modern home in a faraway land.[35] Here, the fantasy of a true *Heimat*
is idealized and introjected, but the loss is—through colonial necromancy—
not irreparable. Rosaldo writes: "Imperialist nostalgia revolves around a paradox: [. . .] somebody deliberately alters a form of life, and then regrets that
things have not remained as they were prior to the intervention. At one
more remove, people destroy their environment, and then they worship nature."[36] Colonialism satisfies this nature-worship by offering ersatz homes in
"natural" settings.[37] The melancholy European subject imagines that his
mythical "Rhein and Neckar" have been destroyed by industrialization, but
that he nonetheless might recapture his lost sense of these in the "foreign,
dark" Indian jungle. Colonial nostalgia thus offers, however disingenuously,
a cure for melancholia. Through spatial and temporal travel, the melancholic
subject can have his lost object returned to him. In this model, home is always there. It is never lost but only hidden, on an alternate, pre-industrial
grid of time and space.[38]

Exotic nostalgia, already present in Benjamin's above-cited reading of
Kafka's childhood photograph and Kafka's "Longing to be a Red Indian,"

is thus based on a paradox—exemplified by variations on the German word *fremd*. Signifying both "foreign" and "strange," this word supplies the root for two terms crucial to understanding exotic nostalgia: first, "alienation" in the Marxian sense (*Entfremdung*) and, second, "the tourist industry" (*Fremdenindustrie*). The paradox of finding *Heimat* in the *Fremde* reveals itself already in the oppositional relation between *Entfremdung* and *Fremdenindustrie*. *Entfremdung*, Marx writes in his 1844 *Economic and Philosophic Manuscripts*, signifies the subject's foreignness (*Fremdheit*) in what he imagines to be his "home."[39] He is alienated from his labor, from the things he creates, and from the things and people that surround him (including himself).[40] *Entfremdung's* non-traditional use of the prefix "*ent-*" heightens this estrangement. Generally, "*ent-*" refers to moving "away from something" or "toward something's opposite," as in *Enthaupten* (taking off someone's head) or in *Entideologisieren* (distancing something from ideology). *Entfremdung*, however, breaks with lexical custom by signifying a state of *increased Fremdheit*.

The *Fremdenindustrie*—which exploded around the time Marx published his *Economic and Philosophical Manuscripts*[41]—promised to liberate subjects from *Entfremdung* by sending them on a journey into the *Fremde*. While Marx theorized alienation, then, the tourist industry began to capitalize on the social and linguistic paradoxes of *Entfremdung*.[42] As Hans Magnus Enzensberger wrote a century later, "Liberation from the industrial world has become an industry in its own right, the journey from the commodity world has itself become a commodity."[43] Alienated Europeans needed only take part in *Fremdenverkehr* (tourism)—making use of *Fremdenbüros* (travel agencies), *Fremdenführer* (travel guides), and *Fremdenbetten* (hotel beds)—in order to experience the authentic way of life that they were denied at home. They began to imagine that only a journey (not, as Marx would have it, authenticated labor) could cure them of their sense of domestic strangeness. The tourist industry, then, emerged as the force apparently capable of reversing the "*ent-*" in *Entfremdung:* by returning this prefix to its customary function and curing the subject's paradoxical *Heimweh nach der Fremde*.

This fantasy of *Ent-fremdung*—of finding an *Ur-Heimat* by going into a primitive *Fremde*—is already present in German Romanticism. As Goethe wrote almost a century before Hesse, in his *West-östlicher Diwan:* "There [in the East] amidst purity and justice I want to penetrate back into the profound origins of the human race."[44] Flaubert expressed similar desires for an authentic home in the East already in *Voyage en Orient* (1849–50): as Jean Bruneau writes, Flaubert imagined the Orient to be his "homeland."[45] By the end of the century, the fantasy of *Ent-fremdung* had become part of popular culture through colonialism's apex, unprecedented middle-class tourism, and the dissemination of paperback travel narra-tives.[46] Paul Gauguin, whose translated Tahitian journals Kafka owned, sent the ringing, widespread message to German and other European ex-oticists in 1901: It was possible, Gauguin claimed, to escape tiresome Eu-rope and settle into a "homeland of freedom and beauty" in "paradis[iacal]" Tahiti.[47]

Fin de siècle German exoticists were, like Kafka, often well-versed in Goethe, Flaubert, and Gauguin, and they continued this tradition of traveling *Ent-fremdung*. Wolfgang Reif, author of the classic study of turn-of-the-century German-language exoticism, argues that turn-of-the-century exoti-cism (as opposed to impressionism or decadence) is distinguished by its "nos-talgic," "regressive" qualities: its fantasy of locating origins and homes.[48] In other words, despite the exoticist's professed "taste" for difference, he is deeply concerned with parlaying this difference into something that will, in the end, become familiar. Fin de siècle writers whose work Kafka knew—Hesse, Bon-sels, Jacques, Robert Müller, Willy Seidel—all attempted, Reif argues, to con-struct an ideal space of home "*in der Fremde*" (in distant lands). They engaged in the "paradox" of exotic nostalgia by relocating the "homeyness" of their homes, lost through "alienation" (*Entfremdung*), in a mysterious, "dark," and "foreign" world.[49]

What these accounts share is a pervading nostalgia: a melancholic de-sire to regain a pre-modern home the traveler imagines to have lost. Bon-sels, whose *Indian Journey* begins ostensibly as a radical hunt for difference, puts a fine point on this when he claims to be suffering from *Heimweh nach der Fremde* and, at the end of his account, claims, like Hesse, to phan-tasmagorically *see* his German *Heimat*—in the middle of India: "There in the evening calm I saw a village from my German *Heimat*. The elder bloomed on the fence, rain had fallen, and the air was cool and moist. High on the gable of a farmhouse, a blackbird sang in the fading sunlight, and the clear sweetness of its voice filled the quiet country with happi-ness."[50] Fritz Hübner, similarly, in a special 1913 edition of *Der Bücher-wurm* devoted to contemporary Austro-German travel literature, especially applauds Hesse's attempt to locate a second home. Hesse dis-covers in India, admirably, Hübner claims, his unfulfilled "feeling for home" (*Heimatgefühl*).[51]

Hanns Heinz Ewers perfectly captures this notion of foreign nostalgia—of *Heimat* in the *Fremde*—in *India and I* (*Indien und Ich*), also from 1911. While walking through an Indian park, he feels an inexplicable *Heimweh*: a "strange, almost melancholy feeling—almost like homesickness."[52] But he does not feel this homesickness for Germany. Rather, he experiences a *Heimweh nach der Fremde*: "this homesickness draws me to precisely this be-witching garden. I feel that I am a foreigner [*Fremder*] here, and I also feel that these humid parks filled with gruesome beauty are my legitimate homeland."[53]

Such confusing cases of exotic nostalgia (Ewers is homesick for a foreign country *while* he is in that foreign country) led contemporary psychoanalysts to speculate on this peculiar phenomenon's unconscious workings. And psychoanalytic theory invented exotic fantasies of its own. Freud claimed already in his 1919 account of the "uncanny" (*das Unheimliche*) that his patients were having nostalgic exotic dreams.[54] He interpreted their unconscious desires as regressive—as a longing to return to the womb: "There is a joke saying that 'Love is home-sickness'; and whenever a man dreams of a place or a country and says to himself, while he is still dreaming: 'this place is familiar to me, I've been here before,' we may interpret the place as being his mother's genitals or her body."[55] Freud's crude equivalence (the foreign country = the mother's genitals) is also evident in the work of the young Freudians Alfred Winterstein and Carl Jung. Winterstein and Jung likewise viewed travel-desire ("*Reiselust*") as expressing the patient's longing to return to the mother. Winterstein speaks bluntly of the foreign country as the maternal Other that has remained mysterious: the male traveler desires to "penetrate [. . .] mother earth" in order to access what she has been withholding from him.[56] Jung's analysis is slightly more subtle, claiming that the traveler-figure embodies an eternally "restless urge" that can "never find its object."[57]

These psychoanalytic theories concerning the desire for the maternal exotic claim to be diagnoses, but it is probably more accurate to view them as both symptom and diagnosis at once. They identify a pre-existing cultural fantasy but participate in it at the same time. What is remarkable is psychoanalysis' and literature's "uncanny" mirroring of each other. The poet and critic Alfred Kerr, in his 1911 defense of the German translation of *Voyage en Orient,* claims that Flaubert heroically depicted a fantastical return to Europe's poetic *Ur*-mother (its "blood" and its "umbilical cords").[58] Robert Müller's protagonist in his 1915 *Tropen: Der Mythos der Reise* (*Tropics: Myth of the Journey*) specifically sees the tropics as his *Heimat* and personal "womb."[59] He experiences in the tropics the "mystery of mothers," and this tropical maternity allows him, phantasmagorically, to live through his own rebirth.[60] In the end, Müller's hero finally acquires his own tropical woman/wife.[61] Like Freud's and Winterstein's versions of "mother earth," this woman corresponds, for Müller, to "Nature" itself.[62]

What these nostalgic accounts have in common—from Hesse to Müller to Jung—is an uncompromisingly positive view of discovering *Heimat* in a foreign world. The only contemporary exception seems to be Freud—who repeats exotic desires in the citation above, yet undermines them in his further insights on the uncanny. According to Freud, the discovery of the familiar in the foreign (or the mother in the exotic lover) ought to give the traveler an uneasy sense of having "been here before" and moreover, through this doubling, a sense of the inevitability of his own death.[63] But the exotic writer tends to welcome this uncanny foreign return without anxiety. Why?

Using Kaplan's terms, we could say that it is precisely the traveler's strong desire to overcome melancholia that allows him to *not notice*—to re-press—the uncanny nature of his return. Hesse, for example, locates a proto-German cultural "paradise" in India in which—despite its resemblances to Germany—he senses no uncanniness. This repression allows him to cure his homesickness. And much more than this. His unproblematic discovery of Germany in India allows him to blot out entirely his memories of pre-journey alienation: He erases an antecedent loss of a paradisiacal Rheinland *Heimat* teeming with "fishermen and maidens." Crucially, Hesse's new Ur-Heimat (India) has persisted over time. It exists and has existed throughout Europe's entire period of modern melancholy. "Our essence and our northern culture" were never really lost, Hesse claims, but rather were simply hidden from us in the present-day South and East. "We" were simply looking in the wrong places.

This nostalgic treatise, I propose, is a nervous defense against home-lessness and *Unheimlichkeit* in all its forms—and is, moreover, decidedly un-exotic (if exoticism is primarily a quest for "difference"). If Asia and Africa are really just metaphors for a pre-industrial German *Ur-Heimat,* then Asia's and Africa's "exotic" difference is only temporal. Their primary cultural claims are effaced through the *coup* of Hesse's (and Ewers' and Müller's) universalizing memory. As Edward Said has argued, the European traveler throughout the modern age has felt that he is "*return*[ing] to the Orient."[64] The traveler, or in Hesse's case, his Germanic people, has always been there before, as if in a Jungian archetypal dream-sequence. Through this act of cultural déjà vu, the nostalgic traveler effectively sub-sumes difference and, in so doing, contradictorily obstructs his own pro-fessed exotic desire.

Nostalgia and Hyper-Nostalgia:
Kafka's *Heimweh nach der Fremde*

As discussed in the introduction, Kafka, despite his attack on "superficial exoticism" in *Richard and Samuel,* also suffered from *Heimweh nach der Fremde*—as evidenced in his "Longing to be a Red Indian" and his love for Schaffstein's *Little Green Books,* which promised a "second home" else-where. These books tell the stories of indigent, lonely Europeans who, by

traveling to Latin America or Africa, find the opportunity to reconfigure
themselves personally and professionally. The story that Kafka called the
"book of rules" for his life, *The Sugar Baron,* repeats precisely this structure (*LF* 532; *BF* 738). The protagonist, a former German officer from the
Franco-Prussian War, squanders everything he has: "Soon after the peace
negotiations, I had to take off my shining lieutenant's uniform and—
without friends or relatives who could help me—I was out on the street,
unemployed, with a mere hundred marks leftover after paying off my
debts [. . .]."[65] By the final chapter of the book (for Kafka, the "most important" chapter), however, the narrator will locate a sense of a new
Heimat (*LF* 532).

Entitled "The Second Home," this final chapter opens with the hero
preparing to climb a mountain above his estates, where, like Hesse on the
Pedrotagalla, he will establish a "monarch-of-all-I-survey" perspective. As
he prepares for this ascent, he simultaneously gains a figurative "bird's-eye-
view" over his former *Heimat* (from which he is now "*entfremdet*"[66] and
which he now remembers visiting):

> I can no longer find my way in the nervous bustle of the stone deserts that
> one calls metropolises. And my eyes are now accustomed to the sun and light
> of the tropics, just as my body is accustomed to the perpetual, stable warmth.
> Snow, ice, and fog, as well as the short days and long nights render me
> melancholy. The one winter that I spent in my homeland [*Heimat*] a few
> years ago ripened my resolve to end my days beneath the always smiling sun
> of the tropics, amidst the perpetual greenery and amidst the people who all
> know me personally and of whom I am master, rather than in Europe,
> where I am only one among hundreds of thousands, only a number.[67]

Here, we have the contemporary model of *Heimweh nach der Fremde* that
so influenced Hesse and even the more circumspect Benjamin. Melancholic because his fantasy of his own home is lost, the despondent European locates a *Heimat* in the developing world. In so doing, he cures
himself of his rootlessness and, what is more, his feelings of alienation and
insignificance: he becomes the beloved master. According to Kafka, this is
the most essential chapter of a book that offered him a book of rules. Why
does he not follow these rules, either actually (by traveling to South America) or fictionally (by creating similarly nostalgic texts)? Why does he, already in 1911, write a response to "external exoticism" that *further* alienates
himself from central Europe?

Kafka's characters never complete the journey to the "second home" because Kafka, in the spirit of present-day anthropological and postcolonial
theory, understands the concept of *Heimat* to be essentially unstable.[68] My

point is not that Kafka's travelers are not nostalgic (they are), but rather that
their idea of "home" (and thus of *nostos*) is unhinged. *Heimat* is not assumed,
as it is for Hesse or Oskar Weber, even as a lost object. Kafka hinted to the
gentile Czech Milena Jesenská in 1920 that being a double outsider (a German Jew in Prague) led him to feel more alienated than others and also to
experience an especially strong longing for home. At the same time, his out-
sider-status led him to examine this concept of home more rigorously—
until it became *entfremdet*. Kafka writes here of (his fellow Prague Jew) Max
Brod, but he could easily have been writing of himself:

> You [Milena] have your homeland [*Heimat*] and can relinquish it, and that
> may be the best thing one can do with a homeland, especially because in so
> doing one doesn't actually relinquish that which is unrelinquishable. But
> [Max] does not have a homeland and therefore cannot relinquish anything
> and must constantly think about searching for it or building it—whether
> he's taking his hat off its hook or lying in the sun next to the pool
> [*Schwimmschule*] or writing the book which you will translate. (*LM* 123; *BM*
> 164, trans. rev.)

Whereas Milena, in Kafka's fantasy, had a homeland to denounce, Kafka
and Brod did not. Jewish nostalgia thus logically transcended gentile nostalgia.[69] The German Jew in Prague needed to search for his home everywhere, be it at the *Schwimmschule* or the hat rack.

Here, we see the ironic fruits of Kafka's outsider status. Extreme nostalgia, in Kafka's description, does not lead to the monarchical discovery of a
second home. Rather, through nostalgia's myopic ardour (at hat racks and
writing desks), it undermines the fantasy of a first home. ("Alas," notes the
mouse in Kafka's late fable, "the world is growing smaller every day" [*GW*
135; *NSII* 343]). Kafka's cultural homelessness manifests itself here as what
we might term a modernist or "absurdist" nostalgia: pushed beyond rea-
sonable limits, nostalgia is transformed into a Chaplinesque quest for a
home at the hat rack. Such a hyper-nostalgia ironically critiques fantasies
of home by overdetermining domestic experience. The overscrutinized familiar world becomes *unheimlich,* and home becomes foreign—not the
other way around.

The Exotic *Heimat:*
Anthropologizing Europe

In the light of this description of a near-sighted search for home, it is not surprising that, during the same 1911 autumn when Hesse appropriates Sri
Lanka from above, Kafka and Brod destabilize central Europe from below.

They describe, midway through *Richard and Samuel's* only completed chapter, a nighttime Munich automobile ride marked by its speed, its lowness ("cellar-like perspectives"), and the blindness of its passengers—whose views of the darkened city are blocked by the large hood of the taxi (*M* 287; *EFI* 198). The driver rattles off the names of "invisible buildings that one ought to be sightseeing" or, more literally, "unseeable sights" ("*unsichtbaren Sehenswürdigkeiten*") (*M* 287; *EFI* 199). The travelers, like blindfolded moviegoers, cannot see the sights: they hear only "tires whir[ring] on the wet asphalt like the apparatus in a cinema." The ultimate effect of this scene is the dislocation and multiplication of eyes. The view from below, the speed of the automobile, and, later, the writers' aesthetic of contradictory stereoscopy all conspire to exoticize Munich: the English Garden, Ludwigstrasse, the Theatiner Church, the Feldherrn Hall, the Pschorr brewery—all of these familiar sites/sights are no longer what they seemed to be.

"Richard"—that is, the *mise en abyme* of Kafka imitating Brod imitating Kafka imitating Brod—finally sums up the way in which the authors' aesthetic project of challenging "superficial exoticism" connects to the anthropological one of exoticizing Europe. Even though he has been in Munich several times before, Richard claims, he is now at once flabbergasted and excited by its strangeness: "I recognize nothing" (*M* 288; *EFI* 199). Kafka and Brod thus succeed in making Europe new and foreign. They manage, as Paul Rabinow puts it, to "anthropologize the West: show how exotic its constitution of reality has been."[70] At the close of Richard's and Samuel's disorienting automobile trip, they rejoin their train, and the themes of perspectival disorientation and domestic exoticism continue. Samuel views peculiar Swiss fences made of pencil-like gray logs that he has "never seen" before; he claims that "every country has novelties to show in the ordinary objects of daily life" (*M* 291–92; *EFI* 202). After Richard falls asleep, Samuel awakens him to show him an unusual Swiss bridge; however, by the time Richard reaches the window, the bridge has already passed out of sight: it "is already past before I peer up" (*M* 292; *EFI* 203). Everything Richard sees from the moving train is with the "faculties of a dreamer": he only hears revelers in the station in Lindau and can't be certain whether he saw or dreamt a solitary man in Württemberg who, at two in the morning, walked out onto his veranda to "cool his head before going to bed" (*M* 294; *EFI* 204). Such scenes accumulate throughout the text, eventually rendering central Europe as ephemeral and disorienting to us as Hesse's Sri Lanka was, when he first arrived, to him.

Work on *Richard and Samuel* stalled in the winter of 1911–12, perhaps because the young writers performed their task of dislocating their own "I"s too well. Kafka, for one, finally found the project of continued self-effacement unbearable. As he writes in his diary on November 19, "every sentence [Max] writes for *Richard and Samuel* is bound up with a reluctant concession on my part" (*D* 122; *Ta* 258). In January 1912, Kafka remarks on the frustrating structure of "mutual resistance" that was the essence of the project but was also detrimental to artistic production: "the one page of *Richard and Samuel* that we finished amidst mutual resistance is simply proof of Max's energy, but otherwise bad" (*D* 162; *Ta* 340). Although frustrated with this particular project, Kafka did not give up on his idea to write a travel novel nor on his attempt to unsettle his central European home—and "*Heimat*" in general—with views from below. Less than one year later, he experienced what he regarded as his literary breakthrough, and he wrote most of the travel narrative, *Amerika*, as well as *The Metamorphosis*. Two years after that, he wrote *The Trial* and, finally, one year before his death, "The Burrow" ("Der Bau"). This late story was the culmination of Kafka's ambition to render internal spaces strange: to discover an exoticism that is not primarily "external" and "superficial."

Kafka's answer to what he and Brod perceived to be an exhausted, "superficial" exoticism was not unique in European modernism. While Hesse, Ewers, and Müller chose to follow European expansion and imperial nostalgia to its logical extremes, Hugo von Hofmannsthal (*Letters of a Returnee*, 1907–8), Arthur Schnitzler (*The Road into the Open*, 1908), Rainer Maria Rilke (*The Notebooks of Malte Laurids Brigge*, 1910), and Thomas Mann (*Death in Venice*, 1911) all exposed this nostalgia as a chimera. These writers, like Kafka, turned the voyage inward, and discovered, contemporaneously with Freud, the exotic nature of "home." But these writers, unlike Kafka, did not so clearly literalize the concept of travel in their internal journeys. By continually employing travelers and travel metaphors, Kafka more methodically questioned the popular assumption that we know where "home" is; that is, that we know of a place where we do not travel. From *Richard and Samuel* onward, Kafka asks, "Where does travel begin and 'home' end?" "Where does the 'foreign' begin?" In "The Judgment," for example, the foreign territory apparently commences with Russia, where Georg Bendemann's friend is dying. But doesn't it actually already begin at the doorway of Bendemann's father's bedroom, or at the limits of his home city, in the river in which he finally drowns? Is not the Samsa living room in *The Metamorphosis*, where Gregor ultimately and conclusively becomes an "animal," foreign terrain?[71]

Kafka's famous, above-mentioned predicament as a double outsider of course stimulated his unique interest in domestic foreignness. But Kafka's subversion of "home" also reaches out toward larger theoretical questions that still concern us today in our increasingly hybridized and migratory world. As Kafka demonstrates, it is always too late for home. The *Reiseanzug* is in the bedroom, "travel" inhabits "dwelling," and "natives" everywhere are, like Gregor, climbing the walls. I am not arguing that Kafka's alienation of home is an effort, as James Clifford ironically puts it, to "make the margin a new center (e.g., 'we' are all travelers)." Rather, I am attempting, with Kafka, to place both "traveling" and "dwelling" in question.[72] By undermining the popular exotic discourse of *Heimat* with *Richard and Samuel,* Kafka starts to strip off exoticism's trappings. He begins to release himself from his, and Benjamin's, nostalgia—while never completely leaving it behind. In fact, the tension between nostalgia and home's destruction runs through Kafka's oeuvre, most notably in his next attempt to write a novel. Kafka became frustrated with *Richard and Samuel,* but he did not give up on his idea to transcend exoticism, both formally and substantially: It is now time for him to go to America.

Chapter Two

The "America" Novel:
Learning How to Get Lost

"Then on top of that I got lost."

—*Karl Rossmann, protagonist of* The Man Who Disappeared

C ritics of Kafka's "America" novel have repeatedly pointed out the
   ways in which it revises and even contradicts the Bildungsroman
   tradition.[1] Written with *David Copperfield* in mind, Kafka's novel
seems to directly oppose the Bildungsroman's structure of progressive
knowledge-acquisition and learning-through-experience. Karl not only
does not learn, he also seems to be amnesiac—in direct contrast to David
Copperfield, whose memory accumulates endlessly, accommodating even
the most picayune details from childhood.[2] Since Karl seems to have forgotten (or repressed) most of his past, he seldom reflects on his actions in
order to learn something and make wiser decisions in the future: Karl thus
repeats the same basic mistake throughout the novel, naively trusting
stranger after stranger (his uncle, Mr. Pollunder, Robinson, Delamarche) as
if he had never before been led astray. The non-progressive, amnesiac structure of Karl's character comes to the fore when, midway through the
novel, he claims that he is fifteen years old—thus, two years younger than
he was in the novel's first sentence (*A* 136; *V* 175).[3]

The Vanishing "I":
Der Verschollene and the Exotic Tradition

Readers sensitive to this assault on the novelistic tradition have overlooked,
however, the ways in which *Amerika* simultaneously counters the exotic

tradition. Exotic literature (in travelogues as well as in novels) generally relied as much on the narrative of personal development as did the Bildungsroman. As I argued in chapter one, many exotic texts likewise
depended on the hero locating a satisfactory *Heimat* at the end: in the words
of Edward Said, on "return[ing]" to an original, temporally regressed
"home."[4] According to the logic of modern melancholia, the traveler
needed only return to this foreign *Heimat* in order to cure himself: relocating home corresponded to recovering one's original, healthy "self."[5] Kafka's
literary era was shot through with such characters, who viewed travel prin-
cipally as a mode of psychological refashioning. Wolfgang Reif refers to this
phenomenon as "*Selbstfindung*" (self-finding or self-discovery) and locates it
throughout exotic, fin de siècle literature: in, for example, Hermann Hesse's
Out of India, Waldemar Bonsels' *Indian Journey,* and Hermann Keyserling's
Diary of a Philosopher (*Das Reisetagebuch eines Philosophen*).[6] One of many
other possible examples is Norbert Jacques' popular *Pirath's Island* (*Piraths
Insel,* 1917), which Kafka owned. Here, the down-on-his-luck Peter Pirath
(whose business is in the red, whose wife is cheating on him) decides to
travel to the South Seas in order to "save" himself. Pirath eventually achieves
a customary form of *Selbstfindung:* He becomes a Crusoean island-master as
well as a harem-owner. At one point, Pirath, crucially, surveys his own plantation through a telescope. Like Hesse on the Pedrotagalla and Kafka's
beloved Oskar Weber above his sugar fields, Pirath proves the importance of
his "self" through his vision: Only this singular perspective can grant meaning and order to the world he has conquered.[7]

　　Kafka's America novel, like *Richard and Samuel,* subverts this fantasy of
Selbstfindung and thereby undermines the typical exotic narrative. Karl can
never "find" himself in America. Instead, he becomes increasingly lost, both
literally and figuratively. This figurative lostness is established, from the very
beginning, in the novel's title. Although Max Brod named the novel
Amerika, Kafka referred to it as *Der Verschollene* (*The Man Who Disappeared*).
Kafka's title thus does not name the protagonist (not *Karl Rossmann* or, as
Jacques might have done, *Rossmann's Continent*), nor does it refer to the
country Karl visits (not *America* or, as in the travelogue from which Kafka
garnered much of his empirical data, *America: Today and Tomorrow*).[8] Rather,
Kafka quite deliberately supplants the name of his character and of the place
that he visits with a subjective *vanishing point:* a perspective that steadily
fades into itself. Kafka's novel, then, from the title page onward, names the
"disappearance" of the traveling self as its theme. *Der Verschollene* may indeed
be a story about exotic nostalgia (Karl wants to locate a new home as much
as do the popular and literary heroes of his day), but it is also a story about
the subversion of this narrative intent. *Der Verschollene* recounts the disappearance—or, as I will argue, the loss—of the traveling "I."

Despite this reversal of exotic *Selbstfindung,* Kafka's novel retains this tradition's narrative structure of lost and found: more specifically, of banishment, disorientation, and, finally, relocation. But in Kafka's novel, this cycle repeats itself—going full circle twice in the first six chapters (the only chapters actually completed and titled by Kafka, and making up two-thirds of the extant text).[9] The first cycle (chapters 1–3) occurs as follows: in "The Stoker," Karl is banished from his childhood home and is eventually taken in by his uncle; in "The Uncle," he settles into his uncle's home; in "A Country House Near New York," he is again banished. The subsequent chapter-grouping (4–6) repeats the same format: in "The Road to Ramses," Karl makes his way to the hotel; he establishes himself both professionally and personally in "The Hotel Occidental"; in "The Case of Robinson," he is expelled. Although none of the remaining chapters were completed and thus do not together form a strict chronology, one could imagine two additional, later groupings: Karl finds a home and job (as servant and "driver" for Brunelda in "A Refuge" and "Brunelda's Departure"), only to lose both of these in an unwritten later chapter; at the end of the incomplete "Nature Theater of Oklahoma," we could extrapolate, Karl will again find a job (as an engineer) and personal contacts (Giacomo, Fanny), only eventually to lose them. This structure of gain and loss, which rehearses the stakes of fin de siècle exotic literature, could conceivably repeat itself ad infinitum in Kafka's novel.

Because of *Der Verschollene*'s formal indebtedness to exotic *Selbstfindung,* it makes sense to re-read Kafka's novel in terms of this tradition. I therefore begin this chapter with a historical deviation, comparing Kafka's *Der Verschollene* to the early travelogues of his two most important literary forbears: Goethe (*Italian Journey,* 1786–88) and Flaubert (*Voyage en Orient,* 1849–51). In both of these texts, we see the roots of the modern exotic structure of *Selbstfindung.* The lost-and-found narrative plays itself out in Goethe's "exotic" Italy[10] and Flaubert's Egypt. These texts were seminal to fin de siècle travel writers because, as discussed in the previous chapter, the 1911 German translation of *Voyage* immediately became a cause célèbre, and, in the same decades, a new Goethe-cult spread across Germany and Austria. In Kafka's specific case, Flaubert and Goethe formed an important constellation in 1911, when Kafka began his first version of *Der Verschollene.* In this year, he re-read Goethe's travel writings and almost certainly read Flaubert's just-published *Voyage* (*D* 56; *Ta* 42–43). Kafka's staging of *Selbstfindung* in *Der Verschollene* thus can be considered a doubled re-staging: a reconfiguration both of the tradition of his day and of the practices of his most important literary predecessors. As I will argue in the second part of this chapter—through a close reading of *Der Verschollene*—Kafka used these writers' early paradigms of lost-and-found in order to re-inscribe them. He

created travel texts—first, *Richard and Samuel* and later *Amerika* (1911–14)—
that placed lostness, not location, at the end of the lost-and-found saga.

Travel-Writing Paradigms:
Lost-and-Found in Goethe and Flaubert

Goethe's importance for Kafka's literary development can hardly be over-
estimated. Brod remembers Kafka's "love of Goethe" and his long-lasting
enthusiasm for Goethe's works: "To hear Kafka talk about Goethe with awe
was something quite out of the ordinary, it was like hearing a little child talk
about an ancestor who lived in happier, purer days and in direct contact
with the Divine."[11] As a young man, Kafka read the culturally conservative
Der Kunstwart, which featured Goethe poems and articles about Goethe
typical of the phenomenon of "Goethe-Worship" (especially pronounced
in turn-of-the-century, German-Jewish Prague).[12] For Kafka, Goethe was
more than just an important literary figure: Goethe, along with Flaubert,
was a model for life. In one of his earliest surviving writings, the nineteen-
year-old Kafka chastises his friend Oskar Pollak—who has just returned
from visiting the Goethe house and National Museum in Weimar—for ap-
preciating Goethe in too literary a way. Pollak's proclaimed interest in
Goethe's study is, for Kafka, precious and false: "a conceit and a schoolboy
idea with just a dash of German lit. [*Germanistik*]—may it roast in hell" (*L*
4; *B* 12). Instead of admiring Goethe's desk, Kafka proposes learning literally to walk in Goethe's footsteps: "But do you know what really is the holiest thing we could have of Goethe's as a memento—the footprints of his
solitary walks through the country—they would be it." Kafka eventually
stood by his word, journeying to Goethe's house and walking around the
property in 1912. As if by ironic plan, he experienced his literary breakthrough with "The Judgment" weeks later, thereby proving that there was
a connection between Goethe and literature that struck deeper than *Germanistik's* conceits.

Kafka had, in fact, already begun following in Goethe's footsteps in
1909, when he traveled to Italy for the first of several times. While in
Malcesine in September 1913, Kafka mentioned *Italian Journey,* telling
his sister Ottla that he was sitting in front of the very same ruined fort
where Goethe had nearly been arrested (as a presumed Austrian spy) in
1786.[13] Kafka was interested, like Samuel Beckett (who, after following
James Joyce to Paris, copied Joyce by wearing shoes that were too
tight), in materializing the metaphor of footstep-following.[14] This desire to *become* Goethe by following the trajectory of his body (not just
writing like him) explains Kafka's fascination specifically with Goethe's
travel writings, especially in the years that Kafka was undertaking his

own travels and beginning his work on *Der Verschollene* (see *D* 56, 60, 176; *LF* 68).

Italian Journey would have been of special interest to Kafka because it offers the eighteenth century's most enduring example of a *Verschollene*-like lost-and-found narrative, beginning with the traveler's deliberate attempt to get lost. Privy Councillor Goethe, suffocating in the atmosphere of the Weimar court, left Karlsbad in the middle of the night on September 3, 1786 to, in his own words, "*lose myself* [*mich zu verlieren*] in places where I am totally unknown." He continues: "I am going to travel quite alone, under another name."[15] Goethe's experiment in getting lost is, on the one hand, a Romantic flight from ennui. He desires, like Baudelaire, to be "anywhere out of *this* world": for Goethe, the claustrophobic world of the Weimar court.[16] This flight is psychological, but also cultural and political. By changing his name (to Möller) he can lose his reputation both as the famous author of *The Sufferings of Young Werther* and as Weimar's respected Privy Councillor. In order to protect his anonymity, Goethe traveled without the most basic necessities of eighteenth-century travel: without a servant, without letters of introduction, and, most importantly, in public postal coaches instead of in a private one. He thus remained essentially undiscovered even in the midst of German expatriate artists in Rome. The vehemence with which he adhered to his disguise expressed the intensity of his desire to get lost.

But Goethe's desire does not preclude its apparent opposite: the desire to find himself. As Richard Terdiman points out in his study of Flaubert's *Voyage,* the complex process of "dis-Orient-ation" fluctuates between the yearning for self-dissolution and for self-re-creation.[17] Goethe's desire to dissolve psychologically and politically contains within it the same reconstructive tendencies Terdiman ascribes to Flaubert. Goethe's claim that he will travel "quite alone, under another name" continues: "and I have great hopes of this venture, odd as it seems."[18] Goethe's "great hopes"—the desired fruits of "losing himself"—are of self-rediscovery through travel. Midway through his journey, Goethe claims to experience a renaissance (a "true rebirth"). This renaissance, he assures us, springs specifically from travel: "Nothing can compare with the new life a reflective individual receives from contemplating a new country."[19] Through losing himself, then, Goethe finds a new and presumably better life. W. H. Auden and Elizabeth Mayer, in their introduction to their magnificent (if inaccurate) English translation of *Italian Journey,* offer a similar narrative of Goethean disorientation and relocation. For Auden and Mayer, Goethe leaves Weimar and loses himself (both name and reputation) in order to be reborn poetically as well as physically/sexually in Italy.[20] Auden and Mayer thereby reinforce

Goethe's fantasy that self-displacement will allow the traveler to, as Said writes, "take hold of" himself in the foreign land.[21]

Complementary to this tension between the lost and found self is the tension between the lost and found Other. Goethe prefigures Dean Mac-Cannell's modern "tourist" in that he thinks he can acquire a "new," more satisfactory ego through travel: In MacCannell's words, modern man suffers from an "existential" sense of "inauthenticity," which he imagines he can attenuate by traveling to a foreign, more "authentic" world.[22] But, as Goethe discovers already in eighteenth-century Venice, this authentic foreignness proves to be as elusive as the traveler's sense of self. Goethe complains upon his arrival that Venice is discursively over-determined: "So much has already been said and published about Venice that instead of a detailed description I shall just give my personal impressions."[23] Goethe protests, here, what Jonathan Culler has termed the overly "marked" nature of the touristic site.[24] Because so many people have written (and "published") about Venice, Venice exists only as a text, not as an imagined Real (read: unmarked) space. Goethe has two choices: he can either mark the site further, adding minutiae to Johann Winckelmann's and others' already-detailed textual maps of Venice, or he can attempt to locate what he calls the "new" Venice, a Venice somehow not yet experienced.

Goethe, not surprisingly, chooses the latter and decides that his tactic for escaping discursive redundancy will be to get lost. Like Walker Percy's American tourists in *The Message in the Bottle* (who stumble upon an Indian religious festival in Mexico), Goethe senses that he must lose his way in order to escape inauthenticity and have what Percy calls an "immediate encounter with being" (for Goethe, this means discovering an astonishingly "new" Venice).[25] Venice is, of course, famous as a disorienting place where, to this day, it is very easy to get lost. But most tourists know this and, unlike Goethe, have a map in hand when departing the hotel. Goethe, however, deliberately leaves guide and map behind: "I hurried out [. . .] without a guide and, noting only the points of the compass [*Himmelsgegenden*], plunged into the labyrinth of the city."[26]

Goethe invades the labyrinth again the following night, this time extending his wanderings ("again without a guide") to the "remoter quarters":

> Toward evening, again without a guide, I lost my way in the remotest quarters of the city. [. . .] I tried to find my way in and out of this labyrinth without asking anyone, again only directing myself by the points of the compass. Finally one does disentangle oneself [*man entwirrt sich*], but it is an incredible maze, and my method, which is to acquaint myself with it directly through my senses, is the best. Also, up to the last inhabited tip of land I have noted the residents' behavior, manners, customs, and nature.[27]

Goethe sets himself twice, deliberately, into the foreign labyrinth. This second time he wanders into a section of the city off the beaten track, a semiotically unmarked (not "published" about) region in the remotest quarters. Acting as ethnographer, Goethe discovers what the modern tourist longs for: pre-"modern" ways and "purer, simpler lifestyles."[28] By traveling to the "last inhabited tip of land," Goethe discovers a human "nature" that, in its simplicity and poverty, causes him, in the end, to cry out to God, "Dear Lord! what a poor, good-natured beast man is!"[29]

Typically for the modern traveler, this discovery of an apparently primitive, uncivilized foreign world encourages the traveler's own *Selbstfindung.* This occurs for Goethe in two ways: first, he gains the authority of an ethnographer ("I have noted the residents' behavior, manner," etc.), and, second, his journey to Venice's unmarked regions resembles Odysseus' successful journey to Hades. Goethe intentionally gives up subjective control ("I lost my way"), but, by doing this, he eventually gains a new, stronger sense of self. Goethe "disentangles" himself from the urban labyrinth simply by relying "directly" on his own "senses." He thus returns to this hotel with a new regard for his own senses and his subjective power ("my method [. . .] is the best"). This vignette represents Goethe's travel program in microcosm. The traveler loses himself—discards guide, name, and identity—only to emerge from the labyrinth of loss with two major finds: an authentic foreign world (the apparently unmarked Venetian fringe) as well as a "new," authorized self. Only after successfully completing this game of lost and found does Goethe (who apparently no longer needs it) buy his first map of Venice.[30]

Using terminology from Freud's *Beyond the Pleasure Principle* (1920) we could explain Goethe's game as a method of "shielding" himself from fear. In such a scenario, Goethe overcomes the greatest travel-fear—the fear of getting lost (cf. *The Odyssey* and even *Hansel and Gretel*)—precisely by getting lost. Like Freud's World War I amputees who dreamt repeatedly of losing their limbs as a mode of psychological inoculation, Goethe pre-emptively loses himself in order to develop a shield protecting him against the trauma of self-loss. Goethe's strategy is, in further terms supplied by *Beyond the Pleasure Principle,* a version of the "fort/da" game. Goethe replaces the Freudian spool, which the child repeatedly tosses behind a curtain and retrieves, with his own body.[31] He throws this body (with the "points of the compass" functioning as security "string") behind the foreign city's curtain and then triumphantly reclaims it, thereby precluding the real suffering of a possible self-loss. We could describe this combination of protective "shield" and "fort/da" as a traveler's insurance policy. The traveler underwrites his own worst fears by realizing them. In so doing, he, like the child in Freud's study, safeguards himself. Goethe could never *really* lose himself, because, as described from the safety of his hotel room, he orchestrates the narrative of loss.

This Venice experience serves as a paradigm for the entire *Italian Journey*. Goethe loses himself but not really. As he writes during his first Rome stay two months later: "Although I am still the same person, I think I am changed to the very marrow of my bones [*bis aufs innerste Knochenmark*]."[32] Here, Goethe imagines doing more than just losing his body in a foreign city: he loses the body's material core. Once again, however, he does not lose himself. *Italian Journey's* economy of return demands that, in the end, Goethe remain "still the same person"—albeit "new" and improved. Nothing could be more opposed to Kafka's sense of self, related in his diary in 1914, over 125 years following Goethe's first journey to Rome ("I have hardly anything in common with myself"), and later, in a conversation with Gustav Janouch ("I am as lonely as—as Franz Kafka") [*D* 252; *Ta* 622].[33]

Over sixty years later, Flaubert relates a Goethean economy of return in his 1849–51 *Voyage en Orient*, whose general renown would have been amplified for the Flaubert-inspired Kafka. Kafka admired Flaubert perhaps even more than Goethe: keeping a copy of *L'Éducation sentimentale* on his desk, referring to Flaubert as his "blood-relation," and even anointing himself Flaubert's "spiritual son."[34] Flaubert's *Voyage*, like Goethe's *Italian Journey* and Kafka's *Der Verschollene*, begins with a narrative of loss. As did Goethe, Flaubert desires to "lose" his self as well as his social-political situation (in his case, deathly boring, bourgeois France).[35] Such a self-loss— or "self-obliteration"—through travel is a necessary first stage in Flaubert's desired project of personal re-creation, of "Oriental renaissance."[36] Like Goethe, Flaubert literalizes his desire to lose himself by actually getting lost, on purpose, in a foreign city. He leaves his guide (his ever-present "dragoman") one January day in 1850 and wanders into the Cairo alleys, a comparable substitute for Goethe's Venetian labyrinth:

> I walk by myself in Cairo, in fine sunshine, in the section between the prison and the Bulak gate [. . .] *I keep losing my way* in the maze of alleys and running into dead-ends. From time to time I come on an open space with the debris of ruined houses, or rather with no houses; hens pecking, cats on walls. Quiet way of life here—intimate, secluded. Dazzling sun effects when one suddenly emerges from these alleys, so narrow that the roofs of the *moucharbiehs* [shuttered bay windows] on each side touch each other.[37]

Flaubert's experience, like Goethe's, consists of losing and finding himself. He wanders guide-less through the foreign labyrinth and discovers an apparently unmarked (not "published" about) section of the city. The neighborhood is both "intimate" and "secluded," apparently outside of touristic, dragomanish discourse. Like Goethe on Venice's "last inhabited tip of land," Flaubert seems to gain entry into an authentic touristic "back space."[38] In this sense, Flaubert, again like Goethe, uses getting lost as a tactic for accessing an authentic realm. Getting lost provides both travelers with an experience apparently beyond the signposts of tour books and guides.

The discovery of such an unmarked foreign space leads, for both travelers, to personal epiphany. Flaubert manages, even without Goethe's "points of the compass," to un-lose himself. He "emerges" without great trouble from the maze of lostness into dazzling sunshine. The extensive critical literature diverges on whether or not Flaubert finally loses or affirms himself in the Orient. Ali Behdad, for example, claims that Flaubert, in the end, "pulverizes" his "self" in the Orient.[39] Lisa Lowe, conversely, emphasizes Flaubert's rather traditional "Orientalist" program of self-assertion. According to Lowe, Flaubert "fetishizes" the Orient in order to stabilize it through stereotype; otherwise, its unknowability would threaten Flaubert's own subjective integrity.[40] Despite Behdad's point that Flaubert (unlike Goethe) actually seems to be trying to annihilate himself through exotic travel (as when he has sex with a plague-infested prostitute), Flaubert's Cairo anecdote emphasizes the ways in which he attempts to orchestrate his loss. In Lowe's terms, he protects himself against the Orient's threatening "absence" precisely by staging his own absence. Playing a "fort/da" game of his own, Flaubert narrates his own re-appearance from the "maze of alleys" and "dead-ends"—thereby emphasizing the temporary, playful nature of his disorientation. He, like Goethe, successfully finds his way out.

Flaubert suggests, toward the end of his "dis-Orient-ing" trip, that he has relocated some (perhaps insufficient) "self" in Egypt. That Flaubert has regained some notion of "self" is implied by his readiness, on his way back home, to lose it again. As he writes to Ernest Chevalier from Rome in 1851: "Well, yes, I've seen the Orient, and it's not enough, since I want to go back. I want to go to India, to *lose myself* in the pampas of America and go to Sudan."[41] I maintain that Flaubert needs to lose himself in India because he never sufficiently did so in Egypt. Instead of losing himself, he acted out a narrative of self-dislocation whose recuperative finale he already knew. Thus, Flaubert ends where he began, eager to begin a Goethean "fort/da" game that might successfully disorient him. Yet this time Flaubert imagines a "fort" without a "da": a narrative of loss that might finally—he hopes—bankrupt the bourgeois economy of *Selbstfindung*.

Der Verschollene: Verirrung without End

As I discussed earlier, Kafka wrote his travel diaries and *Richard and Samuel* with Goethe's and Flaubert's travel writings in mind. Does the same go for

Der Verschollene? Kafka makes pilgrimages to Paris and Weimar in 1911 and 1912, respectively, and he mentions Flaubert and Goethe repeatedly in these years. Of Goethe, he writes in January 1912—while working on the first, discarded version of *Der Verschollene*—"This week I think I have been completely influenced by Goethe, have really exhausted the strength of this influence and have therefore become useless" (*D* 172; *Ta* 358). Later, while writing the extant version of the novel, he turns to Flaubert (cited in part above): "*Éducation sentimentale* is a book that for many years has been as dear to me as are only two or three people; whenever and wherever I open it, I am startled and succumb to it completely, and I always feel as though I were the author's spiritual son, albeit a weak and awkward one" (*LF* 42; *BF* 96). Gerhard Kurz sees in this remark evidence of what Harold Bloom calls the "anxiety of influence": the imperative of a young writer to struggle for his own artistic identity through a confrontation with an idealized poetic father-figure.[42] Although this theory overstates the agonistic nature of Kafka's relation to Flaubert (Kafka often seems to be more interested in *becoming* Flaubert than in defeating him), it nonetheless allows us to see Kafka's *Der Verschollene* as an example of his attempt to continue Flaubert's project in more radical terms. How does *Der Verschollene* move beyond *Italian Journey, Voyage en Orient,* and, as we shall see, *L'Éducation sentimentale?* How does it complete, in a more uncompromising way, Flaubert's attempts at "self-obliteration"?

Goethe's and Flaubert's tales of lost travelers resonate throughout *Der Verschollene,* most notably in the opening scene. Here, Kafka calls attention to Karl's figurative lostness (his banishment from his parents' home) by literalizing it: Karl gets lost. He forgets his umbrella in the boat that brought him to America and thus must leave his suitcase on the deck and return to steerage to look for his umbrella. To emphasize the relationship between Karl's physical and psychological lostness, Kafka employs the reflexive verb "*sich verirren,*" which implies, as I will explore later, both physical and metaphysical errancy: "[Karl] had painfully to find his way down endlessly recurring stairs, through corridors with countless turnings, through an empty room with a deserted writing-table, until in the end [. . .] he *lost himself completely* [*sich . . . ganz und gar verirrt hatte*]" (*A* 4; *V* 8, my emphasis). Karl's complete state of lostness remains with him until he meets the ship's stoker, with whom Karl begins to feel "at home" (*A* 8; *V* 14). But even here, unlike the self-stylized heroes of Goethe's and Flaubert's narratives, Karl does not shed his sense of displacement. As if by way of epithetical introduction, his first words to the stoker are "*Ich habe mich verirrt*" (I've lost my way) (*A* 4; *V* 9). Karl soon realizes that he has lost not only his way but also his suitcase, which functions as a metaphor for Karl's identity (it contains all of his belongings as well as his only photograph of his parents): "But I think my suitcase can't be lost yet"; the "faithful suitcase had perhaps been lost in earnest"; the "loss of the suitcase"; "in case he should have lost his suitcase"; "I'm afraid I've lost my suitcase."[43] Losing his suitcase begins to define Karl as a lost man. Still without mentioning his own name, Karl tells the stoker of the dislocation that has become the defining event of his short narrative life: "*Dann habe ich mich auch noch verirrt*" (Then on top of that I got lost) (*A* 5; *V* 10). Karl repeats his stories of loss neurotically as if, through this ritual of confession, he might expunge them and start to find his way in America.

In the course of the first chapter, it seems that Karl achieves this. Sailors open up the doors separating steerage from first and second class in order to clean the ship, and Karl sees other parts of the ship for the first time. The ship's design, once terribly confusing, becomes more legible. Karl begins to understand the ship's complex "organisation"; as a steerage passenger he had not been able to gain an overview (*A* 11; *V* 19). Karl and the stoker walk along these now navigable corridors—until they reach the Capitain's office, where Karl claims to realize "where [he] was" (*A* 12; *V* 20). This moment of topographical orientation resonates with a psychological one: Karl and his long-lost American uncle "find" each other. They embrace and kiss, and announce: "I'm very glad to have found you" (Karl), "And that's how to find a nephew" (Uncle), "he's found me" (Karl) (*A* 30, 32, 34; *V* 43, 46, 49). The ramifications of these findings are great for Karl's sense of self. Through his wealthy uncle, Senator Edward Jakob, Karl will now have a successful career in front of him. As the nephew of a senator, Karl can now announce his public identity for the first time in the novel: no longer simply the boy who loses his way, he is now "Karl Rossmann," as his passport proves to the onlookers (*A* 24; *V* 36). As we learn at the beginning of the second chapter, Karl has experienced something like a "rebirth" in America (the same metaphor used by Benjamin to describe Rossmann's journey) (*A* 39; *V* 56).[44] Karl was lost, and now is found. As with Goethe, this "rebirth" is tantamount to a reversal of topographical disorientation (*Verirrung*): Goethe, like Karl, literally "disentangles" himself (*entwirrt sich*) on the path to his *Selbstfindung*.[45]

For Karl, however, this disentanglement is not lasting (as it was for Goethe). His uncle banishes him at the end of chapter three, and here, again, he begins wandering about without a sense of orientation: he sets off in a "chance direction" (*A* 98; *V* 127). Although Karl only literally gets lost one more time (in Mr. Pollunder's labyrinthine country house), his adventures are marked, as Mark Anderson has demonstrated, by a perpetual sense of not knowing where he is.[46] Throughout the novel, especially when he has lost his sense of direction, Karl allows himself to be taken blindly from one place to the next: through the ship with the stoker, to

Pollunder's house, to Brunelda with Robinson, and, in the end, with the other recruits to "Oklahama" [*sic*] (*A* 272; *V* 387). In each of these cases, Karl is *taken* somewhere (in a taxi, on a train, on foot). He shows no sign of knowing the way himself. When he travels from New York to Pollunder's country house, Karl falls asleep on the way and thus has no sense of how he arrived. When he finally flees the house, he must trust blind luck in rural upstate New York. Karl's "America" is, as central Europe was for Richard and Samuel, a site of topographical confusion.

Just as Karl Rossmann travels haphazardly through "America," Kafka, the writer, seems to journey randomly through his texts—destructing the idea of the journey as he goes. As Malcolm Pasley's painstaking work on Kafka's manuscripts reveals, Kafka uniquely worked without any preconceived notions of plot lines and character choices. Instead, Kafka entered blindly each night into a world of fictional possibility, allowing his narratives to arise "simply *along the way*."[47] Kafka's breakthrough story, "The Judgment," for example, was originally supposed to be about "a war," Kafka claimed, but then "the whole thing turned in my hands into something else" (*LF* 265; *BF* 394). Here and elsewhere, Pasley sees a "quality of writing *that doesn't know where it is going* and lets itself be carried along by the developing story."[48] Kafka said it best himself, in a comment to Max Brod: "One must write as if in a dark tunnel, without knowing how the characters are going to develop."[49] This tunnel metaphor perhaps explains the illogical extensions of space in Kafka's novel: Pollunder's house ends up containing a large marble chapel, and the ship becomes immeasurably larger the more Karl loses his way (its stairs "recur endlessly" and have "countless" turnings). To really get lost, one needs a big space.

But this triumphant writerly lostness—which ends, like Goethe's, in the author's discovery of himself—is countered by another, less benevolent kind of disorientation. Writing, Kafka claims, can also lead to a state of lostness that never ends. Just before taking a long hiatus from *Der Verschollene* in January 1913, Kafka maintains that, when writing, one can easily "go astray [*man irrt leicht ab*]" and never again find one's way back (*LF* 156; *BF* 250). Less than two weeks later, after finally giving up on *Der Verschollene*, Kafka describes this novel as having literally run away from him: "My novel! The night before last I declared myself utterly vanquished by it. It is running apart on me [*läuft mir auseinander*], I can no longer get my arms round it" (*LF* 171; *BF* 271, trans. rev.). This notion of writing as an endless, unrecuperable motion corresponds to the feelings of many of Kafka's fictional characters, in *Der Verschollene* and beyond. These figures sense that they are, like the 1917 Country Doctor (Landarzt), eternally lost or stranded: "Never shall I reach home [. . .]. Naked, exposed to the frost of this unhappiest of ages, with an earthly carriage, unearthly horses, old man that I am, I go drifting around" (*MO* 161; *DL* 261). Later, the frantic narrator of "A Comment" ("Ein Kommentar," 1922) must ask a policeman the way to the rail station because "I cannot find it myself"—only to hear, instead of directions, the apocalyptic response auguring endless disorientation: "Give it up! Give it up!" (*GW* 183; *NSII* 530). In "The Refusal" ("Die Abweisung," 1920), the melancholic narrator remarks on the impossibility of reaching the border of his country because of the likelihood of losing one's way in the intervening towns: "If one does not get lost [*verirrt man sich nicht*] on the way one is bound to lose oneself [*verirrt man sich*] in these towns" (*GW* 120; *NSII* 261).

As the policeman's and narrator's tones suggest, getting lost implies more than simply losing one's way topographically. The reflexive verb, *sich verirren*, also describes someone who has lost his way morally and spiritually—as in the "lost sheep" (*verirrtes Schaf*) that, in the Book of Matthew, strays from the way of God.[50] Moreover, *sich verirren* calls to mind its substantive, *Verirrung*, which means "going astray," "aberration," "wandering," or "mistake." As Kafka points out four years after finally giving up work on *Der Verschollene*, *Verirrung* refers to errancy in the broadest and most significant sense: to the momentous mistakes of man and God. Kafka claims that humanity's fallen, post-Edenic world is itself a form of cosmic getting-lost, of universal error:

> Destroying this world would be the task to set oneself only, first, if the world were evil, that is, contradictory to our meaning, and secondly, if we were capable of destroying it. The first seems so to us; of the second we are not capable. We cannot destroy this world, for we have not constructed it as something independent; what we have done is to stray into it [*haben uns in sie verirrt*]; indeed, this world is our going astray [*diese Welt ist unsere Verirrung*] [. . .]. (*WP* 103; *NSII* 83)

Kafka poses a paradox. We, like Rossmann and Kafka's wandering "eternal Jew," have strayed onto an "evil" world; this world, moreover, seems to precede us (we "have not constructed it as something independent") (*LM* 147–48; *BM* 198). On the other hand, however, we constitute this world precisely through our straying onto it ("indeed, this world is our *Verirrung*"). The result is a world that we comprise (through our getting lost in it) but do not construct as something separate from us. In the end, we cannot destroy it because it consists in our own errancy, and thus we can never stand outside of it and regard it as an independent object (i.e., something we could destroy). As Wittgenstein claims regarding our relationship to language, we cannot build our own ladder leading us out of language because the ladder, too, is part of that out of which we are attempting to climb.[51]

Karl's disorientation in *Der Verschollene* resonates with this kind of metaphysical displacement. He is astray in the "evil," anarchic world of America (his uncle likens him once to a "lost sheep"), and his sense of self becomes irremediably lost (*A* 39; *V* 56). *Der Verschollene* is thus what I term a provocatively modern *Verirrungsroman,* in which the identity and even the sanity of the traveler remain forever in the balance (it intensifies and extends the project of *Richard and Samuel*). As Kafka probably knew, *Verirrung* brings to light an etymological connection between traveling ("*Reisen*") and madness ("*Irrsinn*") (through the Indo-European root, "*er[e]s*," meaning "to move rapidly, impetuously, or aimlessly"), thereby raising the stakes of young Karl's errancy. This connection between wayward travel and madness was already apparently in the Biblical notion of "*in die Irre gehen*." To speak with Karl's literary descendant, Ralph Ellison's "Invisible Man," Karl does not know "who he is" because he does not know "where he is."[52] Kafka acknowledges the psychological dangers of disorientation throughout *Der Verschollene* and, throughout his life, in his "*Schriftstellersein*" (existence as a writer) (*L* 333; *B* 384). After breaking off work on *Der Verschollene* in 1913, Kafka claims that he only wants to "race through the nights with my pen" even though he might "lose his reason" ("*irrsinnig werden*"); just before returning to this novel one year later, he similarly refers to his "mad [*irrsinniges*] bachelor's life" (*LF* 289, *BF* 427; *D* 303, *Ta* 549). Here, *Irrsinn* relates to the endless, unpredictable, and dangerous journeys of the novel writer—who, like his protagonist, enters onto trajectories that point toward no clear goal.

Finding Oneself (Part I):
Dazzling Sunlight and the View from Above

Lostness begins with the eyes. Both Goethe and Flaubert, when losing their way, remark on how the cities' narrow alleys taper their perspectives. According to Goethe in Venice, "a person walking with arms akimbo will hit against the walls with his elbows"[53] and, as Flaubert notes, this narrowness reduces vision: the roofs on each side of the Cairo alley "touch each other," thereby completely blocking out the sunlight and making it more difficult to see.[54] In both cases, however, this restricting of visual space is countered by an eventual unobstructed panoramic view similar to the one Hesse achieved on the Pedrotagalla (see my chapter one). Goethe climbs the Campanile of San Marco; Flaubert walks to the top of a minaret just outside of Cairo. Their sweeping vistas, typical of the exotic scene of visual mastery, provide them with a sense of direction and of power. Goethe, from the Campanile: "The sunshine was bright, so that I could clearly recognize places near and far without a telescope."[55] Flaubert, from the minaret: "One sees Cairo, the old Cairo almost on the first level, the two large white minarets of Mohammed Ali's mosque, the pyramids, Sakkarah, the valley of the Nile, the desert beyond, Choubra below to the right."[56] These views from above correspond to Flaubert's earlier emergence, on foot, into Cairo's dazzling sunlight. From these perspectives, the travelers learn that their disorientation is temporary and that, in the end, they will be able to gain control over a topography that had begun to engulf them.

This desire for a monarchical view over the foreign world extended into Kafka's turn of the century, when travelers often substituted hotel balconies and skyscrapers for mountains, bell towers, and minarets—but still immediately attempted to gain higher ground.[57] The 1911 travel writers, Kafka and Brod (making notes for *Richard and Samuel*), are no exceptions. Shortly after arriving in Paris in September 1911, the friends step out onto their hotel balcony, ostensibly to view the city. Instead of taking in the sights, however, Kafka only stares at his friend. He does not even see the city with his own eyes. Rather, he watches Brod watching and hears him remark on how "Parisian" the view is. Kafka claims that what he "really saw was only how fresh Max was; how assuredly he fitted into a Paris of some sort that I could not even perceive." In Kafka's memory, Brod steps, like Goethe and Flaubert, from his "dark back room" into literal and figurative "sunlight," and in so doing gains a commanding overview of the foreign city (*D* 454; *Ta* 992). Kafka, conversely, looks at Brod instead of at an imperceptible Paris and thus exchanges the possibility of a panorama for nearsightedness, for the symbolic myopia that will so frequently plague his protagonists. Significantly, Kafka later devotes two pages to describing the Parisian subway (see figure 12). By traveling in these dark, underground tunnels, he claims, foreigners are robbed of their sense of direction. Like Flaubert, they emerge out of the labyrinth into the sunlight, but, unlike Flaubert, they remain confused at the Métro's gates: "it takes a long time, after coming up, for reality and the map to correspond" (*D* 461; *Ta* 1010). Kafka's interest in subterranean disorientation transforms into art twelve years later, in the tangled existential underground of "The Burrow."

Like Kafka's journey to Paris, Karl's adventures in America are marked by his inability to gain a stable perspective—literally or figuratively. As many critics have pointed out, Kafka gained much of the empirical data for his novel from Arthur Holitscher's *America: Today and Tomorrow;* but, as Anderson argues, Kafka's novel resists Holitscher's touristic perspective by constructing a disorienting way of seeing.[58] Whereas Holitscher devotes a good deal of his New York City narrative to orienting himself from atop a skyscraper (e.g., "here is the port at which I arrived," "here is the ship on which I traveled," "here are the streets on which I walked"), Karl spends the entire first chapter of *Der Verschollene* at sea level, gaining no overview of the great city (see figure 13). After catching a quick glimpse of the Statue of Liberty from the deck of his ship, Karl's only other views of the city are through port-holes. These views are typified by their continual restlessness and obscurity. Karl observes boats and ships, but only for the few seconds it takes for them to pass: "little motor-boats, which Karl would have liked to examine thoroughly if he had had time, shot straight past [. . .]" (*A* 17; *V* 26). One of the larger ships moves so close to Karl's porthole that it eclipses completely the daylight.

Karl's views from the portholes oppose him directly to Holitscher. Whereas Holitscher looks down on the ship that brought him ("I catch sight of its four trusty smokestacks"),[59] Karl remains in the ship and looks *up* at the skyscrapers. The juxtaposition is made clearer by Karl's sense that he is not the one doing the looking. Rather, just as the Ceylonese forest seemed to "stare" at Hesse,[60] New York "stares at Karl through the hundred thousand windows of its skyscrapers" (*A* 12; *V* 20, trans. rev.). This underscores Karl's loss of visual orientation: Karl suddenly becomes the sight seen instead of the sightseer. And, unlike Hesse, Karl does not eventually gain the high ground and reverse the voyeuristic economy. Karl's next remark can thus only be meant ironically: "in this room [the ship's office] one knew where one was" (*A* 12, trans. rev.). For a newcomer to New York, the office of a ship in the harbor is precisely where one does *not* know where one is. Karl even experiments with making his vision, already obstructed by the large ships around the portholes, worse: "If one almost shut one's eyes, these ships seemed to be staggering under their own weight" (*A* 11–12; *V* 19). There can be little question about the deliberateness of Kafka's perspectival strategies. He places his hero *inside* of the boat that Holitscher—in the tradition of Goethe, Flaubert, and Hesse—views from above.

In the second chapter, Kafka allows Karl to move above sea level—but never to the heights achieved by Holitscher. Karl steps out onto the sixth-floor balcony of his uncle's house which, unlike Holitscher's skyscraper, is no taller than the tallest building in Karl's hometown (Prague) and thus much shorter than New York's tallest buildings. Karl sees only one of New York's streets. It is extremely congested and chaotic, a tumult of endlessly moving traffic:

> [It] looked like an inextricable confusion, for ever newly improvised, of dis-
> torted human figures and the roofs of all kinds of vehicles, [. . .] all of it held
> and penetrated by a mighty light which the multitudinous objects in the

street scattered, carried off and again eagerly brought back, and that appeared so palpable to the dazzled eye that it was as if a gigantic roof of glass stretched over the street were being violently smashed over and over again. (*A* 39; *V* 55, trans. rev.)

The fragmentation of Karl's view—the dazzling of his eye—brings with it the connotation of a fragmented ego. Whereas Goethe, long before Holitscher, solidified his narrative of *Selbstfindung* through an encompassing view, Karl's splintered perspective leads only to psychic "bewilderment" (*A* 39; *V* 56). Later in the chapter, Karl repeats this scene of visual disorder, which this time takes on cosmic ramifications. From the balcony again, Karl views traffic that seems to be "one small section of a great wheel which afforded no hand-hold unless one knew all the forces controlling its full orbit" (*A* 43–44; *V* 61). Karl's view is again limited: he can never gain an overview of the totality of the forces that control both the city and Karl's movements through it. In the chapter's final scene, Karl rehearses the myopia Kafka had already recorded while visiting Paris with Brod. Driving through the New York streets with Mr. Pollunder, Karl, instead of taking in the sights, only stares at Mr. Pollunder's waistcoat and the gold chain that spans it (*A* 53; *V* 74).

The emotional valences of Karl's experiences of myopia and visual disorientation are mixed. On the one hand, they signify existential *Verirrung* and restlessness: from one porthole, Karl sees "restlessness [*Unruhe*] transmitted from the restless element to helpless human beings and their works" (*A* 17; *V* 27). On the other hand, his visual disorientation signifies the peculiarly modern pleasure of speed and bewilderment: Karl enjoys the "cheerful" motion of waves through the porthole and later speaks of the great "pleasure" he garners from looking at his uncle's traffic-filled street (*A* 11, 41; *V* 19, 57).[61] Whether perceived negatively or positively, however, Karl's perspective always refers back to his sense of disorientation. He sees himself through the shattered mirror of the city's hundred thousand eyes and experiences the strange multiplicity of his eye/I.

Finding Oneself (Part II): Viewing the Woman

According to Mary Louise Pratt, the nineteenth-century traveler's monarchical vision of the landscape (Flaubert on the minaret) traditionally corresponds to this same traveler's commanding view of the "native's" naked body. The strange country "opens up," Pratt writes, as does the "unclothed indigenous bodyscape."[62] Dennis Porter recasts this argument in psychoanalytical terms—claiming that visual pleasure is exemplary of the modern, "perverse" travel tradition. The male traveler who once—like Goethe and Stendhal—yearned for genital intercourse and "love," now fancies voyeurism and visual domination.[63] According to Porter, Flaubert's desire in the Egyptian brothels was "scopophilic": he generally privileged looking over touching. This scopophilia, moreover, was often sadistic, issuing from Flaubert's desire to dominate the female object. For this reason, Flaubert's rhetorical statement at the beginning of *Voyage* could serve as an epigraph for his entire travel book—and perhaps for the visual project of exoticism in general: "How much you would like straightaway to *see* her naked, admit it, naked to the very heart!"[64] Flaubert emphasizes this connection between looking and power during an artful strip-tease performed by the famous Egyptian prostitute Kuchuk Hanem. Flaubert recounts how male Arabs either leave the brothel or (in the case of the musicians) are blindfolded before the prostitutes undress: "the women send away Farghali and another sailor [. . .]. A black veil is tied around the eyes of the child, and a fold of his blue turban is lowered over those of the old man."[65] The naked body, Flaubert emphasizes, is for European eyes only. These eyes observe the disrobing—"Kuchuk [Hanem] shed her clothing as she danced"—with a growing sense of mastery, pleasure, and control.

Hot on the trail of Flaubert, male travelers in Kafka's turn of the century frequently journeyed to brothels.[66] As in Flaubert's case, they often went primarily in order to look. Hesse goes to an Indian brothel in 1911 in order to "*see* Singalese girls," and he gets his wish: "We wanted to see a Singalese dance, for 15 Rps. 6 girls appeared naked and danced, but couldn't dance very well, they were 16–17 years old, spoke all a bit of English, they still sang with a nasal tone, laughing a bit, then we left and went to a Singalese theater."[67] Kafka and Brod, traveling through central Europe in the same weeks that Hesse was in India, visited brothels in Milan and Paris. The day after staring at Brod on the balcony, Kafka goes to a brothel in order to stare at prostitutes (see figure 14). As Brod remembers, Kafka only looks: he does not "touch a girl," does not "even talk to one" (*EFI* 96).

Unlike Flaubert, however, Kafka gains no sense of mastery. As when looking at Brod looking at Paris, Kafka's view is myopic and cropped. He does, like Flaubert, experience initial pleasure in viewing the women ("drawn up in postures calculated to reveal them to best advantage") (*D* 459; *Ta* 1006). But this ends abruptly with an intensification of his myopia and with his discovery that voyeurism's traditional hierarchy can be overturned. The seer becomes the seen:

> It is difficult to view the girls with exactitude because there are too many of them, all blinking their eyes, but mostly because they crowd too closely around one. One would have to keep one's eyes wide open, and that takes

practice. I really only remember the one who stood directly in front of me. She had gaps in her teeth, stretched herself to her full height, held her dress together over her pudenda with clenched fist, and she rapidly and simultaneously opened and shut her large eyes and large mouth. (*D* 459; *Ta* 1006, trans. rev.)

In this depiction, the scopophilic traveler's powerful position of voyeur is undermined because the women get too close to him. Kafka's familiar myopia prevents him from gaining a perspective on the prostitute. She exists as pieces: "gaps in her teeth," "clenched fist," "pudenda," "eyes." Moreover, the *prostitutes'* eyes (mentioned twice—"large" and "blink[ing]"—in this short segment) seem to overpower Kafka's own (which he must struggle to keep open).

Kafka's inability to see corresponds—in contradistinction to Flaubert—to his general sense of self-loss. At the end of the vignette, he employs the passive voice to describe his departure: "I feel myself impelled toward the exit" (*D* 459; *Ta* 1006, trans. rev.). Flaubert, on the other hand, fantasizes that his visit with Kuchuk Hanem (including an eventual "*coup*") has rendered him singular and significant. Before leaving the brothel, he muses: "How flattering it would be for one's pride if at the moment of leaving you were sure that you left a memory behind, that she would think of you more than of the others who have been there, that you would remain in her heart."[68] Kafka surmised, conversely, that brothel tourism undermined his personal significance. In front of the Milan brothel, several days earlier, Kafka notices "heavy traffic between there and the alley, mostly single persons [*Einzelne*]" (*D* 444; *Ta* 968, trans. rev.). The sex tourist is thus not unique but rather is part of a crush of anonymous *Einzelnen*. Moreover, whereas Flaubert's privileged sense of himself as a Frenchman (Egypt's colonizer) is strengthened through his brothel visit, Kafka's nationhood is undermined. The brothel customers, he claims, "lost a sense" of their "nationality" among the prostitutes (*D* 444; *Ta* 969).

The remarkable correspondences between Kafka's Parisian brothel "experience" and the ending of Kafka's beloved *L'Éducation sentimentale* suggest further ironic possibilities. Written weeks after the fact from the quiet of Kafka's Prague desk—perhaps as a future scene for *Richard and Samuel*—the vignette may be as much literary experiment as biographical reality. The final scene of *L'Éducation,* which Kafka refers to specifically in his diaries, takes place similarly in a French brothel (*D* 394; *Ta* 867). Like Kafka's 1911 brothel and his childhood photo (each with their "palm trees"), Flaubert's brothel is artificially exoticized (through the dubious naming, "*la Turque*") (*EFI* 129). Flaubert's Frédéric Moreau, like "Kafka," enters the crowded, faux-exotic house and is immediately overcome with extreme scopophilic pleasure (*"plaisir de voir"*), and Frédéric's pleasure, too, is cut short by its own excesses: he is overwhelmed by the number and proximity of the naked women. Frédéric, again like "Kafka," finds himself standing among a crush of prostitutes, unable to move or speak (*"il devint très pale et restait sans avancer, sans rien dire"*).[69] Fearful and embarrassed, Frédéric—prefiguring his 1911 *Doppelgänger*—runs out onto the street.

The extraordinary similarities between the two texts imply that Kafka crafted his brothel "experience" with Flaubert in mind. Either things happened precisely as Kafka claimed they did (and thus life uncannily mirrored art), or Kafka invented this section of the otherwise largely veracious travel diaries in order to perversely *become* the hero of his favorite novel. Whether the former or the latter is true (or, most likely, a mixture of both), Kafka must have been aware of the correspondences—and thus of himself as a parodic repeat. After all, Kafka sometimes carried a copy of *L'Éducation* with him while traveling (*D* 484; *Ta* 1052–53).

If Kafka's revision of Flaubert is parodic, then it simultaneously criticizes Flaubert's narrative of *Selbstfindung* through voyeuristic control.[70] For Flaubert, the agency of the visually bloated brothel tourist is never in serious doubt. Frédéric flees the brothel precisely because he wants to save his still very strong sense of self. The prostitutes seem to be mocking him, and he wants to rescue his pride. Kafka's traveler, conversely, loses all sense of agency in the moment of self-annihilating visual *jouissance*. "Kafka" is surrounded panoptically by the prostitutes. Their many and varied "eyes," phantasmagorical products of his own scopophilic excesses, reflect, in the end, his loss of sight and self. He feels himself "impelled" toward the door and cannot remember, weeks later in Prague, how he got onto the street. The passive construction in Kafka's text (*"ich [fühle] mich zum Ausgang gezogen"*) opposes Flaubert's active account (*"il s'enfuit"*).[71]

These antipodal psychological grammars underscore Frédéric's intact agency in the brothel and emphasize the still-empowering nature of brothel tourism for Flaubert. However threatened Frédéric felt at the moment of flight, in the end he still recalls the scene as an entertaining moment in his personal "education." Frédéric masters the brothel by transforming it and its prostitutes into a pleasurable narrative that he can repeat at will with his pal Deslauriers (*"c'est là ce que nous avons eu de meilleur!"*).[72] Frédéric emerges from his brothel experience (and from *L'Éducation* itself) feeling masterful, if not "tiger"-like—as did his author in Egypt after sleeping with Kuchuk Hanem for the first time.[73] Kafka's bordello visit, conversely, does not bring him the sense of self that issues from narrative mastery and the pleasures of vitality and male camaraderie. He leaves the building feeling isolated and absurd, never telling his story to his friend, Brod (who is busy doing "the thing" in a back room) (*EFI* 129–30).

Moreover, Kafka never recalls the event in the unfinished narrative of his journey to Paris, *Richard and Samuel.* Kafka's story thus ends once and for all with the "lonely, long, absurd walk home" (*D* 459; *Ta* 1007).

Important to note in terms of both Kafka's development and the construction of *Der Verschollene* is the retrospective nature of this vignette (and of the earlier one on the balcony). Because Kafka wrote both sketches weeks after the experience, these accounts conjoin Kafka's "real" experiences of myopia and self-loss with his interest in re-presenting this disorientation. Kafka's description of his perspectival "lostness" thus is not, in his own mind, inferior to what he called, on a later trip, Brod's "sense of direction." (Losing his way in Leipzig in 1912, Kafka wrote: "Max's sense of direction, I was lost [*Maxens topographischer Instinkt, mein Verlorensein*]" [*D* 466; *Ta* 1021]). Nor is it lesser than Hesse's and Goethe's panoramic perspectives, or Flaubert's visual mastery of the female body. Rather, Kafka's viewpoint is a form of training in what Anderson calls Kafka's new, modern "traveling" style.[74] This style is consistent with Kafka's early theoretical conviction that "apperception" is "not a condition but rather a movement" and that our (often failed) attempts to perceive the world are comparable to the experience of a lost traveler trying to find his way: to a person with no sense of place whatsoever ("*ganz ohne Ortsgefühl*") who comes to Prague "as if to a foreign city" (*NSI* 10–11).[75] Kafka thus never offers us "a Paris" (as Goethe and Flaubert do "a Venice" or "a Cairo"). Rather, he presents readers with a decidedly modern way of (not) seeing an invisible "Amerika"—choosing ground-level myopia over bird's-eye views, blinding proximity over surveyable distance, darkness over light, and motion over stillness (as in Richard and Samuel's "whizzing," nocturnal automobile ride) (*M* 288; *EFI* 199).[76]

The View from Below in *Der Verschollene:* Staring at Brunelda

As Karl works his way down the social ladder (from trust-fund nephew, to elevator boy, to servant for a diva/prostitute), the focus of his vision shifts—in Flaubertian, exoticist fashion—from the landscape of the foreign country (the streets and skyscrapers) to the body of one of its women. In the novel's seventh chapter, the wandering Karl (now dismissed from his job at the Hotel Occidental) finds a temporary home with the diva/prostitute Brunelda—thereby re-starting the cycle of banishment/disorientation and relocation. Brunelda corresponds remarkably to the prostitutes Kafka attempted to view while traveling in Paris and Milan the year before he began *Der Verschollene.* As we learn in one of the novel's later fragments (not included in the first German edition or the

Muirs' English translation), Brunelda works in what seems to be a faux exotic brothel ("Enterprise No. 25") that, like the one in Paris, features "artificial palm trees" (V 383–84). Also, like the Parisian brothel, Enterprise No. 25 is surprisingly "efficiently organized" (Brunelda is even chastised for being late) (D 458; Ta 1006, trans. rev.; V 383–84). She is exaggeratedly obese, calling to mind the "Amazonian" prostitutes Kafka stared at in Paris and Milan (D 459; Ta 1006). Brunelda even repeats some of the gestures of her historical models: a prostitute in Milan "spreads" her legs while sitting in order to let her oversized belly hang shapelessly downward; Brunelda, mirroring, "spread her legs wide where she sat so as to get more room for her disproportionately fat body" (D 444; Ta 968; A 229; V 296). What is more, the Paris prostitute—whose large eyes "blink" and "open and shut" rapidly—menacingly approaches Kafka with a "clenched fist." Brunelda, created just one year later, is uncannily similar: aiming her "glittering eyes" at Karl while panting, glowering, and slowly "advancing her fists" (A 260; V 338).

Like Kafka in Paris (and Flaubert in Egypt), Karl experiences extreme scopophilic desire from the moment he first sees Brunelda, who, when Karl arrives in her apartment, is lying in complete darkness. Karl quickly makes his way to the foot of her couch in order to "see the woman better." Brunelda, her neck and cleavage bare, responds by straightaway complaining about Karl's eyes: "Who is that? [. . .] why does he stare at me so hard?" (A 225; V 292). Karl continues to stare throughout this opening scene, however, and to raise Brunelda's ire: "aware of Karl's wide-open eyes," which had "startled her once already," Brunelda cries out to Delamarche, ordering him to banish Karl from the room. Made uncomfortably hot by the intensity of Karl's look, Brunelda now refers to him only as that boy who was "staring savagely at me" (A 228; V 295). A later reflection sums up the visual tensions that define Karl's relationship to Brunelda: "She couldn't stand him; his eyes terrified her" (A 248; V 322).

The servant, Robinson (whose place in Brunelda's menage Karl is about to take), tells Karl that his future occupation will generate even more desire to see Brunelda: Robinson explains how, early on in his service to Brunelda, he was able to see her naked (A 231; V 298). But he is unable to repeat this pleasure, and this inability produces much of his present longing. He and Karl are banished to the balcony for, again, trying to gain glimpses of Brunelda, and Robinson recalls—when he was previously banished—peeking through the dividing curtain to look illicitly at her. But this led to a beating by Brunelda's lover, so Robinson learned to satisfy himself by watching only Brunelda's shadows on the curtain. Even this, however, proved to be too much for Brunelda, who eventually blocked

Robinson's view (and thus, now, Karl's) by installing a thicker curtain:
Now, Robinson laments, "you can see nothing at all" (*A* 233; *V* 301). As
we learn in a fragment excluded from early editions of the novel, Robinson's and Karl's visual blockade is now complete: they remain on the balcony, seeing nothing at all, and dutifully avert their eyes whenever they get
too close to Brunelda (*V* 356).

At stake in Brunelda obstructing Robinson's and Karl's vision is the traditional balance of visual power in the exotic narrative. In *Der Verschollene*,
the male European traveler on an exotic journey is stripped of the power
once granted Flaubert. He resembles not Flaubert, but rather the blindfolded Arabs. He, too, can see "nothing." More radically, Karl becomes, in
the end, the *object* of the woman's gaze. Like Kafka in the brothel, he feels
the eyes of the female object now turned on him. This begins with
Brunelda's first appearance, when she gazes down from a balcony at Karl
and a small group of men—through opera glasses—until the men "turn
their eyes away from her" (*A* 211; *V* 273). Brunelda has the better viewpoint; moreover, through her look she is able to cause Karl and the other
men to look away.

Brunelda's visual authority increases when she—after surviving Karl's
stares in the apartment—now aggressively and ironically presses the opera
glasses onto his eyes. The opera glasses, which Brunelda once used to view
Karl, now render Karl's vision—in accordance with the novel's governing
structure—confused:

> "I can't see anything," he said, and wanted to get away from the glasses, but
> she held the glasses firmly, and his head, which was buried in her breast, he
> could move neither backwards nor sideways.
>
> "But you can surely see now," she said, and turned the screw.
>
> "No, I still can't see anything," said Karl [. . .].
>
> "When on earth will you ever be able to see?" she said and—Karl's
> whole face now exposed to her heavy breath—turned the screw further.
> "Now?" she asked.
>
> "No, no, no!" cried Karl. (*A* 252; *V* 328, trans. rev.)

This is an ironic commentary on Karl's entire American adventure. First, he,
who has not yet been able to achieve a clear view of anything, claims to
have "good eyes" (and thus to not be in need of opera glasses at all) (*A* 252;
V 327). Second, his inability to see the body of the foreign prostitute now
corresponds—in a farcical upstaging of Pratt's traditional, monarchical male
traveler—with his failure to gain an overview of the American cityscape.
Karl's exaggerated desire to see (he "stares" five times in this chapter alone)
becomes parody in the hands of Brunelda.[77] Kafka pushes Karl's visual de-

sire beyond normal limits, toward absurdity. Wearing the voyeuristic technology of the woman he longs to view, Karl, in the end, "can't see anything." He is blinded by the instrument of his desire. As if to emphasize this
historical reversal of ocular control, Brunelda eventually tires of pressing the
binoculars onto Karl's face and begins to use them for her own pleasure (*A*
253; *V* 328).

This overturning of the traditional hierarchy of seeing—prefigured in
Kafka's Paris brothel visit—deepens the theme of visual *Verirrung* in *Der
Verschollene*. Later, during this same balcony scene, Karl's vision becomes
characteristically cropped and myopic. Instead of gaining an overview of
Brunelda's strange, outlying suburb, he zooms in on street scenes far
below: on a group of men drinking beer, the glitter of musical instruments, and the white face of a political leader. As Brunelda remarks, Karl
is "so busy staring that he's quite forgotten where he is" (*A* 254; *V* 330).
Here, it is Karl's myopia that prevents him—and us (since we also never
achieve a sense of the suburb's, or "America's," layout)—from knowing his
position in the world. Again, Karl is the scopophilic traveler driven to the
point of blindness. He wants hedonistically to see, as does Flaubert, "like
a myopic," but this myopic desire—nourished by visual technology—finally leads to an almost complete visual blockage.[78] And, again, not knowing where he is combines with not knowing who he is. By the end of the
chapter, Karl has decided to give up on his plan to escape from Brunelda.
He stays on as a servant and a prostitute's helper. He naively imagines that
he has found a "refuge" (as Max Brod entitled the Brunelda chapter), but,
as we learn in the novel's final chapter, this is likely not the case. In an unwritten conclusion to the Brunelda episode, Karl has apparently been
given a nickname that corresponds to his present devalued social status:
Karl announces, in the final fragment, that his name is now "Negro" (*A*
286; *V* 402).

Karl's "Refuge"?:
Exoticism and the Return to the Mother

Karl reacts to his visual and psychological *Verirrung* during the Brunelda
episode as did other travelers from the fin de siècle exotic tradition: he
desires to locate a "refuge" in a maternal Other. As Wolfgang Reif has argued, this fantastical quest for the mother's body in journeys to exotic
lands was widespread in the early twentieth century, and literary exoticism was generally marked by a "regressive consciousness." According to
the Freudian and Jungian terms I discussed in chapter one, the traveler desired to locate the foreign yet familiar homeland of the womb (i.e., myth-

ical wanderers such as Gilgamesh, Dionysis, and Christ were searching for the "lost mother"). Using as examples Jacques' 1917 *Pirath's Island,* Müller's 1915 *Tropics,* and Gottfried Benn's 1916 *The Island,* Reif points out how travelers repeatedly transformed exotic lands into the fantasy form of long-lost mothers: The travelers yearned, Reif claims, to enter into "the sheltering-warm unconsciousness of the Great Mother's exposed island-body."[79]

This fantasy of voyaging toward the body of the lost mother lures Rossmann at the precise moments in the text when he is feeling most abandoned. After being banished by his uncle and heading off on his own, for example, Karl attempts to make his parents' image in a photograph "come to life." Unlike his father's photographic likeness, which remains an inert reproduction, the mother's image seems—to Karl—to magically reproduce her feelings for him. Karl's lost mother thus comes mysteriously closer to him: "How could a photograph convey with such complete certainty the secret feelings of the person shown in it?" The mother's photographed hand, moreover, seems to emerge from the background and become real— real enough for Karl to "kiss" (*A* 104; *V* 135). Karl's longing to put his lips to his mother's photograph eventually gives way to a completely regressive, physical desire: growing tired, he lays his face on the now-animate photograph and, with a comfortable sensation penetrating the skin on his cheek, falls asleep.

Karl does not mention his mother again for over 100 pages, until the first Brunelda chapter. Brunelda, as Margot Norris has argued, also embodies some maternal qualities—even if not the purely comforting ones Karl conjures from the photograph. In the psychoanalytical terms employed by Norris, Brunelda is at once the "good" ("nurturing," "oral") and "bad" ("cruel," "cannibalistic") mother.[80] As "good" mother, her substantial body promises the comforts of a refuge: Robinson (Karl's mentor) remembers how she offered him a specifically maternal shelter when she rescued him from the streets. Homeless and hungry, Robinson was comforted by her "beautiful," "enormously wide" body, which encouraged his regressive, oral fantasies: "You felt you could lick her all over. You felt you could gobble her up" (*A* 234–35; *V* 303–4, trans. rev.). Later, Robinson recalls Brunelda's maternal care for him: "If you ever get a chance, Rossmann, you should get her to pat you on the cheek some time. You'll be surprised how lovely it feels" (*A* 240; *V* 310). As "bad" mother, however, Brunelda is tyrannical and devouring. She orchestrates (and enjoys) Karl's beating at the hands of Delamarche and, for her part, draws Karl's body so close to hers that he feels as if he is suffocating—causing him to attempt vainly to escape (*A* 248; *V* 322).

In the ambiguously maternal figure of Brunelda, then, we see how Kafka gives the exotic narrative another turn of the screw. Like the fantasy images of fin de siècle exotic travelers, Brunelda is foreign (exotic) and familiar (maternal) at once. But Kafka perverts the traveler's return "to the Great Mother." Whereas the heroes of *Pirath's Island* and *Tropics* engage in genital sex with the exotic women they meet, Karl—in the style of the perverse traveler—becomes visually fixated on a cruelly maternal prostitute. Moreover, whereas the popular travelers complete their narratives of *Selbstfindung* through sexual satisfaction, Karl loses his already tenuous hold on identity through his unconsummated erotic encounter.

Even if Karl had had intercourse with Brunelda, it is unlikely that he would have imaginatively returned to what psychoanalysts termed "Mother Earth."[81] Rather, Karl would probably have ended up like his traveling literary successor: K. from *The Castle,* who—unlike Karl—does eventually sleep with one of the native women he meets on his travels. The comparison between these novels is warranted because, despite *The Man Who Disappeared's* apparently less "Kafkaesque" themes and style, it contains a rich store of tropes and structures that come into relief in the later novels. In this case, what comes to the fore is *Verirrung:* in the sense of the homesick traveler going sexually astray. As we learn through K.'s very first words in *The Castle* (reminiscent of Karl's first statements), K. has "strayed" (*"mich verirrt"*) into a foreign village (*C* 2; *S* 8, trans. rev.). K. eventually has sex with a native (Frieda), and when he does, he senses (in contradistinction to Jacques' and Müller's heroes) that he is going yet further astray. Sex thus does not return him to a fantasy original state but rather renders him even more foreign—and lost—than before:

> Hours passed there, hours breathing together with a single heartbeat, hours in which K. constantly felt he was lost [*sich verirre*] or had wandered farther into foreign lands [*in der Fremde*] than any human being before him, into lands [*eine Fremde*] so foreign that even the air hadn't a single component of the air in his homeland [*Heimatluft*] and where one would inevitably suffocate from the foreignness [*Fremdheit*] but where the meaningless enticements were such that one had no alternative but to go on and get even more lost [*weiter sich verirren*]. (*C* 41; *S* 68–9, trans. rev.)

Kafka's K., contra Freud, has never "been there before."[82] The exotic journey takes him to a foreign country that has nothing in common with his home. For K., then, the foreign woman no longer represents the possibility (as fantasized by Karl and fin de siècle exoticists) of an uncanny return to origins—or, at the least, of a voyage to a refuge. Rather, contact with the exotic woman produces a disorientation ad infinitum, a continual distancing from all structures of home and self.

Karl as "Negro":
Self-Exoticism and the Closing of the Exotic I/Eye

Der Verschollene ends with the incomplete "Nature Theater of Oklahoma" chapter, which Benjamin sees as essential to understanding all of Kafka's work.[83] Kafka wrote this fragment in late 1914, almost two years after giving up on the last of the three "Brunelda" fragments, and interpreters, whatever their larger methodological frameworks, have generally agreed on one thing: that it is crucial to address Brod's 1927 assertion that Kafka had meant for Karl—in an unwritten ending—to locate in exotic Oklahoma a "profession, a stand-by, his freedom, even his old *Heimat* and his parents, as if by some celestial witchery [*paradiesischen Zauber*]."[84] Brod thus connects *Selbstfindung* with *Heimat*. He claims optimistically that Karl will eventually attain both in Oklahoma. Like the heroes of Kafka's favorite adventure novels and other melancholy early-twentieth-century travelers, the homesick Karl should find a "second *Heimat*."[85] As is so often the case with Kafka's texts, *Der Verschollene* seems—at first reading—to both support *and* not support such an extrapolation. Prominent critics from the 1950s generally agreed with Brod: Wilhelm Emrich pointed out that the "Theater" grants Karl an unprecedented opportunity for self-realization.[86] In a place where "everyone is welcome" and everyone can become what he or she wants to be, Karl can fulfill his childhood dream of becoming an engineer. Here, Karl's "role" and his "self-realization" coincide.[87] Later critics, such as Martin Walser and, more recently, Joseph Vogl, disagree: They point out, among other things, the ominously accelerated "rhythm of Karl's punishment" and the contemporaneity of this fragment with Kafka's famous 1914 punishment narratives (*The Trial* and "In the Penal Colony").[88] As Peter Beicken writes, the Kafka of 1914 "tended toward more tragic endings."[89]

What critics on both sides of the debate fail to emphasize is the way in which what I term the "exotic" structure of Kafka's novel serves to create this debate itself. Indeed, Kafka's supposed words to Brod—that Karl was to find a new "*Heimat*" or a "paradise" in America—are taken directly out of the utopian exoticist context of Kafka's day: out of its rhetoric of a mythical second home.[90] Even Kafka's decision to re-name his protagonist "Negro" at this point in the novel and to send this "Negro" to Oklahoma (and not, say, Alabama) for professional and psychological betterment bears the marks of fin de siècle travel fantasy. Early-twentieth-century Oklahoma—as Kafka probably knew—was viewed as a kind of "promised land" for American blacks.[91] With a large black land-owning class, Oklahoma had approximately forty-five black municipalities—more by far than any state in the Union—and a renowned and successful "Negro Wall Street" in

Tulsa. (This perhaps explains Benjamin's notion that "happiness awaits [Karl Rossmann] at the Nature Theater of Oklahoma.")[92] My contention, like that of the less sanguine group of critics, is that Karl will not locate "happiness" and a "promised land"—not even in Oklahoma. In contradistinction to them, however, I do not ground my reading on Der Verschollene's relation to the 1914 "punishment" narratives (and thus on a perceived progression toward distopia in Kafka). Rather, I want to stress the manner in which Kafka, in response to turn-of-the-century exotic fantasy, attempts to move beyond the binary of utopia/distopia. Instead, he constructs a self that grows increasingly exotic to itself—to the point of its own final silencing (as signaled through the etymology of verschollen, which comes from verschallen, meaning "to die out").[93]

Kafka's attempt to push exoticism beyond its traditional limits manifests itself, as in Richard and Samuel, not primarily in the creation of a strange outside world (although Kafka's fantasy of Oklahoma is strange and exotic enough), but rather within the protagonist's image of himself. Traveling without "identification papers" and having suppressed his real name for a long time, Karl is symbolically identity-less at this point in the narrative (A 282; V 397–98). Accordingly, Karl offers the only name that "occurred to him" when asked to identify himself at the recruitment office: his former nickname, "Negro." Despite the eventual comedy of this scene (the bureau chief cannot bring himself to call this white foreigner "Negro"), Karl's new appellation points to the continued motion of his psychological confusion and encroaching Verschollen-Sein (A 286; V 403). Gerhard Kurz suggestively points out that Karl's name represents his transformation into symbolic "blackness": signifying, in the racialized terms of the turn of the century, the "absence" or opposite of a self.[94] Karl's name thus becomes the material signifier of his psychic lack and, moreover, of his estrangement from this missing self. Twice in the course of the fragment, Karl is referred to by his new name; the second time he sees this name writ large on the announcement board ("Negro, technical worker"), and Karl finds himself wishing that he could go back to his previous name (A 291; V 409). Within Kafka's narrative momentum, however, it is too late.

The dovetailing of "Negro's" symbolic resonance (as absence) with "Negro's" historical significance in early-twentieth-century Oklahoma reveals the depth and multivalence of Kafka's exoticism. Karl's nickname most likely emerges from Holitscher's travelogue, which Kafka seems to have read with great care (as demonstrated by the many details Kafka transplanted directly from this book into Der Verschollene—including Holitscher's warning that the Irish single-handedly control a corrupt New York police force).[95] Holitscher devotes an entire chapter to the horrific treatment of blacks in America (especially the continued practice of lynching), and he even supplies a snapshot of a black man hanging from a tree (see figure 15).[96] Beneath this photograph reads the ironic subtitle, "An Idyll in Oklahama." "Oklahama" is misspelled here exactly as in Kafka's novel (although the spelling is standardized in the English translation), thus leading us to believe that Kafka pilfered it directly from Holitscher. Holitscher's 1911 "idyll" ominously predicts the actual destruction of the Oklahoman Promised Land ten years later. In the space of one night in late May 1921, a mob of whites killed as many as 300 blacks and destroyed—mostly through arson— the prospering black district of Tulsa. As Brent Staples points out, this was "the country's bloodiest civil disturbance of the century."[97]

With the still of the lynched black man and the impending Tulsa riot in the background, "Negro's" journey to "Oklahama" at the end of Der Verschollene loses the blissful qualities attributed to it by Brod and Benjamin. It becomes an augur of death. It is worth noting that Holitscher (a Socialist German Jew) stresses the historical connection between American blacks and European Jews: both were forced to leave Africa and to spend centuries physically and psychologically uprooted.[98] Although Karl is not explicitly Jewish, it is possible that Kafka imagined a symbolic connection between "Negro" and the mythical wandering Jew, a modern-day example of which he had just befriended in Prague (Yitzhak Löwy, the traveling Yiddish actor). If such a speculation holds any validity, then "Negro's" journey becomes doubly ominous. It suggests a voyage to a lynching and, moreover, an ominous train journey in which refugees travel without "Gepäckstück" (luggage) and amid great bureaucratic fastidiousness toward an unclear and foreboding destination (A 296; V 415). "Negro's" final journey is thus doubly shrouded with impressions of ethnic violence and death. The haunting final line of the extant text was, not surprisingly, omitted by Brod in the first edition: It suggests that Karl's future in "Oklahama" might well be the opposite of the paradise Brod imagined for him. As Rossmann's train bound for the Oklahoma Theater passes some powerful mountain streams, we read that "the breath of coldness" causes young Karl's face "to shudder" (A 298, V 419, trans. rev.).

If Karl's final journey symbolizes a voyage unto death, then it also signifies the ultimate stage in his process of self-exoticism: his ultimate Verschollen-Sein (which also signifies being "never heard from again" and "presumed dead"). As this prematurely annihilated self, Karl foreshadows Kafka's musings on his own death eight years after writing the "Oklahama" fragment and two years before he actually died. Kafka's fatal tuberculosis was already well-advanced when he claimed, in this long, tortured 1922 letter to Brod, that—because Kafka is a writer—he has always already been dead. One must experience oneself as dead, he claims, in order to achieve the self-estrangement necessary for good writing. And Kafka does not mean this in the figurative sense of "writing posthumously" (as if one had nothing to lose). Rather, he means it literally—and tries to imagine the details of this literalness. The true writer must orchestrate the viewing of his own corpse. He must see his own dead body. It is this ability to look at his own fully exoticized self that, according to Kafka, defines him as a writer. Instead of using creation's mythical "spark" to bring himself to life, Kafka has used it perversely to "illuminate" his own corpse—a corpse that, in Kafka's logic, was never a living body to begin with. Kafka thus imagines his own strange but pleasant funeral, and how he will describe it: "It will be a peculiar burial: the writer, insubstantial as he is, consigning the old corpse, the everlasting corpse, to the grave. I am enough of a writer to appreciate the scene with all my senses, or—and it is the same thing—to want to narrate it [. . .]" (*L* 334; *B* 385, trans. rev.). The writer, in Kafka's model, is (and always has been) the voyeur of his own dead body. He "narrates" his own never-ending process of illuminating a fully exoticized self. In terms of the discourse of exoticism outlined above, we could argue that this final image represents Kafka's "transcendence" of exoticism because it turns the exotic eye toward the familiar body of the self. The true writer for Kafka is also the supreme exoticist; he desires the uncanny sight of his own corpse.

Kafka wants to write—to describe this scene of utter self-estrangement—with what he calls "total self-forgetfulness" (*L* 334). He can thus only succeed if he, like the chronically amnesiac Karl, learns to disregard himself completely. Here, we see Kafka's radical continuation of Flaubert's unfinished project of self-loss and -obliteration. In Kafka's modern version of the lost-and-found tale, the traveler (like the writer) will never again find himself. He will remain caught in the foreign world's maze and, what is more, can not—like Goethe—remain "always myself."[99] Rather, he becomes something else through getting lost, something that cannot simply be recouped in the form of a "new" and better self. When Karl Rossmann gets disoriented in exotic early-twentieth-century America, he becomes the "black one," becomes "*verschollen*." He is his own Other, his own premature corpse: he is exotic to himself. "Going astray" thus designates, as in the love scene from *The Castle* cited above, getting lost to the point of no return—amid a strangeness so radical that, like Kafka's "America," it is deadly and enchanting at once. As we will see in *The Trial* (and *The Metamorphosis*), Kafka no longer needs to leave home to discover it.

Chapter Three

Traveling at Home:
The Trial and the Exotic *Heimat*

"No one's wearing a uniform, unless you want to call your suit"—he
turned to Franz—"a uniform, but it's more like a traveler's outfit."

—*Josef K.*

The *Trial* (*Der Prozeß*) is clearly not a travel novel in the sense that *Richard and Samuel* and *The Man Who Disappeared* are. In fact, it could be read precisely as an anti-travel narrative. Unlike Richard, Samuel, Karl Rossmann, and K. from *The Castle,* Josef K. does not make a sustained journey from one place to the next, nor does he ever leave his hometown. But K. is continually *in motion,* perhaps even more so than his more obviously traveling counterparts. K. frequently moves from one site to another, and often in one of the city's speedy, motorized taxis. Thus, whether K. is doing standard commuting or traveling to a strange suburb of the courts, his journeys are speedy and abruptly disorienting—such as the first time his uncle pulls him into a cab, calling out to the driver an unfamiliar address (*T* 95; *P* 128). A brief inventory of K.'s "travels" follows, in chronological order:

> boarding house (in city); office (in city center); home; courtroom (in first suburb); home; courtroom (first suburb); office; city streets with uncle; lawyer Huld's home (first suburb); office; Titorelli's attic (suburb diametrically opposite the first suburb); office; lawyer Huld's home; office; cathedral (in city's Cathedral Square); boarding house; stone quarry (open fields on edge of city).[1]

The difference, of course, between Josef K. and the travelers from *Richard and Samuel, The Man Who Disappeared,* and *The Castle,* is that Josef K. travels at home. But this home, as I will demonstrate, has become increasingly foreign. Kafka employs travel here, more radically than in *Richard and Samuel,* as a metaphor for *internal* displacement. Travel becomes so intensive that one need not even leave one's home city in order to take part in it. Considered in the light of the previous two chapters, we now see that Kafka's concentric circles of travel are tightening. The rings of foreignness, beginning with America and *Richard and Samuel's* "Central Europe," now zoom into the walls of Josef K.'s city, his bedroom (where he is arrested), and, by extension, to his structure of self.

Josef K.'s "travels" are not unrelated to the larger themes of *The Trial,* such as K.'s arrest and punishment: The immediate negative effect of K.'s arrest is not incarceration but rather the onset of a series of small—haphazard and frustrating—journeys. Thus, although K. is apparently "at home," his initial punishment is to be forced to suffer the distresses we generally associate with traveling. He has difficulties with "customs," in both senses of the word, and with an apparently foreign bureaucracy: As do Kafka's more evident travelers, Rossmann and K. from *The Castle,* Josef K. begins the novel by searching for his identification papers ("*Legitimationspapiere*") and, immediately afterward, trying to figure out a confusing bureaucratic hierarchy.[2] Like K. in the Castle village (who telephones the Castle offices yet only gets a child's voice), Josef K.'s attempts to reach a member of the bureaucracy with higher authority are continually frustrated. Moreover, like Karl Rossmann (who shares the popular stereotype that the Irish in America single-handedly control the police), Josef K. never adequately understands his home city's power apparatus.[3] (For example, Josef K. watches with astonishment as his own guards, whom he once thought were powerful, get beaten in a storage room.) Similarly, K. is as uncertain of native tipping/bribing rituals as is his later traveling alter-ego, the "man from the country" in "Before the Law." K.'s question in the Cathedral—"Does [the sexton] want a tip?"—recalls both the vain bribes of the "man from the country" as well as Karl Rossmann's uncertainty about American tipping practices (Rossmann absurdly offers an American servant Austrian schillings) (*T* 208; *P* 282). K. indeed plays the role of what he later calls a "*Fremder*" (foreigner) in his home city (*T* 210; *P* 285).

Some of the sparse critical work concerning travel in *The Trial* reflects the long debate surrounding empiricism in Kafka's oeuvre. Early sociological critics such as Klaus Mann and Theodor Adorno stress the negative aspects of K.'s travel—his forced displacement—and relate this to historical, state-sponsored terror: As Adorno writes in 1953, "it is National Socialism far more than the hidden dominion of God that [Kafka's] work cites."[4] K.'s travels, from this point of view, are equivalent to those of a refugee. He becomes a wanderer at home: free to move in his ghetto-like home city yet not free to escape, able to run but not able to hide. Pavel Eisner correctly considers any such prophetically political reading too "superficial" and "timely" but nonetheless also assumes that the novel is essentially historically mimetic.[5] Eisner claims that K.'s city is Prague (despite Kafka's tendency to "wipe" away historical particularity) and that K. is nothing other than a "Prague Jew."[6] K., then, like Kafka, is triply a stranger (religiously, nationally, socially) in Prague's German-Jewish "ghetto."[7] He is a wanderer, a "marginal settler" at home, and becomes, like Kafka, a "martyr" to the cause of *"escaping the ghetto."*[8]

Later critics rightly challenged such empiricist readings as reductionist. Politzer, in an early reaction to Eisner, claims that *The Trial* is no "regional story [*Heimatgeschichte*]" about Prague.[9] Subsequent readings increasingly understood Kafkan motifs, including travel, as divorced from Prague's particular political-cultural topography. Walter Sokel and, later, Gerhard Kurz employed psycho-existentialist methodologies in order to point out that the travel-imagery in *The Trial* (Josef K.'s travels through the city; the arresting guard's "traveler's outfit"; K.'s "album of city sights") functions symbolically: signifying the protagonist's alienation and his sense of impending death, respectively.[10] Laurence Rickels, representing the American deconstructionist school of the 1980s, followed up on Manfred Frank's study of "The Hunter Gracchus" and read Kafka's travel-motif as equivalent to the endless delay of meaning in language.[11] K.'s perpetual travels, in Rickels' reading, correspond to the "process" of eternally deferring signification through reading and writing.

Without contradicting the validity of these opposed approaches, I maintain that the continuing, unsettling force of Kafka's text lies somewhere *between* Adorno's and Eisner's historical-political allegories and Rickels' rigorously non-mimetic account. Kafka's novel purposefully creates, contra Rickels, the terrifying effect of real, historical displacement: a man's "home" is invaded by strangers, and he is forced out of his bedroom. But, pace Adorno, this terror exceeds historical prophecy. It points, rather, toward an intellectual anxiety brought about by the contamination of the categories that inform all forms of displacement and/or travel: "home" and "away." Kafka introduces the problem of political violence and displacement into *The Trial,* but he replaces any allegorical assertion (e.g., "An oppressive regime forces a native [here, perhaps, a 'Prague Jew'] to become a refugee") with a series of theoretical questions: "What is a native?" "Who can claim rights to nativity and to a proper place?" "When is one no longer 'at home'?" "Where do our displacements begin?" Kafka anticipates postcolonial critiques of the opposition between "native" and "foreigner"—or to use the terms of one critic, "dweller" and "traveler"—that inform all questions of "home."[12] Kafka unsettles our fantasies of nativity, albeit without denying them. It is this conceptual disruption—not National Socialism on the one hand or the emptiness of the signifier on the other—that produces the enduringly disturbing effect of his *Trial*.

It is important to note that Kafka's critique of nativity in *The Trial* is not the same as a glorification of displacement. Josef K., like Karl Rossmann before him, gains little pleasure from his banishment and yearns nostalgically for an end to his suddenly itinerant lifestyle. Thus, although Kafka reveals "home" to be a construction of the Law, he does not deny the subject's longing for some version of *Heimat*. As in *The Man Who Disappeared* and the popular exotic novels I discussed in chapter one, the perceived destruction of one's first home carries with it the desire for an elsewhere, for a "second *Heimat*." But what of a novel, like *The Trial*, that can only internalize this exotic nostalgia, whose hero can only hope to locate a second home within the hopelessly alienated first one? This doubled displacement, I will argue, is at the heart of K.'s "proceedings" (*Verfahren*)— which, through endless legal detours, inverts and perverts the very notion of progressive travel. These inversions and perversions are already contained within the German term *Verfahren*: replacing, here, *The Man Who Disappeared*'s similarly governing trope of "going astray" (*Verirrung*). *Verfahren* implies a peculiar kind of "travel" (*fahren*) that—as signaled by the prefix "*ver-*"—"digresses from the course" or, more radically, "turns around into its opposite."[13] *Ver-fahren*'s implication of going the wrong way surfaces in various forms: as an adjective ("*verfahren sein*" = "to be in a hopeless muddle or mess"); as a transitive verb ("*verfahren*" = "to steer [*fig.*] something in the wrong direction"); and, most importantly for my purposes, as a reflexive verb ("*sich verfahren*" = "to lose one's way"). These senses of *Verfahren* imply that K.'s legal "proceedings" are also errant travels that, on a conceptual level, overturn the idea of travel itself. This word augurs the onset of a peculiarly Kafkan form of travel that steers "travel" away from traditional paradigms of faraway voyages and homecomings and, instead, toward an endless network of local loss.

The *Reiseanzug*: The Molestation of "Home"

The Trial's opening scene is striking in both its violence and its apparent absurdity. This scene is upsetting because a man is arrested in his home. But it is doubly disturbing (and darkly humorous) because K. is arrested by what seems to be a tourist, not an officer of the Law. K.'s guard (named Franz!) is dressed like a traveler: "He was slender yet solidly built, and was wearing a fitted black frock, which, like a traveler's outfit [*ähnlich den*

Reiseanzügen], was furnished with various folds [*Falten*], pockets, buckles, buttons and a belt, and thus appeared eminently practical, although one could not quite tell what purpose it served" (*T* 3–4; *P* 7, trans. rev.). Readers have often ascribed this strange outfit—K.'s first assessment of his accuser—to the larger, well-known framework of Kafkan "absurdity." The traveler's outfit points toward a "significance," one reader claims, "that remains hidden from K. as well as from the reader."[14] Supporting this assertion is K.'s own later remark on the suit's ludicrousness: "'What authorities are in charge of the proceedings? Are you officials? No one's wearing a uniform, unless you want to call your suit'—he turned to Franz—'a uniform, but it's more like a traveler's outfit [*Reiseanzug*]'" (*T* 14; *P* 22). Following K.'s own absurdist line of interpretation, another critic argues that the suit is an uninterpretable, incongruous object among many such objects. It points toward a comprehensive strategy of meaninglessness and fragmentation that informs Kafka's entire "modernist" aesthetics.[15] Yet another interpreter concentrates on the suit's symbolic blackness: a figure of death, the *Reiseanzug* uncannily augurs the black frock coats (literally, "walking coats," *Gehröcke*) to be worn by K.'s executioners in the final chapter (*T* 225; *P* 305).[16]

Most immediately striking about the suit, however, are its sexual qualities: its tight fit, excessive folds (pleats, pockets), and accessories (buckles, buttons, belt). As Mark Anderson has argued, this suit is one of Kafka's trademark symbols of *Verkehr,* a conceptual node that, through the word's double meaning, connects "traffic" with "(sexual) intercourse."[17] The guard's suit, as a marker for *Verkehr,* points to what Anderson refers to as the "rape" of K.[18] K., we remember, claims to have been "pester[ed]" or "molested" (*belästig[t]*) in his bed—dressed, like a Kleistian rape victim, only in a blouse-like nightshirt (*T* 65; *P* 88). As we discover later, the man in the traveling suit leaves K.'s room with his usual sexual trophies (K.'s underwear).

If K.'s arrest is also his symbolic rape, then Franz's *Reiseanzug* takes on a new resonance. It represents, paradoxically, both the rapist and the victim—both the phallus and the vagina. As Elizabeth Boa claims, the jacket mirrors the "belted, buttoned, bepocketed" garments of overly masculine film heroes from the German Expressionist era.[19] The jacket's pleats and folds, meanwhile, correspond to the cavities of K.'s body; that is, to possible sites of penetration.

As suggestive as such a reading of K.'s "rape" may be, however, the imagery of "folds" and "pockets"—*not* "holes"—directs us beyond such a narrative of penetration and toward a narrative that resists any fantasy of penetration. As Jacques Derrida argues, the vagina (the mythical site of Western internality) is only an "outside" turned inward.[20] It is not an

internal absence—and thus the opposite of external materiality (skin)—
rather, it is a folding inward of externality. Like the pockets and folds of
the *Reiseanzug,* it is only a surface (skin, cloth) that poses as something
other than surface. What appears to be the valorized inside (of a body,
of a building, of a sign) turns out to be nothing more than an especially
deceptive fold in an outside (in skin, in walls, in signifiers).

This mystifying process of "invagination" applies to the internal space
of K.'s bedroom.[21] He is shocked because outsiders penetrate a space that
he imagines should be protected, first, by the tenets of liberalism central
to a "state governed by law" and, second, by his four walls (*T* 6; *P* 11). As
Boa writes, "The opening of *The Trial* conveys a public intrusion into the
private sphere."[22] But how "private" was K.'s space, even before the intrusion? Is not his fantasy of privacy undermined even before the arrest?
First, K.'s is an urban boarder's room, not a secluded bourgeois home in
the country. As Elias Canetti has already pointed out, the guards, the inspector, K.'s colleagues from the bank, and his voyeuristic neighbors all
seem to penetrate his room (either physically or visually) at will.[23] Second, the door to this room (unlike Gregor Samsa's bedroom in *The Metamorphosis*) is seldom locked. Because K.'s door, like Fräulein Bürstner's,
remains open, guards and other strangers can enter his room whenever
they want to (whether he is at home or not). Just as he and the guards
barge into Fräulein Bürstner's room on the morning of his arrest, so too
could Fräulein Bürstner (or K.'s landlady, or strangers) have been conceivably invading his "private" space regularly during his own long work
days. The unfolding of K.'s internal space thus precedes his arrest (and the
novel itself). Franz's *Reiseanzug* only brings this unfolding symbolically to
our awareness. It provokes our acknowledgement of the public nature of
K.'s privacy.

This opening out of privacy runs through the novel like a red thread—
to the final scene, where K. cannot even find a confidential space for his
death. As Canetti writes, K.'s "last humiliation is the public character of [his]
death," a death that is witnessed by his executioners and strangers (from
windows).[24] But the metaphor of invagination encourages us to question
even Canetti's traditional distinction between public and private—as the
double meaning of the German word *Scham* (denoting both "shame" and
"pudenda") suggests. Being stabbed in the heart by the guards in the novel's
last sentence, K. claims that the "shame [*Scham*] was to outlive him" (*T* 231;
P 312). *Scham's* second meaning was part of Kafka's active vocabulary; he
had already used it to describe the prostitutes' bodies he saw in Milan and
Paris.[25] And even if he intended no pun here, the word's two connotations
overlap. Shame, like the fantasy of invagination, depends on a valorized internal space (privacy, identity, home) that can be invaded. This private

place/part has been denied K. and the other characters throughout the novel (I think of the guards in the lumber room, Block and the lawyer Huld in their respective bedrooms, Titorelli in his attic "home," the cleaning woman in her room). With these steady violations in mind, it is perhaps not, in the context of the entire novel, K.'s "shame" that will outlive him. Rather, he will be survived by the structural impossibility of shame: this is K.'s tragedy. Kafka's *Trial* renders shame impossible by exposing—*not* penetrating—the interiors upon which this emotion depends.

Travel as Trope:
The Metamorphosis as Pre-Text; *Ver-fahren* and *Verirrung*

Kafka thus employs the *Reiseanzug* symbolically, in order to denote a crossing of borders (that never really existed in the first place) and, more importantly, to point toward an intrusion on the protagonist's notion of his own identity. Travel symbolism signals a similar disturbance in *The Metamorphosis* (*Die Verwandlung*)—another narrative that appears to not be about travel at all, even to be an anti-travel narrative. Gregor Samsa is defined precisely by his inactivity. He transforms, infamously, into a "monstrous vermin" in his bed, and then takes the opening several pages simply to make his way out of this bed. He remains in his family's apartment for the rest of the novella—unable, with only three exceptions, to move from his bedroom into the living room. By the end, he is "lying there dead and done for," "motionless," "quite unable to move" (*MO* 121–22; *DL* 193–94, trans. rev.).

But, here, as in *The Trial,* travel takes on the force of a hidden master trope. A small detail functions symbolically, denoting an upcoming traversing of Gregor's private space and a revolution in his personal life: Samsa, we learn on the first page, is a "*Reisender*" (commercial traveler) (*MO* 76; *DL* 115). Why does Kafka make Samsa—someone who moves so rarely in the story itself—a *Reisender?* This profession serves little practical purpose. If Kafka had only desired to keep Samsa out of the house in the novella's pre-narrative, away from the domestic sphere of father, mother, and sister, he could have made him a banker or a businessman with very long hours. But Kafka instead chooses to keep Samsa on the road for days at a time ("on the move day in, day out") and, moreover, to identify him with the constant motion and perpetual unsettledness symbolized by "*Reisender*" (*MO* 77; *DL* 116). More so than in *Richard and Samuel* and *The Man Who Disappeared,* then, travel seems to have, here, as in *The Trial,* a primarily symbolic (not practical) meaning. It denotes impending shifts in the character's psyche and body, and a change in perspective that will render his private arena public and strange.

Gregor's home, like K.'s, immediately becomes a site of penetration. His family freely enters his once locked room just as apples puncture his once integral body. Samsa describes this apparently secure room, on the first page, as an anthropomorphized metaphor for his stable "human" self: "His room, an ordinary human room, if somewhat too small, lay peacefully between the four familiar walls" (*MO* 76; *DL* 115). As if to emphasize the sudden foreignness of this regular human bedroom (which "lay," like Samsa himself, comfortably between four walls), Kafka sends Samsa literally traveling in his room: "crawling all over" a ceiling and walls that are no longer "familiar" (*MO* 101; *DL* 159). Samsa appears, as one critic claims, to be "traveling in his room," and this manic interior motion evokes a state of internal displacement bordering on insanity.[26] Kafka thus employs travel, here, as he did in *Richard and Samuel* and eventually does in *The Trial:* as a metaphor for internal displacement.

Interpreters have generally neglected the peculiarity of Gregor's profession (just as they have overlooked Franz's traveling garments)—choosing instead to interpret the cause and meaning of his metamorphosis. From the story's 1915 publication onward, readers have consistently viewed Samsa's transformation—his unsavory body, including flailing legs and soft, infected belly—as an *externalization* of some internal state. Psychoanalytical critics, for example, speak of a somatic "manifestation" (becoming-visible) of various unconscious conflicts.[27] Marxist interpreters have argued, similarly, that Gregor's transformation expresses his sense of alienation—resulting from years spent at a meaningless job.[28] What these readings fail to see is the possibility of an opposed trajectory: that Gregor's transformation might signify the *internalization* of an outside or exo-tic Other. After all, Gregor does metamorphose into a gigantic insect: the kind of grotesque, disproportionately sized creature that one expects to see in the tropics—with part of the thrill and angst inhering in observing such creatures while still keeping them at arm's length. And the exotic literature that Kafka knew about was rife with vermin: snakes, rats, and bugs. To offer just one prominent example,[29] Flaubert, in bed with an Egyptian prostitute, describes seeing "bugs" on the wall; he proceeds to crush them and then enjoy their "nauseating odor" as it "mingled with the scent of [the woman's] skin, which was dripping with sandalwood oil. I want a touch of bitterness in everything."[30] Although this would constitute an essay in its own right and can't be developed here, I would like to suggest that Samsa's metamorphosis can also be seen as the opposite of externalization: as the incorporation of the exotic. As such, it would be the logical conclusion of Kafka's interest, first voiced in the preface to *Richard and Samuel,* to bring the foreign ever closer to Europe's hearth.

How does this internalization process relate to *The Trial?* Most obvious are two plot points: the traces of exotic primitive life that infect an otherwise modern European city (Leni's webbed fingers and the mythical, nymph-like girls in Titorelli's attic) as well as the above-mentioned appearance of strangers/travelers invading K.'s home. But this internalization also happens on a conceptual level: an outside element (the basic condition for something being exotic) overruns the inside. The novel's opening scene (like the *Reiseanzug* featured in it) serves to confuse traditional distinctions between inside and outside, between "home" and "away." A man dressed like a traveler makes himself at home in K.'s room, sitting down in a chair and eating K.'s breakfast. K., on the other hand, is left symbolically without a proper place: Twice in the opening scene he mentions his desire to sit but is denied each time, either implicitly or explicitly, by the intruders (*T* 5, 13; *P* 10, 21). Sensing perhaps that this physical displacement is the source of his increasing sense of alienation, K. vainly attempts to accustom ("naturalize," *sich einbürgern*) himself to the minds of the guards (*T* 9; *P* 14): K. attempts paradoxically to naturalize himself in the head of a man dressed as a tourist. K.'s absurd predicament allies him with the modern traveler in general—who (like Karl Rossmann) has to contend, from the nineteenth century onward, with large bureaucratic machines that, in quite unnatural ways, propose to "naturalize" foreigners.

K. remains unseated, both literally and figuratively, throughout the entire opening scene—pacing his own rooms like a stranger. Eager to prove his rights of citizenship (and perhaps thereby to regain his proper "place"), K. hurries back to his room to look for his "identification papers." Here, again, Kafka reverses traditional roles: the native, not the traveler, rummages nervously for his personal documents. And K.'s home has become foreign to him. Instead of locating his papers, he at first, comically, finds only his bicycle license. This license to drive or travel ("*Radfahrlegitimation*")—momentarily replacing K.'s identification papers—sets the tone for the novel (*T* 7; *P* 12). It legitimizes K.'s dis-placement, his right to move, not his birthplace or identity. It points toward K.'s status, like Samsa's, as a traveler at home, as a displaced person whose so-called inalienable rights are continually put into question. The bicycle license also foreshadows Kafka's larger question, one he had already begun to pose in *Richard and Samuel* and *The Man Who Disappeared:* Is there any place, any home, to which the banished subject can return? K.'s second guard hints at the foreboding answer: K.'s "*Verfahren*" ("proceedings") as well as his "*Ver*-fahren" (his "travel" that "digresses from the course") have begun. As the guard tells him, "Proceedings [*Das Verfahren*] are under way and you'll learn [*erfahren*] everything in due course" (*T* 5; *P* 9). The fact that K. begins to incessantly travel around the city following this pronouncement suggests that he, like the condemned men Kafka will soon subject to a second legal *Verfahren* (in "In the Penal Colony"), unconsciously and literally incorporates the language of his oppressors.

If K.'s errant traveling signifies the literalization of his proceedings, then his punishment (like Rossmann's) is not waiting for him somewhere later in the novel. Rather, it has already arrived: his "*Ver-fahren*" is his sentence. Theological interpreters have long claimed that K.'s guilt corresponds to his spiritual "going astray" (*Verirrung*), as in Adam's original sin in Eden: the apple that K. eats on the morning of his arrest thus takes on special importance. But such an approach fails to point out that Kafka, here, as in *The Man Who Disappeared*, literalizes spiritual errancy: Like Karl, K. is a figurative "lost sheep," and he is also quite simply lost (*A* 39; *V* 56). The literal and the metaphysical are, here, inseparable: K.'s spiritual straying coincides with the more pedestrian act of losing his way (*sich verfahren* or *sich verirren*).

K. does not get lost to the degree that Karl does, but K.'s sense of topographical confusion is magnified by the fact that he, unlike his predecessor in America, is lost in a place where he *should* know the way. K. regularly finds himself in utterly strange neighborhoods in his home city: the Juliusstrasse court, Titorelli's studio, lawyer Huld's. The site of the first court typifies K.'s general, pervading sense of topographical uncertainty in his home city: "He was given the number of the building in which he was to appear: it was a building on a street in a distant suburb K. *had never been to before*" (*T* 36; *P* 50, my emphasis). This sense of not having "been there before" is amplified by K.'s experiences in the interconnected attic spaces that neither K. nor the reader would ever be able to accurately map. K. must constantly be led: by the washer-woman, by the usher, by Titorelli. Exemplary in this regard is K.'s second visit to the court, when he is led to the attics by the usher, and begins to lose his sense of direction. As the usher points out to K., the theme is again *Verirrung*:

"Surely you haven't already lost your way [*Sie haben sich doch nicht schon verirrt*]?," asked the court usher in amazement, "you go along here to the corner, then right, and straight down the hallway to the door."

"Come with me," said K. "Show me the way; I'll never find it, there are so many ways here."

"There's only the one way," said the court usher [. . .].

"Come with me," K. repeated more sharply. [. . .]

"Don't shout so," whispered the court usher, "[. . .] If you don't want to go back by yourself, then come along with me a ways, or wait here [. . .]."

"No, no," said K., "I won't wait and you have to go with me now." (*T* 72; *P* 97, trans. rev.)

K.'s increasing panic implies that he, like Karl in *The Man Who Disappeared*, understands the stakes of physical disorientation: it carries with it implications of metaphysical wandering. K. does not know "the way," and, as the usher claims with religious overtones, there is "only the one way." K.'s inability to find this way is accompanied, moreover, by a general weakening of his powers of perception. He feels "seasick" on dry land and at home, unable to see or hear beyond an enveloping hallucinatory haze (*T* 78; *P* 105).[31] K.'s lostness thus also implies psychological errancy without actually going anywhere, as in the disruption of perception we generally associate with drug-induced "trips" and madness.

"Journey to His Mother": The Maternal *Heimat* and Death

Like Karl Rossmann and other travelers from the fin de siècle exotic tradition, K. reacts to his general state of *Verirrung* by attempting to locate a "home" that would replace the one he imagines to have lost; this home was often equated with the lost *Heimat* of the mother's womb.[32] For Karl, such a nostalgia is most evident after being banished by his uncle at the end of "A Country House near New York" and, later, during the first "Brunelda" chapter. In the former, Karl tries to conjure his mother's presence through a photograph of her. Later, Karl attempts to replace his absent mother with the ambiguously maternal figure of Brunelda, in and around whom he hopes to find a "refuge."

In a never-completed—and critically neglected—fragment of *The Trial* ("Journey to His Mother"), K. similarly searches for a maternal *Heimat* as an antidote to his topographical and metaphysical lostness. K.'s mother's body, it is important to note, is an especially sheltering home for him because, according to K.'s selective memory, this body has not yet been penetrated and territorialized by his father. K.'s only mention of his father in the entire novel is of this man's absence: he dies young, so young in fact that K., who was perhaps still a baby, never remembered any paternal care (*T* 250; *P* 335). K.'s childhood situation—and his fantasies regarding his mother—is probably best understood psychoanalytically. According to Freud, the pre-oedipal child (which K. either was, or imagines himself to have been, when his father died), does not yet realize that the father—not the mother—possesses the phallus; moreover, he does not yet recognize that this phallic father stakes claims on the mother's body. The *Heimat* of K.'s mother is thus, according to his own pre-oedipal memory structure, still a pure, untrammeled spot. In the terms of the exotic traveler who desires both a mother and an untouched realm, K.'s "*Mutter*" is his utopia (*ou* + *topos* = not + place, thus not a place where someone could already have been). As opposed to the space of his boarding-house room, this private territory has not yet been unfolded. It has not yet been transformed into the public domain of paternity and Law.

With this maternal fantasy in mind, it is not surprising that K. develops what Freud would term a sudden "home-sickness" for his mother almost one year into his case.[33] In the first sentence of this chapter, we discover that K. is suddenly overtaken by an inexplicable desire for his mother: "Suddenly at lunch it occurred to him that he ought to visit his mother." The reasons for this revelation are at first unclear. K. attributes them to unconscious desires ("*Wünschen*") that even he cannot explain (*T* 263–64; *P* 351–52). But K.'s later description of his mother's village leads us to surmise that she represents for him a fantasy *Ur-Heimat,* the psychological and geographical site of his birth. She, like her town, exists before and beyond time: as a "small, unchanging village [*unveränderliche(s) Städtchen*]" (*T* 250; *P* 335).

K.'s nostalgia for the changeless village of his mother's body corresponds to his desire to escape temporality, an escape that would simultaneously signal a freedom from the courts. Unlike the maternal *Städtchen,* K.'s official persecutors are marked by their paternal fascination with punctuality. To give just one example, an official informs K. that he is exactly one hour and five minutes tardy for his first investigation.[34] K.'s journey to his mother, significantly, could result in K.'s missing a similar temporally determined opportunity with the court, which could "turn up any day or hour now" (*T* 265; *P* 353). K.'s visit to his mother thus represents a state beyond "process"—contained in the German word for trial (*Prozeß*)—and proceeding. In this regard, K. correctly reads his actions right before journeying to his mother as subversive (tearing up a letter from a court official and boarding the taxi cab). These actions undermine official temporality in two ways: first, K. possibly misses another future appointment with the court, and, second, through his show of strength, he continues his fantasy that—despite his trial—his social status remains unchanged. (K. reminds himself that even now he is one of the highest officials at the bank and that his mother still thinks he has been, for years, the bank's president.) (*T* 266; *P* 355)

K.'s journey to his mother, then, represents K.'s fantasy of escape: he can break away from temporal and topographical errancy by returning home. If K.'s guilt results in his being served up to disorientation, then the "Journey to His Mother" marks a symbolic restoration of innocence and timelessness. But such a journey is as impossible as a return to Eden (as impossible as in "On the Marionette Theater" by Kleist, whose work Kafka revered). K.'s mother's body is, of course, always already territorialized—*belästigt* (in the view of the child) by a paternal intruder. It is thus not the timeless, unsullied space K. imagines it to be. Rather, it is the latest in a series of concentric circles to be exposed, to be made *un-heimlich*. Perhaps this unbearable insight is precisely what keeps K. from ever arriving at his mother's. (The chapter is never finished; the demystifying, inevitably unhomely encounter with the mother thus never takes place.)

This uncanny journey to the realm of the mother refers symbolically—as in Faust's voyage to the netherworld of the "mothers" and, later, toward the "eternal feminine" (*das Ewigweibliche*)—to a journey unto death.[35] For Freud, similarly, the voyage toward death represents (like the journey to the womb) a return: The "*aim of all life is death*," Freud writes in *Beyond the Pleasure Principle* (1920); the "journey" of life, he continues, is merely an attempt to lengthen the "road to death."[36] Life's voyage, then, becomes nothing other than a series of "*détours*" that postpone the realization of death. Life derails the drive to "return" to an "earlier" state of "lifeless matter" (*Leblosen*)—to become one with, in Goethe's terms, the *Ewigweiblichen*.[37] This state corresponds, in the Freudian model, to an imagined biological Ur-home: a mystical moment before conception during which the organism paradoxically existed albeit beyond time and animation.

K.'s desire for death first surfaces before the corresponding plan to visit his mother. Almost immediately after his arrest, K. is shocked that his guards do nothing to prevent him from committing suicide—even though, just minutes into his proceedings, there would seem to be no reason for him to want to kill himself (*T* 10; *P* 17). K.'s irrational wish to die (he admits that suicide at this point would have been "senseless") springs, perhaps, from the same source as did his unconscious desire to visit his mother: he senses a vague longing for an earlier state beyond his present *Verirrung,* a place that is "lifeless," still, and, for K., utopian.[38] It is a home in death that, because it ends all motion, could possibly relieve K. of the distressing travels initiated by his *Prozeß*. This desire for death, and for an end to motion, offers some insight into K.'s opaque fear in the final chapter (which I will discuss in more detail later): that people will say of him after he is dead that, at the beginning of his case, he only longed to "end it" (*T* 228; *P* 308).

Avoiding "Arrest": Errant Traveling (*Ver-fahren*) and K.'s Defense Strategy

Opposed to K.'s exotic nostalgic for "mother" and death is his attempt to stay in constant motion: to avoid final conviction by, paradoxically, intensifying his state of disorientation. K.'s rapid-fire journeys around his home city (outlined above) may not in fact be completely arbitrary, but neither are these motions predictable or progressive: not directed toward, say, the gate of the Law or, as in the case of Rossmann, toward the (apparently) utopian Nature Theater. K.'s journeys, rather, form a zigzag pattern across the city's grid. Titorelli's home, K. reports, lies in the suburb completely opposite from the first one (*T* 140; *P* 188). K.'s crisscrossing motion—from home to court, to Titorelli's, to the lawyer's—suggests futility and randomness. But there may be a logic to this otherwise inscrutable motion. As another accused man (Block) claims, haphazard motion could contribute to K.'s defense. About to scurry around masochistically on his knees before the lawyer, Block proclaims to K. the utility of his apparently purposeless motion: "let me remind you of the old legal maxim: a suspect is better off moving than at rest, for one at rest might always be on the scales without knowing it, being weighed together with his sins" (*T* 193; *P* 261–62, trans. rev.). As if following Block's advice ahead of time, K. twice makes certain that he (and his uncle) do not stand still while walking the streets in chapter six (K. grabs his uncle's arm to prevent him from "standing still" [*Stehenbleiben*]; in the next sentence, K. again prevents his uncle from "*stehn bleiben*") (*T* 94; *P* 126, trans. rev.). In the terms of *Beyond the Pleasure Principle* outlined above, K.'s (and Block's) continual, non-progressive movement corresponds to a deferral of death. Like the underground creature in "The Burrow" and the other accused men in *The Trial,* K. seems to want to uncover as many *détours* as possible, thereby delaying his inevitable passage toward "lifelessness."[39]

In the legal discourse of K.'s trial, these detour*s* signify a means of deferring final arrest and execution. According to the painter, Titorelli, K. must keep his body and his files in continual motion in order to prevent conviction: Titorelli advises K. to consider an "apparent acquittal" ("*scheinbare Freisprechung*"), which, he insists, can be achieved by maintaining unrelenting physical and textual flux (*T* 156; *P* 211). First, Titorelli would have to physically make the rounds ("*einen Rundgang*") of the judges, sometimes with K. at his side. Second, Titorelli would keep K.'s dossier in permanent circulation, allowing it to wander back and forth from the lower courts to the higher courts to the lower courts again. Citing "traffic" and "jam-ups," Titorelli describes the movement of K.'s files in the same language we could have used to describe K.'s speedy automobile journeys back and forth across the city:

> [The files] remain in circulation [*im Verfahren*]; following the law court's normal traffic [*Verkehr*] they are passed on to the higher courts, come back to the lower ones, shuttling [commuting, *pendelt*] back and forth with larger or smaller oscillations [*Schwingungen*], longer or shorter jam-ups [*Stockungen*]. These peregrinations [*Wege*] are unpredictable. (*T* 158; *P* 214, trans. rev.)

This passage underlines the importance of traveling language (in addition to traveling bodies) for K.'s defense. The direction of these motions (legal as well as physical) is unimportant, but the overall structure of continual detour remains vital. If the legal language surrounding K.'s body is halted— if it does not "remain in circulation"—K., too, will be "arrested," as Titorelli advises: "Someday—quite unexpectedly—some judge or other takes a closer look at the file, realizes that the case is still active, and orders an immediate arrest" (*T* 158–59; *P* 214).

Laurence Rickels has rephrased Titorelli's strategy in the terms of Saussurean linguistics, claiming that such a perpetual slippage between "sign" and "meaning" is, for K., a matter of life and death.[40] If—as Titorelli claims—a judge eventually attentively reads K.'s documents, a fusion of sign and meaning will result: the files will merge with the "verdict" (denoting, literally, "true meaning").[41] This, in turn, will lead to the arrest— the standing still—of K.'s body and, eventually, to his execution. Such a fatal merging is—Rickels argues—also the central theme of the travel narrative that Kafka completed during his two-week break from writing *The Trial*: "In the Penal Colony." Here, the convergence of sign and meaning results in death when the victim is finally "enlighten[ed]" through the writing on his strapped-down body (*MO* 137; *DL* 219). Death issues in both texts from a doubling of the figure of arrest: the arrest of material signs (the files, K.'s moving body) and of K.'s heart (which the executioners aim to stop when they stab it at the end) (*T* 231; *P* 312). In both *The Trial* and "In the Penal Colony," then, the body is bound or held down, and the signs that surround it are stabilized as a verdict that activates the punitive apparatus. The cementing of sign and meaning thus lead to a multiple and final arrest. This sign/meaning consolidation is the goal of Kafka's 1914 legal machineries: it is K.'s assignment, in *The Trial,* to sabotage this merging through the interminable circulation of his own body and its files.[42]

Rickels' 1985 reading of linguistic slippage may seem theoretically capricious today: placed arbitrarily, without historical justification, onto Kafka's *Trial*. But Kafka's *Zeitgeist* as well as his novel call for such a reading. Titorelli's notion of signs in motion, in fact, seems to emerge directly from his era's general crisis of language (*Sprachkrise*), expressed most notably in the work of Fritz Mauthner and Hugo von Hofmannsthal. Mauthner—a Jewish poet, novelist, and essayist—was fin de siècle Prague's first German-language literary celebrity. His later book, *Contributions to a Critique of Language* (*Beiträge zu einer Kritik der Sprache* [1901–3]), was a founding work of modern language philosophy (single-handedly responsible for introducing the term *Sprachkritik* to philosophical discourse). Mauthner viewed language as unreliable—unfortunately so, for his own

Romantic conceptions: for him, language could no longer fulfill its duty as the poet's tool for accurately make sensing of both "reality" and the "self."[43] Hofmannsthal's 1902 "Chandos-Letter" comes to similar conclusions: the fictitious poet, "Lord Chandos," claims that he is giving up writing because of what he perceives to be language's general confusion (*"Wirbel der Sprache"*). Only pure thinking (*not* writing), he claims, can allow a person to achieve peace of mind.[44] These skeptical theories found fertile ground in the young Kafka who, already in 1900, claimed that words were "poor mountaineers and poor miners" capable neither of bringing "treasures" down from the "mountains' peaks" nor up from the "mountains' bowels" (*L* 1; *B* 9, trans. rev.). Kafka's *Sprachskepsis* only increased as he grew older and became increasingly suspicious of language's ability to relate to anything other than itself.[45]

But Kafka's typical fin de siècle language skepticism—appearing in *The Trial* as Titorelli's advice to divorce "sign" from "meaning" (as in Titorelli's apparently meaningless paintings of "heaths")—does not carry through to his main character: Josef K. does not accept Titorelli's recommendation to pursue a defense based on linguistic slippage. On the contrary, K. seems to be aware of the secret, homonymous connection between legal proceedings (*Verfahren*) and errant motion (*sich verfahren*). Keeping bodies and signs in motion, he senses, is part of legal procedure (and not, as Titorelli and Block claim, a way of outmanoeuvring the court). K. thus remains interested, as during his trip to his mother and during his suicide fantasy, in halting both his physical motion and the slippage of sign and meaning: he imagines returning to a simpler style of reading. For this reason, K. asks Titorelli about a nostalgic form of acquittal—the "actual acquittal" (*"wirklichen Freispruch"*), which, as Titorelli claims, only exists in communal memory, in "legends" (*T* 153–54; *P* 207–8).

Even if such an old-fashioned acquittal were possible, however, K. reluctantly acknowledges that it is deeply contradictory (it seems to employ the same rhetoric as do arrest and sentencing). Such an acquittal, Titorelli warns K., would result in the destruction of everything (*"alles ist vernichtet"*): All records, from the accusation to the acquittal itself, in short, the entire text of *The Trial* including its main character, would be completely disposed of (*"vollständig abgelegt"*) (*T* 158; *P* 213–14). But K. nonetheless longs irrationally for such a conclusion, just as he longs later for his mother, as K.'s remark at the end of Titorelli's long speech about "apparent acquittal" and "protraction" (*Verschleppung*) suggests: "'They [the apparent acquittal and the protraction] also prevent an actual acquittal,' said K. softly, as if ashamed of the realization" (*T* 161; *P* 218). K. is ashamed, here, not of the Edenic exposure of his private space and parts (it is already too late for this). Rather, he is ashamed, as he will eventually be at the moment of his death, of his nostalgic desire: he still longs for a legendary, outmoded, and perhaps sentimental "end" to everything—to all textual process and legal proceeding.

Ver-fahren as Perversion: Animal Love

K.'s reluctant strategy of *sich verfahren*—of continually detouring his body and files in order to avoid final arrest—bears a double-edged relationship to the Law. On the one hand, K.'s unpredictable motion confuses the Law's ineluctable "proceeding" toward his death. On the other hand, K.'s deliberate wrong turns (his *Ver-fahren*) often seem to mimic those of the courts. In the case of the courts, such proceedings are often "perverse"—both in sexual terms and in the sense of the Latin root, *pervertere* (*vertere* ["to turn"] + *per-* ["utterly"] = "to overturn," "to subvert," or "to turn the wrong way"). The court's overarching pornological structure (the Law book contains indecent pictures) determines much of its actions, even as it leads to legal deviations that sometimes hamper attempts to convict defendants (*T* 57; *P* 76). Random sexuality continually wastes bureaucratic energy: the guards pilfer K.'s underwear (meaning that the court must contend with K.'s official complaint); the court "Flogger" then tortures these guards overzealously (for two straight days, wearing S&M leather); later, the judges take breaks to philander with a washer-woman; finally, the lawyer Huld makes Block crawl around on his knees. The court is thus "perverse" in two senses: sexually (resulting in legal detours and respites for the accused) and legally (leading to distortions—perversions—of justice that torment accused men such as Block). Mark Anderson and Rainer Stach aptly see the Law as a center of *Verkehr:* of the bureaucratic "traffic" of clients and documents (*Parteienverkehr*) as well as of sexual intercourse (*Geschlechtsverkehr*).[46] But this concept of legal and sexual *Verkehr* should also be extended to the notion of being *verkehrt* (perverse); that is, of traveling wrongly, of "turning the wrong way."

The relation between K.'s strategy of *sich verfahren* and his own perversions comes into relief during his sexual encounter with his neighbor, Fräulein Bürstner. Here, as Anderson demonstrates, K. imitates the guards' molestation of him when he "assault[s]" Fräulein Bürstner. K. indeed explicitly claims to take on the role of the inspector just before he inappropriately grabs Bürstner's body (*T* 32, 31; *P* 47, 44). According to Anderson, K.'s *Ver-fahren,* here, does not serve to confuse the court: rather, it signifies how K. has completely and "unwittingly" taken on the court's own cruel lasciviousness.[47]

But one important aspect of K.'s encounter with Fräulein Bürstner distinguishes his perversions from those of the court. While kissing Fräulein

Bürstner, he does something none of the court officials ever do; he transforms, figuratively, into an animal: "[K.] kissed her on the mouth, then all
over her face, like a thirsty animal lapping greedily at a spring it has found
at last. Then he kissed her on the neck, right at her throat [*Gurgel*], and left
his lips there for a long time" (*T* 33; *P* 48). Anderson reads K.'s "assault" on
his neighbor as a sign of K.'s own degradation: "if K. behaves 'like a dog' it
is because he has been treated like a dog by the court."[48] But becoming a
"dog" in Kafka's writings does not always signify an involuntary disgrace
(contra prominent readings of *The Trial*).[49] As Gerhard Kurz points out,
Kafka often uses animal figures in order to illustrate poetic inspiration—as
"masks for the artist": the animals in "The Burrow" and "A Crossbreed"
("Eine Kreuzung"); Red Peter in "A Report to an Academy"; the vulture
("Geier") from the fragment of the same name; the crows in *The Castle*
(*kavka* means jackdaw in Czech); the mouse-singer, "Josefine"; and the
singing dogs in "Investigations of a Dog" ("Forschungen eines Hundes").[50]
Walter Benjamin correctly notes that animals are the Kafka characters who
have the "greatest opportunity for reflection."[51] Kafka's animals, moreover,
sometimes signify vital, unsubjugated life (as in the panther in "A Hunger
Artist"), and, for Gilles Deleuze and Félix Guattari, "becoming-animal" in
Kafka represents a uniquely creative, liberatory force: "To the inhumanness
of the 'diabolical powers,' there is the answer of becoming-animal: to become a beetle, to become a dog, to become an ape, 'head over heels and
away,' rather than lowering one's head and remaining a bureaucrat, inspector, judge, or judged."[52]

If K.'s animalistic "assault" on Fräulein Bürstner is voluntary, emancipatory, and sexually satisfying (he claims that it rendered him
"*zufrieden*"), then his action cannot be blamed on his own previous
degradation at the hands of the court (*T* 34; *P* 48). My point is that K.'s
attack is an expression of his subjectivity that is not entirely determined
by the courts. As such, his assault is not outside the realm of personal re-
sponsibility (indeed, K.'s later death "like a dog" with a hand on *his*
throat ["*Gurgel*"] suggests an uncanny retribution) (*T* 231; *P* 312). His
aggression signals a form of perversion that even the court accomplices
could not have imagined. As opposed to the student's brutal rape of the
washer-woman on the court room floor (which is not perverse at all,
according to Freudian definitions of perversity as "diverging" from genital intercourse), K.'s attack seems most peculiar: he laps his neighbor's
face and then rests his lips "for a long time" on her neck.[53] What kind
of "assault" is this? And by what kind of strange half-human "animal"?
A vampire that does not bite? A human lap dog nuzzling against a neck?
The eccentricity of this scene distinguishes it from the familiar violent
image of the court: the human rapist. Ritchie Robertson, who—like

most critics—strongly censures K.'s actions as immoral, nonetheless acknowledges the "strange mingling of brutality and poignancy" in this scene; it is, he argues, redolent of K.'s and Frieda's consensual sexual encounter in *The Castle*.[54] K.'s cavalier use of Fräulein Bürstner for his own pleasures of course places him, as critics point out, within the misogynist fin de siècle discourse of Otto Weininger that so influenced Kafka.[55] But K.'s peculiar sexuality also points toward a type of perversion beyond the Law's artless and banal brutalities: perhaps, as we shall see, toward a form of masochism that recurs, in a more extreme form, at the novel's end.

The connection between K.'s per-versions and his possible liberation comes into relief during his tryst with the lawyer's nursemaid, Leni. This scene begins with K. dragging his uncle into the all-enveloping street traffic (*"Straßenverkehr"*) and boarding a taxi bound for the lawyer's (*T* 93; *P* 125); it ends with K. and Leni rolling on the carpet. Here, it is Leni, not K., who is animal-like (animal-like in the loose, Deleuzian sense denoting non-human). But it is this very animality—manifested through Leni's physical "defect"—that begins to attract K.:

> [Leni] spread apart the middle and ring fingers of her right hand, between which the connecting skin extended almost to the top knuckle of her short fingers. In the darkness, K. couldn't discern at first what it was she wanted to show him, so she guided his hand to explore it.
> "What a whim of nature [*Naturspiel*]," K. said, and added, when he had examined her whole hand: "What a lovely claw!" Leni watched with a kind of pride as K. opened and closed her two fingers repeatedly in astonishment, until he finally kissed them [. . .]. (*T* 108; *P* 145, trans. rev.)

This time it is the woman who is the animal/reptile.[56] Leni gives off a stimulating "almost bitter" pepper-like odor; *she* bites and kisses K.'s neck (not the other way around), and she drags him onto the floor (*T* 108; *P* 146). But Leni's animality infects K. Fascinated, he plays with the webbed fingers—pulling them apart and placing them back together again—and kisses them. K.'s reptilian encounter offers him another momentary respite from the patriarchal realm of Uncle and lawyer. A cinematic fade-out sets in immediately after Leni pulls K. to the carpet, resulting in a sizeable gap in the narrative. This textual break lasts, as does K.'s lovemaking with Frieda in *The Castle*, for hours (*T* 109; *P* 146; *C* 41; *S* 68).

This narrative gap—brought on by the woman-animal's infection of K.—is, in political terms, both regressive and potentially subversive. On the one hand, it repeats misogynistic fin de siècle terms labeling the woman (especially the servant girl) as primitive and feral,[57] thus reterritorializing

K.'s journey in the form of a patriarchal voyage toward reified female animality. Furthermore, as with the "Journey to His Mother," this expedition toward the woman's body brings K. to a regressive "unchanging" moment outside of time; that is, toward a derogatory stereotype of femininity that views women as divorced from human history and progress (*T* 250; *P* 335). But K.'s leap beyond time with Leni simultaneously allies him with an aspect of femininity that seems to threaten the Law and its patriarchal minions. K.'s uncle is enraged at K. for his sexual encounter with this "dirty little creature." The uncle connects this with the loss of valuable time: K. was gone for hours ("*stundenlang*"); the lawyer and the Chief Clerk of the court waited for several minutes ("*minutenlang*"); the Chief Clerk waited a while longer ("*noch eine Zeitlang*"); and, finally, the poor uncle himself was forced to tarry in the rain for hours ("*stundenlang*") (*T* 109–10; *P* 146–48). K.'s perverse encounter with Leni thus threatens the courts by puncturing their punctuality. With this in mind, Leni does end up helping K. (as he had originally hoped), but in a way that K. could not have imagined when they first spoke (*T* 107; *P* 143). Together they create a space of strange pleasure: an atemporal, animalistic black hole in the court's legal discourse.

The Travel Guide

Verfahren, as we have seen, has two main meanings in *The Trial:* first, K.'s legal proceedings (and his ineluctable procession toward death) and, second (as *sich verfahren*), the possibility of taking wrong turns (sexual and otherwise). For K., such detours are both dangerous and potentially liberating. When K. is lost in the attics of the courts in the fourth chapter, as discussed above, he is weak and exceedingly vulnerable to attacks from the Law. But his (and his files') general disorienting motion through the city (in "completely opposite" directions) also seems to protect him (*T* 140; *P* 188). As Block and Titorelli suggest, losing one's way saves one from final arrest. K.'s sexual wrong turns—his per-versity (*Ver-kehrtheit,* or in ecclesiastical jargon, *Verirrung*)[58]—with Fräulein Bürstner and Leni are similarly ambivalent. They are imitations of the oppressive law and simultaneously symbols, through K.'s animality, of his capacity for disrupting legal processes.

The tension inherent in *Verfahren*—between proceedings and errant motion—is brought into relief by the travel guide ("album of city sights") that K. carries with him for much of the penultimate chapter (*T* 201; *P* 273). This guide, first, represents K.'s sense of being a tourist in his home town and, second and more importantly, exemplifies precisely the theoretical bifurcation of travel into guided proceedings and errant motion. The tour guide is, within the textual symbolics, a cipher for travel, but it is also a cipher for containing travel. As Georges Van Den Abbeele writes of the historical travel guide, it is a mode of "packaging"—prescribing and thus annulling—"real" travel.[59] K.'s guide, thus, is allied with the Law because it attempts to contain K.'s motion within what Deleuze and Guattari call "superficial" orbits; that is, to keep him on the beaten track of his *Verfahren* and unable to tend to his "own affairs."[60]

The historical travel guide, for which Kafka had a well-known interest (he and Max Brod planned to get rich off of a "new Baedeker" in 1911), was traditionally a kind of insurance policy against getting lost.[61] Looking at the early Baedeker guides that Kafka carried with him on his journeys, one is immediately struck by these guides' overproduction of maps and plans. The 1910 *Austria-Hungary: Handbook for Travelers* (which Kafka owned), for example, contained 143 maps and plans, along with two "panoramas" and six "floor plans" (see figures 11 and 16).[62] Karl Baedeker, in his introduction to this edition, even recommends tearing individual sections out of the thick book, so that the traveler can always have his guide with him and thus prevent moments of lostness.[63]

Baedeker guides, moreover, continually stress the importance of "orientation." The Baedeker *Paris and Environs* used by Kafka features an entire chapter devoted to an "orientation journey." This journey, when taken just after arrival, can help to make "the newcomer familiar with the general physiognomy of the overwhelming city" and thereby save him from "the uncanny [*unheimliche*] feeling of strangeness."[64] Kafka's and Brod's planned "new Baedeker" put an equal—if not greater—emphasis on orientation. The authors claim to want to "revise" Baedeker's system of "maps and plans." In so doing, they will help to give direction to "poorly oriented" travelers (*EFI* 190–1). Like the Baedeker, Kafka's and Brod's guides thus represent a form of traveler's protection: a carry-on guarantee effectively ruling out the possibility of disorientation. Kafka and Brod, correspondingly, offer travelers only *one* plan of travel: "imperative routes, only *one* hotel in each town, only *one* means of travel."[65]

Considering Kafka's historical interest in guides as antidotes to disorientation, we can regard K.'s "album of city sights" as precisely such a symbolic remedy. Like the early Baedeker upon which it was probably modeled, this book likely contains a duplicate of the cathedral in miniature as well as a map guiding readers from one major sight to the next.[66] As such, the album attempts to orient K. both physically and symbolically: it guides his body through the labyrinthine cathedral and, at the same time, instructs him on the importance of the cathedral's many artworks (*T* 205; *P* 278). Moreover, K.'s guide prevents the semiotic slippage Titorelli outlined above. As Rickels argues, the guide likely contains pictures that correspond precisely to the "real" world: "signs" that match up exactly with

"meanings."[67] K.'s German-Italian dictionary (which he consults, originally, in order to lead the Italian around the cathedral) is likewise a system
of one-to-one symbolic correspondence. It, like the guide, suggests that
"signs" and "meanings" can match up. As Titorelli has already made clear,
such a fusion is dangerous for K. If a judge makes this connection (of K.'s
files with his body), it could lead to the arrest of K.'s body—and, eventually, to a verdict and an execution.

K. is unusually dependent upon this guide (he thinks of it repeatedly,
makes sure to remember it before leaving for the Cathedral, and leafs
through it when inside [*T* 205–6; *P* 278–80]). This dependence is under-
standable. K. is as unsettled in this chapter as at any other point in the
novel. He has just dismissed his lawyer (and thus severed his connection
with Leni); he is afraid that he will lose his job; and, moreover, the Italian
businessman whom he was supposed to show around the Cathedral has
not appeared. K. feels more than ever like a foreigner at home, as his
rhetorical question suggests: "What if he were merely a foreigner [*Fremder*]
who wanted to visit the church? Basically, he was nothing other than this"
(*T* 210; *P* 285, trans. rev.). As if to stress symbolically K.'s unsettledness, the
narrator reports at the beginning of the chapter that K. has begun traveling regularly: K. has suddenly and inexplicably been asked to take more
and more business trips for his firm (*T* 200; *P* 271). It is not surprising that
this moment of intense alienation is accompanied by K.'s strongest nostalgic desires. "Journey to His Mother," if it had been finished and included
in the narrative, would most likely have appeared immediately after "In the
Cathedral."[68]

K.'s only moment of random motion (of what Deleuze and Guattari
term "real travel")[69] inside the Cathedral occurs, not surprisingly, at the moment he leaves his tour guide behind. When he leaves the guide on the pew,
his tour of the Cathedral is no longer "packaged." He now discovers, correspondingly, something that would appear in no guide. Carrying only a
flashlight, he walks off into a darkened small side chapel and shines the light
behind the altar. He perceives a painting but, because it is so dark, sees only
its fringe. On this fringe, he notices something that is not represented in his
album of famous art treasures:

> The first thing K. saw, and in part surmised, was a tall knight in armor, por-
> trayed *at the extreme edge of the painting*. He was leaning on his sword, which he
> had thrust into the bare earth—only a few blades of grass sprang up here and
> there—before him. He seemed to be gazing attentively at a scene taking place
> directly in front of him. It was amazing that he simply stood still without mov-
> ing closer. Perhaps he was meant to stand guard. K., who hadn't seen any
> paintings for a long time, regarded the knight for a long time [*längere Zeit*], in

spite of the fact that he had to keep blinking his eyes, irritated by the green glare of the flashlight. Then, as he let the light pass over the remaining portion of the painting, he discovered it was a conventional depiction of the entombment of Christ, and moreover a fairly recent painting. He put his flashlight away and returned to his seat. (*T* 207; *P* 280–1, my emphasis, trans. rev.)

This experience demonstrates precisely what is at stake in the novel's governing tension of *Ver-fahren:* between guided proceedings and errant motion. K.'s apparently random movement (in the dark, in a negligible side chapel) and visual unclarity (he can only "surmise" that he is seeing a knight) leads—as in the earlier encounter with Leni—to a rare moment of pleasure.[70] K. stares at the painting "at length" (reminiscent of the long time he spends with his lips on Fräulein Bürstner's neck and on the carpet with Leni), with rare attentiveness: he experiences "rapture."[71] Having been aesthetically undernourished for "a long time," K. is determined to keep looking even though the glare of the lamp hurts his eyes.

The terms applied by Roland Barthes to photography—the *studium* and the *punctum*—help to elucidate the significance of this critically neglected picture-viewing scene (neglected, perhaps, because K. seems to be dawdling pointlessly before his momentous encounter with the priest). For Barthes, the *studium* corresponds to the picture's main aesthetic or social meaning (that which we "study"), and it usually appears in the center of the composition (here, Christ being laid in the tomb); the *punctum,* on the other hand, is that which breaks (or "punctuates") the *studium.*[72] Often a peripheral detail, it surprisingly catches and holds the glance of the viewer (here, the knight, his sword, the stray blade of grass or two). Important for my reading is Barthes' claim that perceiving the *punctum*—unlike the *studium*—results in a rare devotion redolent of "love" (the *studium* only incites "liking"): The *punctum* rouses "delight" and "pain" (literalized, here, in the pain K. feels in his eyes) (27–28).

To exemplify my point, I refer to Barthes' own reading of the famous 1863 photograph of Queen Victoria seated on a horse. For Barthes, the queen—whose enormous skirt duly drapes the entire animal—is only *historically* interesting (i.e., as a *studium* representing the period of her reign). What really catches Barthes' eye is the queen's kilted groom, standing on the edge of the picture and holding the horse's bridle. This figure causes Barthes to ask eccentric questions that excite him: Is the man there to "supervise the horse's behavior?" "What if the horse suddenly began to rear?" "What would happen to the queen's skirt, *i.e.,* to *her majesty*" (57)? K. asks similar questions (peculiar, inspired) about the knight: Why does he seem to stand so preternaturally still (even for a figure in a painting)? What event has so entranced him? Is he there to stand guard? For Barthes, such questions betray K.'s belief that the figures in the picture have mag-ically "emerge[d]" out of the composition and, moreover, that K. himself imagines entering the world of the picture (57). The kilted groom (not the queen), in Barthes' example, "fantastically 'brings out' the Victorian nature (what else can one call it?)" of the photograph—just as another, 1850 photograph of a stony road to "Beith-Lehem" incredibly evokes the "time of Jesus" (97). Perhaps it is precisely the magical manifestation brought on by the *punctum* that captivates K. The enormous knight and his enormous armor, the sword that bears the terrible burden of this weight, the bare ground broken only by stray blades of grass: these details of an exotic medievalism (not the picture of Christ) conspire to evoke the *other* world for K. *They* enrapture him.

K.'s moment of visual absorption, like the perverse encounter with Leni, offers him a moment of freedom from legal oppression—as well as from the Law's corresponding punctuality. Generally obsessed with exact times throughout this chapter,[73] K. loses his sense of time while looking at the *punctum*. He stares at the knight for an indefinite "*längere Zeit*" and, during this interval, seems to plunge into a realm that defies temporality. In a slip that corresponds to K.'s own desires to puncture time, the narra-tor claims that the clock strikes eleven shortly before K. looks at the paint-ing; afterward, when K. looks at his watch, he sees that it was again eleven o'clock (*T* 206, 210; *P* 279, 285). Brod corrected this apparent error (changing the first reference to "ten o'clock") in the only editions avail-able until 1990. But in so doing he defused a radical atemporality, a possi-bility of stepping outside of time (reminiscent of Karl Rossmann's reverse aging process in *The Man Who Disappeared*). K.'s discovery of the *punctum*, like his encounter with Leni, creates an inassimilable (and pleasurable) temporal gap in the legal processes. In Barthes' terms, the *punctum* serves to "defeat [. . .] Time" by conflating two different pasts with a present ("my present, the time of Jesus, and that of the photographer").[74] In so doing, it emphasizes both the ineluctability of death and the possibility of "ecstasy" (119). The represented subject (for K.: the knight) is alive in the past that was his own life, already dead in the past of the painter (it is a "fairly re-cent" painting), and yet somehow alive again in K.'s present moment of viewing. K. is, in this way, confronted with the reality of death (of the once virile knight)—yet is also treated to a strong feeling of life (of ecstasy) con-nected to his having beheld death. Barthes writes, of another image: "I passed beyond the unreality of the thing represented, I entered crazily into the spectacle, into the image, taking into my arms what is dead, what is going to die" (117). Perhaps K., too, has had the sense of entering into the image, and, moreover, of coming close to what is both dead *and* going to die (the knight). This might account for the curious pleasure—however understated—that brings K. to temporarily halt his frantic movement. He stands still and stares at the knight with the same rapt attention that the latter has reserved for Christ.

When K. finally discovers the *studium*—the picture of Christ and the symbolics of theology (*The Trial*'s most well-known interpretative template)—K. is reterritorialized, by discourses of tour guides and the Law. K. walks away from the painting abruptly (as if suddenly bored by the *studium*'s "conventional[ity]"), picks up his "album," and prepares to leave the Cathedral. But, as at the end of his journey through the attics, K.'s disorientation here leaves him vulnerable. The discourse of the Law punctually returns— in the form of the booming voice of the prison chaplain, who misapprehends (or, better, *correctly* apprehends) K.'s tour guide as an official book (a "prayer book" used, perhaps, in the Law's prisons?) (*T* 212; *P* 288). K. responds to the priest's appellation and, through this acknowledgement, returns to the orbit of patriarchal law. He reverts to a "superficial" conceptual motion that the Law sanctions: an entanglement in the endless hermeneutics of the parable. (We, unlike K., will at this point turn away from the call of the *studium*.)

The stage is now set for K. to surrender to a final cessation of motion— an apparent end to his topographical, sexual, and visual *Ver-fahren*. This arrest will be physical as well as symbolic. K. will eventually stop moving around the city. As the chaplain finally tells him toward the end of the "Cathedral" chapter, K.'s proceedings ("*Verfahren*") will "gradually merge" into his verdict (*T* 213; *P* 289). This fusion of proceedings and verdict leads to the end of K.'s strange travels and to the onset of his apparent stillness in death.

The End as the Beginning: Circularity and Nostalgia

The final chapter, which Kafka called "The End" but wrote simultaneously with the first chapter, begins punctually at nine o'clock in the evening. Two symbolic travelers—reminiscent of the earlier *Reiseanzug,* they wear *Gehröcke*—pick up K. and escort him to the site of his death (*T* 225; *P* 305). This chapter is immediately marked by the increasing limitation of K.'s motion. He walks unusually stiffly in between the two guards. Each one clutches one of K.'s arms stiffly—holding it straight, instead of crooking the elbow—and clasps K.'s hands with an "irresistible grip." Thus grasped, K. imagines his only possible free movement to be that of a fly on flypaper (*T* 226–27; *P* 306–7). The remarkable rigidity of his body is such that, according to K., he can no longer move autonomously. Walking along between the guards, he becomes almost inanimate: "the three of them formed such a close unit that had one of them been struck down they would all have been struck down. It was a unit of the sort seldom formed except by lifeless matter [*Lebloses*]" (*T* 226; *P* 306, trans. rev.).

K.'s progression, on his death march, toward immobility and "lifeless matter" is actually a circular progression. It reminds us of two earlier events in the novel: first, K.'s mention of the possibility of his own suicide in the opening chapter and, second, his fantasized, but never-completed "journey to his mother." Each of these events, I have argued, represent K.'s desire, paradoxically, to progress toward his own past. He longs to *return* to both an inanimate state preceding all life and to the prenatal *Heimat* of his mother's body. Only by so doing can he escape the temporal "processes" of his *Process* (Kafka's non-standard spelling of *Prozeß*). K. is thus nostalgic for origins. More than this, he is nostalgic in the extreme way (demanding death or a return to the womb) that Kafka associates with people who perceive themselves to be outsiders in what should be their own home. In this sense, K.'s radical nostalgia prefigures that of Max Brod (as described by Kafka, in a statement that might have referred to himself as well): Brod, Kafka writes, "does not have a homeland" and therefore "must constantly think about it, search for it or build it" (*LM* 123; *BM* 164).

K.'s radical, circular nostalgia brings to mind, again, similar circularities in Kleist's "On the Marionette Theater" and Freud's *Beyond the Pleasure Principle*. In "On the Marionette Theater," the narrator and his interlocutor long to return to the "paradise" of grace and innocence that precedes human knowledge. When they realize that such a return is blocked, however ("the door to paradise is barred"), they choose instead to "travel around the world"—hoping that paradise has a rear door (i.e., is "somewhere open around the back").[75] Even more apt for Josef K. is Freud's claim, as mentioned above, that the "aim of all life is death." All living beings long to "return" to an unconsciously familiar, inanimate biological state: to return to, in Freud's echo of Josef K., "lifeless matter" (*Leblosen*).[76] K.'s progression toward stillness thus corresponds to Freud's notion that death is a biological homecoming: a "return" to an "earlier state of things," an "*old* state of things," an "initial state" of *Leblosen*.[77] Like the Freudian subject, the homesick K. is now experiencing the *nostos* he longed for when he first—apparently irrationally—imagined taking his own life. Consider, in this regard, K.'s uncannily similar (prostrate) body-position in the first and last scenes. His story begins, like a birth (or a death), in a bed. It ends with him lying flat again, returning, through death, to the lifeless split-second preceding birth. This biological homecoming (the arrest of K.'s blood, his cells, his heart) is augured, in the final chapter's opening paragraphs, by the halting of his external motion.

K.'s return to *Leblosen* signals a return to beginnings that encourages us to read the novel precisely as Kafka wrote it: the last chapter in tandem with the first. As mentioned above, Kafka created the first and last chapters in the same early phase of writing, before the rest of *The Trial*—thereby embedding the notions of circularity and return into the text itself. In an unusual meta-textual narrative moment, K. (like the reader) is given an insight, however dim, into Kafka's conceit. K. abruptly refers to the beginning of his trial in the novel's final pages—as well, perhaps, to his earlier, embarrassingly nostalgic desire, in the opening chapter, to take his own life: "Shall they say of me that at the beginning of my trial I wanted to end it, and now, at its end, I want to begin it again?" (*T* 228; *P* 308).

Radical Masochism and Shame: What "Outlives" K.?

Hidden beneath this last statement is K.'s sense of shame ("What will they say about me after I am gone?"), an emotion that appears again in the novel's last sentence ("'Like a dog!' he said; it seemed as though the shame was to outlive him") (*T* 231; *P* 312). Because "shame" is the final substantive of the novel, it is logically at the center of many debates surrounding the ultimate meaning of K.'s death. For some critics, K. should have taken the knife from his executioners and killed himself, thus rescuing a trace of his autonomy (and saving himself from shame); for others, K.'s refusal to take the knife signals a final (non-violent) resistance to the courts and their brutalities (in this case, K.'s shame is unwarranted). But the victory in each case would be, as Elizabeth Boa states, "pyrrhic."[78] Boa argues that we can instead imagine a third option loosening this critical opposition, related to the "sado-masochistic series" that runs through K.'s narrative. K. seems to be, for the most part, sadistic: he assaults Fräulein Bürstner, pushes the naked Franz (no longer wearing a *Reiseanzug*) under the flogger's rod, and voyeuristically observes Block's ritual humiliations. But by the end of the novel, Boa claims, K. reverses this role—masochistically accepting the "position of victim" and along with it a degree of pleasure (235).

Supporting Boa's argument are two important points: first, K. does not substantially resist his captors (later, he even displays a willingness to oblige), and, second, the entire chapter is stylized as a theatrical sexual game. In contradistinction to the opening, K. makes no objections when the officials arrive at his home. He is in fact dressed and ready for them, pulling on his new, tight-fitting black gloves before they arrive (K. apparently no longer needs instructions, as in the first chapter, on how to dress for court officials). K.'s formal gloves foreshadow the theatrical appearance of the two gentlemen: Wearing only black, they engage in affected, studied courtesies before entering K.'s apartment—leading K. to accuse them of being actors in a theater. But they could just as easily reverse the accusation (K., minus the top hat, is also dressed completely in black and acting as if the entire scene is rehearsed) (*T* 225–26; *P* 305–6). This theater becomes increasingly erotic as the trio, now walking in rigid unity, finally reaches the site of K.'s execution. The gentlemen remove K.'s coat, waistcoat, and shirt—folding them carefully, as if to be used again—and lay K. down on the ground. They prop his head against a boulder and repeatedly shift K.'s body (with K.'s help) as if trying, in vain, to arrange him in an aesthetically pleasing attitude: "In spite of all their efforts, and in spite of the willingness to oblige [*trotz alles Entgegenkommens*] demonstrated by K., his posture remained quite forced and implausible" (*T* 230; *P* 311, trans. rev.). K. thus assists in this attempt to create an appealing tableau. When this staging fails, the gentlemen nonetheless continue their rehearsed formalities—this time by passing the knife back and forth above K.'s bare chest.

This stylized preparation for execution is redolent, for Boa, of "pornograph[y]," or, more specifically, of S & M theater.[79] When the gentlemen finally stab K., they watch his theatrical finale ("*Entscheidung*") with great eagerness: they press against each other (cheek-to-cheek), thus gaining a better view of the blood presumably issuing from K.'s bare breast (*T* 231; *P* 312). The entire chapter, Boa claims, echoes the rhythm of sexual intercourse. The text's cadenced hesitations (K.'s possible shouting to the policemen; K.'s consideration of resistance; K.'s thought of following Fräulein Bürstner) lead inexorably to the "long-delayed, but long-prepared" outcome in the final sentences.[80] This mannered foreplay gives way, Boa continues, to the "thrusting sequence of brief questions" and, following this, the "terrible orgasm suffered by the body into which the knife is thrust." This ending is thus masochistic: the suitable "climax" to K.'s "process of (self-) punishment" (233).

Boa's claim of sexual rhythm goes perhaps too far (a more detailed textual explication would be needed), but her sense of K.'s masochism does not. In an important sense, in fact, she does not push this reading far enough. She claims, finally, that K.'s refusal to take the knife and stab himself marks his escape from the text's general "sado-masochistic" logic.[81] But taking the knife is precisely what K. can *not* do if he is to remain *within* this logic. The masochist can not hurt himself; he needs a dominator/dominatrix to do this.[82] In my reading, K. plays along in the sexual theater because he wants to repeat the explicitly S & M (leather-and-whip) scene that he had previously observed in the "Flogger" chapter. The situation is now reversed. The sadistic voyeur, K., is in the position of the victim. And this is not, for K., an entirely unwelcome development. He had already fantasized in the "Flogger" scene about taking over the masochistic position: He imagines stripping naked and offering himself to the flogger "in place of the guards" (*T* 85; *P* 115). In "In the Penal Colony," moreover, which Kafka wrote in the same 1914 autumn as *The Trial* (and to which readers more readily attribute masochism), the officer reveals a similar desire: he feels "tempt[ed]" to displace the prisoner and assume the masochistic posture on the torture "bed" himself (*MO* 137; *DL* 219).

If K.'s eventual willing death "like a dog" represents his "minimal rebellion against the court,"[83] then it is not because he leaves the Law's sado-masochistic logic. Rather, it is because he intensifies this logic and uses it to serve his own masochistic nostalgia. My view thus emphasizes K.'s agency, however slight, in his own death. In so doing, my reading challenges some dominant interpretations. According to Walter Sokel's reading, for example, K. is guilty because he acts "like a dog" (*hündisch*) when he gives up his struggle against the court, and he, moreover, treats others "like dogs": for these reasons, he must be sentenced to die like one.[84] Later readers have tended to agree that K. is, as Kafka himself once said, "guilty" and thus deservedly punished (guilty of original sin, of forgetting his mother, of relying only on "personal experience") (*D* 343; *Ta* 757).[85] Even readers disagreeing with Sokel's basic tenet (that K. is guilty) nonetheless see *The Trial* as a moral drama, with K. as an *unwilling* casualty: in this case, K. is innocent and is beaten down by a brutal regime.[86] Whether they see Kafka as guilty or innocent, readers generally view K.'s dog-like death as a purely negative punishment—a signal of his final defeat at the hands of the court.

But such readings fail to notice the possibility of masochistic gratification in K.'s punishment, a pleasure that critics nonetheless readily acknowledge in *The Metamorphosis* and "A Hunger Artist" ("Ein Hungerkünstler").[87] Only Sabine Wilke, in a recent essay, has insisted on the masochistic structure of *The Trial* and, moreover, on the possibility that masochism's founding text (Leopold von Sacher-Masoch's *Venus in Furs* [1870]) served as a pre-text. As Wilke demonstrates, the earlier scenes that employ the word "dog" in *The Trial* all suggest that being like a dog means being a masochist. Franz's cries in the S&M "Flogger" scene are explained away as a dog's howls, and Block crawls around on the ground as if he were the lawyer's "dog."[88] More important for my argument, we can now see that K. is masochistic where most other critics claim that he is sadistic: with Fräulein Bürstner, who is perhaps modeled after Sacher-Masoch's fierce, punitive Venus (each rests her elbows on an "ottoman," places her other hand on her hip, gathers her hair into a bun, and looks coldly past her male observer).[89] Continuing in the tradition of *Venus in Furs,* K. submissively licks Fräulein Bürstner "like a thirsty animal." Ultimately, as Wilke points

out, K.'s final utterance corresponds to a similar one from *Venus in Furs:*
Sacher-Masoch describes a masochistic man (Severin) who lies "like a
dog" (*"wie ein Hund"*) before his dominating Venus.[90]

This possibility of K.'s masochistic gratification helps us to understand
K.'s complex sense of "shame." Elias Canetti has argued that K. feels shame
for the same reason he did in the first chapter: because strangers are looking at him.[91] (Sokel, similarly, claims that K.'s desire to "not be espied" is
the "distinguishing mark" of his shame.)[92] K.'s shame thus seems to be the
shame of exposure and invaded privacy: people observe him from a window while he is marched past, stripped down to the waist, and stabbed.
But, as I argued at the beginning of this chapter, Kafka's novel calculatingly
destroys the possibility of this kind of shame (by unfolding the "private"
into the "public"). K.'s shame, then, must be of a different, almost inartic-
ulable sort—connected to his own radical masochism. Unlike the flogger's
victims, he will break the rules of masochism by shamefully demanding his
own death. He is, in this sense, closely allied to the heroes of "The Judgment," "In the Penal Colony," and "A Hunger Artist": his punishment is
also his own performance.[93] He is abetted by theatrical assistants (even if,
as K. laments, they are only tenth-rate ones) (*T* 226; *P* 306). Like the Penal
Colony officer and the suicidal Georg Bendemann from "The Judgment"—whose death, Kafka once told Max Brod, was also a "violent ejaculation"—Josef K. also experiences his death as an ecstatic performance
(with an audience in the windows).[94]

Throughout the novel, as I have demonstrated, K. has desired this
death—either actually (through suicide) or symbolically (by stepping
outside of time in the "unchanging village" of his mother's body) (*T* 250;
P 335). Moreover, like Georg Bendemann's "ejaculation" death, K.'s repeated flirtations with annihilation are connected to pleasure—even
hints of ecstasy (e.g., his love scenes with Fräulein Bürstner and Leni, his
viewing of the *punctum* in the Cathedral). The ending thus represents the
culmination of this series of desire and, more importantly, K.'s longing for
something that goes beyond even the pains and pleasures of masochism.
K. wants to annihilate the terms of masochism (by turning "game" into
"reality") and, in so doing, return nostalgically to an unchanging place
beyond time and (legal) proceedings. K.'s "shame" is thus the shame of
the masochist who wants to, like Sacher-Masoch, finally push masochism
beyond its limits.[95] He desires, as he once claimed to Titorelli, to have
everything destroyed—his case as well as his life. He longs for an acquittal that would transcend all forms of "protraction"—and, moreover, release him from the gigantic bureaucratic proceedings and errant travels
(*Ver-fahren*) that had displaced his subjectivity to begin with (*T* 158–60;
P 213–16).

In Kafka's world, this longing to escape the endless, technologized motion of patriarchal law (sexuality, disorientation, legal process) produces a sense of shame. K.'s violent yet nostalgic longings are anathema to the modern legal world, where absolute acquittals persist only as legends; this explains K.'s shame, earlier in the novel, when he inquires, "softly, as if ashamed," about such an acquittal. In the framework of Kafka's *Trial,* K.'s shame springs from his desire for complete self-effacement: in K.'s fantasy, all documents are completely "disposed of, they disappear totally from the proceedings [*Verfahren*], not only the charge but the trial and even the acquittal are destroyed, everything is destroyed" (*T* 158; *P* 213–14, trans. rev.). K.'s desire in the final chapter now recalls this earlier longing. He wants to end his trial without any form of acquittal at all, by puncturing the Law's all-encompassing text through his own death.

If K.'s radical masochism is nostalgic (pointing toward the changeless state before all proceedings), then his story is also a continuation and intensification of Karl Rossmann's. Rossmann, similarly, sought out a *Heimat* and an end to his errant wandering. Josef K. searches for the same thing, but he does so within the confines of his home town. He, too, is a stranger, but, in my reading, he attempts to escape this state of strangeness by ending his *Ver-fahren* through his own death. But does he really escape? As Kafka's final word—"*überleben*" (outlive)—indicates, one trace of K.'s itinerant past appears to survive his journey to the apparently "unchanging" realm of the dead (*T* 231; *P* 312). As K. attempts to escape to a timeless beyond, his shame trails behind him like the thread dragging after that creature who cannot die, Odradek. Death signals an uncanniness that estranges the subject from itself, in *The Trial* as well as in Kafka's other famous 1912–14 narratives. The dried-up insect corpse from *The Metamorphosis,* for example, is swept away by the indifferent charwoman, but the narrative eerily continues in what appears to be the "dead" Gregor's voice. The officer from "In the Penal Colony," similarly, dies with his eyes monstrously wide open, thus seeming to be grotesquely alert while in extremis. K., likewise, is mortally wounded but not dead by the time we come to *The Trial*'s portentous closing word—which Kafka allows to hang in the air, an everlasting curse on K.'s nostalgic fantasy. This single word keeps him homeless.

Fitting for a homeless man (as for Biblical/mythical scapegoats), K. is executed outside of the city limits: in what Kafka earlier called, in a 1911 diary entry, the liminal realm of the "suburb" (*Vorstadt*). The *Trial* city's suburbs—also the site of K.'s various meetings with the court and his tryst with Leni—are, like K.'s boarding-house bedroom, the place where the familiar and foreign collide. According to Kafka, writing three years before beginning *The Trial,* the suburbs of one's city are *unheimlich*: stranger than any foreign city ever could be. Our suburbs seem "foreign" (*fremd*) to us,

Kafka insists, because the people there live "partly within our city, partly on the miserable, dark fringe of the city that is furrowed like a great ditch, although they all have an area of interest in common with us that is greater than any other group of people outside the city." The suburb, for Kafka, is more exotic than the foreign city because it is at once home's Other and its double. Its people seem to never really be outside the city, but rather on a "fringe" that is at once "miserable, dark" foreign territory *and* "within" our home city. Because of this, Kafka's own 1911 journey to one of Prague's suburbs brings with it a panoply of extreme emotion: "For this reason [because the suburb is both inside and outside the city] I always enter the suburb with a mixed feeling of anxiety, of abandonment, of sympathy, of curiosity, of conceit, of joy in traveling [*Reisefreude*], of virility [*Männlichkeit*]" (*D* 119; *Ta* 253, trans. rev.). With this diary entry in mind, it is not surprising that, three years later, the suburb becomes for Josef K. a site of sexual transformation and also of anxiety. It is *unheimlich*: the city-dweller's pocket turned inside out. Because it is not an *other* place (but only "home" unfolded), it is no place to die. Rather, it is an exotic space that proscribes death's peaceful rest: its denizens include Karl Rossmann and Josef K. and, as we shall see presently, the similarly masochistic and nostalgic "officer" from "In the Penal Colony."

Chapter Four

Savage Travel:
Sadism and Masochism
in Kafka's Penal Colony

"Yes, and then came the sixth hour! It was impossible to grant all the requests to watch from close up. The commandant in his wisdom decreed that the children should be given priority; I, of course, by virtue of my office, could always be close at hand; often I would be squatting there with a small child in either arm. How we all drank in the look of transfiguration on the tortured face, how we bathed our cheeks in the radiance of this justice, finally achieved and already fading! O comrade, what times those were!"

—*The officer from "In the Penal Colony"*

arly readers of Kafka's "In the Penal Colony" ("In der Strafkolonie") decried its shocking, perverse explicitness. As Hans Beilhack wrote in the *Münchner Zeitung* in 1916, Kafka's story was sadistic; its author was a "*libertine* of *horror.*"[1] Otto Erich Hesse, writing in 1921 in the *Zeitschrift für Bücherfreunde,* took Beilhack one step further, claiming that Kafka and his readers were "repulsive" sexual miscreants: "the vileness of the human animal that turns itself on and goes into heat because of such tortures—reported as a matter of course—can only produce disgust."[2]

Even Kafka's admirers felt the need to distance themselves from the story's sexual excesses and from the charge that they, too, were deriving perverse pleasure from it. Kurt Wolff, Kafka's publisher, made it clear that he "loved" the story *despite* its explicitly "*peinliche*" ("painful," "embarrassing," and, in obsolete usage, "by torture") elements: "my love is mixed with a certain dread and horror due to the frightening intensity of the terrible content."[3] Even Kurt Tucholsky, "In the Penal Colony's" first public champion, feared that Kafka's descriptions of needles penetrating a naked man would draw comparisons to the popular sado-masochistic writings of that "perfumed salon sadist [Hanns Heinz] Ewers."[4] But Tucholsky insists that neither Kafka nor his officer-protagonist can be correctly termed a "sadist." Although the story might lead us to recall perverse sexual fantasies from "our" boyhood, "In the Penal Colony's" actual trajectory is political: the story of a military-colonial regime gaining "boundless power" and running amok.[5]

This early attempt to distance Kafka's story, for political reasons, from popular sadism initiated the false separation of sexuality and politics that has polarized readings of "In the Penal Colony" ever since. Following decades of mainly allegorical and text-immanent readings, 1970s psychoanalytic interpreters began to place the story in a Sadean tradition—without, however, adequately addressing the story's treatment of militarism and colonialism. As evidence of Kafka's conscious participation in the pornological tradition, critics cited Kafka's reference to the Marquis de Sade as the "real patron of our era" and also Kafka's professed interest in "torturing and being tortured."[6] Supporting such an argument is Kafka's adoption of Wolff's term, "*peinlich,*" in relation to "In the Penal Colony": "our times in general and my particular time as well have also been *peinlich* and continue to be, and my particular time even more protractedly *peinlich* than the general" (*L* 127; *B* 150, trans. rev.). According to Margot Norris, Kafka is referring here to the *Peinlichkeit* of his own sadomasochistic fantasies and, moreover, to the pornological elements that appear in "In the Penal Colony": the Sadean tropes of torture machines, perpetual motion, and institutions.[7] Peter Cersowsky builds on Norris' argument, arguing that Kafka's story fits into a long "sado-masochistic heritage" including Flaubert, Dostojewski, Byron, Poe, and Octave Mirbeau.[8]

But Walter Müller-Seidel has argued that it is wrong—and even politically suspect—to read "In the Penal Colony" solely in the terms of a sadomasochistic legacy.[9] Müller-Seidel, too, cites "*das Peinliche*" as evidence, but he insists on the importance of Kafka's apparently political reference to the painfulness of "our times in general": according to Müller-Seidel, World War I and the still-existing practice of colonial penal deportation.[10] Kafka's story, Müller-Seidel concludes, is a highly critical meditation on colonial deportation.[11] Building on Müller-Seidel (and incorporating postcolonial theory), recent North American critics have importantly argued that Kafka's story criticizes colonialism—specifically its political, cultural, and linguistic forms of hegemony. In such readings, "In the Penal Colony" is primarily legible as a political (not sado-masochistic) text: Kafka's story, here, reveals the excesses of colonial power.[12]

The problem with such postcolonial readings is that they fail to address the promise of sado-masochistic pleasure that is so central to the story's effect. Just as the earlier psychoanalytical interpretations repressed politics, these political readings repress desire. And perhaps with good reason. For it is precisely the sexual elements that most trouble political readings of "In the Penal Colony": they entice the reader (like Kafka's voyager) with pleasures that are dependent on cruelty. Kafka's delineation of the prisoner's fateful sixth hour, for example, in which the prisoner is "transfigured" through torture, has an undeniably wistful allure: "I [the officer] would be squatting there with a small child in either arm. How we all drank in the transfigured look on the tortured face, how we bathed our cheeks in the glow of this justice, finally achieved and so soon fading! O comrade, what times those were!" (MO 140–1; DL 226). Although one of the most memorable speeches of Kafka's story, this promise of voyeuristic rapture and communal pleasure is absent from postcolonial accounts of the text.[13]

And yet, Kafka's convincing pledge of perverse bliss is precisely what distinguishes his story from an anti-colonial tract and, moreover, what creates the ethical dilemma at the heart of "In the Penal Colony." Without the fantasy of transfiguration, there is only the unmistakably brutal reality of colonialism—only "plain murder" (MO 151; DL 245). But Kafka's promise of ecstasy complicates the textual politics: Enlightened onlookers become sadistic voyeurs who might even, like Kafka's officer, find themselves "tempt[ed]"—"seduced," or, literally, "led in the wrong direction" (verführt)—to get "under the harrow" themselves (MO 137; DL 219). Just as Kafka's story promises perverse raptures to its characters, it is also a siren song to politically committed readers. Russell Berman correctly insists that "there is a deep knowledge in the colonial setting, clearly and inextricably tied to violence and brutality."[14] But more than knowledge, I maintain, pleasure is at stake here. And, what is more, this pleasure troubles all attempts to construct a political reading. In what follows, I allow myself to be seduced by the story's sensual promise, but not in order to crowd politics out of Kafka's story. Rather, I follow the story's sado-masochistic Ver-führungen in order to demonstrate how such "digressions" are integral to a political reading. In Kafka's "colony," politics and perversity become inseparable.

Colonial Discourse/Tropical Rage:
The *Little Green Books* and *Torture Garden*

What is the relation between perverse pleasure and colonial politics in "In the Penal Colony"? In order to further investigate this, we need first to look at some of the popular accounts of colonialism that Kafka knew. Scholars have already cited Kafka's borrowings from Octave Mirbeau's

Torture Garden (1899), in which an explorer is sent by the French imperial regime to observe exotic penal practices.[15] But before discussing this well-known source, I will turn to another, overlooked one: the popular adventure series I referred to earlier, Schaffstein's *Little Green Books* (*Grüne Bändchen*).[16]

Kafka's passion for this series was first discovered by Peter F. Neumeyer in 1971. Neumeyer's investigation—ignored by over thirty years of subsequent scholarship[17]—begins with a peculiar 1916 postcard from Kafka to Felice Bauer, in which Kafka describes these *Little Green Books* and refers to them as "my favorites." Kafka goes on to depict one of them, entitled *The Sugar Baron* and published in 1914 (the same year that he wrote "In the Penal Colony"), in more detail:

> Among [the *Little Green Books*], for example, is one book that affects me so deeply that I feel it is about myself, or as if it were the book of rules [*Vorschrift*] for my life, rules I elude [*entweiche*], or have eluded (a feeling I often have, by the way); the book is called *The Sugar Baron,* and its final chapter is the most important. (*LF* 532; *BF* 738, trans. rev.)

Oskar Weber's *The Sugar Baron: The Adventures of a Former German Officer in South America* (*Der Zuckerbaron: Schicksale eines ehemaligen deutschen Offiziers in Südamerika*) is essentially what its title claims to be (see figure 17). Its eighty-eight pages tell the story of a down-on-his-luck former officer (Weber) who travels to South America in order to reinvent himself. He begins work as a land surveyor, then survives natural disasters and an attempted peasant revolution before ultimately, in the final chapters, making his fortune in sugar. Because I discuss this memoir as well as Kafka's startling, lifelong passion for the entire Schaffstein series in the next chapter, I will limit my present remarks to how these *Little Green Books* represent the fin de siècle practice of colonial sadism. For now, suffice it to say that Kafka mentioned them at least five times, always favorably (once even being moved to tears), and referred to them, in a recently published note, as the "great literature of travel."[18]

"*Vorschrift*" and "*entweichen*" are deceptively complex terms. Possible translations of *Vorschrift* are "specification," "direction," "instruction," "rule(s)," "regulation(s)," "prescription," and Neumeyer renders it as "formula." I prefer "prescription" because it, like the standard English translation ("book of rules") reveals that the *Vor-Schrift* is a system of writing; even more strongly than "book of rules," "prescription" captures the notion of a pre-writing or pre-text, implied by *Vor-Schrift*. Because Kafka experienced these books as a prescription (for literature as well as "for my life"), he also understood them, in the Foucauldian sense, as part of a "discourse" of adventure and colonial-

ism.[19] The *Little Green Books* reproduced a "book of rules" that determined
Kafka's "life," but at the same time a book of rules that he somehow man-
aged to "elude" (*entweichen*). *Entweichen*, unlike more direct forms of resistance, comes from a position of weakness and suggests flight instead of
confrontation (as when a prisoner escapes his prison).[20] Moreover, it implies
making oneself soft (*weich*) and getting out of the way (*ausweichen*): In Kafka's
case, as we shall see, this means uncovering detours and spots for sabotage off
the beaten discursive track.

The *Little Green Books*' colonial *Vor-Schrift* is two-pronged: it prescribes,
first, a typical colonial narrative of "self-discovery" (which I will discuss in
the next chapter) and, second, a systematic sadism. These books are shot
through with scenes of mutilated natives and human-like apes, viewed by
eager German voyeurs. Especially important in relation to "In the Penal
Colony" is, as Neumeyer points out, an old-fashioned machine from *The
Sugar Baron* that plantation owners still use to punish recalcitrant natives.
Oskar Weber recounts the machine's torture process, which traditionally
lasts twelve to twenty-four hours:

> One folds open the top beams like a scissors, sets the feet of the man-to-be-
> punished [*des zu Bestrafenden*] in the cut-outs on the lower beam, folds the
> upper beam closed and fastens the lock and bolt. The man is now trapped
> [. . .] and is, regardless how drunk and murderous, sober and tame within
> 12 to 24 hours. I have seen this "stock" occasionally utilized elsewhere, but
> only by very influential locals; I, as a foreigner, have never placed a man in
> this "stock."[21]

The connection between this machine and Kafka's in "In the Penal
Colony" is admittedly speculative (Kafka's machine is no "stock" but rather
a writing machine).[22] But less speculative are the thematic, discursive connections: a native is tortured in front of a European traveler/observer who
claims to not want to get involved; the torture process lasts at least twelve
hours (in Kafka's story, exactly twelve hours); both victims are transformed
(in *The Sugar Baron*, from murderous to tame; in Kafka's story, from common prisoner to vehicle of redemption) (*MO* 136; *DL* 219).

A similar scene from *Letters of a Coffee Planter: Two Decades of German
Labor in Central America* (*Briefe eines Kaffee-Pflanzers: Zwei Jahrzehnte
deutscher Arbeit in Zentral-Amerika* [1913])—another Schaffstein book by
Weber that Kafka claimed to "especially love"—further supports
Neumeyer's claim (although Neumeyer discusses only *The Sugar Baron*)
(*EFI* 300n30). *Letters of a Coffee Planter*'s narrator (again, Weber) describes
a large metal machine used for shelling and sorting coffee beans. Weber
anthropomorphizes these beans, which lose their "skin" when they are

rolled along a piece of cloth (resembling the penal colony apparatus' vibrating cotton wool, upon which the prisoner's skin is punctured).[23] Like the blood from the penal colony victim's body, Weber's "skinned" beans are eventually steered off into "channels" (*Rinnen*) that lead away from the machine bed into a container. Kafka's penal colony prisoner is similarly shaken and partially skinned; then his blood is conducted "into small *Rinnen*" and finally "into this main channel [*Hauptrinne*] which has a drainpipe into the pit" (*MO* 134; *DL* 215). Moreover, both narratives employ authoritarian legal discourse: in neither case is culpability ever to be doubted. Weber speaks of the coffee beans as if they were animate forebears of Kafka's human condemned man, discursively predetermined for a technologized death (in "*Rinnen*") that, in the end, one can never escape ("*entrinnen*"): "Not one of them escapes its fate. Is it not the same for all of us?"[24]

To cite just one of many more examples of cruelty from the *Little Green Books,* I draw again on Neumeyer, who claimed that Kafka might also have borrowed his central image for "A Report to an Academy" ("Ein Bericht für eine Akademie") from *The Sugar Baron.* Years before witnessing the torture scene described above, Weber recalls shooting an ape while on a pleasure-hunting expedition (see figure 18):

> [The ape] I shot [. . .] from a low palm-tree, fell, still alive, and sat exactly like a man with his back against the trunk. He pressed his left hand against the wound on his chest and looked at me almost reproachfully with big, dark eyes, which protruded from his fear-distorted face; at the same time he screamed and whimpered like a child and searched with his right hand for leaves, which he picked up off the ground, to staunch his wound.[25]

The connections are striking: Kafka's ape, too, is shot from a tree by frivolous colonialists (hard drinkers from "the firm of Hagenbeck") (*NSI* 387; *MO* 188; *DL* 301). After he is wounded, Kafka's ape, likewise, begins to turn human—thereby creating the text's dominant effect of pathos and guilt.

Despite these suggestive links between the *Little Green Books* and Kafka's colonial stories, we can hardly hope—as Neumeyer does—to have located the source for Kafka's accounts of torture. Many possible models for Kafka's "Penal Colony" torture machine, for example, already exist: the planing machines Kafka knew from Bohemian factories; J. M. Cox's "rotary machine" (used in fin de siècle asylums); the sexualized "beating machine" from Regina von Wladiczek's pornographic novel (*The Fever-Schooling of the Amalgamist*); and, most convincingly, the early phonograph as used in law courts to record depositions of defendants and witnesses.[26] But my interest here—as in the following, connected chapter on *The Castle*—moves beyond a debate over sources. I investigate here the *Little Green Books'* sado-masochistic colonial *Vorschrift;* that is, their penchant for perversity, as well as their prototypical attempt publicly to repress this.

Late-nineteenth-century European literature, high and low, tended to displace its sado-masochistic fantasies onto the colonies—most notably (as in *The Sugar Baron*) through the trope of the tortured slave.[27] And colonial sadism was in fact so widespread in the fin de siècle German colonies that it attracted medical attention: "*Tropenkoller*" (tropical rage) was categorized as a "disease of impulsiveness" that supposedly occurred only in the tropics, and that was brought on by a "civilized" person's confrontation with "an 'inferior' race which he regards and treats as half or wholly bestial."[28] The existence of *Tropenkoller* had already been public knowledge—and subject to sharp criticism in the press—for many years. As John Noyes illustrates, disapproving images of colonial sadism appeared in newspapers, journals, and popular magazines throughout the nineteenth century.[29]

This criticism was an important component of what has come to be known as the "New" Imperialism: a liberal reform movement that gained political momentum in the last decades of the nineteenth century.[30] The New Imperialism criticized the traditional hypocrisy of "democracy at home, despotism abroad" and began calling for, among other things, an end to sadistic practices in the colonies.[31] In fin de siècle Germany, public discourse began to view sadism as an "undesireable" and "harmful" excess; it was one of the targets of the *Kaiserreich's* "Colonial Schools for Women."[32] Instruction in these "Colonial Schools" included the planting and harvesting of tropical crops (sugar, bananas, coffee), but the government also expected that the schools' students would act as a sexually "civilizing" force over and against perverse male desire.[33] By the turn of the century, "normalizing" perverse sexual relations had become a prime goal of German colonial policy.[34]

With this New Imperial reform movement in mind (we will later see its resemblances to Kafka's "new commandant"), it is not surprising that the German colonists in the Schaffstein books never claimed to experience any pleasure while torturing.[35] Schaffstein books were, after all, read in the imperial schools and displayed by the *Kaiserreich* at the 1910 Brussels international "Exhibit on Education."[36] They thus obediently repeated the official image of a kinder and gentler form of colonialism.[37] In the context of this policy, it is only fitting that *The Sugar Baron's* protagonist never admits to gratification and vows uprightly after killing the ape "never again" to kill one—thereby repressing his own lust for murder ("*Mordlust*").[38] The narrator from Schaffstein's *In the Hinterlands of German East Africa* (1910), similarly, documents the death of twenty natives (their faces "horribly distorted in death-agony") and even supplies a sketch of a lion maiming an African (see figures 19 and 20).[39] But he, too, denies his own voyeuristic satisfaction, even if this denial is belied by his stylistic vigor. After animatedly describing how an elephant mutilates a native, he insists on his own decency: he would have stopped this slaughter if only he had been able to (but, alas, he found himself stuck in a swamp).[40]

This repressed sadism is part of a larger, New Imperial discourse attempting to eliminate sadistic excess from the colonial realm. This movement was a reaction against the unapologetic Old Imperial sadism, which unabashedly displayed "fantasies of domination, violence, and pleasure" in the colonies.[41] According to this old-style sadism of, for example, Kafka's beloved Gustave Flaubert, real cruelty was only possible in the "Orient," where Europeans had access to the "tremendous" element of the "grotesque": "In the streets, in the houses, on any and all occasions, there is a merry proliferation of beatings right and left. There are gutteral intonations that sound like the cries of wild beasts, and laughter, and flowing white robes, and ivory teeth flashing between thick lips."[42] Before Flaubert's travel notes reached Kafka, they already influenced Mirbeau—whose *Torture Garden* also began in the Old Imperial mode:[43] Mirbeau's French narrator and his sadistic young British lover, Clara, wander through an exquisite Chinese torture garden, with Clara claiming that only "Oriental" cruelty can cause her "whole body" to "quiver in the same way as it does in love"; only the "horror[s] of the Chinese imagination" can create these "pleasing shivers."[44] As will Kafka's Old Imperial "officer," Mirbeau's Chinese master executioner believes that "beaut[iful]" violence is impossible in Europe (where most people "no longer know what torture really is").[45] Only in the Orient is sadism still an art.[46]

Torture Garden's outlandishly explicit celebration of sadism is much more than this. Mirbeau was also an outspoken critic of the Catholic church, the French penal code, anti-Semitism (he publicly supported Alfred Dreyfus), and the New Imperialism, and he likely saw in *Torture Garden*'s exaggerated sadism a possibility for political satire.[47] By pushing the cliché of exotic sadism beyond its normal, acceptable limits, he caricatured "enlightened" Europe's own closeted sadism. Toward the end of the narrative, Clara labels her "Chinese" sadism as critical of "frightful Europe," where, for so long, "we" have "secretly torture[d] in the depths of jails."[48] Mirbeau thus repeats the Nietzschean critique of Europe's clandestine system of discipline, but Mirbeau takes Nietzsche one step further by proposing sadism as a critical practice. By exaggerating sadism's pleasures, Mirbeau parodies Europe's covert ruthlessness.[49] In order to emphasize European cruelty, Mirbeau employs a potent reversal in the final pages of *Torture Garden*: before the eyes of Mirbeau's hallucinating narrator, the face of the Chinese master executioner transmogrifies into that of a well-known French politician.[50]

As enthusiastic as Mirbeau's criticism is, however, it ultimately rings thin because Mirbeau still places only the exotic Other onto the torture block. In the words of Kafka's Old Imperial officer, Mirbeau never gets "under the harrow" himself. But Mirbeau nonetheless offers Kafka a model for, in Kafka's own words, "eluding" a colonial *Vorschrift* that admitted colonial cruelty without admitting any pleasure. Instead of repressing colonial sadism, Kafka, like Mirbeau, proposes a deliberately perverse solution: he renders Old Imperial sadism even crueller, pushing it beyond its traditional limits, toward absurdity. And Kafka's form of *Peinlichkeit* even outstrips Mirbeau's. He now places the eager European—not the recalcitrant native—beneath the machine.

Theater of Domination: Sadism and Old Imperial Power

This historical digression brings us to Kafka's story which, like *Torture Garden,* stages itself *in between* the psychoanalytical and political modes of interpretation: it is, I maintain, Kafka's meditation on the entanglement of sado-masochism and colonial politics at the fin de siècle. This interconnection begins already in "In the Penal Colony's" pre-story, through the figure of the now-dead "old" commandant. In the tradition of Old Imperialism, this commandant maintained his political power through a magnificent sadistic presence. Brazenly phallic (*"straff"*), he instituted a sadistic method of execution (in which the sentence is engraved on the naked prisoner's body) and, what is more, insisted on his own erotic role: laying the naked, condemned man onto the machine's "bed."[51] As Roberta Maccagnani remarked in her treatment of the Marquis de Sade's relation to exoticism, such displays of potency and discipline were essential to imperial sovereignty in the *Anciens Régimes.*[52]

The residue of this "old commandant's" sadistic presence is immediately evident in the commandant's surviving deputy, the officer. At the beginning of the story, this officer's body takes on erotic power for the European voyager ("*Reisender*"), who stares at the officer's captivating uniform: "'Surely these uniforms are too heavy for the tropics,' said the voyager, instead of inquiring about the apparatus as the officer had expected. 'Of course,' said the officer, [. . .] 'but they mean home [*Heimat*] to us; we don't want to lose touch with the homeland'" (*MO* 128; *DL* 204). Peter J. Brenner has accurately delineated Kafka's implicit political criticism here: the uniform corresponds to the European *Heimat*'s essential violence and, moreover, signifies the "exportation" of this violence to the colonies. It thus, Brenner continues, symbolically exposes colonialism's abiding political/moral paradox: "it is not the savages who are barbaric but the representatives of European civilization."[53] But like Müller-Seidel before him, Brenner fails to notice how the voyager, like Kafka's readers, is too distracted to notice this political critique: a sexual narrative—a *Ver-führung*—has already begun to divert both voyager and reader from politics. Having trouble "collect[ing] his thoughts," the voyager ignores the political message and stares, again, at the officer's "tight full-dress uniform, weighed down by its epaulettes and hung about with braiding." This spectacular battledress ("*Waffenrock*")—resembling the costumes worn by officers in parades ("*parademäßig*")—takes precedence over the legal-political apparatus, about which the voyager fails to inquire (*MO* 129; *DL* 206). Like the guard's tight-fitting *Reiseanzug* and the "flogger's" leather vest from *The Trial,* this uniform demonstrates the interconnection of Law, theater, and seduction. As Müller-Seidel warned, it begins to lead us along what appears to be the wrong discursive path.

But these seductions do not distract from a political reading. Rather, they are integral to any attempt to understand the text's politics. Kafka's officer realizes as much. His procedure *must* be a sado-masochistic "*Spiel,*" complete with actors and an audience (*MO* 134; *DL* 215). His political power can only be measured according to his success as a performer; thus, his viewers are as important to him as the executions themselves:

> The day before the performance the entire valley was already packed with people; *everyone* came along just *to look on* [. . .]. Before *hundreds of pairs of eyes*—all the *spectators* [*Zuschauer*] standing on tiptoe right up to the top of the slopes—the condemned man was laid under the harrow by the commandant himself [. . .]. It was impossible to grant all the requests *to watch* from close up. (*MO* 140; *DL* 225–26, my emphasis, trans. rev.).

This "watching" constitutes, as in Maccagnani's Sadean model, the "old" imperial sovereign's power. From the highest officials to the children (whom the commandant allows to come to the front row), everyone is a voyeur; together they constitute a Sadean erotic Panopticon.[54]

This panoptic voyeurism is, as Marcel Hénaff argues, central to Sadean, pornological form, where everything must be theater and must be visible. Although Sade employs no unique perspectival center (no single voyeur crouching in the shadows), there is always an implied "master" libertine, who, like the reader, sees everything. All bodies and all points of penetration must always be exposed. As is the case in Kafka's story, there is no fussing with disrobing: Immediate nakedness is mandatory, and everything is offered to everyone's eye "without mediation."[55] The old commandant's machinery is geared precisely to achieve such an omnivoyeurism: the harrow is made of glass so that "everyone" can "scrutinize the carrying out of the sentence." No effort is spared to get the needles mounted in the glass because "everyone" must be able to "look through the glass and see how the inscription on the body takes place." The officer even invites the voyager to participate: "Wouldn't you like to come closer and take a look at the needles?" (*MO* 134; *DL* 215, trans. rev.). This omnivoyeurism (in which "everyone" sees) is the key to the officer's political success. In these modern times, however, the officer's audience is absent. His "everyone" is reduced to the figure of the voyager, who, luckily for the officer, seems to have a primarily voyeuristic assignment: he "traveled only in order to see" ("*reise nur mit der Absicht zu sehen*") (*MO* 138; *DL* 222, trans. rev.).

The officer seems to realize that his political program (to convince the voyager of the merits of the "old" system) is unavoidably tied to a sexual one (to persuade the voyager to become a voyeur). Thus he pleads with the voyager—"Wouldn't you like to come closer?"—and tries to seduce him into paying more attention. As in the Sadean narratives, the voyeur must also be a sexual actor. While describing the torture process, the officer demonstratively "took the voyager's hand and drew it over the surface of the bed," then linked arms with him, toured him around the apparatus, and, later, pressed him back into his seat and took firm hold of him.[56] The voyager repeatedly demonstrates interest in the torture process and, more than this, flirts with becoming, like one of Sade's libertines, both voyeur and victim at once: he mimics the victim, who will lie down on the machinery, by leaning back in his own chair (*MO* 130; *DL* 209). This coquetry between officer and voyager culminates at the half-way point of the story, when the officer combines Sadean speculative processes with erotic contact.[57] After delineating the staging possibilities of his torture drama from yet another perspective and explaining again the mechanics of pain and transcendance, the officer throws his arms around the startled voyager and lays his head intimately on the voyager's shoulder (*MO* 141; *DL* 226).

As all readers of "In the Penal Colony" know, the officer's seduction does not work. This failure constitutes the story's turning point. The voyager feels deeply "embarrassed," and more importantly he symbolically refuses the proffered role of voyeur: he "looked around impatiently" over the officer's head, "avert[ed] his face from the officer," and "looked aimlessly" around (*MO* 141; *DL* 226–27). By tacitly rejecting the role assigned to him, the voyager also implicitly denounces the entire old colonial system and, on a meta-textual level, destroys the story's sadistic structure.[58] The high political stakes of this formal destruction are immediately clear to the officer. Despite the fact that the voyager has not yet uttered a politically critical word, the officer becomes desperate and aggressive. He seizes the voyager by the hands, turns him around to meet his eyes, and pleads into his face (*MO* 141; *DL* 227). The voyager later notices with apprehension that the officer was "clenching his fists" and, moreover, seizing the voyager by both arms and staring anxiously into his face (*MO* 144–45; *DL* 231, 235). Without the voyager acting as the requisite Sadean viewer-hero, the officer knows that his Old Imperial erotic Panopticon is doomed.

The Politics of Martyrdom: Getting under the Harrow Oneself

After this sexual rejection, the voyager finally denounces the officer politically, and the officer proceeds to go under the torture apparatus himself. Most interpretations—whether theological, psychoanalytical, or deconstructive—have viewed this surrender as the officer's admission that his "old" belief system is bankrupt (be it Judeo-Christianity; the paternal "superego function"; or a system of writing that synchronizes Law and text).[59] But these divergent readings fail to notice that the officer's suicide is also an act of defiance against the explorer and his New Imperial worldview.[60] By welcoming his own torture, the officer demonstrates his belief in the truth of colonial sado-masochistic ecstasy. He thereby paves the way for the old system's political erotics to return to prominence after his death.

The officer's martyrdom is also defiant because, by becoming a victim, he can expose the hypocrisies of the "new" colonialism. Whereas the new colonialism had hoped to transform the officer into a "normal" citizen (sexually and politically), the officer takes this liberal mandate too far by masochistically surrendering his entire masculinity. As in popular caricatures of the German colonists in Africa,[61] Kafka's officer takes literally the "new" directive to submit to a gentler, more feminized form of colonialism: he strips off his uniform and ostentatiously tosses two "ladies' handkerchiefs" to the prisoner, announcing, "Presents from the ladies!" Naked except for his sword and his belt, he proceeds to parody his own castration: He slowly and deliberately takes his sword out of his scabbard ("*Scheide*," also denoting "vagina"), breaks it into pieces, and dramatically hurls all these pieces into the pit (*MO* 148–49; *DL* 240).[62]

These exaggerated displays of emasculation "deeply disturb" the New Imperial voyager (*MO* 151; *DL* 244). Why? I surmise that the traveler fears that this symbolic castration might (like the destruction of the mechanized erotic Panopticon) augur the breakdown of the entire colonial structure. And, as much as the voyager seemed to want precisely this, he must also now realize that his own status and well-being depend upon colonialism. The officer, then, through his self-castration, succeeds in demonstrating what the voyager and the new commandant refused to acknowledge all along: colonialism and sadism depend on one another. The voyager's discomfort reveals (at best) liberal naiveté and (at worst) calculated hypocrisy. This explains the officer's condescending reaction to the voyager, just before the officer strips off his clothes: He smiles at the voyager "as an old man smiles at the nonsense of a child and pursues his own real thoughts behind that smile" (*MO* 146; *DL* 236).

The officer's secret "real thoughts" hint at his hidden plan: to now coax the voyager into the role of the sadist. Only this will allow the officer both to gain the torturer he requires *and* to reveal the moral duplicity inherent in the New Imperialism. The officer's secret plan explains his enigmatic gaze toward the voyager: the officer's eyes "seemed to hold a kind of summons, some call to participate." The nature of this summons is at first unclear to the voyager (*MO* 146–47; *DL* 236–37). But the officer intimates an answer when he attempts to train the voyager to read the machine's newest command, "Be just," which should be inscribed on the officer's body (*MO* 148; *DL* 238). This blueprint, like the contract traditionally agreed upon by a masochist and his torturer,[63] is explicitly a text: "'Read it,' he [the officer] said. 'I can't,' said the voyager, 'I've already told you I can't read those scripts.' 'Just look at it carefully,' said the officer"; as if teaching a child to read, the officer finally traced the letters in the air "with his little finger" (*MO* 147; *DL* 238). But the voyager still claims to be unable to read, and thus refuses to become the officer's torturer.

With this strategy of luring the voyager into sadism stalled, the officer decides to continue his attempt to prove the truth of colonial sadomasochistic ecstasy—without the voyager's help. The officer thus trains the machinery ("it was almost staggering to see how he handled it"), and it obeys him, even to the point that the machine, like Sacher-Masoch's dominatrixes, begins to torture of its own accord. Its harrow magically adjusts itself and then, after the officer lies down beneath it, the bed starts to vibrate, and the designer goes—autonomously—into motion. The officer, for his part, "submit[s]" (*MO* 150; *DL* 242). What follows is not a simple "autoexecution," as some critics claim, but rather a masochistic techno-utopia in which the machine becomes master: it begins to operate on its own.[64] As was the case with Josef K. in *The Trial,* the officer's masochistic trajectory is successful: he finally gets an Other to torture him.

The officer's determined masochism demonstrates the truth of his belief in colonial torture's ecstasies and, at the same time, results in the destruction of this system. This damage is primarily formal and aesthetic, and it precedes the apparatus' oft-cited physical demolition. As soon as the machine becomes the officer's animate master, the omnivoyeurism that had included us as readers begins to destruct. The narrative perspective wanders away from the sexually brutalized body. We, like the voyager, see nothing. The machine is so quiet as to "escape attention," and our eyes follow the voyager's, which veer off toward the soldier and the condemned man. Later, when the machine finally falls to pieces, the cascading cogwheels absorb the voyager's "whole attention" such that he fails to "keep an eye on the rest of the machine." Because he has not seen the machine torturing the officer, it comes as a "surprise" (for us, too) to see the result: a spitted, mutilated body (*MO* 150–51; *DL* 243–44). By getting under the machinery himself, the officer does more than organize the execution of Old Imperialism's last patriarch; he also destroys the perspectival structure upon which this earlier system of erotic domination was based.

This destruction finally allows the officer to achieve his second goal: to reveal New Imperialism's sexual-political hypocrisies. As soon as the machine begins torturing the officer and the old erotic Panopticon is dismantled, the voyager steps into his new role of colonial master: he finds the liberated prisoner "offensive," cannot bear the sight of him, and feels himself siding with the sadist he once denounced. He wants to "protect the officer" and "intervene" on his behalf. More than this, the voyager begins to exhibit his own domineering initiatives, longing at one point to physically "drive" (*vertreiben*) the prisoner and soldier away (*MO* 150–51; *DL* 243–44, trans. rev.). Just as the voyager had initially desired, colonial sadism is now destroyed: both politically (the old torture system can never be employed again) and aesthetically (the erotic Panopticon is dismantled). But this drastic upheaval "disturbs" the voyager, thereby hinting that the new colonialism is not so different from the old. Without sadism's political and perspectival apparatus to protect him, the voyager becomes nervous and unpredictable, telling the soldier and the prisoner (whom he can no longer bear to look at) to "Go home."[65] But as the prisoner (who is already "home") knows, such illogical colonial imperatives depend on a machinery of erotic mastery that is now defunct. He therefore simply "forgot the voyager's command" and does as he pleases (*MO* 150–51; *DL* 243–44).

The voyager's hypocrisy comes into relief in the story's coda, where he repeats the (now empty) colonial gesture that launched the story's plot: fleeing from the island, the voyager climbs into a boat and threatens the prisoner and soldier with a heavy knotted rope (*MO* 153; *DL* 248). This raised hand clearly recalls the hand of the Old Imperial captain, who, for the most trivial of reasons, had struck this same prisoner across the face (*MO* 133; *DL* 213). This final scene demonstrates the coda's political pessimism: no different from the old colonialists, the new, "enlightened" ones still threaten the native with violence and still leave him imprisoned on his island.[66] According to this ending, then, the new commandant's war on colonial sadism accomplishes little. It eradicates Old Imperial *Tropenkoller* only to replace it with another (less obviously brutal) system of discipline and domination.

The Great Madame:
Pleasure and Politics in Colonial Masochism

But Kafka remained dissatisfied with this ending and continued adjusting it through to its 1919 publication. He never explained what bothered him, but I would like to suggest, by way of conclusion, that he was discontented because this ending is too cynical: it does not explore the revolutionary power that colonial, masochistic pleasure evoked earlier in his narrative. As the story now stands, the officer's masochism transforms into a solely political martyrdom that has lost its connection to pleasure: he gets under the harrow only in order to prove the truth of the old system and demonstrate the hypocrisies of the new one. But what about Kafka's earlier promise of transcendence through gratification? Is the officer's martyrdom only political—or also orgasmic? Moreover, does such a perverse politics allow Kafka to find a way of "eluding" the colonial *Vorschrift*, as he had earlier suggested?

The first question is unanswerable since Kafka doesn't tell us what the officer felt. But this makes it all the more surprising that so many scholars uncritically believe the voyager's claim that the officer does *not* receive his "promised deliverance" while being tortured (*MO* 152; *DL* 245). It is worth asking: Why do the same readers who summarily reject the officer's claim that the prisoners experienced transcendence nonetheless accept the voyager's claim that the officer does *not* experience it?[67] The voyager's reasoning is weak: the officer's final "calm and convinced" look suggests, if anything, that he *has* experienced deliverance (*MO* 152; *DL* 246).[68] Whether or not the officer finds what he seeks, he, like Josef K., seems to retain his masochistic belief until the end. Moreover, as I mentioned at the beginning of this chapter, the officer first longs to become like his victim even when the officer's political power is still secure. His actions thus suggest that he actually believes in the truth of what are apparently colonialism's lies. He really thinks that his victims experience ecstasy.

This belief demonstrates the literally per-verse nature of colonialism in Kafka's model: Because the officer believes in the transformative power of sadism, he wants to turn the system upside down. He desires to get under the harrow himself. This is not to say anything good about the officer, but rather to demonstrate how, in Kafka's model, colonialism destructs itself. Because colonialism thrives on a belief in its own brutal deliverance, the officer must trust that his victims transcend: He must ultimately wish for things to be the other way around.

Kafka thus produces a model of colonial mimicry that reverses the standard one delineated by Homi Bhabha. For Bhabha, mimicry is an "ambivalent" mode in which natives unsettle colonizers by imitating them. The colonizers demand that the natives mimic them (the East Indians, for example, should become "British"), but this very imitation undermines the European's sense of self: the native's mimicry is "almost the same, *but not quite,*" and this difference menaces the colonizer's own "narcissistic demand."[69] Kafka in fact depicts such Bhabhian subversive mimicry in "In the Penal Colony" (where the prisoner imitates the voyager) and in "A Report to an Academy" (where the ape becomes a masochistic mimic of the sailors).[70] But it is vital to point out that Kafka also takes the complete opposite tack: for Kafka, the "forlorn" colonist discovers his own pressing need to imitate the native he once tortured.[71] Even at his moment of greatest political power, the Penal Colony officer longs masochistically to become like his victim. Colonial mimicry thus reveals for Kafka, too, colonialism's essential ambivalence. But in Kafka's model the mimicry proceeds from the colonizer: *he* mimics the colonial victim.[72] This "reverse mimicry" reveals colonialism's insecurity and its existential crisis.[73] But more than this, reverse mimicry exposes colonialism's suicidal foundation. Colonialism insists that the victim transcends through torture in extremis. It claims to believe that the inscrutable joys of deliverance are possible only through violence. In order for this colonial ideology to be true (and not just a cynical camouflage for sadism), the officer must perversely want to trade places.

Kafka experienced such reverse colonial mimicry in 1922, when he claimed to be jealous of those who have a "life in the jungle [bush, *Buschleben*]," and in 1909–10, in his "Longing to be a Red Indian" (*D* 416; *Ta* 910). Here, he describes the European narrator's desire to imitate people who—as Kafka knew from his readings in the *Little Green Books*—were on the point of cultural extinction:[74]

> Oh to be a Red Indian, instantly prepared, and astride one's galloping mount, leaning into the wind, to skim each fleeting quivering touch over the quivering ground, till one shed the spurs, for there were no spurs, till one flung off the reins, for there were no reins, and could barely see the land unfurl as a smooth-shorn heath before one, now that horse's neck and horse's head were gone. (*MO* 31; *DL* 32–33)

Critics have often focused on this fragment's depiction of modernity's crisis of representation: how it "efface[s]" the very "object of representation" that it ostensibly sets out to describe.[75] But this representational crisis played itself out, as Kafka knew, against the backdrop of a specific histori-

cal referent: the history of colonial expansion, which set the Indian popu-
lation on the verge of disappearance. The text indeed "proposes" an image
that it later "retracts or suspends," but it does so only within the framework
of perverse late-colonial longing.[76] The European narrator wants
masochistically to enact an ecstatic, self-orchestrated drama of cultural erasure. Only later, in "In the Penal Colony," does Kafka press this vicarious
colonial wish to its logical end.

This longing to become extinct re-appears in Karl Rossmann's (the
"man who disappeared") and Josef K.'s masochistic projects of vanishing,
and finally comes in relief in a fragment Kafka wrote in 1920. Here, Kafka's
narrator desires to die like a savage: "Those savages of whom it is recounted
that they have no other longing than to die, or rather, they no longer have
even that longing, but death has a longing for them, and they abandon
themselves to it, or rather, they do not even abandon themselves, but fall
into the sand on the shore and never get up again—those savages I much
resemble." In the continuation of this vignette, the narrator's masochism
begins to take on a political hue. His desire to throw himself onto the sand
troubles the non-savage workaday world, where daily life, far from the
realm of the wild men, attempts to "go on" despite this series of unsettling,
voluntary deaths: "Anyone who might collapse without cause and remain
lying on the ground is dreaded as though he were the Devil, it is because
of the example, it is because of the stench of truth that would emanate
from him. [. . .] How people do always carry their own enemy, however
powerless he is, within themselves. On this account, on account of this
powerless enemy, they are. . . ." (*WP* 243; *NSII* 241–42, Kafka's text breaks
off). This powerless yet dangerous enemy is the non-savage, the European,
who harbors a secret savage longing to fall into the sand on the shore and
never get up. This weak enemy within gives the lie to Europe's imagined
strength and also to its "enlightened" colonialism. As in Pierre Loti's description of a nineteenth-century Englishman who ecstatically "goes native" (only in order to make the suicidal choice of joining the losing
Turkish army against the British), colonialism seems to produce a colonialist subject who desires to become a victim.[77] In order to maintain this
"truth" (that colonialism is good for the natives), colonialism must produce
colonists who also believe this and who, like Kafka's officer, furtively want
to take the place of the native. Colonialism, in Kafka's account, generates
its own demise.

Three years before Kafka wrote this fragment (and three years after finishing his original version of "In the Penal Colony"), he was still trying to
locate a satisfactory ending to "In the Penal Colony." On August 7–9, 1917,
he wrote a series of alternate endings—one of which demonstrates the
story's connection to the sado-masochistic tradition of "animalisation."[78]

Mirroring Josef K.'s masochism at the end of *The Trial* (as well as Leopold von Sacher-Masoch's hero's in *Venus in Furs*),[79] the voyager desires to become a dog: "'I am [want to be] a cur [*Hundsfott*] if I allow that to happen.' But then he took his own words literally and began to run around on all fours" (*D* 380; *Ta* 822). Like the officer before him, the voyager wants to assume the role of the condemned man, who, at the beginning of the story, is likewise described as "*hündisch*" (dog-like) (*MO* 127; *DL* 203).

In another variation written on the next day, Kafka again displaces the officer's masochism onto the voyager. In this later version, the voyager (or at least a narrator who resembles him) has inexplicably become a laborer for a potentate-like snake known as the "great Madame," who now rules over the entire island:

> we who were to prepare the way [for the great Madame], renowned stone-smashers all, marched out of the bush. "Move!" called our always cheerful commandant, "Move it, you snake-fodder!" Immediately we raised our hammers and for miles around the most diligent smashing began. [. . .] The arrival of our snake was already announced for the evening, by then everything had to be smashed to dust, our snake could not bear even the tiniest pebble. Where is there another snake so sensitive? She is precisely such a unique snake, incomparably pampered by our labor, and thus also incomparably peculiar. (*D* 380–1; *Ta* 824, trans. rev.)

Margot Norris correctly sees in this passage the "severe, cruel woman" from the tradition of masochistic fantasy: Sacher-Masoch's Wanda or Kafka's pampered, despotic Brunelda from *The Man Who Disappeared*.[80] But because Norris views "In the Penal Colony" as solely a sadistic fantasy, she dismisses this masochistic fantasy as "anomalous": inconsistent with the bulk of the text, and thus correctly left out of the published version.

But I maintain that this fragment actually fits into a masochistic logic that Kafka only came across, in a fleeting fantasy, three years after completing his first version of "In the Penal Colony." By August 1917, Kafka had already invented his self-flagellating ape from "A Report to an Academy" and the masochistic narrator who feels like a savage. What is more, Kafka continued recording a series of private masochistic fantasies in his diaries and letters.[81] From this vantage point, I propose, Kafka now sees the importance of colonial masochism to his earlier story, "In the Penal Colony" and, moreover, sees how this masochism reveals the contradictions implicit in colonial ideology. Kafka thus invents his new voyager: no rope-wielding avenger but rather a laborer who moves into the bush, slaving away and preparing to be eaten by the Great Madame. This hallucinatory ending seems, for a moment at least, to provide Kafka with his sought-after conclusion. He effaces his "old" and "new" patriarchs and instead substitutes a cheerful commandant who obediently leads his laborers to the Madame. Instead of benefiting the New Imperial economy ("harbour works, they always keep talking about harbour works!"), the voyager wants to be devoured by the oral mother (*MO* 144; *DL* 233).[82] Laborers crush stones but these (like the laborers themselves) will be consumed for pleasure—not used to expand the economically vital port. This masochistic sexual excess thus harms colonialism's logic in a way that liberal protests do not. Instead of liberal progressivism, Kafka seems to offer us a politics of perversity. Kafka's 1917 coda remains fragmentary, but it still suggests the possibility of a surprising masochistic politics, in which the European's ecstatic submission reveals the "stench" of colonial "truth."

That said, the question of Kafka's (anti-) colonial aesthetic needs more clarification. Noyes has argued (on the models of Loti and Conrad) that masochism can be a "subjective performance of resistance" against colonialism.[83] But how much can we speak of "resisting"—or, in Kafka's words, "eluding"—colonialism in a world where colonial ideology seems to pre-program its own demise? If colonialism's promise of redemption through torture inevitably *produces its own masochism,* then how can we attribute subjective agency when this masochism reveals itself (as it must)?[84] For Kafka, colonialism's radiant brutality creates the desire to submit (*not* the desire to dominate). Kafka addresses this colonial structure/agent problem more thoroughly in his 1922 novel, *The Castle,* the subject of the following chapter. Here, Kafka's focus shifts away from sado-masochism and toward the colonial myth of self-discovery, but the attempt to elude a colonial *Vorschrift* is similar. As in "In the Penal Colony," Kafka's beloved *Little Green Books* serve as a source for *The Castle,* and here, too, Kafka depicts the failure and submission of his would-be colonial hero. But this novel poses, more clearly than "In the Penal Colony," the meta-textual, political-aesthetic questions about the writer himself: Why would Kafka want to create such figures of surrender? How does inventing "failed" heroes allow him to elude a colonial prescription? Might such failures correspond to his own victory as a writer? Is there such a thing as a masochistic narrative of literary self-formation?[85] How does this relate to Kafka's claims regarding a "small" or "minor" literature?

1. Kafka on a trip, site unknown.

2. Kafka (on the right) in Northern Italy, with Max Brod's brother Otto.

3. Riva del Garda (on Lake Garda), where Kafka spent his September 1909 vacation with Max and Otto Brod.

4. "Hotel & Pension Riva" (in the middle, background) in Riva del Garda, where Kafka and the Brod brothers stayed.

5. Kafka on vacation, probably in Riva del Garda (man on right is unknown).

6. Pages from the parallel diaries that Max Brod (left) and Kafka (right) kept during their summer 1911 travels through central and western Europe.

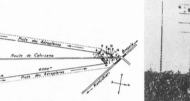

Die Aeroplane in Brescia.

Von Franz Kafka (Prag).

Wir sind angekommen. Vor dem Aerodrom liegt noch ein großer Platz mit verdächtigen Holzhäuschen, für die wir andere Auffschriften erwartet hätten, als: Garage, Grand Büfett International und so weiter. Ungeheure in ihren Wägelchen fettgewordene Bettler strecken uns ihre Arme in den Weg, man ist in der Eile versucht, über sie zu springen. Wir überholen viele Leute und werden von vielen überholt. Wir schauen in die Luft, um die es sich hier ja handelt. Gott sei Dank, noch fliegt keiner! Wir weichen nicht aus und werden doch nicht überfahren. Zwischen und hinter den Tausend Fuhrwerken und ihnen entgegen hüpft italienische Kavallerie. Ordnung und Unglücksfälle scheinen gleich unmöglich.

7.   Photographs from the 1909 air show in Brescia as well as the first lines of Kafka's article, "Die Aeroplane in Brescia."

8. *(left)* The Borghese Gladiator in the Louvre.

9. Clock tower in Brescia. Stereoscopic image that was also in the Emperor's Panorama that Kafka viewed in Friedland.

10. Kafka as a child: "There is a childhood photograph of Kafka, a rarely touching portrayal of the 'poor, brief childhood'" (Walter Benjamin).

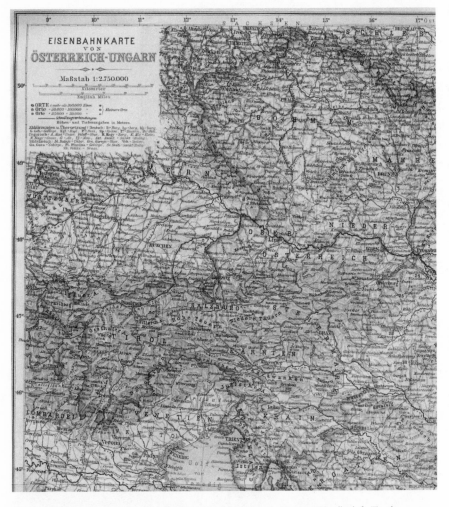

11. A map of central Europe, from the 1910 Baedeker's *Austria-Hungary: Handbook for Travelers* owned by Kafka.

12.   The Métro station Père Lachaise in Kafka's day.

13.   View of Broadway
from above; originally
printed in Arthur
Holitscher's *Amerika: Today
and Tomorrow.*

14. Parisian prostitutes from Kafka's era.

15. Photograph of lynching—ironically subtitled "An Idyll in Oklahama [*sic*]" by Arthur Holitscher in his critical travelogue about America.

ÖSTERREICH-UNGARN

NEBST

CETINJE BELGRAD BUKAREST

Dr. TH. KÜHN
MÜNCHEN
Widenmayerstr. 8

HANDBUCH FÜR REISENDE

VON

KARL BÆDEKER

Mit 71 Karten, 72 Plänen, 6 Grundrissen und 2 Panoramen

ACHTUNDZWANZIGSTE AUFLAGE

LEIPZIG

VERLAG VON KARL BÆDEKER

1910

Alle Rechte vorbehalten.

16. Title page of the 1910 Baedeker's *Austria-Hungary: A Handbook for Travelers*, which Kafka owned; it announces 143 maps and plans, as well as two panoramas and six floor plans.

Ah
4257

Schaffſteins Grüne Bändchen

Der Zuckerbaron

ierundfünfzigſtes der Grünen Bändchen, hrsg.
von Nicolaus Henningſen

17. Cover of *The Sugar Baron* (volume 54 of Schaffstein's *Little Green Books*), the
book that, according to Kafka, "affects me so deeply that I feel it is about myself."

18.   Sketch from *The Sugar Baron,* accompanying the narrator's description of shooting an ape, who, after falling, "sat exactly like a man with his back against the trunk" and "looked at me almost reproachfully with big, dark eyes."

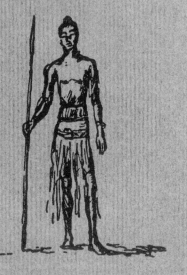

Ah
1257

...steins Grüne Bändchen

Im Hinterlande von
Deutsch Oſtafrika

Drittes der Grünen Bändchen, herausgegeben
von Nicolaus Henningſen

19.   Cover of *In the Hinterlands of German East Africa* (volume 3 of Schaffstein's *Little Green Books*).

20.   Sketch from *In the Hinterlands of German East Africa* (volume 3 of Schaffstein's *Little Green Books*), accompanying the narrator's description of a lion maiming an African.

21.   Sketch from *In the Hinterlands of German East Africa*, featuring the narrator/ protagonist looking out over the edge of a promontory.

22. Passport photo of Milena Jesenská.

Czech overprinted stamps: (top left) agriculture and science issue overprinted for use of air mail, (top right) overprinted Austro-Hungarian stamp, (bottom) Polish stamp overprinted 'Silesia Orientalis'

Czech heller stamps (including special delivery stamp overprinted 'Noviny')

Czech legionnaire stamps

Austro-Hungarian crown stamps

Austrian heller stamps (including an Austro-Hungarian stamp overprinted "German-Austria")

Austrian crown and heller stamps (including an Austro-Hungarian stamp overprinted "German-Austria")

23.   Czech and Austrian stamps of the kind Kafka exchanged with Milena Jesenská (Legionnaire stamps, a special delivery stamp, Austrian stamps overprinted as Czech stamps, a 10-heller stamp overprinted as a special delivery stamp, stamps worth 10 h, 25 h, 50 h, as well as one-crown and two-crown stamps).

53
39/7
Bd.

24.   Cover of *With the Xinqú Indians* (volume 20 of Schaffstein's *Little Green Books*), which Kafka gave to Klara Thein in 1913.

25. The last photograph of Kafka (1923/24).

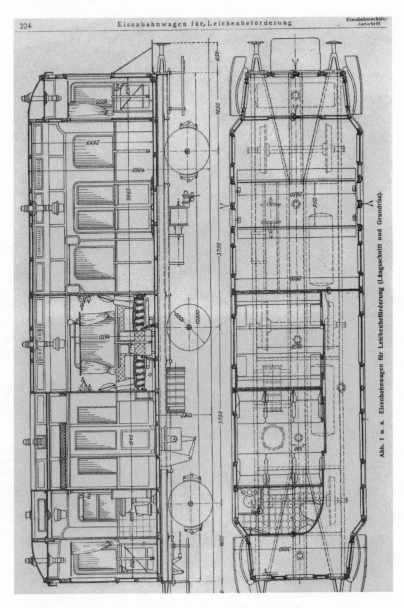

Abb. 1 u. 2. Eisenbahnwagen für Leichenbeförderung (Längsschnitt und Grundriss).

26.   Diagram of an early-twentieth-century *Leichenwagen* (corpse car).

Abb. 6. Einbringen eines Sarges vom [Kopfende aus.

27.   Coffin being loaded into a *Leichenwagen*.

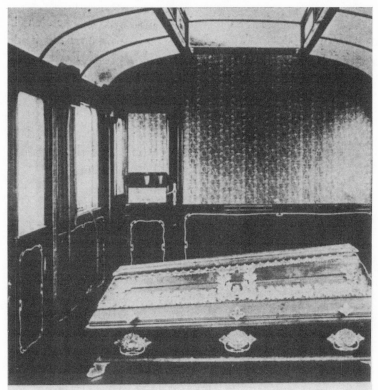

Abb. 3. E'senbahnwagen für Leichenbeföidcirg (Totcni

28. "Death chamber" in a *Leichenwagen*.

Chapter Five

Of Sugar Barons and Land Surveyors: Colonial Visions in Schaffstein's *Little Green Books* and *The Castle*

I am a good boy and a lover of geography.

—*letter to Max Brod, February 12, 1907*

In every issue [of an old newspaper] there was an installment of a novel called *The Commander's Revenge*. I once dreamed of this commander, who always wore a dagger at his side, on one particular occasion even held it between his teeth.

—*the narrator of "Memoirs of the Kalda Railway" (1914)*

R eaders have long puzzled over the profession of the protagonist of Kafka's *The Castle* (*Das Schloß*). Why does Kafka choose to make the faceless hero of his most mysterious novel a land surveyor ("*Landvermesser*")? Since K. never actually does any surveying in the novel (he doesn't even possess any surveying equipment), the choice of profession might seem to be relatively unimportant. But is it? K. is defined throughout by this putative career, which effectively replaces his name. To the other characters (and to the reader), he becomes "*Herr Landvermesser*," the "*ewige* [eternal] *Landvermesser*" or simply "*Landvermesser*" (thus the capitalization in the English translation).[1] Critics seem to agree on the importance of unravelling K.'s profession, but their efforts have led only to

suggestive yet widely differing metaphorical readings. Does surveying signify artistic ambition: observing, writing, and drawing?[2] The process of
reading: delimiting semiotic difference?[3] Messianic promise: rebuilding
Zion?[4] Some readers have questioned K.'s profession even further: claiming that he is not a surveyor at all but rather an impostor.[5] As the son of a
Castle sub-secretary assumes at the onset, K. could well be a "*Landstreicher*"
(vagabond) and *not* a "*Landvermesser.*" Others point out that the term *Vermesser* is already undermined by a grim Kafkaesque irony: it signifies au-
dacity and hubris (*Vermessenheit*) and, most importantly, the possibility of
making a mistake while measuring (*sich vermessen*).[6] Thus, if we take K.'s
profession seriously—as I propose we do—then we must acknowledge
that this designation persists only in the likelihood of its own error. The
Vermesser is *vermessen* and therefore possibly *vermisst sich:* mis-estimates
himself.

Such metaphorical and etymological interpretations have greatly en-
riched readings of *The Castle* (I will return to the crucial connection between surveying and reading in the final section of this essay). For the
moment, however, one cannot help but wonder whether critics, confronted by the opacity of K.'s profession, have missed the trees for the forest. As far as I can tell, only one interpreter has ever attempted to move
behind metaphor and search for a historical land-surveyor figure that
might have influenced Kafka: Peter F. Neumeyer, whose 1971 "Franz
Kafka, Sugar Baron" I mentioned in the previous chapter. Neumeyer argued that Kafka could have borrowed his land surveyor, like his "Penal
Colony" apparatus, from the popular 1914 memoir published in
Schaffstein's *Little Green Books* series: Oskar Weber's *The Sugar Baron: The
Adventures of a Former German Officer in South America* (*Der Zuckerbaron:
Schicksale eines ehemaligen deutschen Offiziers in Südamerika*). Although
Neumeyer does not go far enough—he merely notices influence and does
not attempt a new reading of *The Castle*—he does insist on a possible connection between K. and Weber, who begins his career as a land surveyor
(before making it rich in sugar).[7] As such, Neumeyer's essay serves as a
valuable starting point for gaining some historical footing for K.'s rhetori-
cally slippery profession.

As mentioned in the previous chapter, Neumeyer's investigation begins
with the strikingly peculiar 1916 postcard from Kafka to Felice Bauer,
which I will cite again here, because it is so crucial to my ensuing argument: "Among [Schaffstein's *Little Green Books*], for example, is one book
that affects me so deeply that I feel it is about myself, or as if it were the
book of rules [*Vorschrift*] for my life, rules I elude, or have eluded (a feeling I often have, by the way); the book is called *The Sugar Baron,* and its
final chapter is the most important" (*LF* 532; *BF* 738, trans. rev.). In the

"most important" final chapter, as will become clear later on, the aging erstwhile land surveyor, Weber, climbs a nearby mountain peak in order to survey his property and servants. In a moment of Romantic-Teutonic reflection, he contemplates his own death and voices his desire to be buried on the top of this mountain.

Neumeyer claims that this memoir of a "*Landvermesser*" could have influenced Kafka precisely at the time he was choosing a profession for the hero of *The Castle*. Kafka's first sketch for the novel ("Temptation in the Village," June 1914) features a protagonist traveling to a village and staying in an inn, but he is not yet referred to as a *Landvermesser*. Only after Kafka's reading of *The Sugar Baron* in 1916 does the hero of *The Castle* gain a profession.[8] Neumeyer buttresses his argument with further cases of apparent borrowing from *The Sugar Baron,* as I have demonstrated in the previous chapter, in "A Report to an Academy" and "In the Penal Colony." Weber's moving account of shooting an ape that then becomes uncannily humanlike seems to offer a pretext for the former; for the latter, Weber's interest in machineries of torture resembles that of Kafka's penal colony officer.

Jürgen Born, twenty years after Neumeyer, points out Kafka's peculiar passion for Schaffstein's *Little Green Books,* but he does not investigate this further. He (like other, silent readers of Kafka's 1916 postcard?) understandably categorizes Kafka's enthusiasm as "highly subjective" and emotional, and does not address a possible connection to Kafka's fiction.[9] It is worth noting, however, that Kafka had already used a travelogue, Arthur Holitscher's *America: Today and Tomorrow (Amerika: heute und morgen)* as source material for his first novel, *The Man Who Disappeared (Der Verschollene).*[10] Here, Kafka's love for "travel books" and his "longing for freedom and faraway lands"—as Max Brod puts it in his afterword to the first edition of the novel (which he, as editor, entitled *Amerika*)—indisputably overlapped with his literary production.[11] If Holitscher's travelogue served as literary inspiration, then why not—for both "In the Penal Colony" and *The Castle*—the more popular/national ("*volkstümliche*") *Sugar Baron* as well?[12] New evidence further supports Neumeyer's point by demonstrating that Kafka was thinking about *The Sugar Baron,* again, precisely in the middle of his work on the ultimate version of *The Castle* (February–September 1922). He mailed a catalogue containing the *Little Green Books* to his sister Elli in June 1922 and enclosed the following explanatory note (which was not published in its entirety until 1990): "Schaffstein's *Little Green Books,* from the enclosed catalogue page 10–13 are almost all for Karl [Elli's husband], he knows many of them already; I especially love numbers 50, 54, and 73, do not however own any of them, and would very much like to."[13] Number 54 is *The Sugar Baron,* and number 50 is another memoir by Weber that includes a land surveyor: *Letters of a Coffee Planter:*

Two Decades of German Labor in Central America (Briefe eines Kaffeepflanzers: Zwei Jahrzehnte deutscher Arbeit in Zentral-Amerika [1913]).

Despite this evidence connecting Kafka's readings of the *Little Green Books* with his conception of *The Castle,* what pertained for "In the Penal Colony" also pertains here: any quest for the "real" origin of Kafka's *Landvermesser* remains dubious. The figure of the land surveyor is, as mentioned above, little researched in positivistic scholarship; but we can nonetheless hardly presume to have located *the* source of K.'s profession, just as critics have been hard-pressed to unearth one correct historical model for the Castle.[14] The connection between Kafka's surveyor and the Hebrew word for Messiah (*mashiah,* almost the same as *mashoah,* "land surveyor"), for instance, cannot be overlooked in a quest for sources.[15] As in the previous chapter, my interest here is *discursive:* I want to relate Kafka's protagonist to the ways that land surveying figured in the popular imagination of the fin de siècle. This discourse, as we shall see, encourages us to reconsider Kafka's novel as a response to turn-of-the-century colonial understandings of territory, language, and (technologized) vision. Kafka, I will argue, attempts to "elude" a colonial *Vorschrift* with *The Castle.* But, as with most of his fictions, this escape is plotted from within—and thus is inextricably bound up with the structures it endeavors to avoid.

The Discourse of Land Surveying

Wilhelm Emrich introduced historical-political discourse into the land-surveyor debate in 1957. He argued, to surprisingly little critical echo, that surveying could be viewed as politically subversive.[16] Emrich correctly claims that the arrival of a land surveyor might signify the redrawing of borders and, therefore, challenge the Castle's authority. (This explains the insurgent Brunswick's interest in hiring a surveyor.) As was the case following the dissolution of the Austrian and German empires in 1918, surveying, for Emrich, meant less territory for the governing powers. New, unfriendly neighbors (e.g., Czechoslovakia) depended on land surveyors to draw up their borders and thus, literally, to define themselves as nations. Although Emrich's larger argument (that K. is a revolutionary) founders on a lack of textual evidence,[17] his insistence on the geo-political significance of land surveying in the 1922 novel remains a provocative opening for considering land-surveying's critically neglected historical-political role.[18]

Within the history of European imperialism, however, as depicted in the *Little Green Books* and elsewhere, surveying generally represented— pace Emrich—the opposite of revolution. In the Austro-Hungarian empire, as Kafka certainly knew, the land surveyor was a high-ranking governmental official—carrying with him the special rights and responsibilities of the notary public. More adventurous imperial governments in Spain, Britain, and France, meanwhile, hired surveyors to draw new borders and thereby to recast and solidify their empires' expanding frontiers. The journey of Alexander von Humboldt—who surveyed Latin America at the beginning of the nineteenth century—was, for example, financed by the Spanish crown, as were the voyages of less famous eighteenth- and nineteenth-century European surveyors. The traveling surveyor was often joined by cartographers, artists, botanists, and zoologists, and their communal goal was to demarcate, map, and classify national boundaries. In the colonized areas, as Mary Louise Pratt has written, Europeans were identified precisely as measurers: with their "odd-looking instruments" and "obsessive measurings" (of "heights and distances, courses of rivers, altitudes," etc.).[19] Such actions were far from benign. If we define the modern state as that entity that possesses the exclusive legitimate right to inflict violence within its prescribed borders,[20] then surveying—while itself not a violent act—supplied the geographic parameters for state violence.

This returns us to Kafka's much-loved *Little Green Books,* specifically to the Sugar Baron—who in Oskar Weber's account begins his career in late-nineteenth-century South America as a land surveyor and offers no exception to this profession's reactionary tradition. Like other European contemporaries in Latin America, Weber's Sugar Baron begins his adventure employed by a post-imperial government that continues to cater to European interests. He is hired to parcel up "vacant" land that is eventually to be sold to speculators in coffee and sugar. Making use of the rudimentary engineering skills gleaned from his military service in the Franco-Prussian War, Weber spends seven years at this job. He surveys "abandoned" territories (probably populated by indigenous peoples), in order to ready them for sale to entrepreneurs: "since growing coffee was then a very lucrative business, ownerless [*herrenlose*] governmental estates were being bought up everywhere; these estates [. . .] needed to be surveyed."[21] By taking on these jobs, the hero of the memoir Kafka enthusiastically called his *Vorschrift* becomes a vital cog in the machineries of power.

How familiar was Kafka—beyond having read *The Sugar Baron* and *Letters of a Coffee Planter*—with the historical figure of the traveling *Landvermesser* and, more importantly, with its reactionary context? Kafka was an avid reader of travel literature of all sorts, and his interest in the *Little Green Books* was more sweeping and profound than even Neumeyer acknowledges: Kafka commented on the series five times in the decade from 1912 to 1922—always favorably, being moved to the point of sobbing on December 15, 1913—and he acquired at least seven of the volumes.[22] From the *Little Green Books* (where surveyors play important roles) and from his general travel readings, Kafka was likely familiar with the newly ascendant figure of the journeyman surveyor: as Peter J. Brenner points out in his study of travel literature, "scientific" travelers such as surveyors already outnumbered the more traditional touring gentlemen by the end of the nineteenth century.[23] The connection between surveyors and colonialism would have reached Kafka directly through his Uncle Josef, who worked in territories exemplary of the fin de siècle mania for mapping and remapping: Panama and the Congo.[24] Given the above-mentioned reactionary political use of surveying, it is not surprising that, in the fifth chapter of *The Castle,* the Chairman explains to K. that the village peasants become suspicious ("*stutzig*") when they hear of the Castle's plans to hire a land surveyor: "land surveying is an issue that deeply affects peasants, they scented some sort of secret deals and injustice" (*C* 66; *S* 107).

Kafka, then, would likely have known about the reactionary land surveyor through "scientific" literature, familial relations (in reports from Central America and Africa), and the colonial entertainment industry. In my review of the *Little Green Books* from the years immediately preceding the publication of *The Sugar Baron,* I found six volumes that feature surveyors or surveying. These stories are embedded in an ideology of exploration and exploitation, and the surveyors in them, by plying their trade, help to consolidate post-imperial power.[25] However, surveying in the *Little Green Books* does more than just serve colonial power and land-grabbing. More central to a study of Kafka's novel, surveying simultaneously corresponds to two important aesthetic features. These two formal traits confirm, as we shall see, Edward Said's claim that aesthetics and politics are always intertwined in the colonial arena: that an investment in empire (in this case, the employing of surveyors) is also always an "aesthetic investment."[26]

Colonial Aesthetics I (Plot):
The Business of Self-Discovery

The first of these two aesthetic features is the typical plot design, which I will refer to as the "business of self-discovery." This "business"—which combines financial gain with psychological stabilization—is prominent in the three volumes by Oskar Weber that Kafka claimed in 1922 to "especially love": the aforementioned *Sugar Baron* and *Letters of a Coffee Planter,* and a third book, *The Banana King: What the Offspring of an Indentured Hessian Accomplished in America (Der Bananenkönig: Was der Nachkomme eines verkauften Hessen in Amerika schuf).* Each is the story of an impecunious German going to a faraway country and, following various dramatic setbacks—from fires to volcanoes to revolutions—gaining wealth and personal satisfaction.[27] In each case, the protagonist's economic mastery develops simultaneously with his Bildungsroman-like story of self-discovery. This combination of capital gain and psychological progress is, of course, not new to colonial discourse. Nineteenth-century travelers to the Orient, as Said points out, were often more interested in "remaking" themselves than in "seeing what was to be seen."[28] Richard Hamann and Jost Hermand, similarly, uncover a fin de siècle psycho-economic nexus that they refer to as "imperialism of the soul."[29] Furthermore, Wolfgang Reif argues that Kafka's era featured recurring narratives about heroes gaining an identity through travel,[30] and he points out that many popular and literary authors—Waldemar Bonsels, Graf Keyserling, Hermann Hesse—wrote of alienated Europeans going abroad with the express goal of "*Selbstfindung*" (self-finding or self-discovery). As Keyserling writes in the epigraph to his 1919 *Travel Diaries of a Philosopher* (*Das Reisetagebuch eines Philosophen*), "The shortest path to oneself leads around the world."

This narrative business of self-discovery is, as the Sugar Baron soon discovers, best performed on a blank foreign landscape; that is, on what I call a "negative topos," a place defined by what it is not.[31] The soon-to-be Sugar Baron, for example, remarks at the outset that he chooses South America simply because it is *not* New York: "Should I go to New York like so many other ex-lieutenants before me and there begin a dubious career of washing dishes and the like, or should I [. . .] go to South America?"[32] Ten years before writing *The Castle,* Kafka similarly constructs Russia as a negative, or blank, landscape for Georg Bendemann's "Russian friend" in "The Judgment." Kafka writes to Felice in 1913 that this "friend" is modeled after Kafka's own Uncle Alfred Löwy, the brother of the aforementioned Josef, but only negatively in terms of topography: "[My uncle] is a bachelor, director of railways in Madrid, knows the whole of Europe with the exception of Russia" (*LF* 297; *BF* 435, Kafka's emphasis). For Kafka, then, Russia is like South America for the Sugar Baron: it is a space that is not yet overdetermined by traveling European predecessors.[33] This discursive blankness is important for the soon-to-be Sugar Baron (as well as for the Russian friend, who yearns for self-reinvention through "extraterritoriality") because he wants to redraw himself, as it were, on a clean slate.[34] Like earlier visitors to the Orient described by Said, Weber imagines this foreign world to be an erasable writing pad or, to shift metaphors, an unadorned stage on which to perform his self-fashioning.[35]

This business of self-discovery congeals in *The Sugar Baron,* as elsewhere in the *Little Green Books,* specifically around the act of surveying. The soon-to-be Baron, after surveying for the government and getting rich, finally surveys his own vast properties—thereby transforming them from a negative topos into a positive, particular, inscribed one. Now known simply as "El

Varon" [*sic*] by the "natives," he demarcates, as surveyor, his space of new, private mastery.[36] The hero of *Letters of a Coffee Planter,* similarly, hires a surveyor after he makes enough money to buy an estate. Only after his land is surveyed can the Coffee Planter become a titled landowner, and only after this can he legally move his Indian workers onto his plantation. He can now observe his workers at all times. This panopticism gives him more control over them and, consequently, more power for himself. Political and visual power coincide: as the Coffee Planter claims, "the master's eye fattens the cows" ("*Das Auge des Herrn macht* [. . .] *die Kühe fett*").[37]

Colonial Aesthetics II (Perspective): The "Monarch-of-All-I-Survey" View

In contemporary English, "to survey" also connotes looking down at something from above ("sur" + "vidēre" = "to over-see"). This double meaning of measuring and over-seeing—which extends throughout the *Little Green Books*—coalesces into the second major aesthetic feature in the Schaffstein books: point-of-view. Like the narrative business of self-discovery, perspective in the Schaffstein books relates surveying directly to power. The Schaffstein surveyors invariably attain good views over the lands they traverse, and these superior perspectives correspond to their perceived authority over the natives. Like Hermann Hesse on the Pedrotagalla and other contemporary travelers to Asia, South America, and Africa, the heroes of the *Little Green Books* repeatedly attempt to gain the high ground.[38] This perspective—which Mary Louise Pratt refers to as the "monarch-of-all-I-survey" view—corresponds to the business of self-discovery in the following way: At the outset, the unfortunate European traveler is lost visually, psychologically, and economically—only later gaining a personal and professional identity. Shortly after he acquires this identity, he achieves a singular view from above that confirms both his financial successes and his acquisition of a stable sense of self. The consolidation of his personal and economic "I" thus corresponds with the streamlining of his "eye."

The late-nineteenth-century hero of *Letters of a Coffee Planter* purchases a South American plantation 800 meters above sea level. This height, he claims, offers him a beautiful view and a divine sense of self. He feels as if he is "in heaven" and enjoys a rare, clear vision of a neighboring mountain range: "When the forest permits a vista, one has a beautiful view of the facing cordillera, whose high summits stand out in relief against the rich blue sky."[39] *In the Hinterlands of German East Africa* (1910), similarly, features a hero who gains a sense of himself (as distinct from the natives) by climbing a mountain and looking down.[40] Once at the summit, he surveys an "overwhelming" landscape, a picture of what he terms "indescribable grandeur." The connection between this visual discovery and the protagonist's consolidation of power is emphasized by the sketch that accompanies the description (see figure 21). Here, the fearless adventurer stands on the edge of the promontory and looks out—like Karl Rossmann on the balcony in *Der Verschollene*—through binoculars; his frightened servants, meanwhile, cringe far from the edge. The adventurer is depicted as the single, technologically mediated eye—and thus the uncontested profiteer—in the picture's voyeuristic economy. Moreover, he is present only in order to see, not to be seen. His entire body is covered with clothing (even his eyes are concealed by the binoculars). The cowering, unseeing servants, conversely, are nearly naked. In the end, the narrator is visible only to us, his readers, and only through the other end of the glass. We maintain a perspective even more encompassing than Mecklenburg's, because *we* see *him*. As I will discuss in my conclusion, the readers' position apparently beyond this visual economy renders us the most powerful—but also, paradoxically, the most impoverished—figures in this technologically mediated colonial narrative.

The traveler's ability to see but not to be seen gives him power over both the foreign Other and the foreign landscape. As Pratt argues, the nineteenth-century traveler's sense of visual mastery emerges in conjunction with his ability to transform the foreign landscape into a painting, which, in order to empower him, must not include him. He creates this painting and invisibly views it, so that he is never present inside it. Typical for this "aestheticizing" scene of visual sovereignty is a rhetorical "density of meaning"; that is, an overload of adjectival modifiers, and as demonstrated in the following example from another of Schaffstein's *Little Green Books,* Max Wiederhold's 1913 *The Panama Canal (Der Panamakanal)*, a veritable palette of colors.[41] The German narrator of *The Panama Canal* describes his adventure: a thrilling 1907 journey across the still new and relatively untested canal, culminating in his first-ever view of the Pacific Ocean. As was characteristic for the new century, the setting from which the European directs his gaze is man-made rather than a part of nature: the hotel balcony replaces the traditional mountain peak.[42] The narrator's panoramic view from this technological promontory encompasses the sun setting on the ocean, and he aestheticizes this picture through an overload of color-descriptors:

> The *green* of the near mountains and the *blue* of the distant range become *purple,* which gradually turns into a *violet* and finally transforms into a barely perceptible *gray.* A cloud that shines forth in *red* and *gold* lies atop the mountains at the sea; this cloud sends humanity the final greeting of the sun,

which in the meantime has sunk into the ocean. Before the night covers the earth with its *black* shadows, a *pale green* spreads over the sky, which is then superseded by a shimmer of *gentle pink*. Then it is night.[43]

The dizzying array of color modifiers aestheticizes the landscape by turning it into a densely colored painting (as is fitting for the historical time period of impressionism in visual art). This excessive aestheticizing assists the narrator in his striving toward *Selbstfindung*. It transforms his environment into a discrete, that is, framed, work of art. Furthermore, by demanding the attention of the suddenly overtaxed reader, this dense modification helps to cover up the central contradiction in the narrator's act of self-creation. Like the fully clothed and binoculared hero of *In the Hinterlands of German East Africa,* the narrator describes everything except himself and his standpoint. He is the invisible creator of a landscape that is defined exclusively by his omnipotent yet unseeable eye. He thus paradoxically erases himself in creating the painting that affirms him. As was the case with nineteenth-century colonial postcards of the Orient, the viewer discovers himself by "making" a landscape that cannot include him because—in order to affirm him—it must remain completely Other.[44]

My final example of a European traveler constructing a panoramic view while effacing himself is the most important one for my upcoming discussion of *The Castle.* It issues from *The Sugar Baron,* and exemplifies the way in which the business of self-discovery coincides with the monarchical view (and to aesthetic density). The hero is, at the outset, indigent and visually frustrated, sitting in the lower deck of a ship bound for South America. His personal disorientation, therefore, parallels his inability to gain an overview of the Atlantic Ocean for five long weeks. In direct contrast to this dramatization of visual poverty, *The Sugar Baron's* final paragraphs (part of what Kafka called the book's "most important" chapter) present a now wealthy and self-confident Baron standing high above his own estate. He surveys the same ocean he once saw at eye-level. Now the ocean forms an aesthetically pleasing backdrop for his prodigious property as well as for his final act of narrative business:

I am more than fifteen-hundred meters above the level of the ocean that glimmers toward me in the distance like a broad, silver ribbon. And between it and my standpoint I see an everlastingly green ocean of brush and trees, in the midst of which are the white structures of my estate [*meiner Besitzungen*], with shining, light gray, corrugated roofs, the light green square plots of the sugar cane and corn fields, the darker and more muted meadows, and the small huts of the workers with their brown straw roofs—all lying out there like toys. From this single point, the vista [*Fernblick*] encompasses almost 270 degrees [. . .].

When I first coincidentally became acquainted with this place after the surveying of my property [. . .] I brought ten hard-working men with axes and machetes up here, and I marked for them specifically the individual trees they were to cut down in order to clear the view [. . .]. Every year I have to allow myself the luxury of having the path [leading to the promontory] and the small plateau again cleared of the vegetation which has newly sprung up in the course of the year and interfered with the view.[45]

The connection between panoramic vision and power is explicit. The narrator aestheticizes a realm that clearly belongs to him (his *Besitzungen*). The meaning that Weber produces so densely—hardly a noun goes unmodified—increases his psychological wealth, just as the density of his crops increases his financial well-being.

Because the Baron's psychological business is also the business of economics, his position is inflected with eighteenth- and nineteenth-century notions of land-ownership and class. As proprietor, painter, and observer of the landscape, he achieves a profit through detachment similar to that of Hegel's "master" in *The Phenomenology of Spirit* (*Die Phänomenologie des Geistes*, 1807). The Baron does not, in Hegel's terminology, work on ("*bearbeiten*") the objects of his world; his laborers ("*Arbeiter*") do this. By avoiding proximity to the objects and thus to their threatening otherness—for Hegel, their "independence"—he can enjoy them purely, as "sheer negativity."[46] For instance, the Baron only marks the trees; his servants cut them down. Through the "mediation" of his servants the Baron can "have done with the thing altogether" and, in this way, achieve full "satisfaction in the enjoyment of it."[47] Hegel's notion of pure enjoyment through aristocratic distance invokes, as John Barrell demonstrates, class intonations from the eighteenth-century discourse of "disinterestedness." Barrell associates the "disinterested man" with the "gentleman of landed property"; that is, with the fellow with enough leisure and money to examine the socio-political landscape (because his rental income supposedly frees him from the interestedness of the working world).[48] For Barrell, this man's "elevated viewpoint," his "overview of the whole," signifies class authority because it divides men "into those qualified to observe and those qualified only to be the objects of others' observation" (38, 44, 35). This socio-political privilege is simultaneously an aesthetic license, because the gentleman's "comprehensive" perspective determines the *way* in which society is viewed (35). He configures society from his superior viewpoint as one would a landscape painting. Moreover, through an act of self-effacing legerdemain similar to those of the Schaffstein heroes, the gentleman viewer/painter somehow manages to "occupy, as it were, a position outside the landscape" (31).

The Baron performs precisely such an act of distancing and self-efface-ment. To borrow Nietzche's 1886 terminology, the Baron achieves a pathos of distance (*"Pathos der Distanz"*) by surveying the world beneath him from the perspective of the ruling class's ceaseless *looking down* on subjects and tools (*"aus dem beständigen Ausblick und* Herabblick *der herrschenden Kaste auf Unterthänige und Werkzeuge"*).[49] In his 1887 *On the Genealogy of Morals (Zur Genealogie der Moral)*, Nietzsche equates this kind of pathos with a view from above: with the higher ruling order in relation to a lower order, to a "below" (with *"einer höheren herrschenden Art im Verhältnis zu einer niederen Art, zu einem 'Unten'"*).[50] This distancing allows—as with the Baron and Hegel's "master"—for the eventual elevation (*"Erhöhung"*) of the viewing man: he reaches "ever higher," "more comprehensive states."[51] Such an ele-vation is exactly what the Baron claims for himself, albeit in a far cruder, more personal form. His "eye," that organ of self-distancing, merges with his "I"—a pronoun that appears four times in the second paragraph alone. He organizes the objects on his estate (including his servants' residences) like a collection of "toys" and, at the same time, consolidates his self through a sin-gular, exemplary overview. With his business of personal and professional discovery now complete, the Baron can pronounce, in the final sentences, his readiness to die on this very spot. Again, in this ultimate sense, the nar-rator's self-creation corresponds to his self-effacement. His absence from the painting develops into his absenting himself from life. This final erasure is the ultimate stage of the "master's" figurative blindness and his possible ex-istential bankruptcy, as analyzed by Hegel.[52]

Selbstfindung and Monarchical Vision in *The Castle:* K.'s Failed Business of Self-Discovery

Whether or not Kafka had the *Vorschrift* of *The Sugar Baron* in mind at the moment he invented his own *Landvermesser,* he certainly knew of the his-torical construction of surveyors in the Schaffstein books and elsewhere. Moreover, Kafka's *Castle* suggests that he was also aware of the discursive relationship between "surveying" ("measuring" and "seeing") and identity-construction. As interpreters of *The Castle* ranging from New Critics to post-structuralists have claimed, the major goal of Kafka's land surveyor seems to be to gain a sense of identity. Max Brod first made this claim in 1926, when he reported an alleged conversation with Kafka: In the novel's unwritten ending, K. was to locate a sense of personal and professional sta-bility just before his death.[53] Later critics tended to position themselves as either agreeing or disagreeing with Brod—but few disputed the general assumption that K.'s business in the village was to discover himself. The first round of critics to challenge Brod (in the fifties and sixties) claimed that

K.'s struggle was non-progressive and that *The Castle* was an aggressively modernist anti-Bildungsroman; for such readers, K. learns nothing and does not attain to fulfillment.[54] More sanguine critics from the early seventies returned to Brod's line of thinking, arguing that K. develops in the course of the novel, struggling toward self-completion: he successfully learns "humility and love" by the narrative's end.[55] Post-structuralist readings of the eighties and nineties once more took a gloomier view toward K.'s progress, but again they confirmed that K. is pursuing the elusive goal of self-identity. For example, Charles Bernheimer subtly argues that K. desires—in vain—to render the Castle's confusing semiotic order coherent to his "self" through a "totalizing system of signification."[56] Elizabeth Boa, similarly, uses Lacanian tools to argue that K. "desires absolute recognition of self-identity."[57] Gerhard Neumann claims that K.'s goal—which he fails to achieve—is that of the traditional hero of the Bildungsroman: to create an identity for himself ("*sich eine Identität zu schaffen*").[58]

These methodologically diverse readings suggest—and I agree—that K.'s struggle with the Castle is simultaneously a quest for identity. But I prefer to stress the way in which this narrative of self-discovery is conditioned by the tradition of travel literature. Said's point that the Orient was the nineteenth-century traveler's blank slate of self-discovery is especially fitting for K.'s nameless Castle village—with its generic inns, school, houses, streets, and alleys. At only one point in the novel are "real" places named. K.'s lover, Frieda, mentions her desire to go to Spain or the South of France and, in so doing, jars the reader as much as she does K. (*C* 136; *S* 215). These two sites puncture the text's otherwise strictly unspecific structure and thereby form the exception that proves the rule: the village is the negative topos par excellence.

The village's neutrality opens a space for K.'s business of self-discovery; but at the same time this very blankness thwarts his corresponding desire to order the village and define his position in it. Like many modern travelers, K. wants to locate meaningful patterns in his foreign world. As a surveyor, he longs to map it; that is, to organize its "signs" in a way that can be deciphered. But this village's lack of signs complicates his task. The very negativity that makes the village ideal for self-refashioning renders it nearly impossible to organize and represent as a discrete text. Entangled, extended in space, lacking signposts and maps, K.'s village can be neither framed nor surveyed. As K. remarks disconcertedly, shortly after his arrival, the village's nearly identical little houses extend interminably, as far as the eye can see. The village seems to have no end (*C* 10; *S* 21).

Tim Mitchell, a critic of travel narratives about the Middle East, makes a similar claim concerning foreign cities as perceived by nineteenth-century European travelers. Despite the traveler's desire to order his view of the city, Mitchell claims, he can never adequately "aestheticize" the foreign city and, for this reason, can never sufficiently mark its alterity—its separateness from him. Mitchell's description of the uncontainable negative topos of the nineteenth-century Middle Eastern city uncannily characterizes K.'s 1922 frustrations within the geographically obscure village:

> [The traveler] expected there to be something that was somehow set apart from "things themselves" as a guide, a sign, a map, a text, or a set of instructions about how to proceed. But in the Middle Eastern city nothing stood apart and addressed itself in this way to the outsider, to the observing subject. There were no names to the streets and no street signs, no open spaces with imposing facades, and no maps. The city refused to offer itself in this way as a representation of something. [. . .] It had not been arranged [. . .] to effect the presence of some separate plan or meaning.[59]

The difference in mood between the traditional nineteenth-century travel narrative and Kafka's literary modernism is, as Mitchell's text suggests, not that great. The desire for containment and organization recurs, along with the frustration of this desire. If there is a difference between the two ways of seeing, it resides, first, in Kafka's refusal (or inability) to map the village and, second, in K.'s eventual acceptance of this disorder. As we shall see, K. accedes to a visual chaos for which the nineteenth-century traveler could never have allowed.

The traditional traveler, in Mitchell's description, never stops attempting to organize the chaotic unrepresentability of the foreign city. To achieve this end, he made extensive use of panoramic views, sketchings, and maps. K. has similar desires and plans at the beginning of *The Castle*. We could thus view K.'s struggle with the Castle as precisely a surveyor's desire to gain visual mastery: K. wants to measure, organize, and map the Castle territories according to his subjective blueprints. As Gerhard Kurz argues, K. longs to repeat a moment of visual sovereignty from his rarely remembered childhood.[60] K. resurrects this scene, in which he scaled a high wall in his home village, shortly after attempting (and failing) to climb the Castle hill for the first and last time:

> One morning—the calm, empty square was flooded with light, when before or since had K. ever seen it like this?—he succeeded with surprising ease; at a spot where he had been often rebuffed, with a small flag clenched between his teeth, he climbed the wall on the first attempt. [. . .] He rammed in the flag, the wind filled out the cloth, he looked down, all around, even over his shoulder at the crosses sinking into the earth; there was nobody here, now, bigger [greater, *größer*] than he. (C 28–29; S 49–50)

Kurz's argument is that K. wants to repeat this scene as an adult at the Castle and, in so doing, postpone his own death. Indeed, K.'s desire to overcome death (he symbolically "sinks" the graveyard crosses) relates directly to his narcissistic longing to construct an omnipotent self. K. imagines that his identity will persist over time as long as he can visually contain the Other (here, the dead, and, by symbolic extension, death itself). On this extremely bright day (promising a good view), he scales the wall and makes the megalomaniac claim that no one is "*größer*" than he. K.'s climb reminds us of that earlier purveyor of visual domination, Robinson Crusoe, whom Kafka remembered while working on *The Castle*. As Kafka remarked in a letter to Brod of July 12, 1922, Crusoe illustriously capped off his own self-discovery narrative by planting his flag at the "highest point of the island" (*L* 340; *B* 392).

If K. had repeated this scene of mastery in the Castle village, he would, perhaps, have immediately completed his business of self-discovery.[61] If K. had made it to the top of the Castle hill during his first attempt, he might have (as he later muses) been accepted as the Castle surveyor right away. Furthermore, if this had happened, he would have gained the sense of personal and professional identity that scholars have often cited as his goal. K.'s search (and Kafka's novel) would have ended here—according to the norms of the Bildungsroman-like adventure narrative. But K. famously fails to scale the hill, fails to confront the authorities about his "calling," fails to accomplish his narrative business.

These failures repeatedly correspond to the inability of "*Herr Landvermesser*" to see. In the novel's first paragraph, we learn of the village's darkness, the eternal snow, and the obscurity of the Castle: "There was no sign of the Castle hill, fog and darkness surrounded it, not even the faintest gleam of light suggested the large Castle. K. stood for a long time [. . .] gazing upward into the seeming emptiness" (*C* 1; *S* 7). As the chapter continues, K.'s desire for a clear view is again thwarted—this time not by darkness and fog but rather by his relatively low standpoint: "Here [in the village] the snow rose to the cottage windows only to weigh down on the low roofs, whereas up there on the hill everything soared, free and light, or *at least seemed to from here*" (*C* 7; *S* 17, my emphasis). Because K. is "here" (that is, below) his view remains unclear, as opposed to the omnipotent clarity of the Castle. Everything K. sees and knows from his impoverished standpoint is only appearance (*Schein*) and thus must be questioned.

Opposing the Land Surveyor's view from below is the monarchical perspective of Klamm, a high-level Castle functionary who is also K.'s direct superior. As we learn during K.'s first conversation with the landlady of the Bridge Inn, Klamm has the point of view of an "eagle"; K., conversely, sees the world as a "*Blindschleiche*" (blindworm, a small European lizard [*C* 55;

S 90]).[62] The contrast could not be greater: the *Blindschleiche* sees the world from beneath it and is popularly thought to be blind, due to its tiny eyes. Klamm's eagle is so visually powerful, conversely, as to be panoptic (like Weber's Coffee Planter). One can hide nothing from Klamm (*C* 115; *S* 182). K. realizes this woeful state of affairs in the chapter immediately following the pivotal "Waiting for Klamm" scene, after which K. seems finally to resign himself to never seeing Klamm. In the wake of this period of Beckettian waiting, in which K. vainly attempts to gain a glimpse of Klamm, he finally accepts the fact that only Klamm has the power to see anything and everything:

> The landlady had once compared Klamm to an eagle and that had seemed ridiculous to K., but no longer, he considered Klamm's remoteness, his impregnable abode, [. . .] his piercing downturned gaze, which could never be proved, never be refuted, and his, from K.'s position below [*K.'s Tiefe*], indestructible circles, which he was describing up there in accordance with incomprehensible laws, visible only for seconds—all this Klamm and the eagle had in common. (*C* 115–16; *S* 183–84)

Here, K. accepts the invidious comparison between himself and Klamm. Klamm is above, K. is below ("*K.'s Tiefe*"). Klamm is visible only for moments; K., like the natives in Mecklenburg's *In the Hinterlands of German East Africa,* is always exposed and thus vulnerable. Klamm is the seer, K. the seen.[63] K. is the failed surveyor; Klamm is, for K., the imperial eye/I. (Kafka's certain knowledge of the symbolism of the eagle—as official emblem for the Austro-Hungarian empire—lends historical weight to this connection.)[64]

This brief look at the *Landvermesser*'s visual narrative leads us to the following preliminary conclusion: if Kafka wrote *The Castle* with discursive constructions of the land surveyor in mind, he invented K. as a caricature of this surveyor. Whereas the successful surveyor (e.g., the Sugar Baron) affirms himself and his power by viewing the world from a mountain peak, K. slithers in the village mud. Like the blindworm, named for its tiny, myopic eyes, K. sees the world as looming, larger-than-life figures that perpetually sneak up on him or appear abruptly out of the corners of unlit rooms. Because K. gains no visual high ground throughout the novel, he can never sufficiently organize the village as a view, can never frame or map it. He thus remains *inside of* what he is trying to measure and describe. He is not a distinct subject (the hero of a narrative of self-discovery detachedly observing objects) but a subject who is also an object among objects. Part of the field he attempts to survey, K. is beginning to grasp, however dimly, that he is both subject and object at once.

In my cultural-historical framework, we might argue that the Castle corresponds, as some scholars have suggested, to an "imperial" power.[65] Brod first claimed in 1958 that Kafka's Castle was modeled after a nineteenth-century Austrian colonial outpost. According to Brod, Kafka borrowed this Castle from Božena Němcová's realist novel *Babička* (*The Grandmother*), which portrays nineteenth-century German-speaking nobility living in a castle high above a subjugated, Czech-speaking village. To support Brod's historical reading, we could point out the three central traits that ally Kafka's Castle to the imperial tradition: an overproductive bureaucracy, an omnipresent threat of violence,[66] and an unquestioned *droit du seigneur* that places village women at the mercy of male Castle officials. Although not a straightforward metaphor for empire, the Castle thus bears particular imperial features. But the Castle also lacks the single factor that, in addition to a grand bureaucracy, most clearly defines an imperial power: an army. The Castle does not have any soldiers, nor is it engaged in territorial aggression.

Brod's reading is thus not watertight and has, correspondingly, been subject to critical attacks.[67] Whether or not Kafka actually drew his Castle imagery from a realist account of imperial subjugation is, however, less important for my argument than is Kafka's general concern with imperial rhetoric. My point is that Kafka eschews the broad strokes of imperial history in favor of investigating the particular ways in which empire, conquest, and domination inform our modern ways of seeing. It is no accident that Klamm is referred to as an eagle (with its sharp eyes) and not, say, a lion. Klamm is a seer, as are his secretaries, who serve as additional eyes. In the true spirit of a panoptic, imperial bureaucracy, Momus and other secretaries write down everything they see and then pass it on to Klamm (who may or may not read it), thereby multiplying the apparent effect of Klamm's vision (*C* 113–15; *S* 179–83). If Kafka's Castle is an imperial outpost, then, it is so primarily in the sense that it practices this highly visual form of domination.

Now appearing as the fictional configuration of an unsuccessful imperial surveyor, K. finds his vision failing as the novel progresses. Critics have argued that K. seems less aggressive vis-à-vis the Castle by the end of the novel,[68] but they have failed to relate this shift to K.'s *Blindschleiche* perspective, which becomes progressively more pronounced. After the first chapter, K. never again makes a sustained attempt to walk up the Castle hill or even to view the Castle from the village. Moreover, he stops trying to gain glimpses of Klamm, the Castle's highest officer. Corresponding to this surrender of visual ambition is K.'s acceptance of an extremely limited perspectival scope. He spends the final chapters trapped in interiors (Barnabas' house, the Gentlemen's Inn, Bürgel's bedroom) and, moreover, inside a textual blankness created by Kafka's increasing use of description-free monologues. In the late monological scenes with Olga, Pepi, and Bürgel, K. makes little use of his once-strained eyes. When he sees anything at all, he sees it myopically—for instance, the naked foot of the Castle secretary, Bürgel.

The penultimate scene of the novel, with the Gentlemen's Inn landlady, is exemplary in this regard. K. stares at her dress, then looks inside a giant, deep wardrobe filled with dresses. K.'s vision zooms in on the dim interior, inspecting the clothing—whose various colors he notes. In the final scene, K. is led by Gerstäcker through the "darkness" into a room that was "only dimly illuminated by the fire in the hearth and by a candle stump in the light of which someone deep inside an alcove sat bent under the crooked protruding beams, reading a book" (C 316; S 495). This progression toward darkness and myopia in the novel's last pages suggests an unwritten conclusion that could have led—contra Brod (and Goethe, who called for "more light" on his deathbed)—to more darkness: to the end of what is a thoroughly modernist book, and toward the eventual extinguishing of vision through death. By the closing of the extant text, K. has surrendered his traveling surveyor's desire to achieve subjective distance and visual mastery; instead, he begins to dissolve among the objects of his world. He no longer attempts to frame the Other by scaling the church wall or the Castle hill. Rather, he burrows deeper and deeper into a village world whose old and tattered clothing, as W. G. Sebald has convincingly claimed, augur K.'s own coming decay.[69]

The Politics of Failure

It is instructive to compare this macabre, myopic ending with the final, according to Kafka, "most important" chapter of *The Sugar Baron*. In sharp juxtaposition to the myopic K., the sovereign Weber sits on the edge of a ridge and enjoys a panoramic view. He surveys his vast properties and, in the end, contemplates his own death:

> Here, under the protection of this tree, I want to sleep. No man shall bother me; not even the storm that before long will thunder down from the mountains in the night, at the beginning of the dry season, and which once, in one night, destroyed my coffee plantation, and, with it, my fondest hope. But in the daytime, year after year, the sun will shine upon me; and every day, the whole year long, a small, inconspicuous bird will sing for me its short and wonderfully delicate song, which will be more dear to me than any other singing, under the powerful vault of the giant trees and in the all-encompassing silence of this spot.[70]

The Baron's confident burial wish represents the precise moment in the colonial drama that most attracts *and* repels Kafka. This is the moment of calm finality that Kafka's own forsaken travelers never achieve. Following the death of Bendemann in "The Judgment," the Russian friend is left forever in fictional limbo, yellowing and destitute in Petersburg. The ailing stationmaster from the 1914 fragment "Memoirs of the Kalda Railway" is likewise eternally *in extremis,* stuck on the unfinished line of an unfinished story. The Sugar Baron, conversely, is able to complete his narrative and even demand that it be read. *The Sugar Baron,* one could argue, represents a version of Kafka's own travel novels with a happy ending—not only *The Castle* but also *The Man Who Disappeared.* K. and Karl Rossmann both get good jobs, discover a sense of *Heimat,* and hire reliable servants (*not* K.'s assistants!) who will bury them high above their estates after they die; Franz Kafka, thereby, completes his novels. Max Brod, in his afterword to *The Castle,* claims that Kafka planned similar endings.[71] Why did he never write them?

Neumeyer responds to this question by citing an apparent Oedipal failure now familiar to Kafka scholarship. He claims that Kafka wanted to be like the Sugar Baron (who stands in for Kafka's self-made father, Hermann) but did not have the fortitude to travel to South America, become a land baron, and write his memoirs. *The Sugar Baron,* Neumeyer claims, is "literary wish-fulfillment": It satisfies Kafka's "longings for firmness, competence, direction, self assuredness, and mastery." In his own gloss on *The Castle,* Neumeyer compares K.'s view of the Castle from below with the Sugar Baron's vision from above and concludes that the Sugar Baron is the "lord of what he (literally) surveys."[72] Neumeyer sees *The Castle,* as I do, as a narrative of unsatisfied longings for visual heights; but for Neumeyer this failure is indisputably Kafka's (not just K.'s). He suggests that Kafka wanted to end *The Castle* triumphantly, with K. on top of the Castle hill.[73] The masterful, "most important" finale of *The Sugar Baron,* according to Neumeyer, is thus one that "Kafka himself did not so much (as he says) elude, as it was one that eluded Kafka."

If—as I maintain—Kafka eluded this narrative (not the other way around), then another crucial question presents itself: What could a writer possibly have to gain by creating a failed protagonist? Why would Kafka desire to fail (as Walter Benjamin claimed in his nuanced reading)?[74] Is there not perhaps something to be gained by the creation of an unsuccessful hero? In other words, if K. fails (in his Crusoean task of defining himself through a monarchical perspective), does Kafka in any way "win"? How might Kafka's creation of a "blind" surveyor—a loser in the business of self-discovery—result in his own victory in the business of writing?

My response necessitates revisiting Kafka's claim that *The Sugar Baron* functioned as a *Vorschrift:* a book of rules, a prescription or, literally, a pre-text.

He does not say that it is a pre- (or source) text for *The Castle*. Rather, it is a prescription for his life (*"eine Vorschrift meines Lebens"*). This *Vorschrift* thus extends beyond literature, beyond *The Sugar Baron* and *The Castle*. It is an "ideology," as in Louis Althusser's definition: a linguistic-cultural-political prescription that seems to direct our lives (to the point that even acts of resistance appear to be pre-inscribed).[75] In Kafka's fin de siècle, this *Vorschrift* included the one followed by his maternal uncles and by Weber. It entailed traveling to a faraway country, attempting to make one's fortune and, simultaneously, locating a solid sense of self. Like many young men of his era, Kafka felt strongly tempted by this plot. He imagined living and working in a variety of different places: Spain, South America, the Azores, Madeira, Palestine, and a generic "island" in the south.[76] He longed to participate in the business of self-discovery, complete with its bird's-eye views of sugar cane and its financial successes—as in the above-cited 1907 letter to Hedwig Weiler, which recounts Kafka's hopes of someday working in "faraway countries, looking out of the office windows at fields of sugar cane or Mohammedan cemeteries" (*L* 35; *B* 49).

But Kafka did not travel to faraway countries, and not because, as Neumeyer claims, this plot "eludes" him. Rather, according to Kafka, he eludes or escapes it. The German verb Kafka uses, as discussed in detail in the preceding chapter, is *entweichen,* which means to elude or escape, as in a prisoner escaping from a jail. In this sense, Kafka escapes from colonial ideology; *it* does not elude *him*. He escapes from *The Sugar Baron's* ideological *Vorschrift* by paradoxically not going anywhere at all: he lies low and writes and, more importantly, writes in a certain way. As a writer, he can elude this *Vorschrift* by creating K. (who fails in the business of self-discovery) and also by undermining this prescription's *form:* the monarchical perspective and the corresponding "density" of meaning. This stylistic escape is where Kafka's writerly victory, if there is one, inheres. And, because this is also an escape from ideology, Kafka also eludes in a political sense: both publicly, by resisting imperial aesthetics and traditions, and privately, by resisting a way of life that seems to be thrust upon him.

Revolutions in Style?:
The *Blindschleiche* Perspective
and Linguistic Sparseness

Kafka escapes the monarchical perspective, first, through the *Blindschleiche* point of view and, second, through the opposite of aesthetic density: what I will term—in the spirit of Gilles Deleuze and Felix Guattari— linguistic sparseness. What is this sparseness and what is its significance?

Deleuze and Guattari, following Klaus Wagenbach, argue that Prague German, in Kafka's day, was a "minor" variation on High German. It was linguistically "abstinen[t]," featuring "withered" diction and "sober," "rigid," "dried-up" syntax.[77] Deleuze and Guattari maintain that Kafka elected *not* to enrich this brand of German artificially (as did Brod, Gustav Meyrink, and others from the Prague School), and instead to further "deterritorialize" High German by *increasing* the poverty of this language. They refer to this strategy repeatedly as a possible "line of *escape*" (16, 26, 59, my emphasis). Deleuze and Guattari's point is that Kafka subverts the dominant discourse by deliberately surrendering linguistic territory to it—not by co-opting from it. They oppose Kafka and his "willed poverty" to other "minor" writers such as Brod and Meyrink, who attempt to "reterritorialize" German through expansive prose and comprehensive symbolic networks. (Kafka's "minor" strategies, therefore, are closer to Samuel Beckett's than to James Joyce's: although both Beckett and Joyce wrote in the "minor" environment of Ireland, only the former "resisted the temptation to use language to bring about all sorts of worldwide reterritorializations" [19].)

Deleuze and Guattari, however, strikingly fail to offer a single example of Kafka's *style* in comparison with a "territorializing" style—thus leaving their readers with little idea of the precise form of Kafka's deterritorializing mode, with its so-called syntactical poverty and withered diction. I have chosen two brief textual comparisons almost at random from *The Castle* and from the final chapter of *The Sugar Baron* to serve as such examples. First, I refer the reader back to the description of the Sugar Baron's view from atop his plantation and K.'s comparable account of standing atop the church wall. Focusing only on modifiers, we see a distinct sparseness in Kafka's text: ten modifiers in *The Sugar Baron* versus just one in a passage of comparable length from *The Castle*, demonstrating precisely how Weber bloats syntax while Kafka prunes it. I italicize the modifiers from *The Sugar Baron* and the unmodified nouns from *The Castle*:

The Sugar Baron:

I see an *everlastingly green* ocean of brush and trees, in the midst of which are the *white* structures of my estate, with *shining, light gray, corrugated* roofs, the *light green, square* plots of the sugar cane and corn fields, the *darker* and *more muted* meadows, the *small* huts of the workers and their *brown* straw roofs.

([Ich] sehe ein *ewiggrünes* Meer von Busch und Baum, in das die *weißen* Gebäude meiner Besitzungen mit ihren *hellgrauen, glänzenden* Wellblechdächern, die *hellgrünen quadratischen* Flecke der Zuckerrohr- und Maisfelder, die *dunkleren, matteren* Weiden, die *kleinen* Hütten der Arbeiter mit ihren *braunen* Strohdächern [. . .] liegen.)[78]

The Castle:

He rammed in the *flag,* the *wind* filled out the *cloth,* he looked down, *all around* [in die *Runde*], even over his *shoulder* at the crosses sinking into the earth; there was nobody here, now, bigger than he. (*C* 29)

(Er rammte die *Fahne* ein, der *Wind* spannte das *Tuch,* er blickte hinunter und in die *Runde,* auch über die *Schulter* hinweg auf die in der Erde versinkenden Kreuze, niemand war jetzt und hier größer als er. [*S* 49–50])

If the "meaning" produced by the imperial eye is "dense," then Kafka's meaning, here and elsewhere, is sparse. The distended syntax of the Weber passage offers little space for readerly cohabitation. Kafka's style, conversely, produces a series of bare outposts (flag, wind, cloth) that invite us to journey into the textual space.

Another example comes from the penultimate sentence of *The Sugar Baron,* when Weber, still high above his estate, contemplates his own death. I juxtapose this with the opening chapter of *The Castle,* when K., the blindworm, tries to glimpse the Castle from below. Again, I note the discrepancy in modifiers (nine versus two) in a comparable amount of text, and I italicize the modifiers and unmodified nouns from *The Sugar Baron* and *The Castle,* respectively:

The Sugar Baron:

the *whole* year long, a *small, inconspicuous* bird will sing for me its *short* and *wonderfully delicate* song, which will be more dear to me than any *other* singing, under the *powerful* vault of the giant trees and in the *all-encompassing* silence of this spot.

(das *ganze* Jahr, wird mir ein *kleiner unscheinbarer* Vogel sein *kurzes, wunderbar feines* Lied singen, das mir unter der *mächtigen* Wölbung der Baumriesen und bei der *allgemeinen* Stille jenes Ortes wie kein *anderer* Gesang mir gefällt.)[79]

The Castle:

Keeping his *eyes* fixed on the *Castle,* K. went ahead, nothing else mattered to him. But *as he came closer* [im *Näherkommen*] he was disappointed in the *Castle,* it was only a rather miserable little town, pieced together from *village-houses,* distinctive only because everything was perhaps built of *stone,* but the *paint* had long since flaked off, and the *stone* seemed to be crumbling. (*C* 8)

(Die *Augen* auf das *Schloß* gerichtet, gieng K. weiter, nichts sonst kümmerte ihn. Aber im *Näherkommen* enttäuschte ihn das *Schloß,* es war doch nur ein recht elendes Städtchen, aus *Dorfhäusern* zusammengetragen, ausgezeichnet nur dadurch, daß vielleicht alles aus *Stein* gebaut war, aber der *Anstrich* war längst abgefallen, und der *Stein* schien abzubröckeln. [*S* 17])

Here again we see Weber's distended syntax—which creates for us, as in Wiederhold's *The Panama Canal,* an over-determined picture (bird, song, vault, and even silence are modified, all in one sentence). *The Castle,* conversely, exhibits again the "poverty" of Kafka's diction, and also his thin (albeit elastic) syntax. Kafka's word-choice is concrete and basic (eyes, Castle, town, houses, stone, paint) and radically limited ("Castle" and "stone" are repeated instead of being replaced by synonyms); these few substantives are stretched sparingly across the length of two sentences. The bird's-eye view thus accompanies syntactical density; Kafka's *Blindschleiche* perspective, meanwhile, couples with sparseness.

A Postcolonial Kafka?

Pratt argues that monarchical views and density of meaning are typical of imperial narration (as they are in *The Sugar Baron* and other *Little Green Books*). But does the opposite obtain? Is Kafka's *Castle,* because it escapes a bloated colonial *Vorschrift,* anti-colonial? Does it deterritorialize imperial discourse without attacking it directly? Deleuze and Guattari would say yes and, moreover, argue that the content of *The Castle* mirrors its linguistic subversiveness. *The Castle,* they claim, is exemplarily deterritorializing, psychologically as well as politically: K. arrives in the village without a family, a past, or even a name; he appears to represent a subject uprooted from tradition, desire, and history. More radically than Josef K. from *The Trial,* therefore, K. is "nothing but [deterritorialized] desire."[80] Deleuze and Guattari repeatedly return to metaphors of topography and territory (even though they make surprisingly few references to K.'s corresponding profession). The linguistic sobriety of *The Castle,* they claim, creates a "new map" on which K. practices a strategy of "deterritorializing."[81] Deleuze and Guattari's anarchic land surveyor is, in this sense, not far from Emrich's 1957 revolutionary one: both are capable of questioning the present distribution and (for Deleuze and Guattari) the conceptualization of territory. Kafka's successful "escape" from a colonial *Vorschrift,* therefore, appears to take place in terms of both form and content.

Even K.'s more traditional, nostalgic desires seem to threaten the territorial order. From the first chapter onward, nothing is more remarkable than K.'s quest for a home, but this quest is more the nomad's search for refuge than the colonist's desire for what the Sugar Baron refers to as a "*zweite Heimat.*"[82] In fact, K.'s always-incomplete nostalgia undermines the very binary of "home" and "away" so dear to colonialism. K. gets engaged on just his fourth day in the village, and desires a home for himself and his fiancée, but this home is, first, a cramped room in the Bridge Inn and, later, a spot on the schoolhouse floor. One of K.'s first acts in the Inn room is to nail the letter acknowledging his appointment as land surveyor onto the wall above his and Frieda's bed, thereby marking this

transitory space as his own ("in this room he would be living, so the letter should hang here" [*C* 25; *S* 43]). He is, however, almost immediately
threatened with eviction and soon decides to leave. Later, K. and Frieda
transform the schoolhouse classroom into an uncanny home for their
"family": straw becomes a bed; parallel bars and a blanket transform into
a partition; the teacher's desk becomes a dinner table (complete with
table cloth, coffee pot, flowered cup, box of sardines, bread, and sausage).
Such deterritorializations of public space abound in Kafka. I also think
of Josef K.'s boarding house "home" in *The Trial,* Gregor Samsa's hotels
and his many-doored bedroom in *The Metamorphosis,* and Karl Rossmann's balcony lodging in *The Man Who Disappeared.* The elevators in
the latter novel's Hotel Occidental, moreover, serve as homes for the itinerant lift-boys: they reside in the elevators for almost all of their waking
hours, eat and make love in them, and proudly and somewhat neurotically (in the case of Karl) polish "their" brass bars.

In all of these cases, transitory spaces serve as homes, thereby questioning
the very idea of "home." Kafka's writings, correspondingly, challenge Martin
Heidegger's nostalgic distinction between "building" and "dwelling" (a mere
"building" being where one spends much of one's time and even sometimes
feels "at home," whereas a "dwelling" uniquely offers "shelter" as well as an
authentic homeyness).[83] In *The Castle,* for example, every building is a po-
tential home, but these homes are subject to the randomness of the world—
and thus anathema to the notion of a true shelter. Is Gregor Samsa's flat (and
bedroom sofa) a "dwelling" or a "building"? Which is the underground maze
in "The Burrow"? What about the narrator's shop, surrounded by nomads,
in "A Leaf from an Old Manuscript" ("Ein altes Blatt")? Kafka's fictions undermine the notion of homeyness and instead maintain that shelter is at once
everywhere and nowhere. This diluted concept of dwelling does *not,* as the
cultural anthropologist James Clifford points out, convert the fringe into a
new center (i.e., "'we' are all travelers"); rather, it presents transitory homes
(hotel, flop house, airport) as ubiquitous and therefore as threats to all traditional dialectics of domesticity.[84]

Kafka's fictions place colonial binaries under stress, and this kind of
stress was of course familiar to Kafka, a German Jew living in Prague. The
peculiar nature of Kafka's nationhood placed him somewhere in between
the position of the colonizer and the colonized, and deserves a brief word
of mention. Pre-war Prague was effectively a foreign—that is, Czech—city,
dominated by a small German-speaking ruling class of which Kafka was
part. But Kafka's relationship to Czech-speaking Prague was not only that
of the perceived Austro-German colonialist. His Prague ruling class was
mostly Jewish, and, despite this group's cultural and commercial power, it
had had its own history of being colonized. Provincial Jews, like Kafka's fa-

ther (whose own father was a kosher butcher in the Czech village of Wossek), had been brought under the sway of eastward-spreading Austro-German culture. In the process, they had surrendered a sense of Jewish cultural identity that Kafka famously later tried to regain. In this sense, then, Kafka was colonizer and colonized at once. Kafka's liminal position within the imperial economy makes it difficult to understand him solely in terms of the classical colonial binaries offered by J. A. Hobson and, more recently (and with greater nuance), by Said.[85] Kafka appears to be postcolonial *avant la lettre*.

Kafka's Tears and His "Forlorn" Colonial Reader

But we cannot place Kafka too cavalierly into the camp of the deterritorializers and post- (or anti-) colonialists. Contra Deleuze and Guattari, Kafka's strongly colonial European moment does not allow for this. Like most Austro-Hungarian Jews (who rightly feared German and Czech nationalism in the event of an Austrian defeat), Kafka supported the Austro-Hungarian Empire during the war, sometimes even with unusual passion: registering "sorrow over the Austrian defeats," getting angry with the "stupid" Austrian leadership following the 1914 losses in Serbia, and feeling himself "directly involved in the war" (*D* 314, 322, 351; September 13, 1914, December 15, 1914, November 5, 1915). Scott Spector has pointed out, moreover, that the territorially embattled German Jews of Kafka's Prague were often staunchly anti-liberal—sometimes choosing to retrench within linguistic Germanness or even to expand this Germanness in order to block insurgent Czech deterritorializations.[86] Within this general culture of territorial anxiety, Kafka's diaries, as was typical for his moment, were not strongly critical of colonialism, whether intra-European (Austrian) or extra-European (French, British, German). He was obsessed with Napoleon as a bold adventurer, not as a colonial oppressor (in October 1915 Kafka compiled an exhaustively detailed list of the seventeen reasons why Napoleon lost the war in Russia) (*D* 344–48; *Ta* 757–64).[87] Moreover, Kafka never censured the obvious brutalities in *The Sugar Baron* and elsewhere in the *Little Green Books* he claimed to love. One prominent example of Kafka's uncritical stance is his 1913 diary note, following his reading of the nationalist and sometimes racist memoir *We Boys of 1870/71* (*Wir Jungen von 1870/71*), which recounts the founding narrative of German imperialism (the Franco-Prussian War). After finishing *We Boys*—not only volume thirty-two of the *Little Green Books* series but also the work of the series' co-publisher, Hermann Schaffstein—Kafka writes that he "read with suppressed sobs of the victories and scenes of enthusiasm" (*D* 248; *Ta* 615).

With Kafka's suppressed tears in mind, we see that his escape from *Vorschrift* is not clean. He does refuse to take part in the colonial plot by not traveling to Panama and the Congo like his uncle, and he also reverses some of this plot's traditional aesthetic structures; however, because, as Kafka well knew, ideology often contains its own "negativity," he cannot escape this ideology completely. As Kafka once wrote of his relationship to his era: "I have vigorously absorbed the negative element of the age in which I live [*das Negative meiner Zeit*], an age that is, of course, very close to me, which I have no right ever to fight against, but as it were a right to represent" (*WP* 114; *NSII* 98). Vigorously absorbing his era's "*Negative*" does not create the possibility of direct resistance ("fighting against"); rather, it means that the writer's literary forms of escape will necessarily remain bound up with that which he is attempting to elude.[88] Such a critical double bind informs all of Kafka's writings and is perhaps constitutive of the "Kafkaesque"—of a general structure of self-indictment, entrapment, and duplicity (of judger and judged, jailer and prisoner). But this double bind is most obvious in Kafka's texts with clear colonial references: "In the Penal Colony" and "A Report to an Academy" (and, as I have been arguing, *The Castle*). On the one hand, Kafka exposes brutal colonial apparatuses (the torture machine and the ape's cage, in "In the Penal Colony" and "A Report to an Academy," respectively). On the other hand, however, the victim in each case is no longer the victim by the end: the Officer's "perfect" machine impales *him,* not the imprisoned native, who runs free; Red Peter, the trained ape, eventually becomes a cigar-chomping and wine-drinking orator who hires a chimpanzee call-girl. Moreover, Kafka borrows the plots (of torture and exploitation) that power his narratives from the very "enthusiastic" Schaffstein narratives that his fictions, at the same time, resist.

Even Kafka's conception of his own writing is not completely divorced from territorializing impulses. Kafka's famous letter to his father ("Brief an den Vater"), written just three years before *The Castle,* demonstrates how his writing is, figuratively, an attempt to grab land from an apparently colonial father. Kafka repeatedly compares his father to a hostile, imperial entity—he is "tyrannical," an "autocrat," a "king," a one-man "government" with young Franz as his "slave"—and Kafka claims that his father's body is itself like an empire, "stretching out diagonally" across the "map of the world" ("*Manchmal stelle ich mir die Erdkarte ausgespannt und Dich quer über sie hin ausgestreckt vor*") (*BV* 55, 71, 29, 114–15). Kafka can only consider living in the "regions" not yet colonized by this body, not yet covered by the father's mass or within reach of its imperial extremities ("[*Gegenden,*] *die nicht in Deiner Reichweite liegen*") (*BV* 114–15). These "not very comforting" regions are where Kafka's writing occurs. Kafka imagines his writing topographically: he gains "some distance" from his father's body (the father does not read the son's books) through writing—even if this distance gained is only that of a "worm" (!) fleeing a human torturer (*BV* 85). Writing is thus the site of the son's literary-topographical "attempts at escape" (*BV* 117).

Three years later, on July 12, 1922, midway through *The Castle*, Kafka claims in a letter to Brod that he is always attempting, through his writing, to locate the geographical space of home: "I am away from home and must always write home [write my way home, *immerfort nachhause schreiben*], even if everything home-like has long since floated away into eternity" (*L* 340; *B* 392, trans. rev.). Kafka had already, years earlier, referred to his writing in terms of topography—as if it were not simply words on a page but also a place that he could inhabit. Like more contemporary exilic writers,[89] Kafka claims in April 1918 in another letter to Brod that his writing *is* his home: through his writing, he creates a "*Mondheimat*" (homeland on the moon) and, in so doing, remains beyond the father's imperial reach (*L* 204; *B* 241).

How does such a territorial claim relate to Kafka's so-called deterritorializing style? Do the withered diction and dried-up syntax that eventually appear on Kafka's moon-homeland (on his personal "borderland") signal a form of reterritorialization (*D* 396; *Ta* 871)? Does Kafka's deterritorializing style, active in fringe areas, become his "own"? Kafka's 1915 reading of volume eighteen of the *Little Green Books: Forest-Ranger Fleck's Narration of His Fate During Napoleon's March on Russia and of His Imprisonment 1812–1814* (*Förster Flecks Erzählung von seinen Schicksalen auf dem Zuge Napoleons nach Rußland und von seiner Gefangenschaft 1812–1814*) helps to elucidate this contradiction. Published exactly 100 years after the fact (at the climax of Germany's and Austria's own imperial marches), *Förster Fleck* describes Napoleon's advance on Russia. Kafka read and recalled one especially gruesome scene in his diary: Napoleon's imperial army, starving and madly retreating, blows up some of its own injured forces in a monastery—perhaps in order to spare them further misery or perhaps simply to be relieved of the burden of caring for them. Ranger Fleck, a German traveling with Napoleon, remembers that he and his fellow soldiers felt no compassion for their murdered comrades. Fleck expresses this cold scene in the expansive syntax and dense style typical of the *Little Green Books:* "Our feelings were however already so numbed by the daily spectacle of the most nameless misery and our own misfortunes that we would not have been able to especially concern ourselves with the fate of others" ("*Jedoch waren unsere Gefühle durch den täglichen Anblick des namenlosesten Elends und unseres eigenen Unglücks schon zu sehr abgestumpft, als daß wir uns um das Schicksal anderer noch sonderlich gekümmert hätten*").[90]

Kafka, witnessing this scene as a reader, offers the following sober revision in his diary entry of September 16, 1915: "Read *Förster Fleck in Russia*. Napoleon's return to the battlefield at Borodino. The cloister there. It was blown up" ("Förster Fleck in Rußland *gelesen. Napoleons Rückkehr auf das Schlachtfeld von Borodino. Das Kloster dort. Es wird in die Luft gesprengt*") (*D* 342; *Ta* 754). Kafka increases the desired effect of narrative numbness by not mentioning the actual event at all. Instead of commenting on Fleck's—or Kafka's own?—incapacity for compassion, he understates the macabre event in dry, unadorned prose. Kafka's revision suggests that he could have used this book, and perhaps other *Little Green Books* as well, to practice his "negative" style; that is, his telltale mode of increasing dramatic effect through understatement and the absence of pathetic utterance. The popular text thus offers up the thrilling historical event; Kafka, the author of "In the Penal Colony" and "A Report to an Academy," supplies the chilly, slim staccato. Just as Gregor Samsa never remarks on the cruelty of being assaulted by his father and is, in the end, left to die, Kafka records the heartless explosion at Borodino without affect. Style, here, gains dramatic and also political force. It becomes a private practice of deterritorializing discursive expansion, yet—in opposition to Deleuze and Guattari—it paradoxically signals the simultaneous appropriation of a writerly home.

If Kafka's spare style is also a form of land grabbing, then it is, to continue with the topographical metaphor, a peculiarly gentle form of colonialism. Kafka occupies a liminal terrain—the moon, the borderlands—that is devoid of inhabitants. Moreover, his writing—unlike the dense, colonial style—does not attempt to mark every bit of the fictional world as its own (and *not* the reader's). Like the Sugar Baron, Kafka conquers new territories. But Kafka's spaces are unwanted, marginal regions. Moreover, because they are always only viewed at "eye level," and not from the heights that allow for encompassing views, these realms, like the desolate Steppes, can never be adequately "represent[ed]" (*D* 310, 331; *Ta* 689, 727). Kafka inscribes them only sparsely: we are left, as in *The Castle,* with a faceless hero, an unmapped village, and an only vaguely delineated Castle. Kafka's text is the negative topos revisited, and we readers are challenged the way the colonial traveler is. By creating a terrain that invites readers to project and, through various demarcations, re-fashion themselves, Kafka shifts the political question of colonialism onto the act of reading. We are given a relatively unmarked space (a village, a castle, two inns, a schoolhouse) and are caught between the impulse to impose an overview—*the* interpretation—and to burrow endlessly in the text's details (to become, like K., a subject/object among objects). *The Castle* thus avoids repeating the colonial gesture and instead presents the colonial problem. Kafka confronts us with the dilemma: What is a traveler to do? Do we, like

K., attempt to gain an overview? Or do we—again like K.—lose ourselves among the clothing of the world?

If my reading of *The Castle* is also a form of colonialism—a marking of Kafka's negative topos—then it attempts to be so only in the sense that Kafka imagined all of his readers to be colonialists. In a continuation of the first epigraph to this chapter, Kafka claims (with his usual mix of truth and irony) that his ideal readers are Germans living abroad, specifically in the pre-war African colonies. He is referring explicitly to Max Brod's 1907 mention of him in a journal article (at the end of a list of Prague writers), but Kafka's remarks could just as well relate to his own fictions:

> I don't think I can count much on Germany. For how many people read a review down to the last paragraph with unslacking eagerness? That is not fame. But it is another matter with Germans abroad, in the Baltic Provinces, for example, or still better in America, or most of all in the German colonies; for the forlorn German [*der verlassene Deutsche*] reads his magazine through and through [*ganz und gar*]. Thus the centers of my fame must be Dar-es-Salaam, Ujiji, Windhoek. (*L* 23; *B* 35–36)

Kafka depends on colonial readers because they, unlike the stay-at-home Germans, will read every bit of Brod's article (and thus make it all the way to Kafka's name). Colonial readers are Kafka's ideal readers—*not* because of their ability to achieve monarchical views but rather because of their (colonial?) penchant for reading to the very last word. Kafka's colonists are, in the end, more like K. than like the Sugar Baron's fantasy of himself. The colonial experience leaves them "forlorn"—neither panoptically nor psychologically empowered—and this forlornness turns them into readers. Perhaps, like the heroes of the *Little Green Books,* these colonists unwittingly fall victim to a process of self-creation that relies on simultaneous self-effacement. And it is this paradoxical scene of origination and obliteration—this failure in surveying that means at once "looking out over" and "overlooking" (*übersehen*)[91]—that finally creates the kind of reader Kafka claims to need. Only the colonist, he insists, is sufficiently forsaken. Denied a monarchical view, the colonist, in the end, sees the least. However, in spite of—or because of—this failed attempt at visual mastery, the colonist becomes Kafka's myopic reader par excellence. He learns to read, like the unsuccessful and "blind" land surveyor K., "*ganz und gar.*"

Chapter Six

The Traffic of Writing:
Technologies of Intercourse
in the *Letters to Milena*

In order to eliminate as much as possible the ghostly element between people and to attain a natural intercourse, a tranquility of souls,
[humankind] has invented trains, cars, aeroplanes.

—*letter to Milena Jesenská, March 1922*

As we saw toward the end of the last chapter, Kafka viewed his father's body as imperial. Writing just one year after the collapse of
the German and Austrian empires, Kafka attacks a father he styl-
izes as an emperor. The father spreads his strapping body across the globe,
and not much space is left for the son. For Kafka, this patriarchal body in-
flects all societal structures: religion, education, and, most important, marriage. When depicting the father's expansive body (in the passage cited in
part above from Kafka's "Dearest Father" letter), Kafka specifically names
marriage as the site that this imperial body covers:

But we being what we are, marrying is barred to me because it is your very
own domain. Sometimes I imagine the map of the world spread out and you
stretched diagonally across it. And I feel as if I could consider living in only
those regions that either are not covered by you or are not within your
reach. And in keeping with the conception I have of your magnitude, these
are not many and not very comforting regions—and marriage is not among
them. (*BV* 115)

Marriage is in the realm of the father and thus unattainable for the son. But Kafka nonetheless maintains, earlier in the same letter, that "marrying, founding a family, accepting all the children that come, supporting them in this insecure world" is the "utmost" that a human being can succeed in doing (*BV* 99). Marriage, then, becomes desired territory for Kafka, but at the same time one already hopelessly colonized by the father. Marriage is the son's mode of gaining "independence" (by founding his own family), but it also is his way of reproducing the hated paternal body. Marrying to achieve independence is equivalent, Kafka claims, to a prisoner escaping his prison in order to build an exact replica of the same—conveniently renaming it "pleasure dome" (*Lustschloß*) (*BV* 112–13). Marriage thus contradictorily provides both the greatest possible independence from and "closest relation" to the father (*BV* 113).

In Kafka's paradoxical striving toward marriage, he begins to equate his fantasy of conjugal intimacy with a utopian "second home" not unlike the ones vainly longed for by the exotic travelers discussed earlier. The rare, fulfilling marriage produces such a haven, or at least this is what the journalist Milena Jesenská—Kafka's late-life lover and correspondent—claims in her 1923 essay (otherwise highly critical of marriage): "The Devil at the Hearth" (see figure 22). Unhappily married at the time, Jesenská refers here to the uncommon, healthy marriage as a "home" that protects the loving pair from the world (*LM* 267; *BM* 398).[1] Kafka, who claimed to read Milena's articles as if they were letters addressed to him, responds to Milena's essay by employing the rhetoric of "home" and "away." Kafka claims that there can indeed be successful marriages, but that such "lofty, conscious" bonds must never issue from the "despair of loneliness." Only marriages entered into deliberately and through personal plenitude can lead to true homes; those originating in despair, conversely, will result in permanent exile. "If one loneliness is placed inside another," Kafka writes, "the result is not a home [*Heimat*] but a *katorga* [a punishment of hard labor in Russian exile]" (*LM* 234; *BM* 316).

Kafka's metaphorical juxtaposition of good and bad marriages as *Heimat* and *katorga* produces a rhetoric of domesticity and exile similar to that produced through the juxtaposition of good marriages with writing. Writing, in Kafka's metaphorical system, corresponds to a "Russian"-like exile.[2] Thus the Russian-exiled bachelors from "The Judgment" and "Memoirs of the Kalda Railway" function as, among other things, figures for Kafka's writing. Like bachelorism and failed marriages, Kafka's writing takes place in a "borderland" so liminal that it is not even part of a land known as loneliness: it is situated "between loneliness and community" (*D* 396; *Ta* 871, trans. rev.). Kafka correspondingly tropes writing already in 1914 as that most extreme form of banishment—permanent isolation from all kin:

I waver, continually fly to the summit of the mountain, but cannot stay up there for more than a moment. Others waver too, but in lower regions, with greater strength; if they are in danger of falling, they are caught up by the kinsman who walks beside them for that purpose. But I waver on the heights; it is not death, alas, but the eternal torments of dying. (*D* 302; *Ta* 546, trans. rev.)

Writing, here, is exilic. As opposed to a bad marriage, however, it can produce a kind of home, albeit only on the summit of a mountain or in Russian deportation. Kafka thus told Max Brod in July 1922 that his writing is nothing other than an attempt to "write home," or, better, to write to—and thus create—a home that has always already disappeared ("[*Ich*] *muß immerfort nachhause schreiben, auch wenn alles Zuhause längst fortgeschwommen ist*") (*L* 340; *B* 392). Such a paradoxically unfamiliar "home" subsists in writing and appears only on the margins of earthly domiciles. As in the dialogue Charles Baudelaire's poet-narrator has with his soul, this home is not in Lisbon, Rotterdam, Jakarta, or even on the North Pole: it is "out of the world."[3] It is, as mentioned in the previous chapter, a *Mondheimat*.

By the time Kafka began writing letters to Milena in April 1920, he was still avidly pursuing both kinds of "home": first, the satisfying "hearth" of marriage and sexuality described by Milena in her essay and, second, the exilic home—a redeemed *katorga*—of writing. But these two types of home, these simultaneous journeys, remained mutually exclusive for Kafka for most of his life. This exclusivity produced the dialectical tension underlying both his letters to Milena and his earlier letters to Felice Bauer. As Kafka stressed during his 1914 and 1917 engagements to Felice, his 1919–20 engagement to Julie Wohryzek (which prompted his "Dearest Father" letter), and his 1920–23 relationship with Milena, writing and conjugal intimacy do not mix.[4] Kafka could *either* fulfill that "utmost" of human possibilities—marrying, founding a family, fathering children whom he would support and guide—*or* he could divorce himself from all forms of human intimacy, including the "joys of sex," and become a writer.[5] Kafka expresses the incompatibility of these two paths already in the 1913 letter to Felice I cited in the introduction, where Kafka employs the metaphor of the exotic journey: On the one hand, he imagines forging a new home with his fiancée in the utopian space of the "south" (or, as in his earlier letters to Felice, in Palestine); on the other hand, he desires the "racing" existence of artistic intensity, the internal journey to the edge of madness à la Gregor Samsa (*LF* 289; *BF* 427).

For Kafka, then, there is either the exotic space of the happy marriage (concretized as the fantasy southern *Heimat,* as Palestine) or the near-insanity

of traveling in one's room. There is either the joy of sex and nurturing children in a faraway country or the maniacal resistance to patriarchal law represented by the stay-at-home "bachelor machine."[6] What could possibly
mediate between such polarities? Not surprisingly, the quest for such a mediator between marriage and writing determined much of Kafka's life. As
Gerhard Neumann argues, the only viable mediator for Kafka seemed, paradoxically, to be the source of the original division; that is, the modern communications "media" (e.g., letters, telegraph, telephone) that attempted to
regulate what Kafka called human "*Verkehr*" (traffic, intercourse [social and
sexual], circulation) (*LM* 223; *BM* 302).[7] These media, which enabled human
communication, also tragically enforced the distancing of bodies and, through
an inevitable chain-reaction of miscommunication and misreading, estranged
subjects from each other. The great promises and great shortcomings of the
media thus explain Kafka's passion for and distrust of them (from the written
word to the telegram) throughout his life. The media promised to resolve the
polarity between intimacy and writing, but at the same time they produced
the very space between these two terms. The result for the writer was a series of temporary dwellings, a succession of outposts in the borderlands and
katorgas of the world, that he learns to call "home."

Wolf Kittler has pointed out how various media determined the space
of conflict in Kafka's 1912 breakthrough stories, as well as in "In the Penal
Colony" and *The Castle,* and further critics have noted the "medial" construction of love in Kafka's *Letters to Felice.*[8] Most critics, however, have neglected the role of the media in Kafka's production of modern hope and
despair in the *Letters to Milena* (*Briefe an Milena*).[9] Unlike the German-Jewish Felice Bauer, Milena represented for Kafka an unusually hopeful opportunity to "travel" to a second *Heimat:* toward an exotic Czech gentile
woman (whose foreign-sounding name Kafka liked repeatedly to pronounce) (*LM* 44–5; *BM* 59).[10] Milena, in other words, promised Kafka a
conjugal journey that seemed to reach beyond the territory controlled by
his father. This renewed hope in reaching the utopian space of a woman's
body—combined with Kafka's waning faith in letter writing—led Kafka
to place unusual emphasis on a type of medium generally ignored by
media scholars: the technologies of corporeal transport (automobiles,
steamships, and especially railway trains). As Kafka tells Milena, these are
the prime sponsors of "natural intercourse" and, as such, possible antidotes
to the "ghost[ly]" romantic tragedies he had already suffered through because of the communications media (*LM* 223; *BM* 302). Despite these renewed hopes, Kafka has the experience of Felice behind him, and is more
skeptical than ever of all forms of mediation (even if they do seem to
promise "natural" intercourse). As I will demonstrate in this chapter, Kafka
introduces travel technologies into his *Letters to Milena* in order to extend

his experience of love beyond the agonizing series of promises and disappointments sponsored by semiotic media. But "love" still remains impossible: it subsists now as the by-product of the powerful medial clash between the technologies of "natural" and "ghostly" intercourse.

"Natural" Intercourse: Sex and Trains

By the time Franz Kafka began writing letters to Milena, the new bureaucracies of rail ministry and postal service were firmly in place. Before the mid-nineteenth century, neither Germany nor Austria had a rail ministry, and their postal services were housed together within the *Verkehrsministerium* (transport ministry). In other words, before the 1850s, traveling bodies and traveling letters—or, in the official Austrian jargon, "*Personenbeförderung*" (human transport) and "*Nachrichtenübermittlung*" (information transmission)—were administratively united.[11] The eventual bureaucratic separation of body from information brought with it, by the turn of the century, another, physical separation: bodies and messages no longer necessarily traveled in the same vehicles. With the invention of pneumatic mail, the telegraph, the telephone, and the wireless, information often no longer used traditional vehicles at all. People stopped speaking of "traveling by the night mail," and began to imagine that trains and, later, automobiles were the exclusive province of human bodies.[12]

Such technological and bureaucratic changes led to new ways of thinking about the body's relation—or non-relation—to transported information. According to Kafka, the world was divided technologically into two groups: the technologies encouraging human presence (train, automobile, aeroplane, etc.) and the technologies encouraging absence (postal system, telegraph, wireless, etc.) (*LM* 223; *BM* 301–2). The technologies of presence, Kafka suggests, promote "*natürlichen*"—that is, physical—"*Verkehr*" between humans, while the technologies of absence sponsor a disembodied "*Verkehr mit Gespenstern*" (intercourse with ghosts) (*LM* 223; *BM* 302). On the one hand Kafka desires the "natural" intercourse sponsored by trains; on the other hand, he passionately wants to continue writing letters. For most of the correspondence, Kafka chooses the latter. He is "made of literature," he once wrote to Felice and thus would rather read his lovers' letters than touch their bodies (*LF* 304; *BF* 444). This oft-cited opposition between presence and absence structured Kafka's epistolary relations with Felice and, at the beginning, with Milena.[13]

Kafka wrote "Frau Milena" at least 126 letters between April and December 1920, and throughout these letters, he postpones an ever-promised journey to visit her. This journey, which would achieve physical presence and thus temporarily halt the correspondence, is, significantly, a train journey. As contemporary psychoanalysts speculated, trains had already pervaded the collective fin de siècle unconscious as a symbol of sexuality.[14] Freud claims in 1905 in *Three Essays on the Theory of Sexuality* that this symbolism begins shortly before male puberty, when boys develop "an extraordinarily intense interest in things connected with railways; they subsequently use the rail system as "the nucleus of a symbolism that is peculiarly sexual."[15] Similarly, Karl Abraham reports in 1922 that the sexual neuroses of many of his patients are "related to the danger of finding themselves in a kind of unstoppable motion that they can no longer control." These patients feared locomotion in any vehicle they could not bring to a halt themselves at any time—most notably, Abraham remarks, in railway trains.[16]

For Freud and Abraham, the railway's gender was symbolized by the station and the locomotive, respectively. In his famous *Bruchstück einer Hysterie-Analyse* from 1905 (the "Dora" case), Freud interpreted the station (*Bahnhof*) as a dream-symbol for the "female genitals"; that is, as a site of *Verkehr*. Playing on a possible unconscious connection between the feminized *Bahnhof* and *Verkehr*, Freud coyly remarks: "A '*Bahnhof*' is used for purposes of '*Verkehr*.'"[17] Following Freud's remarks on the feminized station, Abraham argues that the locomotive, correspondingly, is a phallic dream-symbol—thrusting forward ("*Vordringen*") with "inexorable violence."[18] Freud even goes so far as to suggest that the railway's sexual symbolism results directly from the mechanics of turn-of-the-century train travel. The turbulence ("*Erschütterungen*") produced by this early, rather crude system of rails, wheels, and springs, he writes in his *Three Essays,* causes involuntary "sexual excitation" in the traveler's body.[19]

Although Kafka never explicitly connected train travel to sexuality, this widespread cultural fantasy—at once nurtured and diagnosed by psychoanalysis—affected his relations with Milena and, as Mark Anderson has noted, connects his early fiction to the rubric of *Verkehr.*[20] Kafka's interest in the symbolic alliance of modern traffic and sexuality appears in "The Passenger" ("Der Fahrgast"), "Description of a Struggle" ("Beschreibung eines Kampfes"), *The Man Who Disappeared, The Metamorphosis,* and, most obviously, "The Judgment," which ends with the word "*Verkehr*" and the image of motor-bus passing over the drowning protagonist (*MO* 47; *DL* 61).[21] Kafka had "thoughts about Freud" throughout the story and even, according to Brod, imagined a "violent ejaculation" while writing the last line.[22]

Kafka's fascination with traffic and intercourse in the *Letters to Milena* predates his above-cited punning notion that the vehicles of modern *Verkehr* promote human *Verkehr* (*LM* 223; *BM* 302). In an early (May 31) letter in which he, for the second time, rejects Milena's invitation to visit her, Kafka nominally connects the rail system to his two prospective sexual partners: Milena and his fiancée at the time, Julie Wohryzek. Kafka tells Milena that he might change his mind and visit her instead of Julie, as originally planned; in the course of describing his indecision, he leaves out the names "Milena" and "Julie" and replaces them with the names of their respective railway stations. Julie, here, is recognizable only through the word "Karlsbad" and the "short route via Munich," while Milena appears only through the "secret code" denoting "Vienna" and "Linz":

> a telegram arrived "Meet at Karlsbad eighth request written communication." [. . .] Occasionally I look at the telegram and can scarcely read it—as if it contained a secret code, one which effaces the above message and reads: Travel via Vienna! [. . .] I won't do it, even just on the face of it it's senseless not to take the short route via Munich, but one twice as long through Linz and then even further via Vienna. (*LM* 23; *BM* 30–1, trans. rev.)

Railway schedules—the "short route via Munich" and the one "twice as long through Linz!"—stand in for the names of the beloved. The rail route— "Travel via Vienna!"—becomes Kafka's ejaculatory expression of desire.

In this and other early letters, the rail system develops a sexual undercurrent not unlike the one already embedded in the word *Eisenbahnverkehr* ("rail traffic"). Five days following this letter, Kafka warns Milena that a rumored rail strike would cut him off from all "*Eisenbahnverkehr,*" and thus also from all physical intercourse with her (*LM* 35; *BM* 46). Although the strike does not occur, Kafka voluntarily abstains from train traffic: he repeatedly postpones his departure over the course of nearly a month, thereby choosing letter writing over physical presence. He returns to writing, and proceeds to discuss with Milena possible train routes and rendezvous. By including rail schedules in his letters, Kafka contains what appears to be a dangerous, sexualized *Verkehrsnetz* within a ghostly network of codes—and thereby eroticizes the delay of gratification through modernity's chief figure of deferral, writing. If the rail system threatens to transport his body, Kafka will retaliate: he will transpose this network into an order of signs, an endless traffic of letters. We might imagine Kafka sitting at his desk, vigorously fending off *Eisenbahnverkehr* by copying timetables into his missives. Indeed, from another such desk in Prague, months later, Kafka tells Milena that he is studying the timetable she sent him "like a map" (*LM* 210; *BM* 284). This "study"-able timetable, like Kafka's letters to Milena themselves, represents how trains can become texts. Travel, Kafka hopes, might fully be transposed into signs.

Dream: *Eisenbahnverkehr*
versus Letter Writing

On June 14, following his month-long deferral of departure, Kafka relates to Milena two dreams (one a waking dream, the other real), in which he travels to Vienna. These dreams stage Kafka's conflicting, technologized desires for both absence and presence. Here, as in his discussion of timetables, Kafka pits modern, sexualized *Eisenbahnverkehr* against the postal service. Kafka's real dream thus begins with a journey to Vienna. He writes that his body overtook his "own letters, which were still on their way to you" (*LM* 47; *BM* 63). In comparing the relative travel time of body and letter, Kafka here invokes the newly established technocratic difference between human transport and information transmission. Anachronistically, he claims that transport technologies still outpace information technologies: bodies will arrive before letters. For this reason, Kafka, the enthusiastic letter writer, claims to experience "particular pain" (*LM* 47; *BM* 63).

For this first section of the dream, as well as for the entire waking dream, sexualized *Eisenbahnverkehr* holds sway over letter writing. Kafka's dream-body repeatedly appears at some pleasurable site of transit: a railway hotel, railway station, a thoroughfare. In his waking dream, similarly, Kafka finds himself in a hotel near the stations, situated among Milena's house and the arriving and departing trains: "opposite [your house] is my hotel, to the left is the West-bahnhof where I arrive, to the left of that the Franz Josefs Bahnhof from which I depart" (*LM* 47; *BM* 63). The great city of Vienna is reduced to one railway hotel, Milena's house, and, in the terms of contemporary psychoanalysis, two sexually charged train stations. The aroused dream-subject, traveling to meet his beloved, arrives (comes, "*ankomm[t]*") into the center of this *Eisenbahnverkehr*. In the real dream, the city condenses more distinctively into a sexualized metropolis: "wet, dark, an inconceivable amount of traffic [*ein unkenntlich großer Verkehr*]" (*LM* 47; *BM* 63).

In the middle of this dream, Kafka finds himself at another libidinal site of transit: a twilit thoroughfare. This thoroughfare, like the illogically speedy express train before it, allows the dreamer to traffic physically with Milena: "I had one foot in the roadway," Kafka writes, "I was holding your hand" (*LM* 48; *BM* 64, trans. rev.). But here, unlike in the previous scene, new, rival communication technologies appear to challenge "natural *Verkehr*." At the precise moment at which Kafka and Milena hold hands, they are interrupted, ironically, by their own "conversation," which takes on a life of its own: "it" simply "began" and then continued, without Kafka or Milena being able to control it.

This autonomous conversation recalls the lovers' own epistolary conversation, which, according to Kafka, developed independently of and often in

opposition to its own authors (*LM* 223; *BM* 302). Indeed, the dream conversation's insanely fast tempo, punctuated ("*kurzsätziges*") syntax, and
rhythmic clacking ("*klapp klapp*") suggest a telegram—a machine Kafka
often used to communicate with Milena (*LM* 48; *BM* 64). This medium,
inestimably faster than the technologies of human presence, intrudes on the
lovers' physical intercourse. The content of the telegrammatic *klapp klapp*,
Kafka claims, is agony ("*Qual*"), the same word he later uses to describe the
content of all of his correspondence with Milena (*LM* 48, 222; *BM* 64,
301). This agonizing clatter could be dream-shorthand for modern media
traffic—suggesting that this form of traffic, the lightning-fast telegram, is superior to travel technologies and, moreover, anathema to physical intercourse. The lovers are frustrated by the virtually uninterrupted *klapp klapp*
of their own dialogue, which eventually transforms their relationship from
hand-holding into uncomfortable "negotiations" (*LM* 48; *BM* 64). What
began as a seemingly harmless telegrammatic cacophony ends in melancholic separation.[23] The dream thus realizes a nightmare that has secretly
haunted the entire correspondence: modern media technologies sabotage
the lovers' chances for satisfying physical intercourse (and eventually, as we
shall see, reveal how such physicality is always already mediated).

But Kafka's dream, we must remember, began by documenting his desire for precisely such a sabotage: he experiences pain ("*das schmerzte mich*")
when his train-transported body overtakes his letters (*LM* 47; *BM* 63).[24]
Kafka's dream is thus as ambivalent as is its dreamer. It displays Kafka's desire to experience mediated and unmediated physical intercourse at once.
Without the former, he is in pain; without the latter, he experiences agony.
When the dream is over, however, we again see which side Kafka takes
when forced to make a choice. He does not embark on the already long-
postponed journey but rather sits down to write Milena another letter, a
letter about his "horrid" dream (*LM* 47; *BM* 62). Kafka thus enlists agonizing media technologies to tell the story of agonizing media technologies. His only pleasures come from return mail. Two hours after the dream,
he proudly reports, he received "consolation": letters and flowers from
Milena (*LM* 50; *BM* 67).

A Victory for Natural Intercourse,
Then More Letter Pleasure

Kafka's journey to Vienna on June 29 marks, as the letter-addict both desired and feared, the first gap in his correspondence. The "natural" intercourse of trains temporarily shuts down the *klapp klapp* of
communication technologies, and Kafka enjoys, for four days, physical—
and perhaps sexual—intercourse with Milena. In the letters following his

return, Kafka fondly remembers Milena in relation to the sexualized rail system, specifically, as part of the feminized *Bahnhof*. Kafka twice claims that he can only remember Milena's face as it was at the station (*LM* 62, 64; *BM* 82, 85). He remembers her sad station-face ("*trauriges Bahnhof-gesicht*"), and later, when describing the problems he has with customs officials while crossing the border back to Czechoslovakia (Kafka's Austrian visa has expired), he claims that "Milena" spiritually assisted him with the station officials. She becomes his travel angel; as he puts it further, she is the angel of Jews: "*Du Judenengel*" (*LM* 64–65; *BM* 86–87).[25]

With Milena in the role of travel angel, Kafka takes on the job of letter magician. In his first letter upon returning to Prague, he describes missing Milena's physical presence: "*suddenly you were no longer there*; or, better, you were there [. . .], although this kind of being-there was very different from what we knew during the 4 days" (*LM* 61–62; *BM* 82, Kafka's emphasis, trans. rev.). Milena's new kind of being there is a familiar one: she is "there" but only as writing on a page, as an epistolary projection; Kafka claims that he must once again become "accustomed" to this kind of presence. He thus rehabituates himself to letter writing, in the form of the mournful magician. He writes Milena three letters on the day of his return and, in one, imagines conjuring her missing body simply by mailing a letter: "I'm sending you the letter, as if by doing so I could transport you next to me, especially close" (*LM* 62; *BM* 83).

The partnership between travel angel and letter magician, cooperative at the start, grows increasingly contentious. After a couple of weeks of writing optimistically about another meeting, Kafka begins to regard with suspicion his travel angel's facility in transporting his body. He negatively revises his memory of their meeting and resists her entreaties once again: "I won't come [*kommen*]," he writes resolutely and, later, "I cannot come" (*LM* 88, 119, 125; *BM* 117, 159, 167, trans. rev.). This renewed refusal coincides exactly with his reintensified efforts to conjure Milena's body via letters.

On July 30, Kafka announces his refusal to visit for the first time; on this same day, he also initially speaks at length about the material qualities of what he later calls Milena's "beautiful" telegram (*LM* 122; *BM* 162). Like the vampiric ghosts whom Kafka later accuses of having greedily drunk up his and Milena's "written kisses," Kafka claims to imbibe—or suck up ("*auf-saugen*")—Milena's telegram while reading it (*LM* 223, 120; *BM* 302, 161).[26] Kafka later fingers this telegram "constantly" and gains a "special" feeling from having it in his pocket (*LM* 122, 120; *BM* 162, 161). This beautiful telegram—like Milena's beautiful handwriting before it—fetishistically replaces the absent lover's body (*LM* 50; *BM* 67). Months earlier, when Milena complained to Kafka that his face was becoming nothing more to her than "*beschriebenes Briefpapier*" (stationery that has been written on), Kafka defends the pleasures of epistolary absence: "I am so much better off [than you]!" he writes, "the true Milena is here [. . .], and believe me, being with her is wonderful" (*LM* 33; *BM* 44). Fetishistic pleasure thus ameliorates the pain caused by letterary distance. Kafka refuses to visit Milena but is magically able to transfer her essence to him. Through epistolary necromancy, then, the lover is present and absent at once.

Kafka thus separates himself, as letter-writing conjuror, from Milena, the sexualized "angel" of the rails. In these same post-Vienna weeks, Kafka not surprisingly hones his mastery of communication technologies—switching adroitly from letters, to pneumatic mail, to telegrams (*LM* 71, 125, 137; *BM* 95, 167, 183). He blatantly reveals, in a late July letter, his preference for postal over physical intercourse. In response to Ernst Pollak's (Milena's husband) plans to move the couple as far away as Paris or Chicago, Kafka only cares about whether or not he will still be able to write to her once she's there—wondering aloud if she will go to a "place with good mail service?" (*LM* 105; *BM* 140).

Reproducing *Briefverkehr:* Mailing Stamps[27]

The very next day, Kafka makes his clearest statement concerning the importance of the correspondence: "If I receive letters I am right and endowed with everything, and if none were to arrive I would be neither right nor endowed with anything, including life" (*LM* 108; *BM* 144). In other words: I receive letters, therefore I am. Kafka closes this letter about letter writing with what seems to be an off-hand remark about a "great stamp collector" with whom he works. This man, Kafka claims, regularly saves the one-crown Austrian stamps from Milena's envelopes. Now this man has enough of these one-crown stamps, and he wants different ones: "So if you [Milena] could use these other [bigger, blackish-brown] one-crown stamps or some other larger ones for 2 crowns" (*LM* 108; *BM* 144–45). Milena, a writer herself—much more than just Kafka's fantasy agent of *Verkehr*—is lured in by the possibility of more letter traffic: she sends the stamps, Kafka asks for more, and she, in turn, requests more stamps from him (for an anonymous Viennese boy, she claims, who would like to have special Czech congress-stamps) (*LM* 112–13; *BM* 150). A long exchange follows. Kafka's initiation of this stamp swap is important because it is the material correlate to his earlier philosophical statement about self-justification through letters. The stamp exchange is Kafka's attempt to guarantee that he will indeed always be "right" and endowed with "everything." When Milena agrees to participate, Kafka realizes that this vital letter traffic will generate its own momentum.

In the next two-and-one-half weeks, Kafka often writes two letters per day, frequently referring to the stamp exchange. He requests and/or receives from Milena: one- and two-crown stamps, heller-stamps of 10 h, 25 h, and 50 h, "special delivery stamps," "overprinted" stamps, stamps on "thin" and "thick" paper, and a "narrow and reddish-brown" one-crown stamp; in exchange, he mails Czech Legionnaire stamps, and he searches for congress-stamps and special postmarks (see figure 23).[28] Kafka often scribbles his stamp comments in the margins of his letters or adds them on at the end as postscripts. Such apparent marginalizations have led critics and editors to ignore the stamp remarks, so much so that these are included only in the latest, 1983 German edition of the letters. (One section of stamp comments is still excluded from the English translation.) Even in the latest German edition, the editors claim that the stamp dialogue is only important for the dating of the letters; this exchange, they claim, is "certainly unimportant" for the complex unfolding of Kafka's and Milena's relationship.[29]

Assumptions about what is "important" have led the editors to overlook a central aspect of this middle phase of Kafka's correspondence with Milena. His initiation of a stamp exchange represents a further attempt to conjure presence yet remain distant within a vehemently modern techno-logical dialectic. These stamps are, for Kafka, a fetish object valued even more than Milena's "beautiful" telegrams, since Milena has actually touched and even licked the stamps. As Walter Benjamin argues in his 1927 "Briefmarken-Handlung" (collected in *One-Way Street*), the fetishistic value of stamps appreciated at the fin de siècle precisely *because* of the invention of the telegram; Benjamin's point is even more valid in our own fin de siècle of fax and e-mail.[30] As correspondents increasingly replace the material objects they touch (paper, stamps) with invisible, electronic trans-fer systems, they raise the symbolic worth of paper and stamps—especially in love letters. Stamps thus correspond to the "paper" that Kafka famously wanted to "kiss" before sending to Felice in 1912. Although Kafka ac-knowledges that such paper kisses are "miserable"—impoverished substi-tutes for real physical contact—this paper at least remains a medium mutually touched.[31] In the case of the stamps, the shared object has been placed between the lover's fingers, licked, and affixed (gently or firmly) to an envelope. The recipient (or his resident "stamp collector") then re-wets the stamps and delicately peels them off. Even though the lover's arriving stamps are soaked in a dish (not wetted with saliva), they still offer Kafka in 1920 a more potent version of his 1912 "written kisses." They appear to overcome the dialectic of trains and telegrams by creating a physical pres-ence that magically preserves writerly distance (*LM* 223; *BM* 302).[32]

In addition to offering physical pleasure, this stamp exchange supports Kafka's ongoing battle to displace Milena's discourse of trains for his own discourse of mail. He thus introduces the stamp exchange tactically, at the moment when Milena is again encouraging physical presence. An inventory of Kafka's remarks about stamps reveals that he employs them regularly and strategically, not haphazardly, as the editors would suggest. In the nineteen days between July 24 and August 12, 1920, Kafka mentions the stamp exchange thirteen times, and he stresses these remarks by once underlining them in red and blue pencil—something he does at no other point in the correspondence.[33] This tactic allows Kafka to systematically reshape the discourse of the correspondence: from trains and possible rendezvous to stamps and endless letter writing. Kafka's letters were self-reflexive long before the stamp exchange, but now they are *materially* so. Just as the phenomenon of letter writing enters into the texts of his letters from April onward, so too does the letters' outside currency now physically penetrate the envelope. Kafka thus kick-starts a self-perpetuating economy in which the correspondents exchange (fold, separate, lick, press, insert, peel) stamps; in so doing, they carefully fetishize the tender of their relationship.

Perhaps unwittingly, Kafka reveals his secret intentions to Milena the day after she agrees to exchange stamps with him. His goal is to increase letter traffic: "From now on I'm only going to enclose one stamp at a time [. . .] so that I'll be thanked every day"; the daily "thank yous," of course, should come in the form of a letter (*LM* 113, 140; *BM* 150–51, 187). The stamp exchange reads, here, like a ploy for increasing letter traffic. And it seems to work.

As Kafka remarks one day earlier, Milena, too, is writing letters about, among other things, stamps: "And it turns out we really do keep writing the same thing [. . .] I want to die and then you do, I want stamps and then you want stamps" (*LM* 111; *BM* 148). Kafka even begins to imagine that it is Milena—not he—who is responsible for the exchange's momentum. Four days later, after fastidiously asking Milena to replace her usual one-crown stamps with more, lower-priced stamps (25 h), he crosses out this request (but leaves it legible) and then begs Milena to end the torturous exchange: "But no, just forget it, please forget it" (underlined by Kafka in red and blue pencil) (*LM* 120; *BM* 159–60). Again, one week later, Kafka admonishes Milena to "stop wasting stamps" and tells her that, if she does not stop, he will no longer forward the stamps to the stamp collector: "if you continue sending [stamps] I'll stop giving them to the man. I've underlined this request in red and blue, which is the greatest severity I am capable of" (*LM* 144; *BM* 193). But Milena seems to see through Kafka's double conceit: both his attempt to blame the momentum for the exchange on her and his entire story of the great stamp collector. Perhaps suspicious of Kafka's motives, she asks him a question about the stamp collector—"Do you see the stamp collector often?"—and Kafka offers only this defensive and enigmatic response: "There's nothing underhanded about the question although it looks that way" (*LM* 113; *BM* 151, trans. rev.).

Some evidence suggests that Kafka indeed invented the stamp collector, or at least that Kafka experienced him as a fantastic *Doppelgänger*. The man mirrors Kafka uncannily, through the ceiling of Kafka's office. The stamp collector, Kafka writes, "isn't working at all, just looking at the stamps, enraptured, as I am doing with the letters one floor below" (*LM* 145–46; *BM* 195). Moreover, the man uses all of his spare time filling "sheets" and "books" with stamps just as Kafka spends all of his free moments, one floor below, filling sheets with words: "When one sheet is full," Kafka writes, "[. . .] he takes out a new one and so on" (*LM* 156; *BM* 210, trans. rev.). The vampiric letter-addict thus finds his welcomed double, a daytime consumer of stamps. Because of the "stamp collector's" (not Kafka's) voracious appetite, Milena must send more letters *and* more stamps. The fetish objects thus redouble, and Kafka's pleasures do as well.

Kafka's smooth-running media machine first stalls eight days after the initial stamp request. Milena is busily exchanging stamps (Kafka feels compelled to tell her to stop wasting them); but, at the same time, Milena demands more and more adamantly that Kafka visit her (*LM* 144; *BM* 193). Kafka repeatedly refuses. He begins to sense, as he did in Meran, that this refusal will lead her to stop writing to him completely (*LM* 35; *BM* 46). He speaks of this fear on July 31. Shortly after insisting once again that he cannot come to Vienna, Kafka tells Milena that he knows she is turning away from him. He begs her to remember that "a human can't last for long without a heartbeat, and as long as you are turned away how can my heart go on beating? If you could send me a telegram after this letter!" (*LM* 127; *BM* 169). Kafka thus increases the stakes of media technology: a dependency that was once existential ("I receive letters, therefore I am") is now material and biological. Without letters, stamps, and telegrams to caress and "suck up," the media vampire's heart will literally stop (*LM* 120; *BM* 161). Kafka's next letter recounts a dream in which he claims that Milena feels rejected by him; this "*Abweisung*," he fears, will lead directly to Milena halting the correspondence (*LM* 128; *BM* 171). Kafka notes at the end that he feels dreary. He is doubly certain that his epistolary nourishment—Milena's letters and stamps—will stop arriving (*LM* 130; *BM* 173).

Another Promise of Natural *Verkehr;* a Postal Utopia; and the End of the Correspondence

By his own accounts desperate in this last letter, Kafka resorts to a promise of "natural intercourse" in order to guarantee that the material essential to life—letters, stamps, telegrams—will continue to arrive (*LM* 135; *BM*

180). He promises to meet Milena either in Vienna or the Austrian/Czech border town of Gmünd. The theme of these early-August letters correspondingly turns abruptly from stamps to trains. From August 1–3, Kafka mentions train schedules five times—sometimes in exacting detail, as in what he here terms plan number "II": "I likewise leave here at 4:12, but am already (already! already!) in Gmünd by 7:28 P.M. Even if I leave with the morning express on Sunday, it's not until 10:46 [. . .]" (*LM* 131; *BM* 175, trans. rev.). He doesn't really want to be near her, but wants her on the line. So he talks around her. Later in the same letter, Kafka mentions the stamp exchange again, but this old theme is beginning to feel like a fairy tale that has lost its powers to enchant. Kafka knows that he must replace his stamp stories with some new talk of trains: "Yes, you're doing excellently with the stamps (unfortunately I misplaced the special-delivery stamps, the man almost started crying when I told him that). [. . .] I'll even send you some Legionnaire stamps, imagine. I don't feel like telling any fairy tales today; my head is like a railroad station, with trains departing, arriving, customs control [. . .]" (*LM* 132; *BM* 176, trans. rev.).

Kafka allows this flood of train traffic to overfill his suddenly technologized "head" and, what is more, to dilute his desire to tell stories (about stamps). But this cannot weaken his unswerving appetite for composing and receiving letters. In fact, the re-introduction of the theme of "natural intercourse" leads again dialectically to more letter traffic. In the four days following this offer to travel, Kafka writes seven letters and at least three telegrams, and Milena responds. The opposing discourses of trains and telegrams encourage one another again—and again to the final benefit of letter traffic. Kafka reveals his understanding of this dynamic on August 3. Amid more discussions of trains and schedules, he asks Milena to make even more trips to the post office: "answer me by telegram whether you, too, can come. So keep going to the post office in the evening as well [. . .]" (*LM* 134; *BM* 179).

Kafka meets Milena in Gmünd—like the *Mund* (mouth), a site of natural intercourse—on August 14–15.[34] In the months that follow, Kafka mentions farewell *("Abschied")* for the first time and, finally, that winter, severs the correspondence and begs Milena to do the same (*LM* 197; *BM* 266). What brings Kafka to end this correspondence, even though he once claimed that receiving letters endowed him with "everything"? Critics, including the editors of the latest German edition of *Letters to Milena,* have tended to explain this termination according to two contradictory relationship economies: Kafka realized that he could not give Milena the level of sexual intimacy she needed;[35] or, conversely, Kafka wanted the kind of intimate relationship a married woman could never give him.[36] What these opposed readings overlook is the relation of content to form; that is, the connection between Kafka's desire to stop writing letters and the structural exigencies of epistolary exchange. The writer of love-letters desires to be absent and present at once, and modern technologies encourage but do not satisfy these contradictory yearnings.[37] Rather, trains and telegrams set such longings more acutely against one another.[38]

Kafka had a recurring fantasy that would allow him to mend this techno-psychological rift: he would send his own body to his lover. This vision is first articulated by one of Kafka's earliest protagonists, who dreams, in *Wedding Preparations in the Country* (*Hochzeitsvorbereitungen auf dem Lande,* 1906–9), of sending his own "clothed body" to his fiancée while himself staying at home.[39] This fantasy of what Wolf Kittler calls a "postal utopia"—of becoming mail, of becoming a stamp—grows stronger and more literal in the weeks leading up to Kafka's journey to Gmünd, when he first imagines packaging his own body in the mail.[40] Kafka had been sending needed books and other items to Milena (now living in inflationary, post-war Austria), and he claims that he will literally "crawl into [. . .] every item [your list] contains just in order to travel inside it to Vienna [. . .] and please give me as many opportunities to travel as possible" (*LM* 141; *BM* 189). The image here is of Kafka magically shrinking and multiplying himself, then crawling into books and other items, and, finally, mailing these many selves. This vision combines technological fantasy with bureaucratic subversion. It allows Kafka (multiplied) to traffic physically with Milena while, at the same time, maintaining his single, epistolary self. A normal-sized, unshrunk master Kafka, one must assume, serves as writer, packager, and sender.

Kafka's techno-postal fantasy is, of course, never realized. He visits Milena in Gmünd, traveling by train, not parcel post. By Kafka's account, the meeting is unsatisfactory. He returns to Prague and is once again deeply split between body and letters. Unlike the cheerful fantasy of crawling into a postal package, the reality of traveling on a train now causes Kafka great fear. He writes to Milena that he is "afraid of traveling," afraid of coughing uninterruptedly as he had for over an hour the night before. As the now-tubercular Kafka continues, he "wouldn't dream of taking a sleeping car" (*LM* 210; *BM* 285). Traveling, here, again exposes Kafka's body to the world. Instead of revealing the body's sexuality, travel now emphasizes its illness. Now the infected body (not the sexualized one) is on display, but the sudden and unwilling exposure of this body to others—and vice-versa—remains Kafka's central distress. *Eisenbahnverkehr,* he fears, will lead to more non-linguistic physical intercourse, even to death, and again bring about—irrevocably, this time—the end of *Schriftverkehr.*

Travel technologies, Kafka insists, oppose writing even in the most practical sense. As Kafka tells his first epistolary girlfriend, Felice, in 1912, it is not easy to write in moving vehicles: "How do you manage to write in a tram? With the paper on your knees, your head bent that far down while writing? Trams go slowly in Berlin, don't they?" (*LF* 101; *BF* 176). Kafka, similarly, once writes in an electric mountain train during his correspondence with Milena—perhaps with paper on his knees, head bent (he copies the messy letter when he gets home)—but he never writes in a regular railway carriage (*LM* 55; *BM* 74). The "shaking" of the early railway perhaps led, as Freud would have it, to sexual excitement, but it also quite simply got in the way of putting pen to paper.[41] Kafka's protagonist in *Wedding Preparations* suggests as much when, bound for his fiancée's house in a train, he watches a man holding a furiously vibrating notebook: "the note-book trembled, for [the traveler] was not supporting his arm on anything, and the coach, which was now in motion, beat on the rails like a hammer" (*WP* 22; *NSI* 31). Shortly after severing the correspondence with Milena, Kafka extends this material opposition of travel and writing to a conceptual level. He explains his apparent "*Reiseangst*" (travel anxiety) in terms of a fear of not writing (*L* 333; *B* 384). As he tells Max Brod (before a planned trip to Georgental in 1922), part of his mysterious travel anxiety results from his fear of being unable to write: his fear of, through the journey, being "kept away from the desk for at least several days" (*L* 335; *B* 386). *Reiseangst* translates, here, into the end of writing. The travel-phobic Freud argued several years earlier that his own *Reiseangst* (or, more specifically, "*Eisenbahnangst*" [rail-phobia]) denoted a fear of uncontrollable *Verkehr*.[42] Kafka does not deny this, but he adds to this the problem of the possible exception: How do we know when traffic is just traffic, frightening only because it pulls us away from our desks?

In the final months of the correspondence, Kafka grows increasingly aware of this split between traveling (physical) and writing (ghostly) selves, and of this fissure's deleterious effects on him. He is once again in the throes of indecision in his last 1920 letter to Milena—unsure again whether or not to visit her.[43] He sums up his recurring epistolary-existential dilemma—to travel or not to travel—in the form of a letter about a letter and a journey. He writes: "Two people were struggling within me; one who wants to travel and one who is afraid of traveling—both just parts of me, both probably scoundrels" (*LM* 220; *BM* 298, trans. rev.). Kafka's "worst times" are thus brought on, again, by the impossibility of combining traveling and writing selves. The writer-in-love cannot replicate and mail himself to his lover but must, rather, subsist as either the epistolary lover afraid to travel or the traveling lover unable to write.[44] Incapable of being both at once, Kafka chooses to become neither: he stops writing to Milena for over fifteen months.

The Final Letters

When Kafka finally writes again (late March 1922), he is distant and formal, referring to Milena as "*Sie*" (*LM* 223; *BM* 301). He is no longer struggling from within the techno-psychological dialectic of letterary love; rather, he theorizes about it from a temporal and emotional distance. He now sees the technologies that supported his "agonizing" long-distance love affair with Milena as pernicious, even inhuman. As was the case in his breakthrough story, "The Judgment," writing and physical love are here explicitly opposed. The postal system, the telegraph, and the wireless, Kafka claims, alienate bodies from themselves and from each other—thereby permitting lovers only "ghostly" intercourse:

> Writing letters is actually an intercourse with ghosts [. . .]. How did people ever get the idea they could communicate [*verkehren*] with one another by letter! One can think about someone far away and one can hold on to someone nearby; everything else is beyond human power [. . .]. Written kisses don't arrive at their destination; the ghosts drink them up along the way. It is this ample nourishment which enables them to multiply so enormously. Humanity senses this and struggles against it.

"Humanity's" struggle takes the form of innovations in the technologies of transport:

> in order to eliminate as much as possible the ghostly element between people and to attain a natural intercourse, a tranquility of souls, [humankind] has invented trains, cars, aeroplanes—but nothing helps anymore: These are evidently inventions devised at the moment of crashing. The opposing side is so much calmer and stronger; after the postal system, the ghosts invented the telegraph, the telephone, the radiotelegraph. (*LM* 223; *BM* 302, trans. rev.)

For Klaus Theweleit, this letter represents the central techno-psychological shift in Kafka's life: Kafka turns his back on ghostly technologies and instead embraces the "counter alliance" of trains, planes, and automobiles.[45] But if Kafka's anti-ghostly loyalties are as clear as Theweleit would have them be, why did Kafka not actively collaborate with this life-affirming counter-alliance? Theweleit writes that Kafka realized the value of these new technologies "too late"—implying that Kafka had already inwardly decided against the relationship. But how much was Kafka's internal decision—the decision to be no longer "in love"—based on a desire to escape all forms of technological intercourse, especially those at once encouraged and undermined by trains and telegrams? Kafka's "love" for Milena, we must remember, began and ended as self-consciously mediated love. His "kisses" were "written"; his fingers caressed mass-produced, post-marked stamps and telegraph forms. Even during his two rendezvous with Milena, when their *Verkehr* should have been more immediate and "natural," Kafka is aware of the irony implicit in this dialectic: his natural intercourse is *made* possible by new technologies. These supposedly human-friendly inventions of train, plane, and automobile transport people at decidedly unnatural speeds and are, as Kafka insists, devised "at the moment of crashing."

Toward the end of this late letter, Kafka expresses, one final time, his desire to sidestep the dialectic of trains and telegrams by mailing himself. He closes these negative remarks on travel- and communication technologies with the tempting notion that human presence could be magically posted. Kafka suggests that one of his or Milena's letters could arrive miraculously in the form of a pleasing, longed-for "handclasp" (*LM* 224; *BM* 303). Letter transforms here into hand, message into body. This seductive image allows Kafka again to achieve the super-human, the virtual. He stays home and writes, while his body, as in *Wedding Preparations,* travels to his lover. This fantasy is so powerful, so attractive, Kafka continues, that it is the "most dangerous of all," and thus must be guarded against "more carefully than the others" (*LM* 224; *BM* 303). Kafka indeed chooses to guard himself, by abstaining from epistolary love. He writes to "Frau Milena" only seven more times until his death in 1924 (four letters, three postcards) and maintains the formal distance of "*Sie*" all but once. In his final postcard (from December 25, 1923), Kafka acknowledges that his writing seems to have lost its previously thrilling and dangerous capacity for conveying bodies. This ability has deteriorated, Kafka claims, as has his own body. Writing can no longer transport a self. It can barely even convey the most insignificant of messages into the world of threatening and enticing human *Verkehr,* the world of "Frau Milena": "if I write down 'cordial regards,' then are these greetings really strong enough to enter the wild, noisy, gray, urban Lerchenfelderstrasse [Milena's home street], where it would be impossible for me and mine to even breathe?" (*LM* 237; *BM* 321, trans. rev.). This "love" letter, not surprisingly, is Franz Kafka's last.

Coda: Epistolarity and a Fictional Marriage

When Kafka wrote this final postcard to Milena, he was living in Steglitz in Berlin with Dora Diamant, a young Jewish woman from Galicia. Kafka had thus finally completed the longed-for journey from Prague to Berlin as well as toward the satisfactory "home" with a woman. He and Dora had planned another admittedly impossible journey, to Palestine, where they imagined opening a restaurant—with her the cook and him the waiter.[46] But Kafka and Dora (like Kafka and Felice a decade earlier) never made it to the Promised Land. Kafka's condition worsened, bringing the couple first to Prague, then to one sanatorium, and then to another, final one in Austria. Three of Kafka's lifelong journeys, therefore, moved toward a close in 1923: out of Prague, toward a conjugal relationship with a woman, and toward death.

Kafka's and Dora's effective marriage was accompanied by a fictional one that, as did Kafka's endlessly delayed bondings with Felice and Milena, takes place in letters. It performs the precise tensions between travel and writing, between sexual *Verkehr* and epistolary distance, outlined above—albeit this time with a happy ending.

According to Dora, Kafka met a little girl crying one morning in a park because she had lost her doll. Kafka comforted her, "Your doll is just traveling, I know, she sent me a letter." The child was suspicious: "Do you have it with you?" "No, I forgot it at home, but I'll bring it to you tomorrow." Kafka returned home and composed a letter, with the same seriousness he devoted to his writings—be they postcards, letters, or stories. He went back the following day and read the letter to the girl: the doll explained that she had grown tired of living in the same family, and needed a change of air and locale. Although she still thought very fondly of the little girl, she needed to be away from her for a time. She promised to write every day, reporting about her adventures in foreign lands. So Kafka wrote each day, as he had earlier to Milena. And, as he had twelve years before in *Amerika,* he described countries and people that he knew only in fantasy. The doll told of her far-off adventures, of her new school, of the interesting people she met. The child soon forgot about her missing plaything, losing herself in the humorous detail of Kafka's fiction. Continually reassuring the child that she loved her, the doll nonetheless hinted at complications in her life, at her various duties and interests. This game went on for at least three weeks. Kafka suffered terrible anxieties when he thought about ending it. The ending, he knew, must restore order to the girl's life—order that had disappeared the moment she lost her doll. He ultimately decided that the doll would get married. Describing the young man, the engagement celebration, the wedding preparations, and finally all the particulars of the newlyweds' home, the doll told the little girl in the end: "As you see yourself, in the future we will have to do without seeing each other again."[47]

In this epistolary fiction, which survived only in Dora's memory, Kafka achieved what he never could with Milena. Although no trains are mentioned, Kafka reiterates the tension between presence and absence—between conjugal intimacy and letter writing—that produced much of his struggle with Milena. The forces of *Verkehr*—of travel and social intercourse—encourage the doll to become sexual and, in the end, marry. And, here, unlike in Kafka's life, the world of letters does not stand in opposition: rather, the letters are what allow the doll to successfully and considerately grow up and away from her family. Only in Kafka's fiction, then, can letters fulfill their promise of intimacy. The doll can marry because the letters acceptably generate distance from the girl, who represents, here, the retarding force of the family or, more generally, the ever-present debilitating "third" in Kafkan love affairs.[48] It is as if Georg Bendemann had, before the beginning of Kafka's 1912 breakthrough story, informed his "friend" of his coming marriage, stopped writing, and left home with his fiancée. It is as if Kafka, in the dream of unfulfilled travel, had left his family already in 1912 and traveled to Palestine with Felice—creating a new exotic *Heimat* with his lover, beyond the imperial reach of the father, where he could finally stop both traveling and writing.

Perhaps Kafka reached this Promised Land beyond letter writing with Dora, even though the two of them never made it to Palestine, as they had hoped. Like the doll in his story, Kafka finally used letter writing to break away from Milena (and from the little girl in the story) and eventually stopped writing love letters in order to move to Berlin (for Kafka, an ersatz Palestine, where he could live with Dora) (*LM* 236; *BM* 319). What is more, Kafka wrote very few letters to Dora (none have survived), and Dora—unlike Max Brod—agreed to Kafka's earnest request to burn some of the writings that he imagined were torturing him. Dora's above-cited story is the story of the defeat of epistolarity, of the use of letter writing as a means to end letter writing: letters only allow for acceptable separation and are then discarded in favor of conjugal intimacy. But ultimately not even Dora could save Kafka from the eternal noise of the vampiric communications media. Despite Dora the ghosts were already winning, Kafka knew: they had already invented the telegraph, the telephone, and the wireless, and they would continue to thrive long after Kafka stopped writing letters and even long after he was dead. As I will discuss at the end of the next chapter, maybe this fearful knowledge—and Kafka's concomitant desire for a *Heimat* beyond writing—is what made Kafka ask Brod to burn all of his letters and fictions. Literary immortality, Kafka knew, would only create more ghostly intercourse, and never allow him peace. In an irony that Kafka would have understood best, even Dora's memories of the ghosts finally capitulating made their way into print: like a long-lost letter, Dora's memories, too, still circulate; the ghosts, as Kafka predicted late in the exchange with Milena, "will not starve, but we will perish" (*LM* 223; *BM* 302).

Chapter Seven

Travel, Death, and the Exotic Voyage Home:
"The Hunter Gracchus"

"My death boat went off course; a wrong turn of the wheel, a moment's absence of mind on the part of the helmsman, the distraction
of my lovely native country [*Heimat*]."

—*the hunter Gracchus*

As I have argued throughout this book, Kafka often creates nostalgic travelers who—like turn-of-the-century dime-store heroes—
attempt to make their way to "second homes." Karl Rossmann
goes hopefully to America; Josef K. plans to escape the courts by journeying to his mother's house in the country; the Penal Colony officer
wants nostalgically to return to an "old" era; and K. longs to enter the
Castle. Kafka himself imagines second homes in an assortment of loca-
tions (Spain, South America, the Azores, Madeira, Palestine, a generic island in the "south"). But each of these journeys is derailed, infected by
Kafka's telltale discourse of disorientation. This repeated detouring of
nostalgia becomes most evident, toward the end of Kafka's life, in his reflections on the journey toward death. Although not Kafka's last story, the
unpublished fragments now known as "The Hunter Gracchus" ("Der
Jäger Gracchus") were written just months before Kafka's first tubercular
haemorrhage; and they offer us Kafka's most sustained meditation on
death as a disorienting voyage.[1] Death, here, is depicted as the *grand voyage* toward, in Gracchus' words, the "other world" (*Jenseits*) (*GW* 49; *NSI*

309). This other world becomes, as in Kafka's later epistolary musings on
his own death, Gracchus' own longed-for utopian destination.

Nostalgia and Modernity: Paradise Lost

As do Kafka's previous nostalgic journeys, Gracchus' voyage fails, and, even
more so than in *The Metamorphosis* and *The Trial,* Kafka leaves the reason
for the hero's non-arrival obscure. This lack of textual evidence is, at it was
in *The Trial,* troubling: If Gracchus (who apparently has done nothing
wrong) can be sentenced to wander the earth endlessly, then what about
the rest of us? Perhaps this fear explains the hermeneutical urgency surrounding Kafka's text: What has Gracchus done wrong? Why is he never
able to find his way home, or to heaven? When Walter Benjamin first addressed these questions in 1934, he turned to Gracchus' hubristic relation
to the "prehistoric world." For Benjamin, Gracchus' guilt—like that of the
father from "A Problem for the Father of the Family" ("Die Sorge des
Hausvaters")—results from his having "forgotten" the mythical world of
his ancestors.[2] This notion of blasphemous amnesia becomes foundational
for later critics, from the 1950s and 1960s, who emphasize the aspects of
Benjamin's reading that are connected to Judeo-Christian mythology.[3] In
such readings, as in many later ones, Gracchus is found guilty—as a descendant of Adam and Eve—of forgetting God: Gracchus (like all of us) is
guilty of "original sin."[4] Such an interpretation is initially upsetting ("we
are all as guilty as Gracchus"), but it is also liberating in a post-religious
world ("since God is dead, there is no one to punish us").

By the late seventies, on the heels of Derridean post-structuralism, Manfred Frank developed an influential response to Gracchus' guilt that was
similarly troubling and cathartic.[5] For Frank, Gracchus' guilt and endless
wandering issue from the nature of language itself. "Gracchus" is thus a (traditional) story of mythical promise gone awry, but with an important twist:
this promise (of a homecoming in Odysseus' Ithaca or in heaven) must necessarily fail because it is embedded in poetic language. Because metaphorical figuration performs transfers (from signifier to signified, from vehicle to
tenor),[6] Frank begins, a metaphor is always a metaphor of a journey. Journeys, likewise, cannot exist separately from the metaphors/stories that surround them. Thus, journeys determine metaphors and metaphors
determine journeys, and precisely because of this interdependence both
forms of transfer "slip"; that is, neither the traveler nor the metaphor's vehicle can make its way home. More clearly than the earlier errant heroes of
Bateau ivre and *The Flying Dutchman,* Frank claims, the vehemently "modern" "Gracchus" highlights language's and travel's interconnection: Gracchus is a traveler and a writer at once ("Nobody will read what I write

here") (*GW* 50; *NSI* 311). Because Gracchus' journey (like Kafka's story) never ends, Gracchus embodies metaphor's (failed) voyage. "Gracchus" is, Frank acknowledges, not the first narrative to depict the failure of the poetic *nostos,* but it is the first to take this cata-strophe literally. As Frank concludes, "Gracchus" "de-limits" (*ent-grenzt*) the metaphor of the journey of life.[7] Like the interpretation based on original sin, this reading is simultaneously unsettling (we are all homeless in language) and exonerating (everyone is linguistically dislodged, regardless of their actions).

Although I eventually take issue with Frank because his reading minimizes the possibility of Gracchus' historical/political agency, it is important first to expand on his notion of a specifically *nostalgic* fantasy behind Gracchus' journey. Frank argues that "Gracchus" challenges a long tradition of narratives about homecomings, a tradition that begins with *The Odyssey* and the Bible and carries through to psychoanalysis. According to this tradition, travel should provide the character with some form of return, as in the Freudian model, where death denotes the subject's return to an originary moment of anorganic stasis. Religious myths, likewise, promise the alienated ego a return trip: most famously in the legendary Christian chariot of God that will "carry me home." For Elias Canetti (writing just after Kafka), the fantasy of death as homecoming pervades most world religions.[8] Religion promises death in familiar groups, not as isolated individuals: When we die, we will not be alone. The Teutonic tradition, for example, places all men who have died since the beginning of time in Valhalla, where they will feast and imbibe endlessly. Every day they kill each other in battle, but each evening they rise again. The family of warriors thus grows interminably, because mortals are only added, never taken away. Representations of the angels and saints are, likewise, always communal. There is invariably an "enormous number" of these dead souls, Canetti claims, and they are all gathered around God.[9] They are received by Him. Just as they will never leave Him, they will never leave each other. They praise God and gladly surrender all remnants of individuality before his countenance: "This is," Canetti writes, "the only thing that they [the angels and the saints] still do, and they do it together." In a further example, Canetti reminds us that even the devils do not live alienated and alone: medieval Christianity insists that they, too, survive collectively.[10]

Gracchus' death, accordingly, should result in his safe journey to a new, Valhalla-like home. Gracchus confirms this fantasy when, at the moment of his death, he pronounces: "I had been glad to live and was glad to die" (*GW* 51; *NSI* 312–13). Just as he loved his mountainous Black Forest "*Heimat,*" Gracchus is now ready to accept this other world (*GW* 49; *NSI* 309). He recalls gladly stretching himself out on the pallet of his death ship (like the ancient Catullusian hero Kafka once read about) and rejoicing:

"Never had the mountains heard such song from me as was heard then by these four still shadowy walls [of my death ship]" (*GW* 51; *NSI* 312).[11] Death, Gracchus claims confidently, is a homecoming. It will be structurally equivalent to life, Thanatos will be the same as Eros: "I slipped into my winding sheet like a girl into her wedding-dress" (*GW* 51; *NSI* 313).[12]

But the unforeseen happens. Gracchus' death ship takes a "wrong turn," and he is forever denied entry into the "*Jenseits*" (*GW* 49; *NSI* 309). In Frank's terms, Gracchus' "economy of homecoming" is derailed.[13] As with Karl Rossmann in America and Josef K. in the Law courts, disorientation signals, for Gracchus, grave ontological danger (again, through the prefix "*ver-*": Gracchus' ship "went off course" ["*verfehlte die Fahrt*"]) (*GW* 49; *NSI* 309). Like Rossmann and K. from *The Castle,* the disoriented hunter is suspended forever between his first home in "life" (Rossmann's Prague, K.'s pre-narrative "*Heimat,*" Gracchus' Black Forest) and his second home in death ("Oklahoma" [*sic*], the Castle, the *Jenseits*).[14] The Hunter's death ship "*verfehlte die Fahrt,*" and he, an amalgam of Wandering Jew and Flying Dutchman, is kept from ever reaching the longed-for "other world." He thus never achieves death's nostalgic closure. If Gracchus' *Jenseits* is, as Frank claims, "mankind's true *Heimat,*" then Gracchus becomes, in Frank's terms, the prototype of the endless journeyer: suspended between departure and arrival, between signifier and signified.[15] Unlike Homer's and Dante's classical heroes, Gracchus never (even temporarily) reaches the realm of the dead. Instead, like Kafka's other 1917 protagonists, Odradek and the Country Doctor, Gracchus stays forever on "the great stairway" leading up to death (*GW* 49; *NSI* 309).[16] Gracchus thus shifts metaphors but not states, and even this metaphor mixing expresses his modern limbo. He is caught between the wreckage of two discredited metaphorical systems (myth and religion): rudderless on a stairwell, Gracchus lacks a reliable Charon to steer him across (or up) to the *Jenseits.*[17]

Gracchus shares with Kafka's other travelers this confusion between life and death. But he also shares with them their steadfast dissatisfaction with this state. Like Rossmann and K. (for most of *The Castle*), Gracchus retains a resolute belief in a felicitous beyond. Gracchus is Kafka's modern hero par excellence and not only because "God is dead." More significantly, Gracchus is modern because he refuses to accept this apparently given truth. Gracchus has a residual religious desire, a shameless yearning for a heavenly home in the *Jenseits* that renders him "negatively" religious—a state that, as Frank writes, is only possible in modernity: despite the apparent withdrawal of all transcendental goals, Gracchus is still not able to give up his faith in salvation.[18] He cannot properly and comfortably set up a home in this post-religious world. Tortured by archaic memories of a *Jenseits,* Gracchus still requires the theological grammar of grace and divine retribution. This conundrum is typical, Frank writes, of the general spirit of Kafka's work: "beneath dark skies that apparently blanket all hope, there still swells an unquenchable longing—pushing its way past everything attainable, not allowing the ship of life to rest."[19] This surplus of yearning is at the core of Gracchus' tragedy, even the secular one that I will outline now. As in Kafka's oft-misunderstood claim that there is "hope—only not for us," the problem is not the lack of hope but rather hope's unattainability.[20]

"A Bushman Is Aiming His Spear at Me": Colonial Nostalgia

Frank's mytho-poetic approach is not "wrong"; it insists correctly on the protagonist's voracious nostalgia. But his reading is blinkered. It neglects Kafka's deliberate displacement of his synchronic mytho-religious narrative of "homecoming" onto a specific, historical sphere. This history is significant because it points to a political urgency heretofore obscured. Scholars from the early 1970s had already sensed that Gracchus' story—and guilt—might be connected to a socio-political crime beyond original sin. Peter Beicken, dissatisfied with mytho-religious explanations, claimed that Gracchus seemed to be hiding something behind his nonplussed claims of innocence (his claim of being a hunter "in good order" [der Ordnung nach, GW 51; NSI 312]): Beicken maintains that the "basic truth" of Gracchus' guilt inheres in the arena of "real life." But Beicken, like Dietrich Krusche and Hartmut Binder before him, limits his speculations to Gracchus' interpersonal relations—finding Gracchus culpable in his "human inadequacy," his isolation, his "non-relatedness" (Nichtbezogensein).[21] In short, Gracchus' crime is that he keeps to himself. But Beicken does not consider shortcomings beyond this wilful remoteness.[22]

Writing five years after Beicken, Frank himself fleetingly acknowledged the possibility of a broader political guilt. After rupturing his own strictly mytho-poetic schema with a tangential remark concerning the "also imperial-political" motives behind modern travel narration, Frank focuses on a specific object described in the second of the four original "Gracchus" fragments: the only ornament adorning the walls of Gracchus' cabin. Gracchus remarks: "On the wall opposite me is a little picture, obviously of a bushman, who is aiming his spear at me and taking cover as best he can behind a magnificently painted shield" (GW 51; NSI 312, my emphasis). Frank asks the question: Why this peculiar image? Why a bushman? And why a threatening one? This gesture of killing recalls, Frank points out, the earlier image of Gracchus as a wolf and chamois killer. Frozen forever before the bed-ridden hunter's eyes, the bushman's gesture shadows Gracchus in his afterlife "like an affliction"—thus reminding him of his own antecedent violence.

The picture cries out to Gracchus, Frank argues, for the repayment of his "incomprehensible guilt/debt [*Schuld*]."[23]

But there is little further textual evidence to support this reading. Despite Gracchus' excessive protestations, there is no proof that he has not hunted wolves and chamois *der Ordnung nach*. The only thing we can say for sure about the bushman picture, then, is what Frank himself says: it temporarily draws our attention outside of Kafka's text and toward the "political" realm. Specifically, it pulls our imagination toward the era of "colonial fantasy"—of bushmen, shields, and spears—that coincides with Kafka's writing of "Gracchus."[24] Frank thus poses, however briefly, the secular, political question that he otherwise avoided: What has Gracchus done wrong beyond being descended, like all of us, from Adam and Eve? Or beyond being born into a world of slipping signification? Does not this 1917 seafaring European "hunter" in a cabin adorned with a bushman evoke the possibility of other crimes?

Kafka's text already intimates an answer: Toward the end of the first fragment, Gracchus tells us that "the fundamental error of my one-time death grins at me in my cabin" (*GW* 50; *NSI* 309–10). The bushman, who stares at him (perhaps grinning behind his shield), reminds Gracchus of this fundamental "error." But what error? Gracchus has not harmed any actual bushman nor has he committed any obvious colonial crime. A comparison with the more openly colonial "A Report to an Academy" (written almost simultaneously with "Gracchus") is instructive: There, Kafka's seafaring Europeans shoot an African ape and bring him back to Europe under the cruellest of conditions. Gracchus, conversely, captures nothing nor does he (unlike the sailors from "A Report to an Academy" or the explorer in "In the Penal Colony") ever travel to a properly colonial space. The only evidence of Gracchus' contact with the colonies is thus this little image (*"Bild"*) (*GW* 51; *NSI* 312).

In order to better understand Gracchus' mysterious "fundamental error," it is important to analyze this error as an error in relation to a *Bild*. By insisting on the bushman's status as an "image," Kafka emphasizes Gracchus' fantasy relationship to the bushman. His "fundamental error"—which grins mercilessly at Gracchus in his cabin—is thus primarily imaginative.[25] Gracchus has already intimated that the image's painter has likely made a mistake: "On ships one comes across many stupid depictions [representations, *Darstellungen*]; but this [the portrait of the bushman] is one of the stupidest" (*GW* 51; *NSI* 312). Gracchus, here, seems to be criticizing the cliché, "stupid" colonial fantasies that regularly decorate the walls of ships. But if this error is only the painter's (and not Gracchus'), then why does Gracchus also understand the picture to signify *his own* "fundamental error"? How does this picture become *Gracchus'* critical mistake?

To answer this question, we need to take a temporary leap into Kafka's biography, a leap that is more justifiable in "Gracchus" than in most other of Kafka's works because, as scholars have pointed out, Kafka's Czech name, *kavka* (jackdaw), translates into Italian as *graccio* (significant also because Gracchus' bark eventually docks in the Italian town of Riva del Garda). As Hartmut Binder has argued, the image of the bushman seems to be a projection of Kafka's enduring biographical longing for a virile existence in primitive nature: Kafka's first-person narrator from a 1909 fragment claims to have already read a "book about Red Indians" when he was only seventeen, and, three years later, Kafka presented a friend with *With the Xinqú Indians* (volume 20 of Schaffstein's *Little Green Books*), which described a nineteenth-century South American tribe on the verge of extinction (*WP* 221; *NSI* 175; see figure 24).[26] Moreover, Kafka admired one character's "Red Indian" posture; felt "downright detached, like an Indian" at an uninspiring social gathering; told Felice Bauer in 1914 that his heart "is beating with the fury of a schoolboy's after reading tales of Red Indians"; and, in the story "Children on the Country Road," employed "an Indian war-cry" to emphasize the speed and freedom of the running children. This admiration crystallizes in Kafka's own fictional "longing" to be a "Red Indian."[27]

Finally, ten years later, Kafka idealizes a "bushman," like the one hanging on Gracchus' wall. He, too, dreams of living in the "jungle" (bush, *Busch*), claiming that he is "jealous of the happy, inexhaustible nature that labors visibly out of sheer need (as do I), yet always satisfies all the demands its antagonist lays upon it. And so effortlessly, so musically" (*D* 416; *Ta* 910, trans. rev.). Kafka is "jealous" of a primitive life, he claims, and he imagines experiencing it. This is an instantiation of Kafka's ever-recurring "pledge of hope" (*Pfand der Hoffnung*): the infirm, city-dweller—weak with tuberculosis—irrationally imagines becoming the hero of one of his beloved colonial adventure books, and going to live among the Xinqú Indians or the tribesmen of German East Africa.[28] Gracchus' desire is similar: he longs for a primitive life now (in the twentieth century) that would correspond to his primal life then (as a hunter in the fifth-century Black Forest). He hopes to regain his "lovely" and primordial "native country" (*Heimat*), where "there were still wolves" and where his killing and flaying were "blessed" (*GW* 49–50; *NSI* 309–10). Because (as a modern hero) he can't relocate this *Heimat* in the happy hunting grounds of religion, he attempts to find it along "earthly waters."

Kafka's and Gracchus' desires may seem innocent enough, for they merely express the same longing for an alternate world that moved Kafka to tears when he read adventure books. But such longing is based on a "fundamental error" of representation ("*Darstellung*") that resembles the psychoanalytical perversion of fetishism.[29] Like the Freudian fetishist (who denies the absence of the maternal phallus), Gracchus/*kavka* insists on the presence of that which is already absent: the primitive, noble savage, untouched by European influence. This "taking-for-present of what is absent" is Gracchus' (and Kafka's) "fundamental" imaginative error.[30] Both character and author fetishistically deny the loss of a primitive way of life—and want to re-locate it at all costs.

But if Kafka projects his own fetishistic desires onto Gracchus' cabin wall, as Binder maintains, then why does Kafka not satisfy these desires in his fiction? Why does Gracchus not attain a second *Heimat* and instead remain eternally on a rudder-less boat "driven by the wind that blows in the nethermost regions of death" (*GW* 50; *NSI* 311)? I maintain that we can better understand this divergence if we entertain the possibility of Kafka splitting himself into two separate figures: the naïve, utopian *kavka* (appearing in the text as Gracchus) and, on the other hand, Franz Kafka, the writer, who both identifies with and criticizes Gracchus/*kavka*. Gracchus is thus only one aspect of "Kafka": the nostalgic "biographical" Kafka who, as we have seen above, imagined that a colonial adventure novel might be the "book of rules" for his life. Kafka, the writer, meanwhile, distances himself from this unsatisfactory self and thwarts its desires.

If Kafka uses "Gracchus" to deliberately subvert his own and Europe's fantasy, then his story fits into a literary tradition of deconstructing European colonialism from within: from Rimbaud's *Bateau ivre* (1871) to Conrad's *Heart of Darkness* (1902) and Kafka's own "In the Penal Colony" (1914). In each case, the savage finally rises up against the European.[31] What hurts most, in all of these cases, is the imaginary injury: not the threat to the Westerner's body, but rather the eradication of his fantasy of an alternate life. The dream of an "effortless" (if distressed) natural existence somewhere else, which used to comfort the hero in his European malaise, is finally gone. In Gracchus' case, this imaginary punishment is most extreme. Whereas Conrad's Marlowe and Kafka's Penal Colony voyager can return, however disillusioned, to Europe, Gracchus remains adrift, confronted every day anew with his own impossible fantasy. It is fitting that this punishment is imaginary, since Gracchus' "error" was an error of "*Darstellung.*" Just as Gracchus does not capture a real bushman or an African ape, neither does a real post-colonial bushman (like the charging prisoner from "In the Penal Colony") threaten Gracchus. Rather, he is simply sentenced to look, for hundreds of years, at a representation that he now regards as "stupid" (*GW* 51; *NSI* 312). This is Gracchus' only punishment, but it is a significant one: his sole visual stimulation reminds him every day of the preposterousness of his primitivist fantasy. He is caught in a hopeless cliché. His healing, exotic dream of a *Buschleben* (a "life in the bush" that would substitute for his lost Black Forest) is "*dumm,*" and there is no turning away from this (*D* 416; *Ta* 910).

Religion, Colonialism, and "Negative" Nostalgia

This historical disenchantment brings my reading of "The Hunter Gracchus" full circle: connecting the defeat of Gracchus' colonial fantasy with the (traditionally acknowledged) evacuation of his mytho-religious hope. The dovetailing of these two failures speaks to the interdependence of religion and colonialism in the modern world. With God now dead (and heaven undone), Europeans try, like Kafka's Gracchus, to reach the *Jenseits* by ship. Exoticism thus takes up religion's broken promise. As we learn in "In the Penal Colony," the broken-hearted European demands more than just political power from the colonies he dominates; he also calls for soul-salvaging transfiguration ("*Verklärung*") and deliverance ("*Erlösung*") (*MO* 141, 152; *DL* 226, 245). This 1917 sailing European, Gracchus, craves more than a suitable resting place in the land of the "bushman." Shut out by God, he demands a heaven on earth. This displacement of mythological and religious promise onto earthly travel creates the illogical surplus within colonial fantasy. When travelers superimpose heaven onto a "life in the bush," their already ravenous colonial desire becomes even more desperate. This explains the religious aspect of the Penal Colony officer's masochism as well as his stupendous insensitivity to bodies (his own and others') in extremis: with the longed-for redemption always only a few hours away, why quibble over this or that unjust torture?

If colonialism borrows religion's motivating promise of salvation, then it also inherits religion's disappointments. As Kafka made explicit in "In the Penal Colony," European colonialism had already, by 1914, destroyed its own utopian object of desire: the tropics had finally become as disappointing as Europe.[32] "The Hunter Gracchus" takes this disenchantment one step further. Gracchus can neither die as a martyr to his colonial fantasy (as does the officer) nor go back to Europe (as does the Penal Colony voyager). As we learn in the fourth and final fragment, Gracchus continues to sail earthly seas "for fifteen hundred years" (*GW* 52; *NSI* 378). Just as Gracchus illogically hopes for religious transcendence in a modern, godless world, he later hopes to transfer this impossible desire onto earthly travel: he imagines an idyllic second *Heimat* on a 1917 earth torn apart by colonialism and war. Gracchus refuses to accept the truly modern consequences of both a dead God and a frivolous colonialism. It is this nostalgia in spite of itself that sentences Gracchus to endless wandering, on the two metaphorical registers that structure the text: he is incapable of leaving *either* the religious "great stairway" *or* the historical "earthly seas."

Kafka's personal relation to Gracchus' stubborn nostalgia is complex. Whereas Binder claims that Kafka/*kavka* directly transposed his fantasies onto Gracchus/*graccio,* I maintain that Kafka split himself between the utopian *kavka*/Gracchus and Kafka himself, the self-critical writer. In this light, "The Hunter Gracchus" brings the thesis of my entire book into relief: Kafka's naïve fantasies of living high above "Mohammedan cemeteries" and "fields of sugar cane" coexist—as in *The Man Who Disappeared,* "In the Penal Colony," and *The Castle*—with Kafka's own critical investigation of this fantasy (*L* 35; *B* 49). And this examination remains dialectical throughout. Kafka never completely discards his exotic nostalgia, just as he never stops criticizing it. He thus resuscitates this fantasy in "Gracchus" in 1917 and, five years later, in his dream of leading a life in the jungle. This continually dialectical desire for and against exotic nostalgia defines much of what we still understand as the Kafkaesque: Kafka posits a world in which utopia exists, but not for us. Despite the claims of Deleuze and Guattari, Kafka is not completely capable of (or not interested in) discarding nostalgia.[33] Rather, he, like Benjamin, is still investigating modernity's "negative" relation to nostalgia: modernity's failure to discard the longing for the utopian second *Heimat* that is impossible to attain.[34] Kafka does not deny the desire for territory: he chooses to settle into a territory he calls the "borderland," *between* community and isolation, between life and death, between nostalgia and nomadism (*D* 396; *Ta* 871).[35] He cannot discard "home" just as he cannot discard homelessness.

Writing and Dying:
The Contented Death or the Illuminated Corpse?

In Kafka's post-religious, late-colonial world, there is thus no longer any utopia—on heaven or on earth. But this does not keep Kafka, like Gracchus, from longing for a primitive *Buschleben,* a journey to Palestine, or even what he called, in an unusually confident 1914 diary entry, a "contented" death: "On the way home told Max [Brod] that I shall lie very contentedly on my deathbed, provided the pain isn't too great" (*D* 321; *Ta* 708). As in his fantasy of the *Buschleben,* Kafka's desire mirrors Gracchus': he wants a death that is not life's Other but is rather life's complementary twin. Like Gracchus, who gladly wrapped himself into his winding sheet, Kafka boldly claims that he, too, will "rejoice in [his] own death." Kafka thus anticipates Gracchus' own fantasy of contentedly sailing toward the *Jenseits.*

Because he is a writer, Kafka continues, he has an even stronger investment in a contented death than does the fictional Gracchus/*kavka*. Faith in a contented death allows him to live *and* write without fear. This faith, in fact, is what determines the beauty of his writing:

> The best things I have written have their basis in this capacity of mine to meet death with contentment. All these fine and strongly convincing passages always deal with the fact that someone is dying, that it is hard for him to do, that it seems unjust to him, or at least harsh, and the reader is (at least in my opinion) moved by this. But for me, who believe that I shall be able to lie contentedly on my deathbed, such representations are secretly a game; indeed, in the death enacted I rejoice in my own death, hence calculatingly exploit the attention that the reader concentrates on death, have a much clearer understanding of it than he, whom I suppose will loudly lament on his deathbed, and for these reasons my lament is as perfect as can be, nor does it suddenly break off, as does a real lament, but dies beautifully and purely away. (*D* 321; *Ta* 708–9, trans. rev.)

Kafka's Gracchus-like fantasy of a contented death allows him to write "beautifully and purely" and, in so doing, to calmly "exploit" his reader's fear of and fascination with death.[36] Kafka's cynical self-praise refers to the mid-career works that are still viewed as some of his best and most prototypical: "The Judgment," *The Metamorphosis,* "In the Penal Colony," and *The Trial* all culminate in death scenes.

But Kafka's desire to depict death with such beautiful finality (and exploit his reader) wanes from "The Hunter Gracchus" onward, after which he no longer regards depicting death as the ultimate source of his writing's power. Whereas the pre-"Gracchus" heroes appear to die resolutely, if harshly and unjustly, the later, 1917 protagonists (the Country Doctor, Odradek, the Coal-Scuttle Rider) are unable to die. In 1914 Kafka seems to kill Josef K. and the Penal Colony officer,[37] but he then strands his Country Doctor forever in an eternal present tense and on an unfinishable journey.[38] As the Doctor claims at the end, "Never shall I reach home like this" (*MO* 161; *DL* 261). The Coal-Scuttle Rider ("Kübelreiter") is likewise unable to die, flying away in the story's final sentence into the "regions of the glaciers"—where he "disappear[s]" forever, yet seems to survive his own narrative through his present-tense voice (*MO* 198; *DL* 447).

Why does Kafka start depicting this state of limbo so vividly? I propose that this realm of the undead is a logical extension of Kafka's earlier attempt to depict the "exotic *Heimat*" in *Richard and Samuel, The Metamorphosis,* and *The Trial.* There, the exotic appeared, as in "Gracchus," not as an absolutely foreign space, but rather as the domain in between the domestic and the foreign. This middle space of, for example, Gregor Samsa's and Josef K.'s bedrooms is more exotic than traditionally exoticized spaces (Africa, India, South America) because it is at once familiar *and* strange. The undead Gracchus personifies this foreign-domestic space from Kafka's earlier work. Just as *Richard and Samuel's* exotic central Europe challenged the "superficial exoticism"[39] of writings about India and Africa, Gracchus' limbo unsettles the traditional conceptual opposition of (familiar) life and (exotic) death.

As Stanley Corngold has argued, Kafka probably began delineating this radically exotic state of limbo long before "Gracchus," despite Kafka's claims that he was then only interested in describing his characters' actual deaths. Concentrating on what he calls "the metamorphosis of the metaphor" in *The Metamorphosis,* Corngold counters earlier critics, who maintained that Kafka's *Metamorphosis* was uniquely powerful because it "literalized" metaphor.[40] According to such critics, the vehicle (the vermin [*"Ungeziefer"*]) was no longer separate from, or outside of, the tenor (Gregor Samsa). Rather, the vehicle and tenor were united. Samsa was not "like" an *Ungeziefer;* he became one. Through absolute metaphor's contaminating motion, these critics claimed, the distance between terms was effaced. The sentence's tenor—the familiar human term (Samsa)—was irreconcilably mixed with the vehicle—the unfamiliar non-human term (*Ungeziefer*): thus, the story's shocking, disturbing effect.

Corngold takes these critics one step further, claiming that Kafka does not "literalize" metaphor but rather "metamorphoses" it; that is, Kafka suspends the process of metaphorization midway. The fact that a man turns into a bug is unsettling, Corngold admits, but not nearly as unsettling as is a man transformed not completely into a bug and thus caught between man-ness and bug-ness. Gregor's family does not know (as we do not) where to place Gregor: Is he "our son" and "our brother," or is he an insect? If his family only knew how to answer this question, they could better decide how to act. Should they design the room the way an insect would like it or leave it the way their brother/son had preferred? Should they offer him/it Gregor's favorite meals or procure the rancid vegetables favored by vermin? In the end, it is precisely this *unheimliche* indeterminability, this undecidability of a metaphor suspended in the middle of its metamorphosis, that leads even Gregor's mother and sister to turn away from him. As Corngold points out, Gregor's indeterminability issues from the etymology of *Ungeziefer* (which derives, as Kafka likely knew, from the Middle High German word denoting "unclean animal not suited for sacrifice").[41] *Ungeziefersein* thus becomes the expression of Gregor's utterly liminal status. He is exotic unto himself, paradoxically self-strange: "Was he an animal [*Tier*]?" the confounded Gregor asks himself late in the story (*MO* 117; *DL* 185). What is upsetting and powerful in this story, as in "Gracchus," then, is not Gregor's complete Otherness, not his death. Rather it is Gregor's radically exotic state between familiarity and foreignness, between, in the case of "Gracchus," life and death.

In 1914, Kafka might have disagreed with this assertion regarding his story's effects, claiming instead that death itself—not limbo—gave his writing its unsettling force. Eight years later, however, Kafka corrects himself. In a letter to Max Brod written just two years before Kafka's own 1924 death, Kafka imagines living on in a "terrible" state of limbo after he dies. Kafka begins in quotations, as if he were talking to himself:

> "What I have playacted is really going to happen. I have not bought myself off by my writing. I died my whole life long and now I will really die [*wirklich sterben*]. My life was sweeter than other peoples'; my death will be that much more terrible. Of course the writer in me will die immediately, since such a figure has no base, no staying power, is less than dust. He is only barely possible in the broil of earthly life, is only a construct of sensuality. That is your writer for you. But I myself cannot go on living because I have not lived, I have remained clay, I have not blown the spark into fire, but only used it to illuminate my corpse." It will be a peculiar burial: the writer, insubstantial as he is, consigning the old corpse, the everlasting corpse, to the grave. I am enough of a writer to appreciate the scene with all my senses, or—and it is the same thing—to want to narrate it [. . .]. (*L* 334, *B* 385, trans. rev.)

What Kafka is describing here is, as I have argued in terms of *Der Verschollene,* the logical culmination of his project of transcending "superficial" exoticism. The writer does more than depict an exotic Other. He does more even than describe his own corpse. He "illuminates" a contradictory body that has never lived but is nonetheless dead. This body is Kafka's site of alterity beyond compare, and Kafka is "enough of a writer to appreciate" this. Kafka realizes that depicting death (as in his "exploit[ative]" pre-"Gracchus" endings) is too easy: it capitalizes on the reader's vicarious desire for utter difference. Such a strategy does not differ sufficiently from the popular exoticists' attempts to purvey difference through the officially Othered spaces of Latin America, Asia, and Africa. To transcend superficiality, then, Kafka needs to question the finality of alterity and of death.[42] He needs to illuminate the undead corpse.

This radical exoticism is the eternal state of dying that Kafka desires to achieve in his late writing. But what Kafka calls his "real" ego or self ("*mein wirkliches Ich*") does not live happily in this borderland between death and life (*L* 334; *B* 386). Increasingly ill with tuberculosis, Kafka realizes that he has not successfully bought himself off through writing. Because writing means "not death," but rather "the eternal torments of dying," Kafka's late-life fantasies always insist on an end to writing and its endless torments (*D* 302; *Ta* 546). Either he will go to Palestine (where, miraculously healthy, he will work as a waiter), or he will "really die." In both cases, he will leave once and for all this horrible textual limbo that resembles Gracchus' wanderings. Kafka hopes for a death that would—like the fantasy journey to the Promised Land—bring an end to his wandering *and* his writing. As he tells Brod later in the same 1922 letter (in an excerpt from my introduction worth re-citing here):"I may not go out of Bohemia, next I will be confined to Prague, then to my room, then to my bed, then to a certain position in bed, then to nothing more. Perhaps at that point I will be able to renounce the joy of writing voluntarily—voluntariness and joyousness are what count" (*L* 335; *B* 386). Kafka's imagined final state thus brings with it the cessation of writing, the end of metaphor's indeterminate metamorphoses, the end of "dying." Kafka's death, he hopes, will be a reverse voyage into final stillness, as in the Freudian model. Instead of going to Palestine, Kafka will stay home and die. He will never leave Bohemia, Prague, his bed, a certain position in bed, and then will devolve into "nothing."

Just don't get caught half-way. Kafka says as much in his September 13, 1923 letter to Robert Klopstock:"the danger remains that the voyage to Palestine will shrink to a trip to Schelesen. May it at least remain that, rather than end up as the elevator trip from the Altstädter Ring to my room" (*L* 380–81; *B* 445). Either Palestine or death, but not—like the protagonist of Kafka's "The Businessman" ("Der Kaufmann")—an elevator ride: caught between here and there (*MO* 22; *DL* 23). Kafka's final journey, like Gracchus', must remain a regressive voyage: past the exotic space of language, toward an original *Heimat* in a nothingness. Even more than a "life in the jungle," this final voyage proffers Kafka an ultimate respite from sites of transit, from the middle ground of endless dying.

This nostalgic desire for a second home beyond words clarifies the trajectories of Karl Rossmann in America, K. in the Castle village, the hunter Gracchus on the earthly seas, and Kafka himself as he plans his late-life impossible journey to Palestine. As Kafka writes to Milena Jesenská in 1923, apparently referring to the 1922 letter to Brod, he never really thought he could go to Palestine. Rather, the journey to "Palestine" is dependent on—and, in a certain sense, equivalent to—lying in bed and dying: it is the fantasy of a man who knows that he will never leave his bed again. Kafka sums up: "If I'm never going to leave my bed why shouldn't I go at least as far as Palestine?" (*LM* 236; *BM* 319). Death and Palestine, these become the goals of Kafka's exotic nostalgia. Both promise an end to writing, and also help us to understand the irony of Gracchus' apparent complaint that "nobody" will read what he writes. I maintain that this is precisely what Kafka desires when he asks Max Brod to destroy his works. For only by having his writing destroyed could Kafka avoid immortality; that is, the torturous condition of being *like* a dead man.[43] By having no one read what he writes, Kafka might achieve a thorough, emancipatory nostalgia. The power of Kafka's desire, however, is equalled only by his knowledge that writing—as I will investigate in the epilogue—denies its own silencing. Even after the body dies, writing effaces the resting place toward which its author hopefully pointed.

Epilogue

Kafka's Final Journey

The failed nostalgic journeys of Kafka's protagonists—Karl Ross-mann, Josef K., the Penal Colony officer, K. from *The Castle*—mirror Kafka's own never-completed utopian journeys, about which he fantasizes even more as he gets closer to death. His earlier dreams of emigrating to Spain, South America, the Azores, and Madeira begin to solidify into the enduring late-life fantasy of Palestine: like Moses, Kafka wants to travel to the Promised Land before he dies (*D* 394; *Ta* 867). He moves in with the young Galician Jew, Dora Diamant, and begins learning Hebrew in preparation for an eventual journey. Palestine appears over and over again in his late letters and diaries: he watches a film about it, struggles through a Hebrew novel by a Palestinean writer, even sets an approximate date for his trip (October 1923) (*D* 395; *Ta* 870; *L* 388; *B* 453; *LM* 236; *BM* 319). But such a voyage was, for Kafka, always impossible. Kafka claims later, "[I] wanted to go to Palestine. I would certainly not have been up to it, am also fairly unprepared in He-brew and other respects; but I had to give myself something to hope for" (*LO* 84; *BO* 146). Palestine was the ultimate u-topia: one cannot travel there; one can only "trace one's way [to Palestine] with a finger across the map" (*L* 201; *B* 237, trans. rev.).

But the failure of the dying man's utopian journey leaves him living in fear of limbo. Kafka is afraid that, like the hunter Gracchus, he will never find a place to rest, will wander endlessly, will never "really die" (*L* 334; *B* 385). His hopes thus shift—logically, for Kafka—to the destruction of his writing. Because writing signifies eternal dying (an endless postponement of death), only writing's final destruction can save the writer. Kafka imag-ines that—by preventing the endless, posthumous circulation of his texts—he might finally gain a resting place (not unlike the Sugar Baron's in South America). "Nobody will read what I write here," Kafka writes hopefully,

imagining that this anonymity, like Gracchus', will grant him a posthumous peace (*GW* 50; *NSI* 311). Writing's annihilation might allow him to
cease being what he had chosen to become: a writer, prowling the exotic
space between life and death. If no one reads his writing, Kafka imagines,
he might escape Gracchus' limbo—and the ghosts that inhabit it—and
reach death's Promised Land.

Letters/Literature:
An Intercourse with Ghosts

Kafka's fear of an exotic limbo in writing issues at least partially from his
relation to writing's "ghosts." Kafka already acknowledged his "own ghost"
to Milena Jesenská in 1922, claiming that he had nourished it through his
prolonged "intercourse with ghosts"; that is, through letter writing (*LM*
223; *BM* 302). Letter writing, according to Kafka, depends on two spectres: the absent self and the absent interlocutor. Beyond these two, there is
a vast community of ghostly offspring watching, listening, and devouring:
"Writing letters [. . .] means exposing oneself to ghosts," who vampirically "drink up" our letters and multiply immensely. Letter writing is thus
never a private exchange; it is staged before a voracious and ever-prolifer-
ating group of ghostly readers.

For this reason, epistolary exchange serves as a model for literature itself. Letters and literature share the same Latin root in the plural form of
"letter" (as in letter of the alphabet, *litterae*), and only our relatively new,
university-sanctioned, "scientific" form of literary studies has constructed
the strict separation of literature from letters (now deemed "private" and
"autobiographical").[1] But Kafka insisted that letters are *not* private, that
ghostly readers hover above them, and that, finally, the literary and epistolary modes always mix. Kafka's published writings are almost always letters
of a sort, addressed "to" someone (*Meditation* to Max Brod, "The Judgment" to Felice, *A Country Doctor* to his father). His letters, conversely, were
often directed over the head of the addressee, toward a spectral readership,
and he sometimes simply mailed (unpublished) literature instead of a letter: for example, his only copy of a story manuscript ("Before the Law")
to Felice; his diaries (which contained many unpublished fictions) to
Milena; and his "Letter to his Father" (now seen as a literary work in its
own right) to Milena instead of his father.[2] Kafka seemed to understand,
long before Jacques Derrida, that literature is always a ghostly missive that
may or may not arrive at its destination.[3]

Unlike Derrida, however, Kafka had no sense that this ghostly "letterary" interchange might be playful.[4] Because Kafka was afraid of ghosts (especially his own), he wanted Brod to destroy his manuscripts and thus

prevent his posthumous wandering. For Kafka, being a ghost meant being, like the angels in Wim Wenders' *Wings of Desire,* greedily hovering at the fringes of life, "waiting and lusting" vampirically after human sensuality (*LM* 225; *BM* 304). In order for Kafka to free himself finally from such ghostly *Verkehr,* he sensed that he had to interrupt the stream of letters nourishing his own and others' spectres. Kafka thus started with the epistles themselves, claiming in late January 1922 to bask in the warmth engendered by a "whole pile" of letters going up in flames (*L* 317; *B* 369). But he can only "escape" these ghosts if he destroys his literature, too—once vowing to Dora that he would "burn everything that he had written" in order to "free his soul from these 'ghosts.'"[5]

One need not claim to know anything about the afterlife to argue, like Maurice Blanchot, that Kafka seemed to have a "right" to literary mortality: a right to have his sense of a ghostly afterlife taken seriously.[6] A look at Kafka's fictions from 1917 (the year of his first tubercular outbreak) reveals a consistent and disturbing fear of becoming a ghost. The hunter Gracchus is dead but "to some extent [. . .] alive too" (*GW* 49; *NSI* 309). The Country Doctor, likewise, finds himself in a state of limbo: Naked and "exposed to the frost of this unhappiest of ages," he is trapped at the midway point of an never-ending journey and an interminable story (*MO* 161; *DL* 261). In these works (as well as in "A Problem for the Father of the Family" and "The Coal-Scuttle Rider"), we see Kafka's ongoing fears of immortality distilled.

Immortality's Curse:
Scheintod, Herzstich, and the Everlasting Writer

Kafka's fictional fears of joining the ranks of the undead had some scientific justification: a widespread fin de siècle fear of the *Scheintod* ("apparent" or "premature" death). The first *Scheintod* (and concomitant escape from the coffin) was recorded in 1357, but the *Scheintod* only appeared as a collective fear in the nineteenth century.[7] According to Edgar Allan Poe and others, the prematurely dead man looked exactly like a dead man but was still alive.[8] He maintained an intact nervous system, blood circulation, and all other vital functions (albeit at an undetectable minimum). In order to keep from inadvertently burying someone alive, doctors (still working without EKGs and EEGs) relied on, among other things, the *Herzstich* ("perforation of the heart" with a stiletto-like blade), which supposedly spared the deceased a possible rise from the grave. Contemporaries of Kafka who feared being buried alive or aimlessly wandering the earth specifically requested the *Herzstich;* their ranks included Gustav Mahler, Arthur Schnitzler, and, in a graphic 1910 account, the father of the hero

of Rilke's *The Notebooks of Malte Laurids Brigge*.[9] Kafka's famous protagonist, Josef K., likewise died through a *"Herzstich"*: three years before Gracchus begins wandering the earth, two impeccably dressed men thrust a
"long, thin, double-edged" knife into Josef K.'s heart and turn it there
twice (*T* 230–31; *P* 311–12). This heart perforation seems to spare Josef K.,
unlike his literary descendants, the death-like trance of the undead.[10]

Kafka sensed that he, too, might need to protect himself from a *Scheintod*. In 1911, he took part in a "discussion of *Scheintod* and *Herzstich*"
("Mahler asked for a *Herzstich,*" Kafka notes), and, approximately seven
years later, he created a fragmentary meditation on the in-between state of
the *Scheintoten:* "not even in our thoughts should we wish to be alive and
in the coffin without any chance of return" (*D* 443; *Ta* 966; *WP* 430; *NSII*
142). But since Kafka was "made of literature"—existing as "nothing but
one single word"—his real worries centered on the possibility of a literary
Scheintod; that is, an undead state brought about by "letters" remaining in
circulation after the death of the body (*LF* 304; *BF* 444; *LM* 25; *BM* 33).
For Kafka, letterary traffic tragically determined *and* outlived physical
death, as we learn in the "Dream" fragment connected with *The Trial*: Josef
K. hops into his grave, only to see his own name on the gravestone above
him racing across "with mighty flourishes" (*MO* 186; *DL* 298). In the main
text of *The Trial,* K. imagines (in addition to twice considering suicide) that
he might finally end his trial only through scriptive annihilation (*T* 158; *P*
213–14). K. longs for this radical halt to textual circulation, just as Kafka
would later request from Brod the conflagration.

Two years before his death, Kafka wrote the long letter to Brod cited
in the preceding chapter, which describes a death scenario that, I think,
Brod should have considered to be part of Kafka's famous last testament.
In fact, this 1922 letter was written between the two extant versions of
Kafka's testament and, as such, forms a middle panel in the triptych of
Kafka's final requests to Brod. This middle panel supplies two possible images of Kafka's death, depending on which decision Brod makes: either the
"terrible" image of the writer illuminating his own corpse or the "joyous"
one of the writer and his writing perishing at the same triumphant moment (*L* 334–35; *B* 385–86; see chapter seven). The two actual testaments,
written on either end of this letter, outline the necessary legal narrative.[11]
In the first, 1921 testament, the lawyer Kafka lays the groundwork for realizing the blissful image, the double annihilation—by giving Brod the
right to retrieve all of Kafka's writings "in my name" (*T* 266; *EFII* 365).
The second testament, from November 1922, completes this legal project
by naming the recipients now holding the wayward letters ("Frau Felice
M, Frau Julie née Wohryzek, and Frau Milena Pollak"). Kafka finally closes
all legal loopholes by outlawing "exceptions," even using rare underlining

to emphasize this: "everything without exception," "without exception and preferably unread," "all these things without exception" are to be "burned, and I beg you to do this as soon as possible" (*T* 266–67; *EFII* 422). In this last testament, Kafka allows six of his printed works to "stand," but he hopes that they, too, will eventually sink out of sight, get *verschollen* or "lost," like Karl Rossmann in America.[12]

Corpse/Corpus:
The Prospects of Burning

The problem with ghosts is that they, like Hamlet's armor-clanking father, are immaterial and material at once. As Kafka knew, writing is, similarly, both an imaginary corpus and a substantial body of work. His fascination with writing's materiality is well-known: he obsessed over his and others' handwriting, the quirks of the typewriter, the typeface of his published works, the stationery that he and his epistolary lovers touched and kissed, and, finally, Milena's 1920 telegraph, which he fetishized, carrying it around with him and fingering it in his pocket. But Kafka was equally attentive to the opposite trajectory—the human body's transformation into a readable sign. He repeatedly imagined the body metamorphosing into messages, into pieces of mail. Already in *Wedding Preparations in the Country,* Kafka's protagonist dreamt of sending his own clothed body to his fiancée while he himself (the writer) stayed at home (*WP* 11; *NSI* 17). This fantasy of becoming mail grew stronger and more literal in the course of Kafka's career, culminating, as discussed in chapter six, in his desire to crawl into every object he sent to Milena in 1920 (*LM* 141; *BM* 189).

But if the body is also a text, then the burning of one's writings will solve only half of the problem. For, as Kafka knew, bodies, like that of the hunter Gracchus, can continue to create meaning long after they have "died." At first glance, then, it is surprising that Kafka neglected to include his body in the "everything" that Brod was to burn.[13] Following centuries of illegality (encouraged by the Roman Catholic Church), cremation had in fact become legal again in Europe in the 1870s. Just five years before Kafka's birth, modern Europe's first crematorium opened in the German city of Gotha (a few hours' train ride from Prague). In the course of Kafka's lifetime, crematoria expanded commensurately with both Rome's weakening and the rail system's burgeoning, which increased the supply of clients from far away.[14] "Cremation societies" promoted the practice of cremation on hygienic and land-conservationist grounds, but the populace's long-standing worries about the *Scheintod* could not have been far beneath the discursive surface.[15] George Bernard Shaw (whom Kafka admired) points ironically to the fears of the living, that they will someday be outnumbered by the living dead: Cremation is necessary, Shaw asserts, because the dead might one day "crowd the living off the earth if [earthly burial] could be carried out to its end of preserving our bodies for their resurrection on an imaginary day of judgment."[16] Even more certainly than the *Herzstich,* cremation irrefutably countered such fears: it guaranteed that the body, reduced to ash, would not wander after death. As cremation became a more regular practice, the *Herzstich,* not surprisingly, faded into historical obscurity.

Why did Kafka not ask to have his physical body—like his body of work—burned? Perhaps he realized that the annihilation of his corpse would not save him from immortality. Whereas writing's materiality *can* be destroyed (Kafka knew this from burning manuscripts and letters at various points in his life),[17] the body's immateriality cannot. The body carries on posthumously because the writer (who cannot die) has already memorialized it. As Blanchot argues, writing is paradoxically that which makes us dead when we are still alive and immortal when we are dead: the body's death through writing is what makes it unable to die.[18] Cremations and burials, Kafka knew, are not final. They are games for ghostly writers, who, through ritual, achieve a Pyrrhic victory over death. The spectral writer "narrates" and "appreciates" the funeral of "I myself," as Kafka told Brod, even going so far as to "illuminate" his own body (*L* 334; *B* 385, trans. rev.). Kafka does not require that his body be burned (nor did he, after 1914, ever again perforate a heart in his fiction) because he knew that such a ceremony only supplies *more* nourishment for the ghosts. And the futility of burning a body suggests, anew, something about the pointlessness of burning writing: If writing, like a body, persists in ghostly form after its destruction, then why bother destroying it? As Kafka writes to Milena several months before penning his final testament, "nothing helps anymore" (*LM* 223; *BM* 302). Perhaps this, too, was a (contradictory) secret message to his surviving friends: my writing will feed the spectres whether you burn it or not.

Final Journey:
Leichenwagen and Imperial Message

Since Kafka did not ask anyone to burn his corpse, no controversy surrounds his survivors' decision to transport it from the Kierling sanatorium near Vienna—where he died on June 3, 1924—back to Prague (see figure 25). I have not been able to reconstruct the journey of Kafka's body, but the general history of corpse-transport in the 1920s provides us with the ground for some speculation. Kafka's corpse would have been initially sent to the sanatorium's mortuary and then soldered shut inside a metal coffin (according to international transport regulations).[19] This hermetically sealed coffin was then probably placed inside a second one (again, according to regulations) and then, on June 5, slipped into a horse-drawn hearse (Kierling was too rural for motorized hearses, which first appeared in Austria in 1922).[20] This hearse would have proceeded to the Franz Josef Bahnhof in Vienna, where the coffin would have been placed in either a regular freight car (alone or with several other coffins) or in a special, more expensive "corpse car" (*Leichenwagen*) (see figures 26–27).[21] The primarily financial choice between freight car en masse, freight car alone, and *Leichenwagen* would have been left to Kafka's family and friends.[22]

Regardless of which of these routes Kafka's mourners finally chose, the possibilities for Kafka's last train journey uncannily re-create Kafka's own earlier vision of a phantasmagoric life after death: the corpse lives on through art—perversely "illuminated," "appreciated," and "narrated." The fin de siècle freight cars and, especially, *Leichenwagen* were designed to provide this kind of decadent allure to the deceased's final ride. When loading corpses, the freight cars were specially decorated: black cloth somberly trimmed their walls, and a chalk cross adorned their outside panels.[23] The *Leichenwagen,* introduced to the general public in 1905, took this aestheticizing impulse even further.[24] As a 1905 promotional article in the *Eisenbahntechnische Zeitschrift* (*Technical Railway Journal*) claimed, the new *Leichenwagen* even kept the deceased's tastes in mind: their goal was to create a more "pious space" for him or her. This piety materialized itself in a highly stylized "death chamber" where, in true decadent style, art was the only god: the room was stripped of all "denominational markers" but nonetheless retained a seductive "chapel-like character" (see figure 28).[25]

As in Kafka's fantasy of his own death, the proper "illumination" of the dead person produced death's perverse and mystical appeal. The *Eisenbahntechnische Zeitschrift's* description of the lighting system reads like the background setting for a decadent, exoticist novel, on a par with Mirbeau's *Torture Garden*. First, sunlight enters the death chamber through the *Leichenwagen's* ceiling: "Violet arabesque glass"—inserted laterally in the roof—"tints the penetrating streams of sunlight a faint blue, so that the white ceiling and wall areas are overlain, shimmering, with a delicate blue veil." The side lighting complements this illumination from above: "the mostly subdued light entering through the permanently frosted side windows gently animates the darkened wall areas beneath, relieving these of their sepulchral appearance." When the sun goes down, the "blue hue of the lampshade" creates the same "effect" as the skylight, leading to the desired "uttermost elegant, peaceful mood." This ambience lighting is finally "supported most effectively by the [death chamber's] wainscoting." The author describes this illuminated wainscoting in elaborate detail: from the "white, fireproof pegamoid, framed with slender black ebony-mouldings" to the pattern on this pegamoid, which, designed especially for *Leichenwagen,* "displays a crown with funereal plumes protruding downward and, between these individual crowns and boughs, a garland winding its way in and out."[26] In the center of all of this is the coffin, resting on a podium. With the "illuminated" and displayed dead body as the scene's focal point, the *Leichenwagen* completes Kafka's earlier vision of a "terrible" death: the corpse never really dies, nor does it ever make it to Palestine. Rather, it is lit up, turned into art, and thus forced to continue functioning as a sign in the exotic space between life and death. But a sign of what?

Kafka's transported corpse functions as the initial, un-authorized, posthumous letter sent to his readers: the coterie of some 100 devotees awaiting his body in Prague. When the coffin arrives, it is again displayed, on a bier, and Brod and Johannes Urzidil read eulogies. Kafka's body immediately begins to create meaning, if only through the probably apocryphal story (later vehemently refuted by Brod) of two women, each claiming to be Kafka's wife, fighting at his open grave.[27] Not long after this corpse completed its journey to its first "readers," Kafka's literary corpus began to make the trip as well. Authorized by the first part of Kafka's testament, Brod starts to request and, later, demand that everything "in the way of diaries, manuscripts, letters, sketches" be returned to him. Already by July 17 (just one month after Kafka's burial), Brod announces publicly, in *Die Weltbühne,* the surprisingly expansive breadth of Kafka's (textual) remains.[28]

Kafka's body arrives in Prague as does Gracchus' in Riva: as a ghost. It is a missive without a dispatcher or, more accurately, a package mailed by Kafka's mourners to themselves. His body is a text, but not one that Kafka has written or sent. It is a text without a master, a message mailed by recipients. Authorless, Kafka's corpse prepares his very first readers for the eventual difficulties of reading his writing. Like the emperor in Kafka's exotic parable, "An Imperial Message" (a travel story, and the final story Kafka's mourners read aloud at his funeral), Kafka's dead body exists at once as missive and corpse. His body, like the emperor's, is ostentatiously displayed "before all the spectators of his death" (*MO* 175; *DL* 281). At the same time, his valued words (whispered, over the years, into the ears of Brod and other messengers) are now traveling back toward Prague. In the story as in life, the imperial originator is dead by the time the mail arrives. The message is always delivered without author/ity. And the recipients of the imperial message, like the "forlorn" German colonists Kafka imagined living in German East Africa, read this message "through and through" (*L* 23; *B* 35). Like Kafka's body, his writings are the message from a dead emperor, or, with Kafka's final journey in mind, the message *is* the dead emperor: an undecipherable text sent by mourners to themselves in a time of need. We are this spectral "throng," Kafka insists, and the corpse/corpus—even though it is our own—is never safe with us (*MO* 175; *DL* 281). We travel with it and drink it up "along the way." This nourishment is precisely what enables us "to multiply so enormously," read and travel even more, and, in so doing, bring "wrack and ruin to the souls"—living or dead—"of the world" (*LM* 223; *BM* 302).

Notes

Introduction

1. Rolf Goebel uses the phrase "textual traveler" in relation to Kafka in his *Constructing China: Kafka's Orientalist Discourse* (Columbia, SC, 1997), 1. In this sense, Kafka resembles Kant, who barely left his home town and never left Prussia yet, in the polemical formulation of Thomas de Quincey, read *no* books other than those describing voyages and travels (*The Works of Thomas de Quincey* [Cambridge, 1877], 9:450). Cf. Willi Goetschel, *Constituting Critique: Kant's Writing as Critical Praxis,* trans. Eric Schwab (Durham, NC, 1994), 31, 193n43.
2. Barthes refers to this "releas[ing]" detail as the "biographème" and gives as examples "Sade's white muff, Fourier's flowerpots, Ignatius' Spanish eyes" in Barthes, *Sade, Fourier, Loyola,* trans. Richard Miller (New York, 1976), 9.
3. "The Second Home" is the title of the "most important" chapter of the Schaffstein book that seemed to Kafka to be "about myself" (*LF* 532; *BF* 738), Oskar Weber's *Der Zuckerbaron: Schicksale eines ehemaligen deutschen Offiziers in Südamerika* (Cologne, 1914), 83.
4. This cousin was traveling through Prague in 1906. Kafka finds him intriguing and finally persuades him to stay on another day so that Kafka can introduce him to Brod (*L* 22; *B* 34).
5. Cited in Max Brod, *Franz Kafka: A Biography* (New York, 1995), 119.
6. According to Brod, Kafka often quoted Flaubert's sentence, "ils sont dans le vrai" (Brod, *Franz Kafka,* 98).
7. Brod, *Franz Kafka,* 100.
8. Brod's afterword to the first, 1927 edition of Kafka's *Amerika* (Frankfurt a. M., 1991), 260.
9. Laurence Rickels, "Writing as Travel and Travail: *Der Prozess* and 'In der Strafkolonie,'" *Journal of the Kafka Society of America,* 5 (1985): 32. Despite the lack of a comprehensive analysis, sporadic references to travel and the traveler figure do appear throughout the secondary literature. I will address these at the pertinent points in my argument.
10. Oskar Weber, *Zuckerbaron,* 83.
11. Waldemar Bonsels, *Indienfahrt,* in *Wanderschaft zwischen Staub und Sternen: Gesamtwerk* (Munich, 1980), 3:44.

12. Allen Thiher has noticed a similar relation between travel and writing in the stories from Kafka's *Nachlaß*: "Here we might lay hold of one of the basic rules of Kafka's textual games: forward motion generates the spaces to be filled by that motion. This motion, moreover, points to the power of mere going to generate the metaphors that in turn appear to valorize the going itself, whatever be the goal of this movement" (Allen Thiher, "The *Nachlaß:* Metaphors of *Gehen* and Ways Toward Science," in *Kafka and the Contemporary Critical Performance,* ed. Alan Udoff [Bloomington, 1987], 258).

13. Gilles Deleuze and Félix Guattari, *Kafka: Toward a Minor Literature,* trans. Dana Polan (Minneapolis, 1986), 35; Charles Grivel, "Travel Writing," *Materialities of Communication,* ed. Hans Ulrich Gumbrecht and K. Ludwig Pfeiffer (Stanford, 1994), 254 (Grivel's emphasis).

14. Scott Spector argues that "Zionism" and "marriage" converge in Kafka's fantasy during his correspondence with Felice Bauer (Scott Spector, *Prague Territories: National Conflict and Cultural Innovation in Franz Kafka's Fin de Siècle* [Berkeley, 2000], 143).

15. One of the most brilliant analyses of Kafka's use of the postal system *against* Felice remains Michel Cournot's "Toi qui as de si grandes dents . . . ," *Le Nouvel Observateur* (April 17, 1972), 59–61. Other discussions of letters, travel, and technology appear in my chapter six, "The Traffic of Writing."

16. Grivel, "Travel Writing," 254.

17. In *The Interpretation of Dreams* (1900) Freud first refers to travel as a dream-symbol for death: death is the "undiscover'd country from whose bourn no traveler returns." Seventeen years later, in the *Introductory Lectures on Psycho-Analysis,* Freud specifies that "dying is replaced in dreams by *departure,* by a *train journey."* He refers to the colloquial notion of death as "the last journey" as well as to the ancient rituals in which one always *journeys* to the "land of the dead": in Ancient Egypt, for instance, *The Book of the Dead* "was supplied to the mummy like a Baedeker to take with him on the journey." See *The Standard Edition of the Complete Psychological Works of Sigmund Freud,* ed. James Strachey (London, [1953–74]), 4:255 and 15:153, 161.

18. This tendency to identify Kafka's work with a cramped, static existence within Prague began with the excellent pioneering work of Klaus Wagenbach, who wrote in 1958 what remains the most influential critical biography of Kafka's early years. As Wagenbach points out, Kafka was born "early enough to experience the labyrinth of the former [Prague] ghetto, the Josefstadt. The house names are indicative of the ghostly life that reigned in its narrow, tortuous streets until the turn of the century: 'The Mouse Hole,' 'The Left Glove,' 'Death,' 'Gingersnap,' and most curiously of all, a little house called 'No Time.'" Wagenbach insists on a connection between this cramped world and Kafka's writing: "For Kafka, the 'unnatural isolation' of Prague had serious consequences. In his work the city limits are almost never crossed; nature seldom emerges and then only in a sketchy

fashion. In this 'lifeless' sphere, the experience of things becomes much more intense and painful" (Klaus Wagenbach, *Franz Kafka: Eine Biographie seiner Jugend, 1883–1912* [Bern, 1958], 68, 93; the translation [slightly revised] is from Wagenbach, "Prague at the Turn of the Century," in *Reading Kafka: Prague, Politics, and the Fin de Siècle*, ed. Mark Anderson [New York, 1989], 27, 48).

19. There is now a travel guide available for literary pilgrims: Wagenbach's *Kafkas Prag: Ein Reiselesebuch* (Berlin, 1993) (translated into English as *Kafka's Prague: A Travel Reader* [Woodstock, N.Y., 1996]). Among the other writers arguing that the effect of the Kafkaesque depends on the restrictive topography of Prague (past and present) are Kafka's Prague contemporary, Pavel Eisner, and Kafka's Prague descendant, Milan Kundera (Pavel Eisner, *Franz Kafka and Prague* [New York, 1950]; Milan Kundera, "Somewhere Beyond," *Cross-Currents* 3 [1984]: 61–70).

20. Lukács devalues Kafka's work from a Marxist perspective as a prototypically "sick," politically "static" modernism (as opposed to Thomas Mann's "healthy," "progressive" social realism). Picking up on Lukács' metaphor of motion, I demonstrate throughout this book that, although Kafka's fictions are not "progressive," they are nonetheless not "static." Rather, Kafka offer us the motion of "eluding": escaping pre-scribed itineraries, discovering ways off of beaten discursive paths. For more on the stakes involved in "eluding," see especially my chapters four and five (Georg Lukács, "Franz Kafka oder Thomas Mann?," in *Wider den Mißverstandenen Realismus* [Hamburg, 1958], 86, 90). For the Marxist opposition to Lukács' views on Kafka, see Theodor Adorno's various remarks on Kafka, most concentrated in "Notes on Kafka," in *Prisms,* trans. Samuel and Shierry Weber (Cambridge, MA, 1981), 243–71.

21. As Rudy Koshar points out, the nineteenth century gave rise to modern tourism for a number of reasons but most notably because of the development of the railroad and because capitalism was now "unleashed" (leading to an unheard-of "capital accumulation" that created "both the necessity and the means for innovative leisure practices") (Rudy Koshar, *German Travel Cultures* [New York, 2000], 2–3). I would add to this list the unprecedented colonial expansion of the nineteenth century: by the final third of the nineteenth century, virtually the entire world was under European dominance and thus open to tourism. Koshar offers an excellent introduction to the vast literature on travel and tourism (1–18). I would like specifically to mention Dean MacCannell's groundbreaking sociological study, *The Tourist: A New Theory of the Leisure Class* (New York, 1976) (to be discussed in chapter one) and James Buzard's in-depth discussion of the early years of middle-class tourism (specifically, the attempt of the "traveler" to distance himself from the "tourist") in *The Beaten Track: European Tourism, Literature, and the Ways to Culture, 1800–1918* (Oxford, 1993), 1–79. On the development of the railway and its effect on the way the traveler saw the world, see Wolfgang Schivelbusch's classic *The Railway*

Journey: The Industrialization of Time and Space in the 19th Century (Berkeley, 1986).

22. *Palestine and Syria,* the first extra-European Baedeker guide, appeared in 1875. Cook started bringing travelers to Palestine already in 1869, just three years after the first Cook tour of America.

23. As MacCannell writes, "for moderns, reality and authenticity are thought to be elsewhere" (MacCannell, *The Tourist,* 3).

24. See *EFI* 95, 104, 119, 137, 182, 189, 191. As Hannelore Rodlauer points out in her dissertation on Kafka's Paris diaries, Kafka and Brod oriented themselves according to their Baedeker's *Paris* "in order to best use their available time in the terms of a conventional 'educational journey' [*Bildungsreise*]" (Hannelore Rodlauer, "Kafkas Pariser Tagebuch," Ph.D. diss., Vienna, 1984), 214.

25. Brod, *Franz Kafka,* 120–21.

26. K.'s uncle (whose Panama hat marks him as a traveler) tells K. that taking a trip to the countryside is the best way for him to get beyond the court's reach (*T* 88, 93–94; *P* 118, 125–26).

27. In a certain sense, the Romantic era, too, is characterized by voyages—mundane and fantastic—and I will discuss Goethe's travel diaries in depth in chapter two. Another example is the paradigmatic poem in English, Wordsworth's *Prelude,* which is framed through a walk in the Lake District (Wordsworth even wrote a travel guide for the Lake District, "A Guide to the Lakes"). Another famous Romantic poem, Coleridge's "Rime of the Ancient Mariner," forms a supernatural counterpart to Wordsworth's travels through natural landscapes: Coleridge takes us to the mythic land of ice, the same exotic wasteland that Caspar David Friedrich repeatedly paints. This said, however, modern travel differs remarkably from Romantic travel in its middle-class, everyman nature. Three major nineteenth-century developments—the invention of the railway, the expansion of colonialism, and the wide-ranging marketing of travel by Cook and Baedeker—conspired to make travel a more encompassing popular reality in Kafka's era than in Goethe's and Wordsworth's. By 1900, the nondescript middle-class bureaucrat—Franz Kafka—would inevitably find himself traveling, even against his will, as one of the first in a long series of twentieth-century "accidental tourists." I thank David Clark for pointing out the connection to Wordsworth and Coleridge.

28. Malcolm Bradbury, "The Cities of Modernism," in *Modernism: 1890–1930,* ed. Malcolm Bradbury and James McFarlane (Harmondsworth, 1976), 101.

29. Paul Fussell, *Abroad: British Literary Traveling Between the Wars* (New York, 1980), 11.

30. Kafka's 1909–12 travel itinerary was as follows: September 1909 (Riva-Brescia-Desenzano); October 1910 (Paris); December 1910 (Berlin); January-February 1911 (Friedland-Reichenberg); August-September 1911 (Munich-Zurich-Lucerne-Lugano-Milan-Stresa-Paris-Erlenbach); June-July 1912 (Leipzig-Weimar-Jungborn).

31. According to the editors of the Fischer critical edition, Kafka left behind 188 pages of travel notes from his 1911 and 1912 trips alone (*Ta¹* 49–74). Published in the form of the critical edition, these pages convert to 127 pages (*Ta* 931–1057). This does not include Kafka's 1909 essay on the air show he witnessed in Brescia (Italy) nor does it include his brief "Notizen zu Paris," probably written down in Prague in preparation for his 1910 trip (for these two texts, see *EFI* 17–26 and 50–51). An English translation of the critical edition of the travel diaries has not yet appeared; the current translation follows Brod's older (lightly censored) version and can be found in *D* 427–87.

32. Brod, *Der Prager Kreis* (Stuttgart, 1966), 110.

33. Anthony Northey correctly points out that this was not the first such essay published in German (as three different biographers have claimed). Rather, Kafka's essay fits into a burgeoning, early twentieth-century trend of writing about airplanes and dirigibles (Anthony Northey, "Myths and Realities in Kafka Biography," in *The Cambridge Companion to Kafka,* ed. Julian Preece, 189–90 [Cambridge, 2002]).

34. For a detailed depiction of Kafka's and Brod's two trips to Paris (including numerous photographs of early-twentieth-century Paris), see Hartmut Binder's *Kafka in Paris: historische Spaziergänge mit alten Photographien* (Munich, 1999).

35. Brod, *Franz Kafka,* 105 (my emphasis).

36. Brod, *Prager Kreis,* 110.

37. With the exception of a couple of entries from around May 1909, the diaries do not begin until after Kafka's September journey with Brod; they finally become regular—and regularly dated—in 1910. For an account of the genesis (and dating) of Kafka's diaries, see *Ta¹* 85–97.

38. See Hartmut Binder's critique of Brod's theory (Binder, *Kafka in Paris,* 119).

39. Cf. Malcolm Pasley's essay on Kafka's travel diaries, in which he agrees with Brod's claim that Kafka's travel writing led to his fiction writing (Malcolm Pasley, "Kafka als Reisender," in *Was bleibt von Franz Kafka?,* ed. Wendelin Schmidt-Dengler [Vienna, 1985], 1–15).

40. Binder employs the above Kafka citation (*D* 50) in an attempt to invert Brod's and Pasley's argument. Since Kafka claims that he can only properly travel *after* he writes well at home—Binder argues—Kafka must have used his Prague diaries as a way of practicing for his travel writing (not, as I am arguing, the other way around). But—contra Binder—Kafka's stated goal is a general improvement in "perception"; and, as Kafka's next citation from my main text demonstrates, this perception is not ultimately aimed at a discernible reality (e.g., the Paris or Milan of 1911) but rather at what Kafka calls "true description"—a kind of writing that is free from the objective "experience" of the foreign worlds to which he actually travels (Binder, *Kafka in Paris,* 120).

41. Cf. Pasley, "Kafka als Reisender," 6.

42. The remarks of René Dumesnil (whose Flaubert book Kafka had already
    given to Brod) concerning Flaubert's *Notes du voyage* point toward what
    might have drawn Kafka to Flaubert's travel writing: "Les années d'ap-
    prentissage de son dur métier se confondent chez lui avec les années de
    voyage. Le voyage n'est qu'un complément de la preparation au métier—
    un complément indispensable. Il faut apprendre à bien voir, à observer.
    [. . .] 'Je sais voir,' disait Flaubert, 'et voir comme les myopes, parce qu'ils
    se fourrent le nez dessus'" (René Dumesnil, introduction to *Voyages,* by
    Gustave Flaubert, ed. Dumesnil [Paris, 1948], 1:viii; cited in Pasley, "Kafka
    als Reisender," 11).

43. Gerhard Kurz likewise sees this passage as prototypical of Kafka's travel writ-
    ing style (Gerhard Kurz, "Einleitung: Der junge Kafka im Kontext," in *Der
    junge Kafka,* ed. Kurz [Frankfurt a. M., 1984], 7–39 [here, 30–32]).

44. The sparse additional scholarly work on Kafka's travel diaries concentrates
    primarily on Kafka's journeys to Paris: Hannelore Rodlauer's dissertation
    ("Kafkas Pariser Tagebuch") and article ("Kafkas Paris," *Etudes Germaniques*
    39 [1984]: 140–151), as well as Hartmut Binder's more recent, above-men-
    tioned *Kafka in Paris.* See also Rodlauer's "Die Paralleltagebücher Kafka-
    Brod und das Modell Flaubert," *Arcadia* 20 (1985): 47–60 and Binder's
    *Kafka in neuer Sicht: Mimik, Geste und Personengefüge als Darstellungsformen
    der Autobiographie* (Stuttgart, 1976), 35–76.

45. Pasley, "Kafka als Reisender," 6. Wolfgang Jahn was the first to remark on
    the cinematic aspects of Kafka's style, in *Kafkas Roman "Der Verschollene"
    ("Amerika")* (Stuttgart, 1965). Later, Mark Anderson (*Kafka's Clothes: Or-
    nament and Aestheticism in the Habsburg Fin de Siècle* [Oxford, 1992], 115–22)
    and Hanns Zischler (*Kafka geht ins Kino* [Hamburg, 1996]) also discuss the
    "filmic" aspects of Kafka's style.

46. It is important to note that this "little motor-car story" is only a transition
    piece between Kafka's travel writings and his mature prose. As Kafka is
    quick to point out, it too retains some of the "disconnected starts" typical
    of his travel observations (this story, too, remains "homeless" [*heimatlos*]).
    Despite (or because of) this piece's residual travelogue-like faults, however,
    it encourages Kafka to set his sights on a more continuous, seamless form
    of fiction: he now imagines writing something "large and whole, well
    shaped from beginning to end" (*D* 104–5; *Ta* 226–27).

47. Anderson, *Kafka's Clothes,* 119.

48. In Benjamin's original German, film allows us "gelassen abenteuerliche
    Reisen [zu] unternehmen" ("Das Kunstwerk im Zeitalter seiner techni-
    schen Reproduzierbarkeit," in *Gesammelte Schriften* 7[1] [Frankfurt a. M.,
    1989], 376; English translation in *Illuminations* [New York, 1968], 236).
    Deniz Göktürk similarly describes film as an ersatz form of travel in her
    study of German representations (including Kafka's) of America between
    1912 and 1920 (Deniz Göktürk, *Künstler, Cowboys, Ingenieure: Kultur- und
    mediengeschichtliche Studien zu deutschen Amerika-Texten 1912–1920* [Mu-
    nich, 1998], 1–22).

49. Brod, *Franz Kafka*, 132.

50. Kafka mentions his desire for this kind of writing obliquely in his travel diaries, when describing the Milan Galeria—"there was nothing to arrest the sweep of the eye"—and, later, when sweeping his own writerly eye over the Borghese Gladiator in the Louvre: "your eye is lured along the rigidly extended leg and flies securely over the inexorable back to the arm and sword raised toward the front" (*D* 443, 460; *Ta* 967, 1008, trans. rev.; see figure 8).

51. Kafka had already admired the "*Ruhe*" of Goethe's style in a December 19, 1910 diary entry (*D* 31; *Ta* 135).

52. Anderson, *Kafka's Clothes*, 120.

53. See Klaus Wagenbach's commentary to his edition of "In the Penal Colony" (Franz Kafka, *In der Strafkolonie. Eine Geschichte aus dem Jahre 1914. Mit Quellen, Abbildungen, Materialien aus der Arbeiter-Unfall-Versicherungsanstalt, Chronik und Anmerkungen von Klaus Wagenbach* [Berlin, 1975]) and Walter Müller-Seidel, *Die Deportation des Menschen: Kafkas Erzählung "In der Strafkolonie" im europäischen Kontext* (Stuttgart, 1986). Other recent important cultural-historical contributions (not pertaining primarily to "In the Penal Colony") are Ritchie Robertson's *Kafka: Judaism, Politics, and Literature* (Oxford, 1985) and Sander Gilman's *Franz Kafka, the Jewish Patient* (New York, 1995).

54. Rickels, "Writing as Travel and Travail," 32–40. The long tradition of formal analysis gained much of its impetus from Friedrich Beissner's 1952 *Der Erzähler Franz Kafka* (in which he comes up with his theory of "*Einsinnigkeit*" as Kafka's central narrative principle) and Martin Walser's 1961 *Beschreibung einer Form*. Perhaps its most elegant formulation appears in Stanley Corngold's *Franz Kafka: The Necessity of Form* (Ithaca, NY, 1988).

55. See Elizabeth Boa, *Kafka: Gender, Class, and Race in the Letters and Fictions* (Oxford, 1996), 133–47; Karen Piper, "The Language of the Machine: Kafka and the Subject of Empire," *Journal of the Kafka Society of America* 20 (1996): 42–54; Paul Peters, "Witness to the Execution: Kafka and Colonialism," *Monatshefte* 93 (2001): 401–25; and Rolf Goebel, "Kafka and Postcolonial Critique: *Der Verschollene*, 'In der Strafkolonie,' 'Beim Bau der chinesischen Mauer,'" in *A Companion to the Works of Franz Kafka*, ed. James Rolleston (Rochester, NY, 2002), 187–212.

56. Rainer Nägele, "Introduction: Reading Benjamin," in *Benjamin's Ground: New Readings of Walter Benjamin*, ed. Nägele (Detroit, 1988), 9. Scott Spector cites Nägele, as well, as a critical credo for "sav[ing] the text." Spector holds to this principle in his careful examinations of texts by various near-forgotten Prague writers, but, because of the broad historical sweep of his book, he does not offer close readings of Kafka's fictions (with the exception of some excellent pages on "Jackals and Arabs" and "A Report to an Academy") (Spector, *Prague Territories*, 34, 191–93).

57. See Goebel's *Constructing China* for a thorough discussion of Kafka's fascinating "Chinese" stories—which I do not handle in depth here—in the terms of the history of German Orientalist discourse.

58. Anderson, "Kafka in America: Notes on a Travelling Narrative," in *Kafka's Clothes*, 98–122. According to my research, the first critic to address Kafka's interest in the multiple meanings of *Verkehr* (here, the connection between epistolary and sexual "intercourse") was Charles Bernheimer, in 1982. Later, Gayatri Spivak emphasized the importance of the Marxian notion of "commerce" contained within Kafkan *Verkehr*. Rainer Stach then identified the connection between legal and sexual "traffic" in Kafka (Charles Bernheimer, *Flaubert and Kafka: Studies in Psychopoetic Structure* [New Haven, CT, 1982], 152–61; Gayatri Spivak's remarks are found in "Discussion [of Stanley Corngold's "Consternation: the Anthropological Moment in Literature"]," in *Literature and Anthropology*, ed. Jonathan Hall and Ackbar Abbas [Hong Kong, 1986], 192; Rainer Stach, *Kafkas erotischer Mythos: Eine ästhetische Konstruktion des Weiblichen* [Frankfurt a. M., 1987], 145–57).

59. Müller writes: "Why do I speak so much about the tropics [*Tropen*]? The savage doesn't know of them, only the Northerner does; they are for him the trope [*Tropus*] for his ardor and the burning fever in his nerves" (Robert Müller, *Tropen: der Mythos der Reise: Urkunden eines deutschen Ingenieurs* [*Tropics/Tropes: Myth of the Journey*] [Paderborn, 1990], 185). Kafka knew of Müller, whose *Tropen* was originally published in 1915, because Müller was one of the earliest reviewers of *The Metamorphosis*. Kafka commented on Müller's review in an October 7, 1916 letter to Felice Bauer (*LF* 517; *BF* 719–20).

60. In this regard, I will discuss the theoretical work of James Clifford, Caren Kaplan, Dean MacCannell, Paul Rabinow, and Renato Rosaldo.

61. Walker Percy, *The Message in the Bottle* (New York, 1975), 86.

62. Xavier de Maistre, *Voyage autour de ma chambre* (Lausanne, 1794).

Chapter One

1. Walter Benjamin, "Franz Kafka: On the Tenth Anniversary of His Death," in *Illuminations*, 118–19; *Benjamin über Kafka. Texte, Briefzeugnisse, Aufzeichnungen* (Frankfurt a. M., 1992), 16.

2. Benjamin, "Franz Kafka: On the Tenth Anniversary of His Death," 118.

3. According to Klaus Wagenbach, Kafka was approximately four years old at the time of this photograph—not six, as Benjamin claims (Wagenbach, *Franz Kafka: Bilder aus seinem Leben* [Berlin, 1994], 28).

4. For a concise summary of the various definitions of literary exoticism, see Wolfgang Reif, "Der Exotismus und der exotistische Roman," in *Zivilisationsflucht und literarische Wunschräume: Der exotistische Roman im ersten Viertel des 20. Jahrhunderts* (Stuttgart, 1975), 1–35.

5. "The taste for the exotic feeds on cultures that are experienced as distant and different, whether remote in space or in time," *Encyclopaedia of World Art* (New York: McGraw-Hill, 1983), 297.

6. Cf. Chris Bongie, "An Idea Without a Future: Exoticism in the Age of Colonial Reproduction," in *Exotic Memories: Literature, Colonialism, and the*

Fin de Siècle (Stanford, 1991), 1–33. The later chapters of Bongie's book discuss the "exotic memories" of Jules Verne, Pierre Loti, Victor Segalen, and Joseph Conrad.

7. For Dauthendey (in South America), see Hans Christoph Buch, *Die Nähe und die Ferne: Bausteine zu einer Poetik des kolonialen Blicks* (Frankfurt a. M., 1996), 115–21. For Jacques (who toured Japan), see Günther Scholdt, *Der Fall Norbert Jacques: Über Rang und Niedergang eines Erzählers (1880–1954)* (Stuttgart, 1976). For Kellermann, see the dedication to his publisher, Paul Cassirer, on the first page of Kellermann's memoir, *Ein Spaziergang in Japan* (Berlin, 1911).

8. For Kellermann's description of geishas, see *Ein Spaziergang in Japan,* 46–48.

9. According to MacCannell, travelers desire to pass through several stages of "front spaces" in order to reach the "authentic" back space of the foreign land. This authentic space motivates touristic desire, but the prevalence of "staged authenticities" (e.g., the "authentic" back room of a Provence tavern constructed especially for the tourist) continually undermines the reality of back spaces. For MacCannell, this touristic desire for authenticity is a symptom of modern alienation, a reaction to the domestic alienation characteristic of the post-industrial Western world: "the generalized anxiety about the authenticity of interpersonal relationships in modern society is matched by certainty about the authenticity of tourist sights" (MacCannell, *The Tourist,* 101–2, 14).

10. For Bonsels' plague-infested Bitschapur and his Bombay brothel vignette, see Bonsels, *Indienfahrt,* in *Wanderschaft* 3:126–27 and 3:97–100, respectively.

11. Hesse's desire to locate a "primitively authentic" Sri Lankan whorehouse (as opposed to an inauthentic "European" one, which he carefully avoids) resembles Bonsels' above-cited attempt to penetrate India's back spaces (Hermann Hesse, *Aus Indien: Aufzeichnungen, Tagebücher, Gedichte, Betrachtungen und Erzählungen* [Frankfurt a. M., 1982], 178). For more on brothel tourism and its connection to the modernist desire for authenticity, see John Zilcosky, "Franz Kafka, Perverse Traveler: Flaubert, Kafka, and the Travel Writing Tradition," *Journal of the Kafka Society of America* 23 (1997): 80–87.

12. Regarding Kafka, Gilles Deleuze and Félix Guattari speak of an "immobile voyage that stays in one place." This voyage, they continue, "takes place in a single place, in 'one's bedroom,' and is all the more intense for that" (Deleuze and Guattari, *Kafka: Toward a Minor Literature,* 35, 95n12).

13. Norbert Jacques, *Heiße Städte: Eine Reise nach Brasilien* (Berlin, 1911). The Flaubert debate is recorded in *Pan* 1 (January 16, 1911), 181–88, *Pan* 1 (February 1, 1911), 226–34, and *Pan* 1 (July 15, 1911), 591–93.

14. For Kafka's strong interest in Flaubert's travel writings, see Pasley, "Kafka als Reisender"; Rodlauer, "Die Paralleltagebücher Kafka-Brod und das Modell Flaubert"; and Kurz, "Einleitung: Der junge Kafka im Kontext," in *Der junge Kafka,* 25–32.

15. Kafka did not initially propose a novel but rather only that he and Brod keep parallel travel diaries. Hartmut Binder claims that the project eventually shifted from this primarily non-fictional one to a primarily fictional one during the friends' journey (Binder, *Kafka in Paris*, 121). But any such shift was minor: As my discussion in this chapter will reveal, the *fictional* device at the heart of Kafka's original idea (each traveler would imagine the world from the *other traveler's* perspective) also governs the form of the eventual novel (through "contradictory stereoscopy").

16. Brod, *Prager Kreis*, 111.

17. Max Brod and Franz Kafka, "Erstes Kapitel des Buches, 'Richard und Samuel,'" *Herder-Blätter* 1 (May 1912): 15–25. I cite from the most recent edition of "The First Long Train Journey," in *EFI* 193–208.

18. Brod, *Prager Kreis*, 111.

19. Concerning the bed as a symbol of intimacy and domesticity, I think of Penelope's test of Odysseus upon his return home in Book 23 of *The Odyssey*.

20. Brod, *Prager Kreis*, 110–11.

21. Brod, *Prager Kreis*, 110 (Brod's emphasis).

22. Anderson, *Kafka's Clothes*, 102.

23. Zischler, *Kafka geht ins Kino*, 50–60. One obvious example countering Zischler's claim is "Richard's" quotation early in *Richard and Samuel:* "we really see only as far as the first floor of all the buildings" (*M* 287; *EFI* 198). This first appeared in *Brod's* notebooks (*EFI* 74).

    One of Kafka's diary entries suggests that, exceptionally, he wrote the final "Richard" entry (*M* 292–96; *EFI* 203–6) by himself on December 8, 1911 (*D* 131; *Ta* 281). See James Rolleston, "Die Romane," in *Kafka-Handbuch*, ed. Hartmut Binder (Stuttgart, 1979), 2:406. But even if Kafka did write a version of this entry alone, we have no way of knowing whether these exact words made their way into the published text (especially since Brod was explicitly "not pleased" with Kafka's draft) (*D* 132; *Ta* 282).

24. Hartmut Binder, *Kafka-Kommentar zu sämtlichen Erzählungen* (Munich, 1975), 93.

25. For Pratt, the "monarch-of-all-I-survey" view has three defining qualities: (1) the landscape is "aestheticized"; (2) "density of meaning" is sought; (3) a relation of "mastery" is constructed between seer and seen. Aesthetics and ideology thus combine to create what Pratt terms a "rhetoric of presence" (Mary Louise Pratt, *Imperial Eyes: Travel Writing and Transculturation* [New York, 1992], 204–5).

26. For Goethe and Flaubert, see my chapter two; for Hesse, see the next paragraph. Pratt also cites British explorers from the 1860s who were looking for the source of the Nile (e.g., Richard Burton and John Speke) (Pratt, *Imperial Eyes*, 201–8).

27. Hesse, *Aus Indien*, 105.

28. Hesse, *Aus Indien*, 178.

29. Bonsels, *Indienfahrt*, 44.

30. Hesse, *Aus Indien,* 32.

31. Caren Kaplan, *Questions of Travel: Postmodern Discourses of Displacement* (Durham, NC, 1996), 33–57. Kaplan has her sights set on Malcolm Cowley's commemoration of expatriate Euro-American writers in the period between the two World Wars, *Exile's Return: A Literary Odyssey of the 1920s* (Harmondsworth, 1982) and on Paul Fussell's similarly celebratory description of the period, *Abroad.*

32. Cf. Fred Davis, *Yearning for Yesterday: A Sociology of Nostalgia* (New York, 1979).

33. Kaplan, *Questions of Travel,* 33; for more on nostalgia as an illness, see Davis, *Yearning for Yesterday,* 1–7.

34. Kaplan, *Questions of Travel,* 33–34.

35. Renato Rosaldo, *Culture and Truth: The Remaking of Social Analysis* (Boston, 1993), 70; cited in Kaplan, *Questions of Travel,* 34.

36. Rosaldo, *Culture and Truth,* 69–70.

37. Dean MacCannell equates modern travelers' exotic nostalgia with a desire for "naturalness" in *The Tourist,* 3.

38. Cf. MacCannell, *The Tourist,* 3.

39. See the section entitled "Entfremdete Arbeit und Privateigentum" ("Alienated/Estranged Labor and Private Property"), where Marx claims that the modern subject "only feels himself in himself [*fühlt sich bei sich*] outside his work, and in his work feels outside himself. He is at home when he is not working, and when he is working he is not at home" (Karl Marx, *Marx/Engels Gesamtausgabe,* ed. Institut für Marxismus-Leninismus [Berlin, 1982], 1(2):363–75 [here, 367]).

40. Already alienated/estranged from his labor, man is also alienated, Marx writes, from "nature," from "himself," and from his "*species*" (Marx, *Marx/Engels Gesamtausgabe,* 1(2):369 [Marx's emphasis]).

41. The railway, first developed in the 1830s, was vital to the development of middle-class tourism. Not surprisingly, the first modern travel guidebooks were published in England and German in that same decade. For a concise summary of the history of the rise of middle-class tourism, see Koshar, *German Travel Cultures,* 1–5.

42. On the tourist's desire to escape alienation through travel, see MacCannell's *The Tourist:* "it is through sightseeing that the tourist demonstrates better than by any other means that he is not alienated from society" (68). See also 17–37, 55.

43. Hans-Magnus Enzensberger, "Eine Theorie des Tourismus," in *Einzelheiten I. Bewusstseins-Industrie* (Frankfurt a. M., 1964), 196.

44. "Dort [im Osten], im Reinen und in Rechten/ Will ich menschlichen Geschlechten/ In des Ursprungs Tiefe dringen" (Johann Wolfgang von Goethe, *Westöstlicher Diwan* [1819; rpt., Munich, 1958], 9).

45. Jean Bruneau, *Le "Conte Orientale" de Flaubert* (Paris, 1973), 79.

46. For a reading of the socio-psychological importance of popular literature in the *Kaiserreich,* especially Karl May's exotic adventure novels, see Jochen

Schulte-Sasse, "Karl Mays Amerika-Exotik und deutsche Wirklichkeit: Zur sozialpsychologischen Funktion von Trivialliteratur im wilhelminischen Deutschland," in *Karl May*, ed. Helmut Schmiedt (Frankfurt a. M., 1983), 101–29.

47. Paul Gauguin, *Die Aufzeichnungen von Noa Noa* (Wetzlar, 1982), 96, 64.
48. Reif, *Zivilisationsflucht*, 15. Reif opposes exoticism (which is more closely allied to expressionism) to the decadent, "impressionistic" travel accounts that preceded early-twentieth-century German-language exoticism. Good examples of the impressionistic traveler are, for Reif, Albrecht von Qualen in Thomas Mann's 1903 "Der Kleiderschrank" and Rainer Maria Rilke's self-stylized life: both live in hotels and do not want to arrive anywhere (36). Bernhard Kellermann's *Das Meer* is typical of the impressionist travel novel, in which the hero never wants to arrive but instead exclaims "let's discover *new things!*" (37). Reif's working definition of exoticism is that it expresses nostalgic desires for a regressive utopia: for a primitive world better than the European one (71). Novels such as Joris-Karl Huysmans' *A rebours* (1884) are thus not exoticist because they are not interested in the formation of "simpler and more primal worlds" but rather go "so to speak 'à rebours' through a purposeless refinement and the technology of completely artificial worlds" (86).

The few other monographs devoted to German-language exoticism either do not focus, as does Reif, on the early twentieth century, or they limit themselves (like Wolfgang Kubin's book on China) to one exotic region only. See Anselm Maler, *Der exotische Roman: bürgerliche Gesellschaftsflucht und Gesellschaftskritik zwischen Romantik und Realismus* (Stuttgart, 1975); Daniela Magill, *Literarische Reisen in die exotische Fremde: Topoi der Darstellung von Eigen- und Fremdkultur* (Frankfurt a. M., 1989); Wolfgang Kubin, *Mein Bild in Deinem Auge. Exotismus und Moderne: Deutschland—China im 20. Jahrhundert* (Darmstadt, 1995).
49. Reif, *Zivilisationsflucht*, 13.
50. Bonsels, *Indienfahrt*, 217.
51. Fritz Hübner, "Reise-Impressionismus," *Der Bücherwurm. Eine Monatsschrift für Bücherfreunde* 3 (Reiseheft) (July 1913): 263.
52. Hanns Heinz Ewers, *Indien und Ich* (Munich, 1919), 178–79 (originally published in 1911).
53. Ewers, *Indien und Ich*, 178–79.
54. Freud probably began "The Uncanny" as early as 1913, shortly after Kafka and Brod toured central Europe and Hesse traveled to India. For the genesis of "The Uncanny," see *The Standard Edition of the Complete Psychological Works of Sigmund Freud*, 17:218.
55. Freud, "The Uncanny," in *Standard Edition*, 17:245. Cf. Freud's account (also in "The Uncanny") of repeatedly losing his way while visiting an Italian town; each time he gets lost, he emerges, as if against his will, in this town's red-light district.

56. Alfred Winterstein, "Zur Psychologie des Reisens," *Imago. Zeitschrift für Anwendung der Psychoanalyse auf die Geisteswissenschaften,* 1. Jahrgang, Heft 1 (March 1912), 502.

57. Discussing mythical heroes such as Gilgamesh, Dionysus, Hercules, Christ, and Mithras, Jung writes: "That these heroes are almost always wanderers has a clear psychological symbolism: Wandering is an image of longing, of the restless urge that can never find its object because it is searching, without knowing it, for the lost mother" (Carl Jung, "Wandlungen und Symbole der Libido: Beiträge zur Entwicklungsgeschichte des Denkens" [2. Teil], *Jahrbuch für psychoanalytische und psychopathische Forschungen* 4 [1912]: 249).

58. Alfred Kerr, "Jagow, Flaubert, Pan," *Pan* 1 (February 1911): 222.

59. Müller's hero senses that he has experienced the lush heat of the tropics before, but only in dimmest memory: "Where, where had I gone through this tropical condition, this scene of will-less growth, where, where?"; later he refers to the tropics as that "great race [sex, *Geschlecht*] of primal nature, mother and whore at once." Finally, toward the end, when wandering into a deserted grotto, he claims to have discovered his "second womb": "The second womb! [. . .] When you miss the first one,—you can still live here in the spare" (Müller, *Tropen,* 15, 23, 169). For Müller's connection to Kafka, note 59 in my introduction.

60. Müller, *Tropen,* 24.

61. Shortly before acquiring his lover, Zana, Müller's protagonist threatens, "Either I get a *Weib* or I pulverize the village" (Müller, *Tropen,* 135).

62. See Reif's analysis of *Tropen* in *Zivilisationsflucht,* 121–45 (here, 135).

63. Freud, *Standard Edition,* 17:241–43, 246–47.

64. Edward Said, *Orientalism* (New York, 1979), 167 (Said's emphasis).

65. Weber, *Zuckerbaron,* 5.

66. Weber, *Zuckerbaron,* 84, 83.

67. Weber, *Zuckerbaron,* 83.

68. See, for example, James Clifford's attempt to unsettle the traditional dualism between "dwelling" and "traveling" in "Traveling Cultures," in *Cultural Studies,* ed. Laurence Grossberg, Cary Nelson, and Paula Treichler (New York, 1992), 96–116.

69. Kafka's attitude here crucially refines Zygmunt Baumann's oft-cited interpretation of Kafka's position as a double-outsider in Prague. Baumann claims that Kafka's outsider-ness led to his remarkably clear-eyed capacity for depicting alienation and homelessness, but this same stranger-status seems to be responsible for Max Brod's powerful nostalgia at the hat rack and Kafka's sometimes sentimental attraction to colonial adventure stories. In Kafka, we see a heightened awareness of alienation (as Baumann would have it) but also a heightened nostalgia. See Zygmunt Bauman, "Excursus: Franz Kafka, or the Rootlessness of Universality," in *Modernity and Ambivalence* (Ithaca, NY, 1991), 85–90.

70. Paul Rabinow, "Representations are Social Facts: Modernity and Post-Modernity in Anthropology," in *Writing Culture,* ed. James Clifford and

George E. Markus (Berkeley, 1986), 241. I thank Monika Shafi for direct-
ing me toward Rabinow during her response to an earlier version of this
argument at the MLA Convention in Chicago (December 1999).

71. "War er ein Tier, da ihn Musik so ergriff?" (Was he an animal, that music
could move him so?) (*DL* 185; *MO* 117).

72. Clifford, "Traveling Cultures," 101. I think, furthermore, of how Kafka's protagonists repeatedly locate "homes" on the road—suggesting that "traveling"
is as unstable a concept as is "dwelling" (e.g., in *The Castle,* K.'s and Frieda's
cramped room in the Bridge Inn; also in *The Castle,* K.'s and Frieda's carefully arranged residence on the schoolhouse floor; in *Amerika/Der Verschollene,* Karl Rossmann's homey elevator in the Hotel Occidental; also in
Amerika, Karl's balcony bedroom outside Brunelda's apartment).

Chapter Two

1. Marion Sonnenfeld first referred to the "America" novel as a *Bildungsroman*
("Die Fragmente 'Amerika' and 'Der Prozeß' als Bildungsromane," *German
Quarterly* 35 [1962]: 34–46), but Mark Spilka correctly pointed out that
Kafka's novel is a modern revision of the Dickensian *Bildungsroman* tradition: it displays a "surge toward moral dissolution" and the "replacement of
all sympathetic fervor with anxiety, or with the objective depiction of despair" (*Dickens and Kafka: A Mutual Interpretation* [Bloomington, 1963],
174). Peter Beicken claimed that Kafka uses elements of the *Bildungsroman*
only to rob these of their traditional function and significance: Kafka fails
to present an unambiguous doctrine of either "upbringing" or "education
[*Bildung*]" (*Franz Kafka: Eine kritische Einführung in die Forschung* [Frankfurt
a. M., 1974], 254). Finally, in 1983, Jürgen Pütz fully examined the specific
ways in which Kafka's novel revises the Bildungsroman tradition (*Kafkas
Verschollener—ein Bildungsroman* [Frankfurt a. M., 1983]).

2. For the theme of forgetting in *Der Verschollene,* see Walter Sokel, "Das
Labyrinth und Amerika," in *Franz Kafka—Tragik und Ironie* (Munich and
Vienna, 1964), 311–29.

3. Max Brod's edition (the only one available through 1983) "corrects" Karl's
age in the opening sentence of the novel to sixteen (he is seventeen in
Kafka's original), thereby neutralizing some of the novel's fundamental
non-progressivity.

4. Said, *Orientalism,* 167.

5. See my discussion of melancholic nostalgia in chapter one. Said also points
out how colonial travelers generally viewed their journeys as ideal opportunities for "remaking" themselves in a new, better form (Said refers here
specifically to Alexander Kinglake's 1844 *Eothen, or Traces of Travel Brought
Home from the East* [Said, *Orientalism,* 193]).

6. Reif, "Exotismus im Reisebericht des frühen 20. Jahrhunderts," in *Der
Reisebericht: Die Entwicklung einer Gattung in der deutschen Literatur,* ed. Peter
J. Brenner (Frankfurt a. M., 1989), esp. 443–51.

7. Norbert Jacques, *Piraths Insel* (Berlin, 1917), 171–72, 217–18. The narrative of *Selbstfindung* recurs not only in Weber's *Sugar Baron* but also throughout Kafka's treasured *Little Green Books,* where the heroes often achieve psychological and professional fullness in faraway lands. For more on the general discourse of *Selbstfindung* in the *Little Green Books,* see my chapter five.

8. Arthur Holitscher's *Amerika heute und morgen* (which I discuss later in this chapter) first appeared in installments in the 1911–12 *Neue Rundschau,* where Kafka likely read it. Later, Kafka acquired the seventh edition, printed in 1913. Many critics have discussed Kafka's use of Holitscher as source material. The earliest to do so were: Jahn, *Kafkas Roman "Der Verschollene" ("Amerika");* Gerhard Loose, *Franz Kafka und Amerika* (Frankfurt a. M., 1968); and Alfred Wirkner, *Kafka und die Außenwelt: Quellenstudien zum 'Amerika'-Fragment* (Stuttgart, 1976). Other, above-mentioned examples of travel narratives named after their destinations are *Indian Journey, Hot Nights in Brazil, A Stroll through Japan, Out of India,* and *Voyage en Orient;* below I will discuss Goethe's *Italian Journey.*

9. See Wolfgang Jahn's claim that the two halves of this part of the text completed/titled by Kafka (chapters 1–3 and 4–6) form two separate narratives of banishment (Jahn, "*Der Verschollene (Amerika),*" in *Kafka-Handbuch,* ed. Hartmut Binder, 2:410–11).

10. For the construction of Italy as an exotic space for Northern Europeans in the eighteenth century, see the body of work by Chloe Chard, who argues that eighteenth-century Italy—due to the "major symbolic and geographical transition" figured by a journey over or around the Alps—was a unique site of "drama and excess": the "*mise-en-scène* of the forbidden." See Chard's introduction to *Transports: Travel, Pleasure, and Imaginative Geography, 1600–1830,* ed. Chloe Chard and Helen Langdon (New Haven, CT, 1996), 6; "Effeminacy, Pleasure and the Classical Body," in *Femininity and Masculinity in Eighteenth-Century Art and Culture,* ed. Gill Perry and Michael Rossington (Manchester, 1994), 153; *Pleasure and Guilt on the Grand Tour: Travel Writing and Imaginative Geography, 1600–1830* (Manchester, 1999), 91.

Eric Downing has demonstrated how this exoticization carried on into Kafka's fin de siècle, in Downing's examination of Wilhelm Jensen's "Gradiva" (famous as the subject of Freud's first sustained analysis of a literary text). As Downing points out, this story, which describes the journey of a German archaeologist to Italy, consistently constructs the "link between the African and the Italian sun"—thereby endowing Italy with all of Africa's "implicitly racist (and racistly erotic) shadings" (Eric Downing, "Dead Woman Walking: Jensen's 'Gradiva'" [paper presented at the annual meeting of the American Comparative Literature Association, San Juan, Puerto Rico, April 2002]).

The most obvious and enduring example of the eighteenth-century exoticiziation of Italy comes from Goethe himself, in Mignon's song about Italy in *Wilhelm Meisters Lehrjahre* (1795–96): "Kennst du das Land, wo die

Zitronen blühn [. . .] ?" (Do you know that land where the lemon blossom grows?).

11. Brod, *Franz Kafka: A Biography,* 122. For a full-length comparative study of Kafka and Goethe, seen through the shifts in German literature from Goethe to Kafka, see Bert Nagel's *Kafka und Goethe: Stufen der Wandlung von der Klassik zur Moderne* (Berlin, 1977).

12. See Wilfried Barner, "Jüdische Goethe-Verehrung vor 1933," in *Juden in der deutschen Literatur: Ein deutsch-israelisches Symposion,* ed. Stéphane Moses and Albrecht Schöne (Frankfurt a. M., 1986), 127–151, and Eduard Goldstücker, "Die Prager deutsche Literatur als historisches Phänomen," in *Weltfreunde: Konferenz über die Prager deutsche Literatur 1965,* ed. Goldstücker (Prague, 1967), 29.

13. In this postcard, Kafka describes attempting to locate the exact spot from which Goethe had sketched the Malcesine castle in 1786—before the Italian police accosted him: "The castellan showed me the spot where Goethe did his drawing, but this spot did not correspond with [Goethe's] journal and so we could not agree about that, any more than we could about Italian" (*LO* 7; *BO* 20). Kafka's postcard thus playfully adds another layer to the confusions already present in Goethe's text: as Kafka knew, Goethe's Malcesine story of mistaken identity was already a doubled or even tripled case (traveling as Möller, the Frankfurt-born Goethe was taken for an Austrian and for a spy); Kafka—the Jewish, Austrian-Czech aspiring writer—arriving at the castle as a tourist 150 years later, lightheartedly imagines himself in the role of the classical German writer; to confuse matters more, he miscommunicates with the Italian castellan—in broken Italian—about the spot on which this great writer is meant to sit.

14. This anecdote is included in most biographies of Beckett, including James Knowlson's recent *Damned to Fame: The Life of Samuel Beckett* (New York, 1996), 108.

15. Johann Wolfgang von Goethe, *Letters from Goethe,* trans. Dr. M. Herzfeld and C. A. M. Sym (Edinburgh, 1957), 164; *Goethes Briefe: Briefe der Jahre 1786–1805* (Hamburg, 1964), 9 (my emphasis).

16. "N'importe où! N'importe où! pourvu que ce soit hors de *ce* monde" (Charles Baudelaire, "Anywhere out of the world—N'importe où hors du monde," *Petits Poèmes en Prose* [*Le Spleen de Paris*] [Paris, 1958], 213 [my emphasis]).

17. In Terdiman's reading, Flaubert desires to both dissolve into the Orient and to absorb it into his reconfigured self. Dis-Orient-ation is, for Terdiman, both resistant to and complicit with Orientalism. Flaubert's desire for self-loss, in Terdiman's reading, is eventually overcome by self-reclamation: Flaubert returns to France with a reinvigorated sense of self, as the writer now capable of *Madame Bovary.* This profitable economy of self-loss also functions for Goethe, who only begins his mature work after returning from Italy. See Richard Terdiman, *Discourse/Counter-Discourse: The Theory and Practice of Symbolic Resistance in Nineteenth-Century France* (Ithaca, NY, 1985), 227–57.

18. Goethe, *Letters from Goethe,* 164.

19. Goethe, *Italian Journey,* trans. Robert R. Heitner (Princeton, NJ, 1994), 121, 120.

20. Auden and Mayer claim to witness this benevolent transformation in portraits from around the time of Goethe's journey: through the "striking" difference between Goethe's "over-refined, delicate, almost neurasthenic" pre-Italian face and the "masculine, self-assured" post-Italy one, which belongs to a "man who has known sexual satisfaction" (W. H. Auden and Elizabeth Mayer's introduction to their translation of *Italian Journey,* by J. W. Goethe [New York, 1970], 16). I have chosen Robert Heitner's translation over Auden/Mayer's because the former is much more accurate (if less elegant). For the extensive flaws in Auden/Mayer's translation, see Thomas P. Saine's brief discussion in the preface to Heitner's translation of *Italian Journey* (8–9).

21. Said, *Orientalism,* 193.

22. MacCannell, *The Tourist,* 16, 3.

23. Goethe, *Italian Journey,* 58.

24. Jonathan Culler, "The Semiotics of Tourism," in *Framing the Sign: Criticism and Its Institutions* (Norman, OK, 1988), 153–167 (here, 161).

25. Percy, *The Message in the Bottle,* 52 (discussed in Culler, *Framing the Sign,* 163–64). Consider also Roland Barthes' description of losing his way in Japan in *Empire of Signs* (London, 1983), 33–36.

26. Goethe, *Italian Journey,* 59; *Italienische Reise* (Munich, 1978), 68.

27. Goethe, *Italian Journey,* 60; *Italienische Reise,* 70.

28. MacCannell, *The Tourist,* 3.

29. Goethe, *Italian Journey,* 60.

30. Goethe, *Italian Journey,* 120, 60.

31. Freud, "Beyond the Pleasure Principle," in *The Standard Edition of the Complete Psychological Works of Sigmund Freud,* 18:27–28, 15. A modern revision of Goethe's lost-and-found story is Walter Benjamin's in his *Berliner Chronik,* where he connects the experience of childhood itself with the sensation of being lost in a city: he remembers "the dreamy recalcitrance with which I accompanied [my mother] as we walked through the streets," looking at the city with a gaze that saw "not a third" of what it took in. According to Benjamin, "it was thirty years before the distinction between left and right had become visceral to me, and before I had acquired the art of reading a street map" (Benjamin, "A Berlin Chronicle," in *Reflections,* trans. Edmund Jephcott [New York, 1978], 3–60 [here, 4]).

32. Goethe, *Italian Journey,* 120; *Italienische Reise,* 146.

33. Gustav Janouch, *Conversations with Kafka,* trans. Goronwy Rees, 2nd ed. (New York: New Directions, 1971), 70.

34. *LF* 179, 315, 42; *BF* 281, 460, 96. For Kafka's general enthusiasm for Flaubert, see Wagenbach, *Franz Kafka: Eine Biographie seiner Jugend,* 159–61. For Kafka's specific interest in Flaubert's travel writings, see note 14 in chapter one.

35. For Flaubert's desire to escape the ennui that he generally associated with death, see Terdiman, *Discourse/Counter-Discourse,* 231–33, and Jean-Paul Sartre, *L'idiot de la famille: Gustave Flaubert de 1821 à 1857* (Paris, 1988), 2:1107 ff. (cited in Terdiman, 232n11).

36. "Self-obliteration" is Terdiman's phrase; the term "Oriental renaissance" is Edgar Quintet's and dates from 1842 (*Discourse/Counter-Discourse,* 237, 234). For a further discussion of Flaubert's Oriental renaissance, see Bruneau, *Le "Conte Oriental" de Flaubert,* 23, 32–33.

37. Gustave Flaubert, *Flaubert in Egypt: A Sensibility on Tour* (New York, 1996), 77 (my emphasis).

38. MacCannell, *The Tourist,* 101–2.

39. Ali Behdad, *Belated Travelers: Orientalism in the Age of Colonial Dissolution* (Durham, NC, 1994), 67.

40. Lowe employs Homi Bhabha's idea that the Orient is not "the Orient" per se but rather that which inheres in between Orient and Occident and thus opens up, for Western travelers, a terrifyingly inexplicable/unknowable conceptual absence. This fear-inducing absence, Lowe argues, causes Flaubert to attempt to materialize the Orient in the form of a stereotype and (like the Freudian fetishist) obsessively repeat this form. Later, Lowe concedes that the mature Flaubert seems to criticize Orientalism in his *Salammbô* (Lisa Lowe, *Critical Terrains: French and British Orientalisms* [Ithaca, NY, 1991], 75–101 [for her discussion of fetishism, see 86–87]).

41. Flaubert, *Oeuvres complètes* (Paris, [1971–75]), 13:137 (my emphasis).

42. Kurz, "Einleitung: Der junge Kafka im Kontext," in *Der junge Kafka,* 26.

43. *A* 5, 8, 9, 31; *V* 10, 14–16, 44, trans. rev. Karl eventually re-locates his suitcase at the end of the "Country House near New York" chapter only to again lose possession of it at the end of "The Case of Robinson" (*A* 95, 193; *V* 123, 251).

44. Benjamin writes of Rossmann's "*Neugeburt*" (rebirth) in "Franz Kafka: Zur zehnten Wiederkehr seines Todestages," in *Benjamin über Kafka,* 17; English translation in "Franz Kafka: On the Tenth Anniversary of His Death," 119.

45. Goethe, *Italian Journey,* 60; *Italienische Reise,* 70.

46. Anderson, *Kafka's Clothes,* 108–9.

47. Malcolm Pasley, "The Act of Writing and the Genesis of Kafka's Manuscripts," in *Reading Kafka,* ed. Mark Anderson, 206 (Pasley's emphasis).

48. Pasley, "Act of Writing," 209 (my emphasis).

49. Max Brod, "Uyttersprot korrigiert Kafka," *Forum* 43/44 (1957): 265.

50. See Matt. 18:12 (where the reflexive verb, "*sich verirren,*" is used). *Verirrung*—which refers to literally and metaphorically lost sheep—appears throughout the Bible, for example, in Ezek. 34:12 and Ps. 119:176 (all references are to the Luther translation).

51. Wittgenstein thus recommends that a follower come along and, after climbing the ladder Wittgenstein has built (through the *Tractatus*), throw the ladder away (Ludwig Wittgenstein, *Tractatus Logico-Philosophicus* [bilingual edition] [London, 1961], 150).

52. Ellison's protagonist sees a man lost in the New York subway and muses, in relation to his own "lost," "invisible" self: "Perhaps to lose a sense of *where* you are implies the danger of losing a sense of *who* you are. That must be it, I thought—to lose your direction is to lose your face" (Ralph Ellison, *Invisible Man* [New York, 1972], 564 [Ellison's emphasis]).

53. Goethe, *Italian Journey,* 59.

54. Flaubert, *Flaubert in Egypt,* 77.

55. Goethe, *Italian Journey,* 61.

56. Flaubert, *Oeuvres complètes,* 10:469. As Behdad remarks, Flaubert "indulged" here "in his imperialist fantasy of all-seeing" (Behdad, *Belated Travelers,* 58). Before this, Flaubert recorded a similar view from high above Cairo: "From there [the top of a minaret] I have Cairo beneath me; to the right the desert, with camels gliding on it and their shadows beside them as escorts; opposite, beyond the plains and the Nile, the Pyramids" (Flaubert, *Flaubert in Egypt,* 46).

57. See the previous chapter for a discussion of the colonial history of the "monarch-of-all-I-survey" view. Fin de siècle travel guides and travelogues generally recommended that modern travelers (like their eighteenth- and nineteenth-century predecessors) immediately gain a good viewpoint upon arriving in a foreign city. Arthur Holitscher, for example, recommended surveying New York from a skyscraper, and the Baedeker guide that Kafka used in Paris listed the best places for viewing Paris from above (Arthur Holitscher, *Amerika: heute und morgen* [Berlin, 1912], 57–58; Karl Baedeker, *Paris und Umgebungen* [Leipzig, 1896], 49).

58. Anderson, *Kafka's Clothes,* 104–13. For more on Kafka and Holitscher, see note 8 above.

59. Holitscher, *Amerika,* 58.

60. Hesse, *Aus Indien,* 106.

61. Just one year earlier, while riding the subway beneath Paris' streets, Kafka likewise enjoyed the "calm [*ruhige*], pleasant sense of speed" (*D* 460; *Ta* 1009).

62. Mary Louise Pratt, "Scratches on the Face of the Country; or, What Mr. Barrow Saw in the Land of the Bushmen," *Critical Inquiry* 12 (Autumn 1985): 124.

63. Dennis Porter, "The Perverse Traveler: Flaubert's Voyage en Orient," *L'Esprit Créateur* 29 (1989): 24.

64. Flaubert, *Oeuvres completes,* 10:443 (my emphasis). Porter writes, regarding this passage: "such a visual pursuit of nakedness of and beyond the unclothed body is a recurrent motif in the *Voyage*. The perverse scenario of this and other passages anticipates in a more explicit way Frédéric Moreau's [the hero of *L'Éducation sentimentale*] experience of women. It even suggests that that wayward hero's famous 'N'est-ce que ca?' is less the lament of a disabused idealist than that of an embittered fetishist who compulsively repeats in disgust and anger his encounter with non-phallic woman" (Porter, "Perverse Traveler," 30).

65. Flaubert, *Flaubert in Egypt,* 117.

66. Cf. Reif, "Exotismus im Reisebericht des frühen 20. Jahrhunderts," 445.

67. Hesse, *Aus Indien,* 178 (my emphasis).

68. Flaubert, *Flaubert in Egypt,* 119.

69. Flaubert, *L'Éducation sentimentale,* in *Oeuvres complètes,* 3:398.

70. For a theoretical discussion of the uses of parody for political critique (in Butler's case, a critique of gender politics), see Judith Butler, "Conclusion: From Parody to Politics," in *Gender Trouble: Feminism and the Subversion of Identity* (New York, 1990), 142–49.

71. *D* 459; *Ta* 1006; Flaubert, *L'Éducation sentimentale,* in *Oeuvres complètes,* 3:398.

72. Flaubert, *L'Éducation sentimentale,* in *Oeuvres complètes,* 3:399.

73. Flaubert, *Flaubert in Egypt,* 117.

74. Anderson, *Kafka's Clothes,* 113–22.

75. Anderson mentions Kafka's essay (originally written as a private response to Max Brod's published article, "On Aesthetics") in *Kafka's Clothes,* 100; Stanley Corngold discusses it in greater depth (and offers the first full English translation) in *Complex Pleasure: Forms of Feeling in German Literature* (Stanford, 1998), 125–29.

76. As Jörgen Kobs points out in his detailed study of Kafka's narrative form, Kafka similarly limits the perspective of his protagonists as part of a deliberate aesthetic strategy (Jörgen Kobs, *Kafka: Untersuchungen zu Bewußtsein und Sprache seiner Gestalten,* ed. Ursula Brech [Bad Homburg, 1970], 98–531). In the words of the priest from *The Trial* (speaking to Josef K.), Kafka's characters cannot see "two steps" in front of them (*T* 214; *P* 290).

77. See *A* 225, 228, 236, 254, 263; *V* 292, 295, 306, 330, 343.

78. See René Dumesnil's introductory comments to *Voyages,* by Gustave Flaubert, 1:viii.

79. Reif, *Zivilisationsflucht,* 75, 61. Müller's protagonist literally imagines that the tropics are the reincarnation of his mother's "womb" (see note 59 in chapter one).

80. Margot Norris, *Beasts of the Modern Imagination: Darwin, Nietzsche, Kafka, Ernst, & Lawrence* (Baltimore, 1985), 114–16.

81. Winterstein, "Zur Psychologie des Reisens," 502. See also Freud, "The Uncanny," in *Standard Edition,* 17:245.

82. Freud, *Standard Edition,* 17:245.

83. Benjamin, "Franz Kafka: On the Tenth Anniversary of His Death," 120.

84. *A* 300; the German version can be found in Brod's afterword to the first, 1927 edition of Kafka's "America" novel (Kafka, *Amerika,* ed. Max Brod [Frankfurt a. M., 1991], 260).

85. Weber, *Zuckerbaron,* 83.

86. Emrich sees in the Theater in Oklahoma the "image of a life unmotivated and free of purpose, a life in which play and work, theater and reality, childhood and vocation unite and become reconciled in a world-play, in which 'everybody,' taken on and enabled to play his natural role, could ex-

press his true being that 'cannot but be loved'" (Wilhelm Emrich, *Franz Kafka* [Frankfurt a. M., 1957], 258; translation in Emrich, *Franz Kafka: A Critical Study of His Writings* [New York, 1968], 315).

87. "Rolle und Selbstverwirklichung fallen zusammen" (cited in Peter Beicken's summary of the secondary literature [Beicken, *Franz Kafka,* 260]).

88. Martin Walser, *Beschreibung einer Form* (Munich, 1961), 98. As Josef Vogl writes: "Ultimately there is nothing to support the assumption that Karl Rossmann's entrance into the Theater of Oklahoma is about his salvation, self-becoming [*Selbstwerdung*], and self-realization" (Josef Vogl, *Ort der Gewalt: Kafkas literarische Ethik* [Munich, 1990], 31).

89. Beicken, *Franz Kafka,* 260.

90. See my chapter one, and Theresa Mayer Hammond, *American Paradise: German Travel Literature from Duden to Kisch* (Heidelberg, 1980). On the utopian nature of exotic novels in general, see Reif, "Die Reise in den Urzustand," in *Zivilisationsflucht,* 36–77.

91. Brent Staples, "Unearthing a Riot," *New York Times Magazine* (December 19, 1999).

92. Benjamin, "Franz Kafka: On the Tenth Anniversary of His Death," 119.

93. Cf. Anderson's mention of *verschollen*'s etymology in *Kafka's Clothes,* 104.

94. Kurz writes: "Negro: the black one. When Karl gives up his name, he is not heard of again [is presumed dead, *verschollen*]" (Gerhard Kurz, *Traum-Schrecken: Kafkas literarische Existenzanalyse* [Stuttgart, 1980], 158). Remarking on how American racist discourse defines whiteness in terms of completeness and blackness in terms of fragments and parts, Arthur Holitscher points out that— in America—a "white" person is utterly white whereas "blackness" is determined by only a "drop of black blood" (Holitscher, *Amerika,* 363).

This conception of whiteness as complete and blackness as fragmentary (or even as absence) is also present in late-nineteenth-century colonial discourse. As David Spurr writes (commenting on an 1877 remark by H.M. Stanley), Western colonial writing tended to conceive of the African Other "as absence, emptiness, nothingness, or death" (David Spurr, "Negation," in *The Rhetoric of Empire: Colonial Discourse in Journalism, Travel Writing, and Imperial Administration* [Durham, NC, 1993], 92–108 [here, 92]).

95. Commenting on the power of the Irish in America, Holitscher writes mischievously, "How long does one have to live in America before one can become an Irishman?" (Holitscher, *Amerika,* 351). Cf. *A* 4; *V* 9.

96. Holitscher also wrote about the oppression of American blacks in a novella with which Kafka was probably familiar: Holitscher, "Scab," *Die neue Rundschau* 24 (1913): 1267–1280 (cf. Göktürk, *Künstler, Cowboys, Ingenieure,* 35n75).

97. Staples, "Unearthing a Riot," 64.

98. Holitscher agrees wholeheartedly with the young black man who tells him: "'We [Blacks and Jews] are in the same boat!' [. . .] Our fates are very similar. And both of us even come from Africa, the Jews as well as we Negroes'" (Holitscher, *Amerika,* 365).

99. Goethe, *Italian Journey*, 120.

Chapter Three

1. This is the chronology of what are listed as "completed" chapters of *The Trial* in the Fischer critical edition. The Fischer edition distinguishes between these and the "fragmentary" chapters, which take place at the following additional sites: at home; in a city restaurant; in a carriage on the way to Elsa's; in the office; in a taxi on the way to K.'s mother's.

   The more recent Stroemfeld facsimile edition of *The Trial* does away with chronology (since Kafka never gave the chapters/fragments a final order) and makes no distinction between what the Fischer editors term "completed" and "fragmentary" chapters. In the Stroemfeld edition, all sixteen of the chapters/fragments are presented as individual booklets and are collected in one slip box. The many new ordering possibilities render K.'s "travels" even more chaotic.

2. See *A* 14, *C* 4, and *T* 7; *P* 12. This trouble with "*Legitimationspapiere*" prefigures Kafka's own later difficulties in Europe's early (post–World War I) days of passports: Just as Karl Rossmann cannot produce his "identification papers" when detained by a policeman in upstate New York, so too is Kafka (lacking a proper visa) detained by Austrian agents at the Czech/Austrian border upon returning from visiting Milena Jesenská in Vienna in July 1920 (*A* 214; *V* 277; *LM* 64–67; *BM* 86–90).

3. For a popular account of apparent Irish-American control of the police and the connection to Kafka's America novel, see note 95 in chapter two.

4. Adorno claims to be following Klaus Mann's "insiste[nce] that there was a similarity between Kafka's world and that of the Third Reich" (Adorno, "Notes on Kafka," in *Prisms*, 259). For an overview of early sociological approaches to Kafka, see Beicken, *Franz Kafka*, 214–25.

5. Pavel Eisner, "Franz Kafka and Prague," *Books Abroad* (Summer 1947): 267.

6. Eisner, "Franz Kafkas *Prozeß* und Prague," *German Life and Letters* 14 (1960): 17, 20.

7. Eisner, *Franz Kafka and Prague*, 21.

8. Eisner, *Franz Kafka and Prague*, 8, 79; "Franz Kafka and Prague," 267 (Eisner's emphasis).

9. Heinz Politzer, *Franz Kafka, der Künstler*, (Frankfurt a. M., 1965), 247 (originally published in 1962).

10. *T* 3, 201; *P* 7, 273. See Sokel, *Franz Kafka—Tragik und Ironie*, 138, 145 (originally published in 1964); Kurz, *Traum-Schrecken*, 160, 183.

11. Laurence Rickels, "Writing as Travel and Travail"; Manfred Frank, *Die unendliche Fahrt: Ein Motiv und sein Text* (Frankfurt a. M., 1979), 17–37.

12. See Clifford, "Traveling Cultures." For a neo-Marxist perspective (which "many Marxists might find abhorrent") on the fragmentation of home (and of narrative authority), note Arjun Appadurai on global disjuncture: "This is not to say that there are no relatively stable communities [. . .].

But it is to say that the warp of these stabilities is everywhere shot through with the woof of human motion, as more persons and groups deal with the realities of having to move or the fantasies of wanting to move" (Arjun Appadurai, *Modernity at Large: Cultural Dimensions of Globalization* [Minneapolis, 1996], 201n1, 33–34).

13. *Wahrig Deutsches Wörterbuch*, 1986 edition, s.v. "*ver-*."

14. Ritchie Robertson, "*Der Proceß*," in *Franz Kafka: Romane und Erzählungen*, ed. Michael Müller (Stuttgart, 1994), 137.

15. David H. Miles, "'Pleats, Pockets, Buckles and Buttons': Kafka's New Literalism and the Poetics of the Fragment," in *Probleme der Moderne*, ed. B. Bennett, A. Kaes, and W. J. Lillyman (Tübingen, 1983), 331–42.

16. Kurz, *Traum-Schrecken*, 160.

17. Anderson, *Kafka's Clothes*, 159.

18. "The arrest is an intrusion into [K.'s] intimate life, almost a rape" (Anderson, *Kafka's Clothes*, 161).

19. For example, Ernst Lubitsch's film *Die Bergkatze* (1919) (Boa, *Kafka*, 189n16).

20. Derrida speaks of this notion of "invagination" at several points throughout his work, but probably his first reference of consequence is from his 1977 "Living On / Border Lines": "By definition, there is no end to a discourse that would seek to describe the invaginated structure of [Maurice Blanchot's] *La folie du jour*. Invagination is the inward refolding of *la gaine* [sheath, girdle], the inverted reapplication of the outer edge to the inside of a form where the outside then opens a pocket. Such invagination is possible from the first trace on. This is why there is no 'first' trace" (Jacques Derrida, "Living On / Border Lines," in Harold Bloom et al., *Deconstruction and Criticism* [New York, 1979], 97).

21. Derrida, "Living On / Border Lines," 97.

22. Boa, *Kafka*, 188.

23. According to Canetti, the most upsetting aspect of K.'s arrest is its "being public" (Elias Canetti, *Kafka's Other Trial: The Letters to Felice*, trans. Christopher Middleton [New York: Schocken, 1974], 64–65).

24. Canetti, *Kafka's Other Trial*, 72.

25. Max Brod deleted Kafka's remark on the Milan prostitute's *Scham* from his editions of Kafka's diaries; it has still not been translated into English (*D* 459; *Ta* 969, 1006).

26. Caitriona Leahy, "Reisen in einem Zimmer, oder: die Wände hochgehen," in *Reisen im Diskurs*, ed. Ann Fuchs and Theo Harden (Heidelberg, 1995), 87–101. Leahy points out that Kafka's mad room-traveling was foreshadowed by Xavier de Maistre's *Voyage autour de ma chambre* (1794) and Charlotte Perkins Gilman's "The Yellow Wallpaper" (1892). For more on the affinity between Kafka and Gilman, see Boa, *Kafka*, 120–33.

27. These conflicts include Gregor's desire to punish himself (for having usurped his father's dominant role in the family) (Kaiser), his masochistic "self-hatred" (Neider) and his latent "death drive" (Landberg). See Hellmuth Kaiser,

"Franz Kafkas Inferno: Eine psychologische Deutung seiner Strafphantasie," *Imago* 17 (1931): 41–103; Charles Neider, *The Frozen Sea: A Study of Franz Kafka* (New York, 1948), 77–78.; Paul Landsberg, "Kafka et 'La Metamorphose,'" *L'Esprit* 72 (1938): 671–684. For an overview of the criticism, see Beicken, *Franz Kafka,* 261–72 and Stanley Corngold, *The Commentator's Despair: The Interpretation of Kafka's "Metamorphosis"* (Port Washington, NY, 1973).

28. Beicken summarizes Marxist interpretations of this story in Beicken, *Franz Kafka,* 265–66. See also Kenneth Hughes (ed.), *Franz Kafka: An Anthology of Marxist Criticism* (Hanover, NH, 1981).

29. Another example is Waldemar Bonsels' best-selling *Indienfahrt* (*Indian Journey*), which is rife with *Ungeziefer.* In one especially explicit account, Bonsels describes how bloodthirsty Indian rats maul a helpless kitten:

> A dainty little kitten, hardly realizing the danger, sprang into the moonlight, gracefully leaping. Two shadows, perceptible only by their furtive movements, followed swiftly—a few moments later and the little thing was torn to shreds. At its heartrending cry of distress, its mother made a desperate effort to come to the rescue. I looked on horrified, as the dreadful assailants fixed their teeth in her body. With screams of pain, *such as I had never heard from a cat,* she writhed upon the floor. (my emphasis)

Even more frightening, to the narrator, than the image of the foreign horde tearing apart a kitten is the uncanny transformation of the kitten's mother. In the midst of the squeals of the rats, she emits an expression of pain that, for Bonsels, does not sound like a cat's. He implies that she, like another cat in the fray, has been infected psychologically by the rats: "Out of its mind [*wie von Sinnen*]" with pain, the cat suddenly became for him "monstrous [*ungeheuer*]." (Bonsels, *Indienfahrt,* in *Wanderschaft,* 3:18–20). The use of *ungeheuer,* here, has the same etymological echo that it does in the first sentence of Kafka's *Metamorphosis: geheuer* issues from the Middle High German *gehiure,* which is related to "home" and means, specifically, "belonging to the same settlement."

If Bonsels' cat is *ungeheuer* (*not* belonging to the same settlement as the narrator), it is not *ungeheuer* to the same degree that Kafka's *Ungeziefer* is. Bonsels' narrative—unlike Kafka's—limits its own unsettling force in two ways. First, Bonsels' narrator is always safely distanced from the grotesque, foreign element. Observing the rats from a distance, he is never in danger of getting ill or being bitten himself. His own human body, unlike Gregor's, is not itself the site of the uncanny transformation. Secondly, this narrative takes place in a faraway land. The grotesque vermin (rats, but also various bugs and snakes) upset his temporary home in India, but not his true *Heimat* in Germany. Unlike Kafka's novella, then, *Indian Journey* is a kind of uncanny tease. It offers its audience only as much alterity as it can handle (indeed, precisely enough to make *Indian Journey* a best-seller). In the end, however, it assures its bourgeois readership that the grotesque Other is quite far away, both literally and conceptually, from "home."

Kafka's beloved *Little Green Books*, first published in 1910, contained many similar descriptions of *Ungeziefer* in exotic realms. See (all published in Cologne, by Schaffstein): Karl von den Steinen's 1912 *Bei den Indianern am Shingu*, 21; Förster Fleck's 1912 *Erzählung von seinen Schicksalen auf dem Zuge Napoleons nach Rußland und von seiner Gefangenschaft 1812–1814*, 91; Oskar Weber's 1913 *Briefe eines Kaffee-Pflanzers: Zwei Jahrzehnte deutscher Arbeit in Zentral-Amerika*, 9; and esp. K. Wettstein's 1911 *Durch den brasilianischen Urwald: Erlebnisse bei einer Wegerkundung in den deutschvölkischen Kolonien Süd-Brasiliens*, 6–8, 18, 22, 28, 35–36, 42, 57.

30. Flaubert, *Flaubert in Egypt*, 119, 220.

31. Cf. the similar phrasing in Kafka's earlier "Description of a Struggle," where we learn of a man who is suffering from "a seasickness on dry land" (*DS* 60; *NSI* 89, trans. rev.).

32. See chapter one for a general discussion of the second home (and the fantasy of the lost-and-found mother) in exotic fin de siècle literature. For the specific case of Karl Rossmann, see chapter two.

33. Freud, "The Uncanny," in *The Standard Edition of the Complete Psychological Works of Sigmund Freud*, 17:245.

34. *T* 43; *P* 59; for further examples, see *T* 37, 103, 196; *P* 52, 138, 266.

35. Johann Wolfgang von Goethe, *Die Faustdichtungen* (Munich, 1989), 338–41, 526.

36. Freud, *Beyond the Pleasure Principle* (*Jenseits des Lustprinzips*), in *Standard Edition*, 18:38, 41, 40.

37. Freud, *Standard Edition*, 18:39, 38; *Freud-Studienausgabe*, ed. Alexander Mitscherlich, Angela Richards, James Strachey (Frankfurt a. M., [1969–75]), 3:248.

38. Jean Baudrillard points out a connection between the Freudian death drive and utopia that matches precisely with K.'s own u-topian desire to die: "[The death drive] dissolves assemblages, unbinds energy and undoes Eros' organic discourse by returning things to an inorganic, *ungebunden*, state, in a certain sense, to utopia as opposed to the articulate and constructive topics of Eros. Entropy of death, negentropy of Eros" (Jean Baudrillard, *Symbolic Exchange and Death* [London, 1993], 149).

39. Freud, *Standard Edition*, 18:39.

40. Rickels, "Writing as Travel and Travail," 32, 33.

41. Rickels' use of "ver-dict's" literal meaning is dubious since Kafka never once uses the German word "*Verdikt*" (instead employing "*Urteil*") in *The Trial*. Suggestive as this connection between "verdict" and "meaning" is, it depends on importing the word "verdict" into the German text. I thank an anonymous reader at Palgrave for pointing this out (Rickels, "Writing as Travel and Travail," 33).

42. The K. of the later chapters seems to learn intertextually from "In the Penal Colony," which Kafka began mid-way through *The Trial*: K. only

consults with Titorelli on a full-blown traveling defense and begins to travel more frantically in the second half of *The Trial.*

43. For more on Mauthner and his importance for Prague culture in Kafka's era, see Christoph Stölzl, "Prag: Die Verhältnisse um 1900," in *Kafka-Handbuch,* ed. Hartmut Binder, 1:86–88.

44. Hugo von Hofmannsthal, "Ein Brief," in *Sämtliche Werke,* ed. Ellen Ritter (Frankfurt a. M., 1991), 31:54.

45. For a description of writing's loss of authority for Kafka after 1917, see Corngold, "Kafka's Double Helix," in *Franz Kafka: The Necessity of Form,* 105–36.

46. Rainer Stach, "Eros, Macht und Gesetz: Der Verkehr der Behörden," in *Kafkas erotischer Mythos,* 145–57; Anderson cites Stach in his discussion of *Verkehr* in *The Trial* (Anderson, *Kafka's Clothes,* 155n16).

47. Anderson, *Kafka's Clothes,* 163, 162.

48. Anderson, *Kafka's Clothes,* 162.

49. In addition to Anderson, see Stanley Corngold: "And, indeed, the outcome for Josef K., who has evidently conducted his trial badly—obtusely, faint-heartedly—is to be stabbed to death 'like a dog,' an unteachable dog" (Corngold, *Franz Kafka: The Necessity of Form,* 236).

50. Gerhard Kurz, "Figuren," in *Kafka-Handbuch,* ed. Hartmut Binder, 2:120.

51. Benjamin, "Franz Kafka: On the Tenth Anniversary of His Death," 132. The original reads: "unter allen Geschöpfen Kafkas kommen am meisten Tiere zum Nachdenken" (*Benjamin über Kafka,* 30–31).

52. Deleuze and Guattari, *Kafka: Toward a Minor Literature,* 12.

53. For Freud's definition of perversity, see his "Three Essays on the Theory of Sexuality," in *Standard Edition,* 7:125–245.

54. Robertson, *Kafka: Judaism, Politics, Literature,* 110.

55. For the importance of Otto Weininger's best-selling, misogynist *Sex and Charakter* (*Geschlecht und Character,* 1903) for Kafka, see Anderson, *Kafka's Clothes,* 194–216. Further in this cultural-historical vein, Elizabeth Boa sees Fräulein Bürstner as a prototypically independent "New Woman"; in Boa's view, K.'s actions are part of a cultural "mean rage against the New Woman, whose escape from stereotypes proves difficult if not impossible to accept" (Boa, *Kafka,* 197).

56. Leni's fingers could also signify the human "degenerate" as represented, for example, in the deformed fingers and toes from Paul Gauguin's 1880s/1890s "Eve" paintings, about which Kafka (a reader of Gauguin's Tahitian journals) likely knew. Like Gauguin's Eves, Leni has a "defect," is a "whim of nature." This notion of the "degenerate" is of course not far apart from notions of the "animal" (the non-human) in exclusionary nineteenth- and twentieth-century discourses (as National Socialism finally bears out). (See, among other Gauguin paintings, *Ève—pas écouter li li menteur* [1889], *Ève bretonne* [1889], *Ève exotique* [1890], and *Te nave, nave fenua* [1892].) I thank Sander Gilman for the reference to Gauguin.

57. Weininger's *Sex and Character* generally devalued women as purely instinctual, sensual, and unreflective beings, for whom "emotion" and "thought"

were one and the same (not separate categories as they were for men). Max Brod's *A Czech Servant Girl (Ein tschechisches Dienstmädchen,* 1909) comments specifically (as did Freud, in scattered remarks) on the excessive sexuality of servant girls. For more on *A Czech Servant Girl* and its possible connection to Kafka's depictions of women, see Spector, *Prague Territories,* 174–77.

58. In Paul's letter to the Romans (during his discussion of the depravity of the gentiles), sexual *Verirrung* refers to perversity, explicitly to homosexuality: "their men, in turn, giving up natural intercourse [*den natürlichen Verkehr*] with women, burn with lust for one another; men carry on disgracefully with men, and they are paid the wage of their perversion [going astray, *Verirrung*] in their own person, as is fitting" (Rom. 1:27; my translation from Martin Luther's German).

59. Georges Van Den Abbeele, "Sightseers: The Tourist as Theorist," *diacritics* 10 (December 1980): 2–14.

60. Deleuze and Guattari, *Kafka,* 45.

61. Kafka and Brod named their prospective series "*Billig*" (On the Cheap) and planned to issue titles such as "On the Cheap through Switzerland," "On the Cheap in Paris," etc. (Brod, *Franz Kafka: A Biography,* 120–21). The entire text of Kafka's and Brod's sketch (not yet translated into English) is entitled "Unser Millionenplan 'Billig'" ("Our Plan to Make Millions 'On the Cheap'") (*EFI,* 189–92).

62. Karl Baedeker, *Österreich-Ungarn (nebst Cetinje Belgrad Bukarest): Handbuch für Reisende* (Leipzig, 1910).

63. Baedeker, *Österreich-Ungarn,* v–vi.

64. Baedeker, *Paris und Umgebungen,* 48.

65. Brod, *Franz Kafka,* 120 (Brod's emphasis); cf. *EFI* 190.

66. Baedeker employs precisely this mode of "guiding" the tourist through museums. See, for example, Baedeker's guide to central and northern Germany (Baedeker, *Mittel- und Nord-Deutschland: Westlich bis zum Rhein: Handbuch für Reisende,* 22nd edn. [Leipzig, 1887]), which guides the tourist, artwork by artwork, through the Altes Museum in Berlin; this (or a slightly updated edition) was likely the guide that Kafka carried with him on his journeys to Weimar and Leipzig in 1912 (and perhaps later to Berlin, when visiting Felice Bauer or moving in with Dora Diamant).

67. Rickels, "Writing as Travel and Travail," 33.

68. According to Kafka's diary entries from December 1914, he was beginning his "mother chapter" in the same days that he was finishing "In the Cathedral" (*D* 320–21; entries from December 8 and 13). The logic of the Fischer critical edition of *Der Prozeß* (which, unlike the more recent Stroemfeld slip-box version, orders chapters according to the chronology of their creation) would thus likely position "Journey to His Mother" immediately after "In the Cathedral."

69. Deleuze and Guattari, *Kafka,* 45.

70. There is a similar randomness leading up to the sexual encounter with Leni: K. meets her in a dark hallway, and he allows himself to be led blindly

until they reach the door of the lawyer's empty office (where the love scene occurs) (*T* 104; *P* 139–40).

71. Stanley Corngold uses this term to discuss Karl Rossmann from *The Man Who Disappeared,* but I think that it also pertains to *The Trial's* K. (whose rapture, like Rossmann's, often seems to issue from fatigue). See Corngold, "Rapture in Exile: Kafka's *The Boy Who Sank Out of Sight,*" in *Complex Pleasure,* 121–38.

72. Roland Barthes, *Camera Lucida,* trans. Richard Howard (New York, 1981), 26–27.

73. K. arrives at work at seven o'clock *("um sieben Uhr"),* plans to meet the Italian around ten *("etwa um zehn Uhr"),* arrives punctually *("pünktlich")* at the Cathedral, waits at least half an hour *("zumindest eine halbe Stunde")* for the Italian, and, later, looks at his watch *("sah auf seine Uhr")* (*T* 201, 203, 206, 210; *P* 272, 276, 279, 285).

74. Barthes, *Camera Lucida,* 96, 97.

75. "Doch das Paradies ist verriegelt und der Cherub hinter uns; wir müssen die Reise um die Welt machen, und sehen, ob es vielleicht von hinten irgendwo wieder offen ist" (Heinrich von Kleist, "Über das Marionettentheater," in *Über das Marionettentheater: Aufsätze und Anekdote* [Frankfurt a. M., 1987], 7–16 [here, 11]).

76. Freud, *Beyond the Pleasure Principle (Jenseits des Lustprinzips),* in *Standard Edition,* 18:38, Freud's emphasis, trans. rev. Freud's German reads *"zum Leblosen zurückzukehren"* (*Studienausgabe,* 3:248). Freud uses the term *zurückkehren* because he views life (i.e., the organic) as something that has come out of the inorganic (i.e., from "unsere[r] Erde und ihr[em] hältnis zur Sonne" [*Studienausgabe,* 3:247]). Hence the idea of return: "Der konservativen Natur der Triebe widerspräche es, wenn das Ziel des Lebens ein noch nie zuvor erreichter Zustand wäre" (*Studienausgabe,* 3:248).

77. Freud, *Standard Edition,* 18:37–38 (Freud's emphasis).

78. Boa, *Kafka,* 234.

79. Boa, *Kafka,* 234.

80. Boa, *Kafka,* 233.

81. K.'s "refusal of the knife becomes a refusal of the Janus-like position which sado-masochism represents" (Boa, *Kafka,* 235).

82. Deleuze correctly points out, in his reading of Sacher-Masoch's *Venus in Furs,* that the masochist's torturer is generally not a "truly sadistic torturer" but rather only a dominator/dominatrix who has been trained by the masochist (who needs a well-trained torturer to fit into *his* masochistic fantasy). Moreover, a "genuine sadist could never tolerate" a masochistic victim (i.e., one who gained pleasure from the torture). See Gilles Deleuze, "Coldness and Cruelty," in *Masochism* (New York, 1991), 40–41.

83. Boa, *Kafka,* 235.

84. Walter Sokel, "Franz Kafka, *Der Process* (1925)," in *Deutsche Romane des 20. Jahrhunderts,* ed. Paul Michael Lützeler (Königstein, 1983), 117.

85. Peter Beicken discusses, in his review of the secondary literature, the various ways in which critics have traditionally understood K.'s guilt (Beicken, *Franz Kafka*, 275–84). In a later publication, Stanley Corngold argues that K. is guilty because he relies too much on "personal," "lived experience"— at the expense of writing, or, more specifically, of a kind of writing that is not beholden to experience (Corngold, *Franz Kafka: The Necessity of Form*, 245, see also 246–49).

86. According to Mark Anderson, K. suffers under both the "nightmarish" "criminal justice system" and the "sexual ethics of the patriarchal society": this legal and social system has the awesome power to "corrupt everything, even the accused men it persecutes without reason and will finally execute" (Anderson, *Kafka's Clothes*, 169, 171).

87. For *The Metamorphosis*, see Ruth Klüger Angress, "Kafka and Sacher-Masoch: A Note on *The Metamorphosis*," *MLN* 85 (1970): 745–46; F. M. Kuna, "Art as Direct Vision: Kafka and Sacher-Masoch," *Journal of European Studies* 2 (1972): 237–46; Anderson, "Kafka and Sacher-Masoch," *Journal of the Kafka Society of America* 7 (1983): 4–19. For "A Hunger Artist," see Norris, "The Fate of the Human Animal in Kafka's Fiction," in *Beasts of the Modern Imagination,* 101–17.

88. *T* 84, 195; *P* 114, 265. Sabine Wilke, "'Der Elbogen ruhte auf dem Kissen der Ottomane': Über die sado-masochistischen Wurzeln von Kafkas *Der Process," Journal of the Kafka Society of America* 21 (1997): 75, 77.

89. Wilke, "Der Elbogen," 74.

90. Wilke, "Der Elbogen," 69.

91. Canetti, *Kafka's Other Trial,* 71–72.

92. Sokel, "Franz Kafka, *Der Process,*" 117.

93. This story grouping opposes Sokel's, who (failing to notice K.'s masochism) sees K. as disconnected from Georg Bendemann (Sokel, "Franz Kafka, *Der Process,*" 120). For more on masochism and performance, see Deleuze's claim that masochism "always has a theatrical quality" (Deleuze, "Coldness and Cruelty," 55). Deleuze borrows this notion from Theodor Reik, who argues that masochism corresponds to the "staging of a drama" (Reik, *Masochism in Modern Man,* trans. Margaret H. Biegel and Gertrud M. Kurth [New York: Farrar, Straus, 1949], 49).

94. Brod, *Franz Kafka,* 129.

95. See Sacher-Masoch's contract with his dominatrix, Wanda, which gives her the "right to torture you to death by the most horrible methods imaginable" (Leopold von Sacher-Masoch, *Venus in Furs,* in *Masochism* [New York: Zone, 1991], 279).

Chapter Four

1. Hans Beilhack, "Fünfter Abend für Neue Literatur," in *Münchner Zeitung,* November 12, 1916, rpt. in *Franz Kafka: Kritik und Rezeption zu seinen*

Lebzeiten 1912–1924, ed. Jürgen Born (Frankfurt a. M., 1979), 121 (Beil-hack's emphasis).

2. Otto Erich Hesse, "Franz Kafka, In der Strafkolonie," *Zeitschrift für Bücher-freunde,* March/April 1921, rpt. in Born, *Franz Kafka: Kritik und Rezeption zu seinen Lebzeiten,* 97.

3. Kurt Wolff, *Briefwechsel eines Verlegers* (Frankfurt a. M., 1966), 49.

4. Kurt Tucholsky [Peter Panter, pseud.], "In der Strafkolonie," *Die Weltbühne,* June 3, 1920, rpt. in Born, *Franz Kafka: Kritik und Rezeption zu seinen Lebzeiten,* 94.

5. Tucholsky, "In der Strafkolonie," 95. Otto Erich Hesse immediately coun-tered Tucholsky by claiming that, even though "In the Penal Colony" in-deed seems to criticize a political "lust for power," the story remains primarily sadistic and "sensational[ist]" (Hesse, "Franz Kafka, In der Strafkolonie," 97). Beilhack, likewise, claimed that Kafka's fascination with what is "loathsome and disgusting" cancels out the story's otherwise "po-litical" connections to our "men-murdering epoch" (Beilhack, "Fünfter Abend," 121).

6. Janouch, *Conversations with Kafka,* 131; *Gespräche mit Kafka,* 2nd ed. (Frankfurt a. M., 1968), 180; *LM* 214; *BM* 290.

7. Margot Norris, "Sadism and Masochism in Two Kafka Stories: 'In der Strafkolonie' and 'Ein Hungerkünstler,'" *MLN* 93 (1978): 430–47 (ex-panded version in Norris, *Beasts of the Modern Imagination,* 101–17 [here, 102, 107]). "Pornology" is Gilles Deleuze's term; I employ this throughout this chapter to denote a kind of erotic language that, as in the work of Sade and Masoch, goes beyond pornography's "elementary functions of order-ing and describing" (Deleuze, "Coldness and Cruelty," 18).

8. Peter Cersowsky, "Das Erbe des Sadomasochismus," in *Phantastische Liter-atur im ersten Viertel des 20. Jahrhunderts* (Munich, 1983), 183–209. Most re-cently, building on Norris and Cersowsky, Mark Anderson has argued that the decorative arabesques on the Penal Colony victim's body can be read as signs of theatrical sado-masochism and "play" (*Kafka's Clothes,* 175).

9. Müller-Seidel specifically criticizes Cersowsky for neglecting the story's manifest political landscape (Müller-Seidel, *Deportation des Menschen,* 141–42 and 182n124).

10. Müller-Seidel, *Deportation,* 17–25. Müller-Seidel builds on the pioneering historical work of Klaus Wagenbach in Wagenbach's edition of Kafka's "In the Penal Colony" (Wagenbach [ed.], *In der Strafkolonie. Eine Geschichte aus dem Jahre 1914*). Müller-Seidel, like Wagenbach, claims that Kafka's fic-tional voyager is probably modeled after the German jurist, Robert Heindl, who was commissioned by the German Colonial Ministry to in-vestigate deportation practices in New Caledonia and other European penal colonies (Müller-Seidel, *Deportation,* 80–87, 108–10). Heindl pub-lished his findings in 1912 in *Meine Reise nach den Strafkolonien* (*My Journey to the Penal Colonies*).

11. Müller-Seidel speaks of the text's thoroughgoing "critical vision, which cannot be gained from the perspective of a single character but rather through the text in all of its perspectives" (Müller-Seidel, *Deportation*, 135). See also *Deportation*, 145.

12. For Karen Piper, Kafka "condemn[s]" the colonial system and moreover ultimately opens up the possibility of postcolonial liberation (Piper, "The Language of the Machine: Kafka and the Subject of Empire," 47). Although Rolf Goebel does not allow for Piper's optimism, he similarly sees "In the Penal Colony" as a narrative of a "victim of colonial power" being oppressed by the "ideological language" of the colonists (Goebel, "Kafka and Postcolonial Critique," 201). Paul Peters relies less on postcolonial theory than do Piper and Goebel (arguing that "In the Penal Colony" is more akin to the anticolonialist classics of Fanon, Césaire, and Memmi than to the discourse-centered work of Said, Bhabha, and Spivak) but comes to a similar conclusion regarding the close connection between Kafka's fiction and colonialism: the "landscape of colonialism," Peters claims, is the "actual historical topography" for Kafka's story (Peters, "Witness to the Execution: Kafka and Colonialism," 401).

13. In Elizabeth Boa's brief discussion of "In the Penal Colony," she briefly mentions the coexistence of colonial and sadistic tensions in this story. But because her interests primarily concern representations of the male body in the crisis of "modernity," she does not fully investigate, in "In the Penal Colony," the specifically colonial aspects of sadism.

    In her conclusions about the story, Boa correctly points out that Kafka ultimately rejects a Sadean pornological structure by not having his Penal Colony traveler become a "sadistic voyeur" (the observer/reader figure central to Sadean aesthetics). But Boa fails to notice the story's equally essential masochistic structures, without which, I maintain, we cannot adequately interpret the story's finale (Boa, "The Double Taboo: The Male Body in *The Judgment, The Metamorphosis,* and *In the Penal Colony*," in *Kafka,* 107–47 [Boa discusses "In the Penal Colony" on 133–47]).

14. Russell Berman, *Enlightenment or Empire: Colonial Discourse in German Culture* (Lincoln, NE, 1998), 232.

15. Mirbeau's narrator's original commission was to go to Fiji and Tasmania to "study their systems of penal administration" (Octave Mirbeau, *Torture Garden,* trans. Michael Richardson [Sawtry, Cambs, England, 1995], 64).

16. *Schaffsteins Grüne Bändchen,* ed. Nicolaus Henningsen (Cologne: Schaffstein, 1910–70). By way of general introduction, it is important to note that the *Little Green Books'* connection to German colonialism is remarkably unsubtle: Appearing first in 1910 and sometimes used as *"Sachliteratur"* in imperial German schools, these volumes offered entertaining, detailed descriptions of how to plant and harvest the exotic crops (sugar, coffee, bananas) grown in the colonies. Notable in this regard are some of the volumes that I will discuss either here or in the following chapter: *The Sugar Baron, Letters of a Coffee Planter,* and *The Banana King.* Moreover, the

Little Green Books also instructed future colonialists on how to hunt exotic wildlife and discipline "savages," as part of a thrilling colonial adventure(in, for example, *In the Hinterlands of German East Africa* [*Im Hinterlande von Deutsch-Ostafrika*, 1910] and *Through Brazil's Tropical Forest: Experiences of a Reconnaissance Mission in the Ethnic-German Colonies of Southern Brazil* [*Durch den brasilianischen Urwald: Erlebnisse bei einer Wegerkundung in den deutschvölkischen Kolonien Süd-Brasiliens*, 1911]). More brutal and direct were the lessons taught by *The Battle against the Herero: Images from the Campaign in the Southwest* (*Im Kampfe gegen die Hereros: Bilder aus dem Feldzug in Südwest*, 1911), and, after the outbreak of World War I, *How We Liberated East Prussia* (*Wie wir Ostpreußen befreiten*, 1915).

17. Peter F. Neumeyer, "Franz Kafka, Sugar Baron," *Modern Fiction Studies* 17 (Spring 1971): 5–16. The only subsequent mentions I have found in the secondary literature are two very brief ones in Beicken's *Franz Kafka*, 287, 337 and one brief one in Binder, *Kafka in neuer Sicht*, 627n304. See also my "Of Sugar Barons and Banana Kings: Franz Kafka, Imperialism, and Schaffstein's *Grüne Bändchen*," *Journal of the Kafka Society of America* 22 (1996): 63–75.

18. Kafka's personal library as well as the books that he refers to in his diaries and letters are expertly indexed by Jürgen Born in *Kafkas Bibliothek: Ein beschreibendes Verzeichnis* (Frankfurt a. M., 1990). For Kafka's personal collection of and references to the *Little Green Books* (he owned at least seven of them), see *Kafkas Bibliothek*, 145–48, 175 ("the great literature of travel"), 180, 217. For the reference to Kafka's tears, see *D* 248 (diary entry from December 15, 1913). Recently, the Stuttgart antiquarian Herbert Blank collected most of the books from Kafka's library documented by Born (including many of Schaffstein's *Little Green Books*) (Herbert Blank, *In Kafkas Bibliothek: Werke der Weltliteratur und Geschichte in der Edition, wie sie Kafka besaß oder kannte* [Stuttgart, 2001]).

19. Although this term undergoes revision in Foucault's work, I will take "discourse" to mean the quotidian reflection of what he calls an *episteme*: the "fundamental codes of a culture," the "historical *a priori*," the "positive basis of knowledge" in a specific historical moment. This definition issues from Foucault's first attempt at articulating discourse, from *Les Mots et les choses: Une archéologie des sciences humaines* (Paris, 1966); English translation from *The Order of Things: An Archaeology of the Human Sciences* (New York, 1973), xx–xxii. He outlines his notion of discourse further in *L'ordre du discours* (Paris, 1971); English translation in "The Discourse on Language," appendix to Foucault, *The Archaeology of Knowledge*, trans. A. M. Sheridan Smith (New York, 1976), 215–37.

20. *Wahrig Deutsches Wörterbuch*, 1986 edition, s.v. *"entweichen." Entweichen* is rendered in the standard English translation of *Letters to Felice* as "avoid," which is inadequate because it does not contain *entweichen's* suggestion of a possible liberation.

21. Weber, *Zuckerbaron*, 29.

22. Neumeyer discusses this example and admits, likewise, that the link between the two machines is speculative, but his essay remains primarily positivistic: he does not investigate discursive correlations. Nonetheless, another of Neumeyer's connections is worth mentioning. He points to similarities between another piece of machinery in *The Sugar Baron* (a sugar press; see figure 14) and Kafka's "Penal Colony" apparatus: The former twists and turns a piece of cane until it expels syrup, redolent of the expelled blood from "In the Penal Colony," which also leads—for the viewers—to purifying "sweet[ness]" (Neumeyer, "Franz Kafka," 10–13; Weber, *Zuckerbaron*, 17). Unnoted by Neumeyer, Kafka might also have been influenced by Weber's terminology of "pressing out" or "crushing" *(auspressen):* the Sugar Baron's press cannot satisfactorily "crush" the syrup out of the cane *("die Auspressung [war] ungenügend");* the penal colony's torture machine, similarly, can no longer adequately "crush" a scream out of its victim ("Heute gelingt es der Maschine nicht mehr, dem Verurteilten ein stärkeres Seufzen auszupressen") (Weber, *Zuckerbaron*, 17; *DL* 226).

23. Weber, *Briefe eines Kaffee-Pflanzers*, 36.

24. Weber, *Briefe eines Kaffee-Pflanzers*, 37.

25. Weber, *Zuckerbaron*, 11.

26. For the machines in Cox and Wladiczek, see Klaus Wagenbach's notes in his expanded, 1995 edition of Franz Kafka, *In der Strafkolonie: Eine Geschichte aus dem Jahre 1914*, 77–9, 113–15; for the phonograph, see the fascinating discussion by Wolf Kittler in "Schreibmaschinen, Sprechmaschinen. Effekte technischer Medien im Werk Franz Kafkas," in *Franz Kafka: Schriftverkehr*, ed. Wolf Kittler and Gerhard Neumann (Freiburg, 1990), esp. 116–41.

27. For example, Hermann Glaser cites an article from the popular German magazine *Die Gartenlaube* (entitled "A Disgrace to the Nineteenth Century") that describes voyeurism at a slave auction in late-nineteenth-century Dutch Surinam ("The male or female slave is immediately compelled to discard all clothing") and, later, brutal sadism ("Yes, it is scarcely believable, but in Surinam there are [European] ladies who do not hesitate to examine and scrutinize the thighs of their slaves to see whether the depths of their wounds are in good relation to the guilders they have paid; ladies who rub Spanish pepper into bloody limbs"). See *Querschnitt durch die Gartenlaube*, ed. Heinz Klüter (Bern, 1963), 158–60; cited in Hermann Glaser, *Literatur des 20. Jahrhunderts in Motiven* (Munich, 1978), 1:135. John Noyes discusses this citation in relation to colonial sadism and masochism in *The Mastery of Submission: Inventions of Masochism* (Ithaca, NY, 1997), 117–18.

28. Noyes, *Mastery of Submission*, 127.

29. Noyes, *Mastery of Submission*, 127–38 (includes reproductions of some of these images).

30. As Chris Bongie points out, the New Imperialism began to gain the upper hand in 1876, during the British debate surrounding the Royal Titles Act,

which was to proffer the title of "Empress of India" to Queen Victoria. Although the Old Imperialists won this battle (Victoria became Empress),
the liberal opposition acquired a moral momentum that led to reforms in
official colonial policy in the last decades of the century. As Bongie argues
(and as I will discuss in relation to Kafka's story), the New Imperialism's
apparently modern notion of enlightened colonialism had, however, contradictions of its own: "Ridding the Empire of its imperial vestiges is the
paradoxical imperative of the New Imperialism, as it engages in and is engaged by a process of rationalization that must (in theory, to be sure) lead
to the transformation of an enlightened despotism into an even more lu-
minous paternalism, one better suited to the global pretensions of colonial
power in the age of the New Imperialism" (Bongie, *Exotic Memories*,
36–38).

31. The New Imperialism insisted that the "founding contradiction of the Old
Imperialism—the two-fold postulate of democracy at home and despotism
abroad—had to give way, or at the very least be represented as giving way,
to a more 'civilized' relationship between metropolitan and peripheral territories" (Bongie, *Exotic Memories*, 36–37).

32. Noyes, *Mastery of Submission*, 127, 129. As Noyes points out, the German
Colonial Society (founded in 1887) and the German-Colonial Women's
League (1907) "provided free passage to South-West Africa for prospective
settler-wives" (129).

33. Noyes, *Mastery of Submission*, 129. Sabine Wilke elaborates on the same
point: "the training of women for service in the colonies culminated in pro-
viding the settler with the cozy atmosphere of a German household and
keeping him from fraternizing with the natives. This project is intimately tied
to the strict prohibition of miscegenation" (Sabine Wilke, "The Colonial
Pedagogy of Imperial Germany: Hegelian Dialectics, Hermeneutics, and
Masochism," in *Competing Imperialisms*, ed. Elizabeth Sauer [forthcoming]).

   Moreover, the women's (sexually) civilizing influence was to help with
the general New Imperial re-direction of male libidinal energy away from
sadism and toward what Chris Bongie terms economic "rationalization"
and "efficiency" (the latter being the modern "watchword" of the New
Imperialism) (Bongie, *Exotic Memories*, 37, 41).

34. Noyes, *Mastery of Submission*, 127–28.

35. This fact cements the Schaffstein heroes' position within a "new" colonial
discourse that demanded that sadism be repressed. Further, contemporaneous examples of German colonial sadism (and its more or less successful
repression) include Frieda von Bülow's aptly named 1895 *Tropenkoller* (a
critical account of the brutal German colonialist, Karl Peters) and Gustav
Frenssen's 1906 *Peter Moor's Journey to Southwest Africa*. See John Noyes,
"National Identity, Nomadism, and Narration in Gustav Frenssen's *Peter
Moor's Journey to Southwest Africa*," in *The Imperialist Imagination: German
Colonialism and Its Legacy*, ed. Sara Friedrichsmeyer, Sara Lennox, and Su-
sanne Zantop (Ann Arbor, MI, 1998), 87–105.

36. Cornelia Schneider, "Die Bilderbuchproduktion der Verlage Jos. Scholz (Mainz) and Schaffstein (Köln) in den Jahren 1899 bis 1932" (Ph.D. diss., Frankfurt a. M., 1984), 66. Schaffstein's *Little Green Books* were, the publishers claimed, the first series devoted to *Sachlesen* ("history, geography, natural history") in German schools, and the publishers advertised for these books' continued use in schools into the 1930s and beyond (Severin Rüttgers, *Schaffsteins Grüne Bändchen im Schulunterricht und als Klassenlektüre* [Cologne, 1930], 1).

37. The official policy against sadism in the colonies foreshadows the Nazi prohibition against sadism in Auschwitz three decades later. For the Nazi legal regulations against sadism in Auschwitz (including the 1943 charges filed by the government against the Head of the Auschwitz Political Department) and the attempt to enforce what would seem to be a more orderly and domestically acceptable form of genocide, see Rebecca Wittmann, "Holocaust on Trial?: The Frankfurt Auschwitz Trial in Historical Perspective" (Ph.D. diss., Univ. of Toronto, 2001), 127–39. With this particular connection between colonial and National Socialist discourse in mind, it is interesting to note that Schaffstein's *Little Green Books* became favorites of the Nazi Wehrmacht—sent along (like Karl May books) as *Feldpostausgaben* (military editions) for the soldiers to read on the front. This *Feldpostausgabe* stamp can still be seen on 1940s reprints of some of the *Little Green Books*.

38. Weber, *Zuckerbaron*, 10, 9.

39. Adolf Friedrich zu Mecklenburg, *Im Hinterlande von Deutsch-Ostafrika* (Cologne, 1910), 47, 11.

40. Mecklenburg, *Im Hinterlande von Deutsch-Ostafrika*, 59–60

41. Noyes, *Mastery of Submission*, 117.

42. Flaubert, *Flaubert in Egypt*, 42–43. Throughout his notes and personal letters from the Orient, moreover, Flaubert regularly revels in looking at the tortured and ill bodies of the "natives": a beaten "black behind" (33), rotten teeth (114), lepretic genitalia (40), plague-sores (118). As Ali Behdad argues, however, Flaubert seems to exaggerate his sadistic perspective, and even to drive perverse clichés to absurd extremes (as in Flaubert's trumped-up remake of what he calls "the old comic business of the cudgeled slave") (Flaubert, *Flaubert in Egypt*, 33). Flaubert pushes his perversity beyond colonialism's traditional limits; in so doing, he ends up by (perhaps unconsciously) parodying the very colonial system that made space for his sadism to begin with. Flaubert's desire is, says Behdad, "transgressive" because of its excess: he over-produces sadism and thereby "transcend[s] the power relations of Orientalism" that had prepared the stage for his fantasies. Flaubert thus turns cliché into pornographic over-indulgence. (Behdad, *Belated Travelers*, 65).

   And Flaubert, like Kafka's officer (and unlike the heroes of the *Little Green Books*), toys with the idea of perhaps ultimately becoming one of the beaten, one of the injured native bodies. Flaubert does more than just attempt to "go native" by dressing like an Egyptian (as evidenced by the only surviving photograph of Flaubert in Egypt); he also courts "native" infections, encouraging illness, through deliberately reckless sex. As he writes after having sex with a "crazy," plague-stricken Egyptian prostitute: "On the matting: firm flesh, bronze arse, shaven cunt, dry though fatty; the whole thing gave the effect of a plague victim or a leperhouse" (Flaubert, *Flaubert in Egypt*, 40; cf. Behdad, *Belated Travelers*, 145n13). Flaubert sadistically penetrates this powerless foreign Other, but she might, in turn, penetrate his body with her disease. How much of her Otherness—her insanity, her infection, her proximity to death—will he be able to contain? As Behdad argues, sadistic pleasure becomes, in the end, less important to Flaubert than these self-exposures to death (Behdad, *Belated Travelers*, 66–68).

Comparable to Flaubert's attempt at Oriental self-obliteration is T. E. Lawrence's, whose homosexuality and masochism Kaja Silverman investigates in "White Skins, Brown Masks: The Double Mimesis, or With Lawrence in Arabia," in *Male Subjectivity at the Margins* (New York, 1992), 299–338.

43. Long viewed as the primary source for the sadism in Kafka's story, *Torture Garden* has, however, yet to be seen as a source for "In the Penal Colony's" specifically *colonial* sadism. See Binder, *Kafka-Kommentar zu sämtlichen Erzählungen*, 174–81.

44. Mirbeau, *Torture Garden*, 106, 125.

45. Mirbeau, *Torture Garden*, 153, 152.

46. As we read in *Torture Garden:* "[T]he Chinese alone know the divine secret" of artful torture (Mirbeau, *Torture Garden*, 153–54).

47. For more on the politics of Mirbeau and his *Torture Garden* (especially in relation to the Dreyfus Affair), see Müller-Seidel, *Deportation*, 143–45; Anderson, *Kafka's Clothes*, 177–78; and Brian Stableford's introduction to the latest translation of Mirbeau's *Torture Garden*, 10–11. Anderson, too, sees *Torture Garden* as a political "parody" (albeit of European decadence, not of colonial sadism) (177).

Kafka was also a supporter of Dreyfus, who was imprisoned on the French penal colony, Devil's Island, from 1895 to 1899. In a letter to Max Brod, Kafka wrote of the "fight for Dreyfus" *("Kampf für Dreyfus")* (*L* 348; *B* 402). See Gilman, *Franz Kafka, the Jewish Patient*, 68–88.

48. Mirbeau, *Torture Garden*, 139.

49. As Clara points out to Mirbeau's narrator, European sadism is by no means limited to Europe: "I'm sure you think the Chinese are fiercer than us? Not at all! We English? Ah, tell me about it! And you French?" She then goes on to recall seeing the French bury thirty fleeing Algerians in the hot desert sand (with only their heads protruding) until they died of dehydration. She then remembers how the English slit the throats of the "little Modeljar princes" on the temple steps in the sacred city of Kandy, the former capital of Ceylon (Sri Lanka) (Mirbeau, *Torture Garden*, 140–41).

50. This leads the narrator to think of "the [European] judges, the soldiers and the priests who, everywhere [. . .] continued death's work" (Mirbeau, *Torture Garden*, 189–90).

51. The steel belt on the engraving part of the old commandant's machinery "*strafft sich sofort* [. . .] *zu einer Stange*" (stiffens immediately to form a rigid bar) and then begins to cut and spray acid into the prostrate man's skin (*MO* 134; *DL* 215). On the phallic nature of the old commandant, Clayton Koelb writes: "This 'Straffheit' of the machine, which is really just a reflection of the 'Straffheit' of the old Commandant and his ethic, an ideal of 'straffe Zucht,' rigid discipline, is thus both sexual and authoritarian" (Clayton Koelb, "'In der Strafkolonie': Kafka and the Scene of Reading," *German Quarterly* 55 [1982]: 512).

52. The sovereign based his power on his "dominion over bodies and his capacity for their total subjection" (Roberta Maccagnani, "Esotismo-erotismo—Pierre Loti: Dalla maschera erotica alla sovranità coloniale," in *Letteratura, esotismo, colonialismo,* ed. Anita Licari, Roberta Maccagnani, and Lina Zecchi [Bologna, 1978], 68). Cited in Bongie, *Exotic Memories,* 38.

53. Peter J. Brenner, "Schwierige Reisen: Wandlungen des Reiseberichts in Deutschland 1918–1945," in *Reisekultur in Deutschland: Von der Weimarer Republik zum "Dritten Reich,"* ed. Peter J. Brenner (Tübingen, 1997), 129.

54. For more on Sade's erotic Panopticon, see Marcel Hénaff, *Sade: The Invention of the Libertine Body,* trans. Xavier Callahan (Minneapolis, 1999), 109. See also Peter Cersowsky's claim that Kafka's Penal Colony traveler is an instantiation of sado-masochism's prototypical "voyeuristic observer" (Cersowsky, *Phantastische Literatur,* 198–201).

55. Hénaff, *Sade,* 106, 109. One of many examples of Sade's exposure of everything, from all possible angles, is an early scene in part one of *Juliette,* where Juliette tells us that "the tableau was comprised in this manner" and then goes on painstakingly to describe the convoluted positionings and penetrations of herself, the Mother Superior, Télème, Laurette, Volmar, Flavie, and Ducroz. Since everyone is involved in the orgy, no one (least of all Juliette) could have witnessed all of this on his/her own; but this omnivoyeurisitc perspective is nonetheless related, throughout the narrative, to the reader (Marquis de Sade, *Juliette,* trans. Austryn Wainhouse [New York, 1968], 57).

56. *MO* 130, 132–35; *DL* 208, 212–13, 216–17.

57. On sadism and speculative processes, see Deleuze: "The essential operation of sadism is the sexualization of thought and of the speculative process as such" (Deleuze, "Coldness and Cruelty," 127).

58. As Elizabeth Boa points out, the voyager refuses to accept the pornological position of "viewer-hero" (which had been filled, in Mirbeau's *Torture Garden,* by Clara) (Boa, *Kafka,* 145). Boa borrows this term from Susanne Kappeler, *The Pornography of Representation* (Oxford, 1986), 59.

59. For a summary of the first (traditional theological interpretations), see Beicken, *Franz Kafka,* 288–89; for an example of the second, see Norris,

Beasts of the Modern Imagination, 113; for an example of the third, see Allen Thiher, *Franz Kafka: A Study of the Short Fiction* (Boston, 1990), 59.

60. Cf. Koelb, who likewise sees in this suicide an act of defiance against the voyager. (Koelb, "In der Strafkolonie," 519).

61. Noyes, *Mastery of Submission,* 120–38.

62. The officer thus ostentatiously surrenders what Noyes would term his "imperial male sexuality" (Noyes, *Mastery of Submission,* 114).

63. For the importance of the contract (outlining the dominator's/dominatrix's powers over the masochist) see Leopold von Sacher-Masoch's appendix to *Venus in Furs* ("Two Contracts of Masoch," in *Masochism,* 277–79), and Deleuze, "Coldness and Cruelty," 91–102.

64. See Norris, *Beasts of the Modern Imagination,* 113. In contrast to Norris' claim of an autoexecution, note Kafka's description: When the strapped-down officer can no longer reach the crank (to start the designer), the designer inexplicably starts on its own ("hardly were the straps in place when the machine began to operate"). Later, we learn that the machine develops something like a consciousness: it "notic[es]" its own performance (*MO* 150, 152; *DL* 242, 245).

65. In later fragments of "In the Penal Colony," not included in the published version, the voyager beats the two stragglers with his fists and then imagines that a "good old miller back home in the north" might grind these "two grinning fellows" to death between his millstones (*D* 380; *Ta* 824).

66. As Goebel points out, it is not altogether clear that this man is a native of the island, but Boa correctly asserts that he does seem not to be European: his "bulging" (*wulstig*) lips are a "racist marker suggesting African features" (*MO* 131; *DL* 139) (Goebel, "Kafka and Postcolonial Critique," 201; Boa, *Kafka,* 139).

67. For example, Müller-Seidel speaks suspiciously of the officer's assumptions: "the transfiguration and redemption" that the officer "believes to perceive" in the faces of the condemned men is "not verified by a single character in the story." But at the same time Müller-Seidel seems to believe the voyager's equally unconfirmed assumptions about the officer: "But when the officer could verify such an absurd redemption through his own death, this precisely does not occur" (Müller-Seidel, *Deportation,* 122).

68. Stanley Corngold writes: "Who says—and on what authority—that the officer found no trace of the promised redemption? The officer remains convinced; he has not registered the shortfall in the promised redemption" (Corngold, "Allotria and Excreta in 'In the Penal Colony,'" *Modernism/Modernity* 8 [2001]: 290).

69. See the chapter entitled, "Of Mimicry and Man: The Ambivalence of Colonial Discourse," in Homi Bhabha, *The Location of Culture* (New York, 1994), 85–92 (here, 86, 88).

70. See Goebel's use of Bhabha's theory of mimicry in relation to "In the Penal Colony" in Goebel, "Kafka and Postcolonial Critique," 199–200.

71. See Kafka's 1907 letter to Max Brod, in which he writes of the "forlorn" German colonists in "Dar es Salaam, Ujiji, Windhoek" (*L* 23; *B* 35–36). I discuss this passage in depth at the end of the following chapter.

72. Cf. Silverman's notion of "the double mimesis" in *Male Subjectivity at the Margins,* 299–338. See also note 42 above.

73. For an account of colonialism's existential crisis (but not a discussion of mimicry), see Jean-Paul Sartre's preface to *The Wretched of the Earth,* by Frantz Fanon (New York, 1963), 7–31.

74. Two of many possible examples of this theme of extinction from the *Little Green Books* occur in volumes three and twenty: Mecklenburg's 1910 *In the Hinterlands of German East Africa* and Steinen's 1912 *With the Xingú Indians (Bei den Indianern am Schingu).* In the former, the narrator witnesses an "authentically original" Watusi (Tutsi) celebration directed by a "Negro prince"; the narrator claims that his experience has been especially meaningful because the Watusi will soon be forced to "give way" to the domination of Europeans (25, 34). In the latter, explorers/ethnographers tell of one of the world's last populations still managing to evade "civilization" and still leading the "primal, simple life of the 'Stone Age'"(5). Kafka seemed to have been especially interested in this latter book: he presented a copy to a friend in 1912, just two years before he wrote "In the Penal Colony" (Binder, *Kafka in neuer Sicht,* 127).

    Concerning Kafka's interest in cultural extinction, see also his description of one of the "last large battles that the American government had to wage against the Indians," written on the same day and in the same notebook as Kafka's final (unpublished) variation of "In the Penal Colony" (August 9, 1917). Here, Kafka writes of a legendarily brutal General Samson, who struck fear into the hearts of the few Indians who were still left to resist the American government: "The shout, 'General Samson!' was almost as effective as a musket against a lone Indian" (*D* 382; *Ta* 827, trans. rev.).

75. Anderson, *Kafka's Clothes,* 103.

76. Anderson, *Kafka's Clothes,* 103.

77. Pierre Loti, *Aziyadé,* trans. Marjorie Laurie (London, 1989) (originally published in 1879). For a discussion of colonial masochism in *Aziyadé,* see Noyes, *Mastery of Submission,* 107–9.

78. Cersowsky, *Phantastische Literatur,* 200.

79. See my discussion of Josef K.'s masochism in chapter three.

80. Norris, *Beasts of the Modern Imagination,* 114

81. In the words of Red Peter, the ape, "One watches over oneself with the whip; one flays oneself at the slightest sign of resistance" (*MO* 194; *DL* 311).

    Kafka's own masochistic fantasies are legend, as is his sense that both writing and reading are the reward for this pain. His most graphic torture fantasies—such as being yanked upward through a house, "bloody and ragged" until all that remains is the empty noose, "dropping the last fragments of me when it breaks through the roof"—are never far from his conception of literature (*D* 224; July 21, 1913). Reading is akin to taking part in a violent internal journey: to smashing, with an ax, the "frozen sea inside us" (*L* 16; January 27, 1904 letter to Oskar Pollak). Writing corresponds to the body's most painful physical experiences (it is a "birth, covered with filth and slime, and only I have the hand that can reach to the body") as well as to a peculiar desire to literally incorporate language (*D* 214, 134; February 11, 1913, December 8, 1911). When Kafka sits down at the desk to write, he feels the same pain as he would feel falling down and breaking both of his legs (*D* 29; December 15, 1910). One month after writing the above-cited alternate endings to "In the Penal Colony," Kafka describes writing (letters) as a form of bleeding to death, in which the correspondents' "throats, our poor pigeons' throats, one here, one there, are cut. But so slowly, so provocatively, with so little blood, so heartrendingly so hearts-rendingly" (*L* 140, letter to Brod, mid-September 1917, trans. rev.). This notion of writing painfully yet pleasurably "on one's own body" is finally literalized in "In the Penal Colony": the officer's body should be, through writing, tortured and redeemed. For more examples of Kafka's masochism, see also his diary entry from September 16, 1915, as well as Pietro Citati's biography, *Kafka* (New York, 1990), 27–28.

82. For the connections between the New Imperialism and economic efficiency, see Bongie, *Exotic Memories,* 40–46.

83. Noyes, *Mastery of Submission,* 114.

84. Cf. Kafka's later (1920) aphorism: "The animal wrests the whip from its master and whips itself in order to become master, not knowing that this is only a fantasy produced by a new knot in the master's whip-lash" (*WP* 41; *NSII* 119).

85. In this regard, see Judith Butler's argument concerning the subject's "stubborn attachment" to its subjection in "Stubborn Attachment, Bodily Subjection: Rereading Hegel on the Unhappy Consciousness," in *The Psychic Life of Power: Theories in Subjection* (Stanford, 1997), 31–62.

Chapter Five

1. *"Landvermesser"* appears in the text 112 times, almost as often as *"Schloß"* itself, which appears 189 times (Heinrich P. Delfosse and Karl Jürgen Skrodzki, *Synoptische Konkordanz zu Franz Kafkas Romanen,* vols. 2 and 3 [Tübingen, 1993], 1137).

2. Marthe Robert, *The Old and the New: From Don Quixote to Kafka* (Berkeley, 1977), 18.

3. According to Charles Bernheimer: "[K.] is a land-surveyor in the sense that his vocation is to delimit differences, to map out boundaries, in order to establish the symbolic principle relating possession to authority, ownership to its origin, material presence to an absent but recuperable presence. His ambition is to be a successful reader of the symbolic structure binding Cas-

tle and village, and he feels that his very existence depends on this success" (Bernheimer, *Flaubert and Kafka*, 198).

4. Helga Göhler, *Franz Kafka: "Das Schloß"* (Bonn, 1982), 52; Robertson, *Kafka: Judaism, Politics, Literature*, 228–35.

5. Sokel, *Franz Kafka—Tragik und Ironie*, 403–5.

6. Erich Heller, "The World of Franz Kafka" (1952), rpt. in *Twentieth-Century Interpretations of "The Castle,"* ed. Peter F. Neumeyer (Englewood Cliffs, NJ, 1969), 70.

7. Weber's memoir could well be fictional, since he wrote another "memoir" about a South American coffee planter (*Letters of a Coffee Planter*) that tells a different life story. The important thing for my argument, however, is not the "truth" of Weber's account and its depiction of land-surveying but rather the book's connection to the general turn-of-the-century discourse surrounding land surveying.

8. Neumeyer, "Franz Kafka, Sugar Baron," 9–10.

9. Born, *Kafkas Bibliothek*, 228.

10. Wirkner, *Kafka und die Außenwelt*, 14–40.

11. See Max Brod's afterword to the first, 1927 edition of Kafka's *Amerika*, edited by Max Brod (Frankfurt a. M., 1991), 260.

12. Born, *Kafkas Bibliothek*, 228.

13. Kafka's note to Elli is excerpted in *EFI* 300n30 and published in its entirety in Born, *Kafkas Bibliothek*, 180.

14. For possible historical sources for Kafka's Castle and village, see Binder, *Kafka-Handbuch*, 2:442–43, and Beicken, *Franz Kafka*, 337.

15. Evelyn Torton Beck, *Kafka and the Yiddish Theater: Its Impact on His Work* (Madison, WI, 1971), 195.

16. Emrich, *Franz Kafka* (Frankfurt a. M., 1957), 300–303.

17. Walter Sokel and, later, Stephen Dowden correctly argue against Emrich and any such benevolent reading of K. They point out that K. often seems to be interested only in his own well-being—not in the needs of the community (Sokel, *Franz Kafka—Tragik und Ironie*, 165, 414, 419 [cited in Binder, *Kafka-Handbuch*, 2:462]; Stephen Dowden, *Kafka's Castle and the Critical Imagination* [Columbia, SC, 1995], 30–31, 34–35).

18. The few recent scholars who address the historical-political framework of *The Castle* generally focus on Kafka's connection to fin de siècle Jewish culture and politics (Zionism, the Yiddish theater, Messianism). See, for example, Harold Bloom's introduction to *Franz Kafka's "The Castle"* (New York, 1988), 1–22; Robertson, *Kafka: Judaism, Politics, Literature*, 218–72; and David Suchoff, *Critical Theory and the Novel: Mass Society and Cultural Criticism in Dickens, Melville, and Kafka* (Madison, WI, 1994), 136–77.

19. Pratt, *Imperial Eyes*, 17. See also Pratt's entire chapter, "Science, planetary consciousness, interiors," in which she discusses Linnaeus and the general eighteenth- and nineteenth-century European desire to classify the world (15–37).

20. The state, according to this definition, is a form of power separate from ruler and ruled, and also from the economy. It exists primarily as *territory*, and as the corresponding exclusive right to commit violence within this territory's boundaries. See Quentin Skinner, *Foundations of Modern Political Thought*, 2 Vols. (New York, 1978), and Nicos Poulantzas, *State, Power, Socialism* (London, 1978); both are cited in Pratt, "Scratches on the Face of the Country," 126n16.

21. Weber, *Zuckerbaron*, 18.

22. Kafka's library and reading notes included works about the North Pole, the South Seas, Greenland, Iceland, Mexico, Italy, Russia, Central and South America, Africa, the United States, England, Scotland, East Prussia, and Germany. All of the travel books owned by Kafka—including the Schaffstein volumes—are indexed in Born's *Kafkas Bibliothek*, 144–48. To review the books mentioned in Kafka's letters and diaries, see the index to *Kafkas Bibliothek* (235–55), where all of the books to which Kafka refers are listed according to the author's name. See also note 18 in chapter four.

23. Peter J. Brenner refers to this development in his aptly titled chapter on the nineteenth-century German travel writers Alexander von Humboldt and Adelbert von Chamisso: "Die Vermessung der Welt" (Surveying the World), in Peter J. Brenner, *Der Reisebericht in der deutschen Literatur* (Tübingen, 1990), 443–90 (here, 445).

24. Josef Löwy was active in a commercial venture in Panama, and then held important colonial posts in the Congo (for nearly twelve years) and, later, in China. During Löwy's (and Kafka's) lifetime, the Panama Canal region was surveyed, measured, and occupied—first unsuccessfully by the French (for whom Löwy likely worked), and later by the Americans. The Congo was assigned to King Léopold of Belgium during the 1885 Berlin conference. One of Léopold's driving desires was to build the Congo Railway, for which Löwy was the chief of commercial sections (Anthony Northey, *Kafka's Relatives: Their Lives and His Writing* [New Haven, 1991], 9, 15–30).

25. Surveyors appear in the following *Little Green Books* (all published in Cologne by Schaffstein): Carsten Borchgrevink, *Festes Land am Südpol: Erlebnisse auf der Expedition nach dem Südpolarland 1898–1900* (1911), 53; Sven Hedin, *Über den Transhimalaja* (1911), 96–99; Mecklenburg, *Im Hinterlande von Deutsch-Ostafrika* (1910), 37; Weber, *Zuckerbaron* (1914), 55–6, 87; Weber, *Briefe eines Kaffee-Pflanzers* (1913), 54, 58, 61–2; Wettstein, *Durch den brasilianischen Urwald* (1911), 6–7, 29, 48. In Wettstein's *Durch den brasilianischen Urwald* (*Through the Brazilian Jungle*), to offer just one example, the narrator recalls his earlier pleasures of "surveying and hunting" in colonial Africa (a theme later repeated at the outset of Kafka's "A Report to an Academy") (48).

   For more on the general pro-imperial stance of the *Little Green Books* and the Schaffstein Verlag, see note 16 in chapter four.

26. Said writes: "The great cultural archive, I argue, is where the intellectual and aesthetic investments in overseas dominion are made" (Edward Said, *Culture and Imperialism* [New York, 1993], xxi).

27. In *The Banana King*, the German protagonist is born in a German settlement in the United States, not in Germany. Except for this difference, however, the plot is the same: the young Samuel Rath heads off to Latin America penniless, looking to get rich through colonial crop production.

28. Said, *Orientalism*, 193.

29. This term connects psychological colonialism to the burgeoning fin de siècle interest in travel and travel writing (Richard Hamann and Jost Hermand, *Impressionismus*, 2nd ed. [Munich, 1974], 14–30).

30. Reif, "Exotismus im Reisebericht des frühen 20. Jahrhunderts," 447–51.

31. Susanne Zantop similarly refers to colonies, in the German imagination, as a "blank space for a new beginning, for the creation of an imaginary national self freed from history and convention—a self that would prove to the world what 'he' could do" (Susannne Zantop, *Colonial Fantasies: Conquest, Family, and Nation in Precolonial Germany, 1770–1870* [Durham, NC, 1997], 7). David Spurr likewise delineates the colonial fantasy that the conquered world is a blank, "negative" space—lacking both history and individuality (Spurr, "Negation," in *The Rhetoric of Empire*, 92–108). See note 94 in chapter two.

32. Weber, *Zuckerbaron*, 5.

33. For Kafka, Latin America is not a blank landscape, because of Josef Löwy's work in Panama. But Kafka equates the adjective "Russian," as he writes in a January 1912 diary entry, with an experience of "extreme solitude"; three years later, he defines Russia as a symbol that is emptied out, a site of eternal erasure: "The infinite attraction of Russia. It is best represented not by Gogol's troika but by the image of a vast river of yellowish water, which sends waves—but not too high ones—breaking all round. Windswept, desolate heaths upon its banks, blighted grass. *Nothing can represent it; everything rather effaces it [Nichts erfasst das, verlöscht vielmehr alles]*" (*D* 165, 331; *Ta* 348, 727, my emphasis, trans. rev.). Correspondingly, the Stationmaster in Kafka's 1914 fragment "Memoirs of the Kalda Railway" claims that Russia is the ideal spot for him because of its barrenness: it creates an inimitable and welcome "solitude ringing in my ears" (*D* 303; *Ta* 549).

34. Gerhard Neumann, *"Das Urteil": Text, Materialien, Kommentar* (Munich, 1981), 147–48. Neumann borrows the term "extraterritoriality" (*Exterritorialität*) from Ina-Maria Greverus, *Der territoriale Mensch: Ein literatur-anthropologischer Versuch zum Heimatphänomen* (Frankfurt a. M., 1972). For more on Kafka and extraterritoriality, see note 35 in chapter seven.

35. As Said points out the Orient is, for many travelers, "dead and dry—a mental mummy"; it is something travelers, from Alexander Kinglake to Gustave Flaubert, want to "remake" or to "bring to life" (Said, *Orientalism*, 193, 185).

36. Weber, *Zuckerbaron*, 87.

37. Weber, *Briefe eines Kaffee-Pflanzers*, 54, 61–62, 32–33.

38. Hesse, *Aus Indien*, 105–6. For further examples, see Pratt, *Imperial Eyes*, 201–27.

39. Weber, *Briefe eines Kaffee-Pflanzers*, 57.

40. Mecklenburg, *Im Hinterlande von Deutsch-Ostafrika*, 36–37.

41. Pratt, *Imperial Eyes*, 204.

42. Pratt, *Imperial Eyes*, 216.

43. Max Wiederhold, *Der Panamakanal* (Cologne, 1913), 59–60, my emphasis.

44. According to Malek Alloula, in his study of the colonial postcard, the representation was never allowed to reveal the viewer: it never exposed the embodied eye that made the picture possible (Malek Alloula, *The Colonial Harem*, trans. Myrna and Wlad Godzich [Minneapolis, 1986]). Tim Mitchell discusses Alloula in *Colonising Egypt* (New York, 1988), 26.

45. Weber, *Zuckerbaron*, 87–88.

46. G. W. F. Hegel, *Die Phänomenologie des Geistes*, ed. Hans-Friedrich Wessels and Heinrich Clairmont (Hamburg, 1988), 133; G. W. F. Hegel, *Phenomenology of Spirit*, trans. A. V. Miller (New York, 1977), 116.

47. Hegel, *Phänomenologie*, 133; *Phenomenology*, 116.

48. John Barrell, *English Literature in History 1730–80: An Equal, Wide Survey* (New York, 1983), 33. I thank David Clark for pointing out this connection with Barrell.

49. Friedrich Nietzsche, *Jenseits von Gut und Böse*, in *Kritische Gesamtausgabe*, ed. Giorgio Colli and Mazzino Montinari (Berlin, 1968), 6(2):215; Friedrich Nietzsche, *Beyond Good and Evil*, trans. Walter Kaufmann (New York, 1966), 201 (my emphasis).

50. Nietzsche, *Zur Genealogie der Moral*, in *Kritische Gesamtausgabe*, 6(2):273; Nietzsche, *On the Genealogy of Morals*, trans. Walter Kaufmann and R. J. Hollingdale (New York, 1966), 26.

51. Nietzsche, *Jenseits*, 215; *Beyond*, 201. It is important to note, Nietzsche places the modern notion of being disinterested (*désintéressé*) firmly within the moralizing herd instinct (*Genealogie* 274; *On the Genealogy* 26). However, Nietzsche's assertions regarding the pre-historic nobility nonetheless resemble Barrell's description of the disinterested man of the eighteenth century: both figures lay claim to a form of supra-human, in Nietzsche's words, "self-surmounting" point of view that purports to be at once more "distanced" and more "comprehensive" than the commoner's (*Jenseits* 215; *Beyond* 201).

52. Hegel writes, for example: "[The master's] truth is in reality the unessential consciousness and its unessential action" (*Phänomenologie*, 134; *Phenomenology*, 117). Alexandre Kojève famously argues that, by the end of the "master/slave" dialetic, the master loses and the slave wins: "In the long run, all slavish work realizes not the Master's will, but the will—at first unconscious—of the Slave, who—finally—succeeds where the Master—necessarily—fails" (Alexandre Kojève, *Introduction to the Reading of Hegel* [New York, 1969], 30).

53. See Brod's afterword to the first, 1926 edition of Kafka's *Das Schloß*, edited by Max Brod (Frankfurt a. M., 1968), 347.

54. These critics include Heller, "The World of Franz Kafka" (1952); Politzer, *Franz Kafka, der Künstler* (1965); Robert, *L'Ancien et le nouveau: de Don Quichotte à Kafka* (Paris, 1963); and K.-P. Phillipi, *Reflexion und Wirklichkeit: Untersuchungen zu Kafkas Roman "Das Schloß"* (Tübingen, 1966). Cf. Binder, *Kafka-Handbuch*, 2:463.

55. Richard Sheppard summarizes his own and John Winkelman's positions as follows: "Winkelman and Sheppard claim [. . .] that K. must be liberated from this artificial identity—so that his true self can be revealed, and the power of his proud will can be overcome through humility and love" (cited in Binder, *Kafka-Handbuch*, 2:461).

56. Charles Bernheimer, *Flaubert and Kafka*, 198.

57. Boa, *Kafka*, 253.

58. Gerhard Neumann, "Kafka's 'Schloß'-Roman: Das parasitäre Spiel der Zeichen," in *Franz Kafka: Schriftverkehr*, 208.

59. Mitchell, *Colonising Egypt*, 32–33. See also Mitchell's entire opening chapter (1–33), where he further argues that the traveler desires to re-present the Other as an object and, in so doing, to define himself as distinct from this object. By making photographs, drawings, and maps, and by situating himself on top of Egypt's pyramids or minarets, the traveler can "organize" an otherwise disorderly view. In so doing, he can see the foreign world "as a picture," an object from which he is distinct. Organizing the "objectness of the other" means here, as in the Schaffstein narratives, putting the Other into a frame. When the Other becomes a self-enclosed object or "work," the traveler can confirm his separateness and thereby claim the identity that marks the success of his psychological business.

60. Kurz, *Traum-Schrecken*, 159–60.

61. K. seems to be on the same trajectory of self-discovery as are the heroes of the three Schaffstein novels Kafka claimed to "especially love": K. begins the novel poor and unemployed (resembling a *Landstreicher* or vagabond more than a *Landvermesser*); he has no friends or family (his rumored wife and child are left at home); and he hopes to gain an identity (both personal and professional) in the foreign land.

62. In the original English translation, the Muirs rendered *Blindschleiche* as "snake in the grass," thus effacing Kafka's deliberately visual opposition.

63. K.'s only view of Klamm occurs in the third chapter, at which point the mighty Klamm's body is revealed to be pedestrian and unimposing. But the "reality" of K.'s sighting is later called into question by Olga, the sister of Barnabas (a Castle messenger): Olga claims that people are continually mistaking others for Klamm—confusing him with various Castle officials and village secretaries (such as Momus). Because Klamm functions as a locus for subjective "yearning," Olga claims, he takes on a "variety of shapes" in different people's "imaginations"—thereby putting K.'s, and any other, apparently authentic Klamm-sightings in doubt ("ein so oft ersehnter und so selten erreichter Mann wie es Klamm ist nimmt in der Vorstellung der Menschen leicht verschiedene Gestalten an") (*C* 181; *S* 286; see also *C* 176–77; *S* 277–79).

Klamm, conversely, claims to maintain a more accurate view of K. He keeps a figurative (and panoptic) "eye" on K. at all times *("Ich behalte Sie im Auge")*; he does this perhaps with the metonymic help of his many spying secretaries (*S* 187; *C* 118, trans. rev.).

64. I thank Mark Anderson for bringing this connection to my attention.

65. Brod, "*The Castle; Its Genesis*," in *Franz Kafka Today,* ed. A. Flores and H. Swander (Madison, WI, 1958), 161–64. See also Sokel, who claims that the Castle resembles an "alliance of the Austrian aristocracy and Austrian bureaucracy, that ruled over the peasants of [Czech] Bohemia" (Sokel, *Franz Kafka— Tragik und Ironie,* 397; cited in Suchoff, *Critical Theory and the Novel,* 168).

66. Although we never see the police in *The Castle,* the schoolmistress suggests calling them to remove K. from the schoolhouse, and before that K. compares his possible status in the administration with that of the village policeman (*C* 133, 23; *S* 210, 41). Moreover, the villagers' fear of the Castle may be a justified fear of violence: the villagers' deformities (heads flattened at the top, as if they had been "beaten") suggest some form of violence from above (*C* 22; *S* 39).

67. Guido Kisch, "Kafka-Forschung auf Irrwegen," *Zeitschrift für Religions- und Geistesgeschichte* 23 (1971): 339–50.

68. Ronald Gray, *Kafka's Castle* (Cambridge, 1956), 78–81; John Winkelman, "An Interpretation of Kafka's *Das Schloß,*" *Monatshefte* 64 (1972): 115–31; Richard Sheppard, *On Kafka's Castle* (London, 1973), 182–87.

69. W. G. Sebald, "The Undiscover'd Country: The Death Motif in Kafka's *Castle,*" *Journal of European Studies* 2 (1972), 33–34; cf. also Gray, *Kafka's Castle,* 131–32.

70. Weber, *Zuckerbaron,* 88.

71. Brod's afterword to Kafka's *Das Schloß,* 347.

72. Neumeyer, "Franz Kafka, Sugar Baron," 14, 15.

73. The final chapter of *The Sugar Baron,* Neumeyer claims, is an ending that Kafka longed for but "could never have written" ("Franz Kafka, Sugar Baron," 15).

74. Walter Benjamin, June 1938 letter to Gershom Scholem, published in *Benjamin über Kafka,* 88; translation in Benjamin's "Some Reflections on Kafka," in *Illuminations,* 145.

75. For Althusser, the subject can never avoid ideology, since "the category of the subject is constitutive of all ideology" and moreover all ideology "has the function (which defines it) of 'constituting' concrete individuals as subjects." Within this constricting double constitution, resistance is difficult to imagine. Althusser, however, challenges himself and his readers to attempt to "break" with ideology through a "subject-less" discourse: "while speaking in ideology, and from within ideology we have to outline a discourse which tries to break with ideology, in order to dare to be the beginning of a scientific (i.e., subject-less) discourse on ideology" (Louis Althusser, "Ideology and Ideological State Apparatuses," in *Lenin and Philosophy* [New York, 1971], 127–86 [here, 171, 173]).

76. See *L* 25; *B* 37; *LM* 236; *BM* 319; *LF* 289; *BF* 427.
77. Deleuze and Guattari, *Kafka: Toward a Minor Literature*, 22, 26.
78. Weber, *Zuckerbaron*, 87.
79. Weber, *Zuckerbaron*, 88.
80. Deleuze and Guattari, *Kafka*, 52.
81. Deleuze and Guattari, *Kafka*, 78.
82. Weber, *Zuckerbaron*, 83
83. Martin Heidegger, "Building Dwelling Thinking," in *Poetry, Language, Thought*, trans. Albert Hofstadter (New York, 1975), 145–61 (here, 145–46).
84. Clifford, "Traveling Cultures," 101. A contemporary example of how the borders between "dwelling" and "traveling" blur is the 1993 film by Philippe Lioret, *Tombés du Ciel (Lost in Transit)*. The action takes place almost entirely in a Paris airport, in the no-man's land between the runway and the customs gate. People without proper papers, denied admittance to "France," live in an abandoned storage area. Here, they demarcate their own "private" spaces with curtains and piles of belongings. They remain here for years, rasing families and engaging in intimate, yet public, acts.
85. In the case of Said, I am referring to *Orientalism* and, specifically, to James Clifford's criticism of *Orientalism:* that, despite Said's efforts to the opposite, he still sometimes drifts toward an essentialist and inaccurately rigid notion of Occident and Orient. It is worth further considering, in the context of my argument about Kafka: where might fin de siècle Jewish-German Prague fit into something known as the "Occident"? (James Clifford, "On *Orientalism*," in *The Predicament of Culture: Twentieth-Century Ethnography, Literature, and Art* [Cambridge, MA, 1988], 255–76.)
86. Spector writes: "Each and every one of the 'humanists' of the Prague circle [of German-Jewish literati], while diverging from one another in every other way conceivable, set himself in opposition to the liberalism he saw to be at the root of his contemporary dilemma" (Spector, *Prague Territories*, 34; see also 3–4, 13–16, 33–34).
87. Kafka garnered this information from a painstaking reading of the *Memoirs of General Marcellin Marbot* as well as of Paul Holzhausen's *The Germans in Russia 1812: Life and Suffering during the Military Advance on Moscow*. He also read, as we shall see below, volume 18 of Schaffstein's *Little Green Books: Forest-Ranger Fleck's Narration of His Fate During Napoleon's March on Russia and of His Imprisonment 1812–1814*.
88. Note the affinity here between Kafka's notion of "escape" and the respective claims of Theodor Adorno/Max Horkheimer and Michel Foucault that historical resistances can only take place within the very socio-linguistic "cultures" or "discourses" that they are working to transform. For Adorno and Horkheimer, the resistant "style" of "great" art is always threatened by the hegemonic "culture" that precedes it. Culture attempts to homogenize style and, in so doing, endeavors to neutralize style's critical capacity for "discrepancy" and "self-negation" (Adorno and Horkheimer, *Dialektik der*

Aufklärung: Philosophische Fragmente [Frankfurt a. M., 1969], 139). For Foucault on the relation between "discourse" and resistance, I am thinking of the later permutations of Foucault's notion of discourse—as in the "Method" chapter in volume 1 (*La volonté de savoir*) of *Histoire de la sexualité* (Paris, 1976); English trans. *The History of Sexuality: An Introduction* (New York, 1980). Here, Foucault argues that apparent resistances can never function outside of the framework of "power." Power resides in resistance even as it resides in oppression: "Power is everywhere not because it embraces everything but because it comes from everywhere." Resistance occurs, in other words, only within power's network. Moreover, such resistance can never be predicted, categorized, organized, or united in common cause: "instead there is a plurality of resistances, each of them a special case" (*The History of Sexuality*, 93, 96). For an elaboration on this point (and Foucault's "Method" chapter), see Culler, *Framing the Sign*, 57–68.

89. For emigré accounts of writing "home" (in the autobiographical work of Theodor Adorno and Edward Said), see Kaplan, *Questions of Travel*, 117–22.

90. Fleck, *Förster Flecks Erzählung*, 32.

91. Throughout *The Castle*, Kafka moves back and forth between the two possible meanings of *übersehen*: "to survey/look out over" (*S* 60, 122, 422; *C* 36, 76, 269) and "to overlook" (*S* 10, 388; *C* 3, 247). I thank Rebecca Comay for bringing up the importance of *übersehen*.

Chapter Six

1. For more on Milena Jesenská's life and writing, see the following biographies: Margarete Buber-Neumann, *Milena* (New York, 1988); Jana Černá, *Kafka's Milena* (Evanston, IL, 1993); Mary Hockaday, *Kafka, Love, and Courage: The Life of Milena Jesenská* (London, 1995).

2. Kafka writes of living through "what is for Europe so extreme an experience of solitude that one can only call it Russian" (*D* 165; *Ta* 348). For more on Russia as a metaphor for isolation, see note 33 in chapter five.

3. Baudelaire, "Anywhere out of this world—N'importe où hors du monde," 211–13.

4. If he marries Felice, Kafka tells her and later her father, he would lead a "monastic existence," and the husband and wife would see each other for only one hour per day (*LF* 309, 313; *BF* 451, 457).

5. "When it became clear in my organism that writing was the most productive direction for my being to take, everything rushed in that direction and left empty all those abilities which were directed toward the joys of sex, eating, drinking, philosophical reflection, and above all music. I atrophied in all these directions" (*D* 163; *Ta* 341).

6. Gilles Deleuze and Félix Guattari refer to Kafka's "machine célibataire" as follows: "[Kafka] knows that all the lines link him to a literary machine of expression for which he is simultaneously the gears, the mechanic, the op-

erator, and the victim. So how will he proceed in this bachelor machine [. . .]?" (Deleuze and Guattari, *Kafka: Toward a Minor Literature,* 58).

7. Neumann writes: "It is the 'media' that draw the subject into their game and, in the worst case, obliterate it; media that show a double face: the circulation of language and writing on the one hand, the succession of images on the other—those elements that, hovering between people, give significance to life and simultaneously alienate the living from one another" (Neumann, "Kafka's 'Schloß'-Roman," 201).

8. Wolf Kittler focuses especially on the early Kafka narratives (written before and during the Felice correspondence) in which letter writing opposes and/or prevents physical contact: *Hochzeitsvorbereitungen auf dem Lande, Das Urteil, Der Heizer,* and *Die Verwandlung* (W. Kittler, "Schreibmaschinen, Sprechmaschinen," esp. 84–107). Others discussing media in Kafka's *Letters to Felice* are Cournot, "Toi qui as de si grandes dents . . ."; Friedrich Kittler, *Discourse Networks 1800/1900,* trans. Michael Metteer (Stanford, 1990), 359–63, and *Gramophone, Film, Typewriter,* trans. Geoffrey Winthrop-Young and Michael Wutz (Stanford, 1999), 222–28; Bernhard Siegert, *Relays: Literature as an Epoch of the Postal System,* trans. Kevin Repp (Stanford, 1999), 207–64; and Marjorie Rhine, who argues that Kafka constructs a media-sponsored "post"-modern *jouissance* ("'Post'-Modernity in Kafka's *Briefe an Felice,*" *Journal of the Kafka Society of America* 18 [1994]: 35–40). My argument extends these discussions of mediated love to Kafka's *Letters to Milena* and, more importantly, stresses the importance of other media generally ignored by scholars of media and technology: railway trains (the medium of corporeal transport) and, later in the chapter, postage stamps (a fetishistic medium promising presence in absence).

9. Theweleit briefly discusses media in the *Letters to Milena,* but he focuses more on the *Letters to Felice* and more on the misogynistic Orphean dynamic between Kafka and his lovers than on the technologies of intercourse (Klaus Theweleit, "Gespensterposten. Briefverkehr, Liebesverkehr, Eisenbahnverkehr. Der Zug ins Jenseits: Orpheus 1913 in Prag," in *buch der könige* [Basel, 1988], 1:976–1055). I address Theweleit's remarks at the close of this chapter. After I finished an earlier version of this chapter ("The Traffic of Writing: Technologies of 'Verkehr' in Franz Kafka's *Briefe an Milena,*" *German Life and Letters* 52 [July 1999]: 365–81), I read Scott Spector's excellent pages on the *Letters to Milena,* which contain further insights into Kafka's mediated "love" correspondence with Milena—without, however, focusing on the technological nature of this correspondence (Spector, *Prague Territories* [Berkeley, 2000], 217–33).

10. Referring to Milena's original role as Kafka's translator into Czech (this is why they started corresponding), Spector refers to her Slavic, gentile exoticism: "the creative power of [Kafka's] German text faces the feminine Czech translation, reproductive and at the same time seductive, sexy in its exoticism and as a result of the exaggerated imbalance of power" (Spector, *Prague Territories,* 220).

11. See Heinrich von Stephan, *Geschichte der Preußischen Post: Nach amtlichen Quellen bis 1858 bearbeitet von Dr. H. v. Stephan. Neubearbeitet und fortgeführt bis 1868 von K. Sautter* (Berlin, 1928), 1:470. Cited in W. Kittler, "Schreibmaschinen, Sprechmaschinen," 83.

12. This fantasy of no longer traveling by the night mail persisted despite the fact that letters indeed traveled in trains (out of sight, in separate compartments from humans) and, later, in automobiles.

13. In the *Letters to Milena,* I maintain, the two terms eventually begin to function dialectically. Spector also sees a dialectic in the *Letters to Felice,* but this, Spector points out, is a dialectic that only results in more and more powerful writing (the "becoming-real" of Kafka's writing) (Spector, *Prague Territories,* 145). I am more interested in a technological dialectic, which, as we shall see, creates, however fleetingly, a longed-for third term: a media-sponsored presence-in-absence that inheres both inside and outside of "writing."

14. It is noteworthy that Freud connects his own *Reiseangst* (travel anxiety) to sexuality and that he specifically relates this to having seen, when he was between two and two-and-a-half years old, his own mother naked in a train. As Freud writes to Fliess on October 3, 1897: "my libido toward *matrem* was awakened, namely, on the occasion of a journey with her from Leipzig to Vienna, during which we must have spent the night together and there must have been an opportunity of seeing her *nudam* [. . .]. You yourself have seen my travel anxiety at its height" (*The Complete Letters of Sigmund Freud to Wilhelm Fliess, 1897–1904* [Cambridge, MA, 1985], 268).

15. *Three Essays on the Theory of Sexuality* (*Drei Abhandlungen zur Sexualtheorie*), in *The Standard Edition of the Complete Psychological Works of Sigmund Freud,* 7:202. The German text reads: "Den Vorgängen auf der Eisenbahn pflegen sie [Knaben] ein rätselhaftes Interesse von außerordentlicher Höhe zuzuwenden und dieselben im Alter der Phantasietätigkeit (kurz vor der Pubertät) zum Kern einer exquisit sexuellen Symbolik zu machen" (*Freud-Studienausgabe* [Frankfurt a. M., (1969–75)], 5:107.)

Writing just two years before Freud, Otto Weininger also directly connects travel (if not explicitly train travel) to eroticism: the desire to travel (*Reiselust*) expresses, for Weininger, "indeterminate longing" (Weininger, *Geschlecht und Charakter: Eine prinzipielle Untersuchung* [Vienna, 1903], 317n1).

16. The German text reads: "Ihre Angst bezieht sich auf die Gefahr, sie könnten in eine unaufhaltsame, ihrem Willen nicht mehr gehorchende Bewegung geraten. Die gleichen Patienten pflegen auch Angst vor der Fortbewegung in irgendeinem Fahrzeug zu produzieren, das sie nicht jederzeit nach Belieben zum Stehen bringen können. (Eisenbahn usw.)" (Karl Abraham, *Psychoanalytische Studien* [Frankfurt a. M.: 1971], 2:102).

17. Freud, *Fragment of an Analysis of a Case of Hysteria,* in *Standard Edition,* 7:99; *Bruchstück einer Hysterie-Analyse,* in *Studienausgabe,* 6:166.

18. Abraham, *Psychoanalytische Studien,* 2:103.

19. Freud, *Standard Edition,* 7:201–2; *Studienausgabe,* 5:106–7.

20. Anderson, *Kafka's Clothes,* 19–49, 98–122. For more on *Verkehr* and its importance for Kafka, see note 58 in my introduction.

21. The main characters of "The Passenger," *Richard and Samuel,* and *The Metamorphosis* are all sexually stimulated (or in the case of Gregor Samsa's pubescent sister, Grete, sexually awakened) during train or tram travel—thereby echoing Freud's theory of mechanical, train-induced *Erregung* (excitation).

22. *D* 213; *Ta* 461; Brod, *Franz Kafka: A Biography,* 129.

23. Although other factors lead to the lovers' melancholy separation in the dream (Milena's frustrating vagueness; Kafka's incessant pushiness; Kafka's intrusive companions), the deterioration of the relationship begins with the telegrammatic clamor that then continues for the entire dream (*LM* 48; *BM* 65).

24. In his preference for letter transport over human transport, Kafka prefigures the wise Catalonian in Gabriel García Márquez' 1967 *Cien Años de Soledad,* who claims: "The world must be all fucked up when men travel first class and literature goes as freight" (*One Hundred Years of Solitude* [New York, 1971], 368).

25. Fewer than six weeks later, Kafka explicitly connects his Jewishness to *Verkehr,* using the metaphor of the "eternal Jew" to describe his own sexuality: "This drive [*Trieb*] had something of the eternal Jew—senselessly drawn along, senselessly wandering through a senselessly obscene world" (*LM* 147–48; *BM* 198, trans. rev.). Kafka's benevolent "angel of Jews" foreshadows (part of) Benjamin's reading of Paul Klee's "Angelus Novus": the angel who "would like to stay, awaken the dead, and make whole what has been smashed" (Benjamin, "Theses on the Philosophy of History," in *Illuminations,* 257).

26. In the following letter, Kafka's letter vampirism becomes human vampirism: "I see you bent over your work, your neck bared, I'm standing behind you, but you don't know it—please don't be frightened if you feel my lips on the back of your neck" (*LM* 123; *BM* 164–65).

     For more on Kafka's epistolary vampirism, consider the following remarks: "I'm tilting my head way back, drinking the letters, aware only that I don't want to stop drinking"; "I read [your letters] [. . .] the way an animal dying of thirst drinks"; and "one used to drink up the letters and immediately feel [. . .] ten times thirstier" (*LM* 18, 45, 170; *BM* 23, 60, 231, trans. rev.).

     Kafka's vampirism in *Letters to Milena* is mentioned by Mark Anderson ("Kafka's Unsigned Letters to Milena Jesenská," in *Reading Kafka,* 248–50) and by Deleuze and Guattari (*Kafka,* 29–30). Anderson correctly remarks, as I discuss later, that the letters function as fetishistic substitutes for Milena's body (248). However, both Anderson and Deleuze/Guattari focus on vampirism as a lack, either of identity (Anderson) or of lifeblood (Deleuze/Guattari)—not as the desire for a magical surplus, for an excessive presence within absence generated by necromantic postal manipulations.

27. Kafka writes of *"Verkehr in Briefen"* (communication/intercourse by letter) in a February 17–18, 1913 letter to Felice and later in a March 1922 letter to Milena (*"durch Briefe* [. . .] *verkehren"*) (*LF* 197; *BF* 304; *LM* 223; *BM* 302)

28. These stamp remarks appear on the following pages (cited in the order I have mentioned them in the text): *LM* 108, 146, 120, 155–56, 132, 158, 146, 140, 112–13; *BM* 144–45, 195, 159–60, 210, 176, 213, 195, 204 (this last citation is missing from the English translation), 187, 150–51. Additional stamp comments can be found on *LM* 108, 111 (*BM* 145, 148) and also in Kafka's April 1921 letter to his sister Ottla (*L* 277; *BO* 117).

29. Jürgen Born and Michael Müller, "Kafkas Briefe an Milena: Ihre Datierung," *Jahrbuch der deutschen Schillergesellschaft* 25 (1981): 514.

30. "There is, it is known, a stamp-language that is to flower-language what the morse alphabet is to the written one. But for how long will the flowers continue to bloom between the telegraph poles? Are not the great artistic stamps of the post-war years, with their full colours, already the autumnal asters and dahlia of this flora? Stephan, a German and not by chance a contemporary of Jean Paul, planted this seed in the summery middle of the nineteenth century. It will not survive the twentieth." Benjamin, of course, has been proven wrong by the beginning of the twenty-first century—but only barely. And his insistence on the fetish value of stamps (and "regular" mail) carries even more validity now than it did in his own day. See Walter Benjamin, *One Way Street and Other Writings* (New York, 1979), 94; Benjamin, "Einbahnstraße," in *Gesammelte Schriften,* 4(1):137.

31. "Darf ich Dich also küssen? Aber auf diesem kläglichen Papier?" (May I kiss you then? But on this miserable paper?) (*LF* 51; *BF* 107).

32. There is a legal/criminal parallel to this production of a magical presence in lovers' discourses: the saliva on stamps has become a DNA source in forensic investigations.

33. The English-language edition of *Letters to Milena* fails to note this peculiarity in the manuscript.

34. Cf. Vincent Kaufmann, *Post Scripts: The Writer's Workshop,* trans. Deborah Treisman (Cambridge, MA, 1994), 27.

35. Rotraut Hackermüller, *Kafkas letzte Jahre 1917–1924* (Munich, 1990), 44–48.

36. Max Brod, *Franz Kafka: A Biography,* 230–31; Born and Müller, "Kafkas Briefe an Milena," 517–19. The least objectionable reading is Born and Müller's. They suggest, through paraphrases from Kafka's letters, that Kafka distanced himself from Milena as a reaction to Milena's own distancing—especially her refusal to leave her husband. They emphasize Milena's initial refusal: "[Milena] apparently [attempted slowly to distance herself somewhat. The fact that she was unable to disengage herself from Ernst Pollak (as she had already written to Kafka in mid-July) also contributed to the way the relationship was left to die away" (518). Born and Müller's con-

clusion is based on the last lines of Kafka's mid-April 1921 letter to Max Brod (*L* 273; *B* 318): "Kafka closes this letter to his friend with the realization that Milena was unattainable; he would have to resign himself to this" (Born and Müller, "Kafka's Briefe an Milena," 519). But this explanation, like the others based on the psychodynamics of the relationship, is belied by Kafka's valorization of imagination and language over the apparent realities of an epistolary love relationship. Earlier in the same letter to Brod, Kafka wrote that Milena was *"unerreichbar"* (unattainable) only because he *created her* as such: "I can love only what I can place so high above me that I cannot reach it" (*L* 273; *B* 317). Willy Haas, in the first essay about *Letters to Milena* (from 1952), foreshadows my critique of the explanation based on relationship economics. He argues that the accepted break-up excuse (that Milena "loved her husband too much to leave him") is a transparent one; Haas, however, does not go on to consider the possibility that the structure of letterary love itself could be the source of the split (Willy Haas, afterword to Kafka's *Briefe an Milena,* ed. Haas [Frankfurt a. M., 1952], 215).

37. A recent article on business travelers in *The New York Times Magazine* contains the following Kafka-like confession: "Perhaps the strangest thing [. . .] is when I'm sitting here next to my wife, and I'll call up her voice mail in Massachusetts to leave a message" (*New York Times Magazine* [March 8, 1998], 40).

38. Freud writes in *Civilization and Its Discontents* (*Das Unbehagen in der Kultur*) (1930): "If there had been no railway to conquer distances, my child would never have left his native town and I should need no telephone to hear his voice; if traveling across the ocean by ship had not been introduced, my friend would not have embarked on his sea-voyage and I should not need a cable [*den Telegraphen*] to relieve my anxiety about him" (*Standard Edition,* 21:88; *Studienausgabe,* 9:219).

39. The passage reads: "Ich brauche nicht einmal selbst aufs Land fahren, das ist nicht nöthig. Ich schicke meinen angekleideten Körper nur. Also ich schicke diesen angekleideten Körper" (I don't even need to go to the country myself, it isn't necessary. I'll send my clothed body. So I'll send this clothed body) (*WP* 11; *NSI* 17, trans. rev.).

40. W. Kittler, "Schreibmaschinen, Sprechmaschinen," 83.

41. Freud, *Three Essays on the Theory of Sexuality,* in *Standard Edition,* 7:201–2; *Drei Abhandlungen zur Sexualtheorie,* in *Studienausgabe,* 5:106–7.

42. Freud writes: "A compulsive link of this kind between railway-travel and sexuality is clearly derived from the pleasurable character of the sensations of movement. In the event of repression, which turns so many childish preferences into their opposite, these same individuals, when they are adolescents or adults, will react to rocking or swinging with a feeling of nausea, will be terribly exhausted by a railway journey, or will be subject to attacks of anxiety on the journey and will protect themselves against a repetition of the painful experience by a dread of railway-travel [*Eisenbahn-*

angst]" (*Standard Edition,* 7:202; *Studienausgabe,* 5:107). For Abraham's similar, 1922 definition of "*Eisenbahnangst,*" see his *Psychoanalytische Studien,* 2:102. For Freud's personal "Reiseangst," see note 14 above.

43. I employ here the most recent dating of the letters, by Jost Schillemeit (in the 1983 Born/Müller edition, this is the penultimate 1920 letter, not the ultimate one). See Schillemeit, "Mitteilungen und Nicht-Mitteilbares: Zur Chronologie der *Briefe an Milena* und zu Kafkas 'Schreiben' im Jahr 1920," *Jahrbuch des freien deutschen Hochstifts* (1988): 253–303.

44. As Kafka notes in his *Letters to Felice,* desire intercepts fantasy when lovers attempt to write letters to one another in the other's presence: "I [. . .] will suffer on those evenings from the disadvantage of not having the sense to allow you to finish writing your letters to me; instead, I shall come up to you, take the hand that is trying to write, hold it, and refuse to let it go" (*LF* 109; *BF* 188).

45. Theweleit, *buch der könige,* 1:1026.

46. Felix Weltsch, *Religion und Humor im Leben und Werk Franz Kafkas* (Berlin, 1957), 39.

47. This citation and the ones preceding it in this paragraph are from Dora Diamant, "Mein Leben mit Franz Kafka," in *"Als Kafka mir entgegenkam . . .": Erinnerungen an Franz Kafka,* ed. Hans-Gerd Koch (Berlin, 1995), 177–78. I paraphrase the entire doll story from Diamant's account. Cf. also the paraphrase of Diamant in Citati's biography, *Kafka,* 297–98.

48. Not only Kafka's father is, according to Kafka, preventing him from attaining conjugal intimacy. In his *Letters to Milena,* there are two other obvious "thirds" that stand in the way: Kafka's fiancée at the time he meets Milena, Julie Wohryzek, and Milena's husband at the time, Ernst Pollak. In more conceptual terms, this third is constituted by the communications media themselves, the "ghosts" that always travel in the spaces between the lovers—like the mysterious "third" next to the lover in T. S. Eliot's *The Waste Land.* Since Eliot wrote the longest part of his poem in 1921, just after Kafka and Milena made their major break, and because *Letters to Milena* and *The Waste Land* seem to speak to one another, I cite the entire pertinent stanza from *The Waste Land*'s Section V ("What the Thunder Said"):

> Who is the third who walks always beside you?
> When I count, there are only you and I together
> But when I look ahead up the white road
> There is always another one walking beside you
> Gliding wrapt in a brown mantle, hooded
> I do not know whether a man or a woman
> —But who is that on the other side of you?

Gerhard Neumann (borrowing terminology from Michel Serres) complicates the question of the "third" in Kafka's writing: He argues that the "noise of the third" (or "*le bruit parasite*") does more than just disturb communication between two partners: it—like the noisy, vampiric media in *Letters to Milena*—is also precisely what renders this communication possible in the first place (Neumann, "Kafka's 'Schloß'-Roman," 213; see also 214–21).

Chapter Seven

1. Kafka never finished "Gracchus," and the manuscript now exists only as a series of fragments. In order to provide for clearer citation, I follow Malcolm Pasley's division of the text into four fragments (*GW* 47–55; see also *GW* xiv–xv)—even though Hartmut Binder is right to notice a very brief fifth fragment (*NSI* 311) (Binder, "'Der Jäger Gracchus': Zu Kafkas Schaffensweise und poetischer Topographie," *Jahrbuch der deutschen Schillergesellschaft* 15 (1971): 375–440). Kafka began this story in December 1916 and last worked on it in April 1917 (see *NSI*¹ 88–89). His first tubercular hemorrhage was in August 1917.

2. Benjamin connects both Gracchus and Odradek's "father of the family" with Josef K., through their common senses of guilt: "[Odradek] prefers the same places as the court of law which investigates guilt. Attics are the places of discarded, forgotten objects. Perhaps the necessity to appear before a court of justice gives rise to a feeling similar to that with which one approaches trunks in the attic which have been locked up for years" (Benjamin, "Franz Kafka: On the Tenth Anniversary of His Death," 133; see also 131–32).

3. For an overview of the early criticism of "The Hunter Gracchus," see Beicken, *Franz Kafka,* 315–18.

4. Rainer Nägele, "Auf der Suche nach dem verlorenen Paradies: Versuch einer Interpretation zu Kafkas 'Der Jäger Gracchus,'" *German Quarterly* 47 (1974): esp. 66–67.

5. See Frank, *Die unendliche Fahrt,* esp. the chapter entitled "'Der Jäger Gracchus': Variationen einer modernen Phantasie" (17–37).

6. In I. A. Richards' terminology, the "tenor" is the thing designated, and the "vehicle" is the metaphor itself: "My love [tenor] is a rose [vehicle]." See I. A. Richards, *The Philosophy of Rhetoric* (New York, 1936), 96, and also Corngold, *Franz Kafka: The Necessity of Form,* 55.

7. Frank, *Die unendliche Fahrt,* 164.

8. Elias Canetti, *Masse und Macht* (*Crowds and Power*) (Frankfurt a. M., 1996). Although *Masse und Macht* was first published in 1960, Canetti began it over three decades earlier. See esp. the section entitled "Die unsichtbaren Massen" (The Invisible Crowds), 46–53.

9. Canetti, *Masse und Macht,* 50.

10. Canetti, *Masse und Macht,* 49. Franz Rosenzweig's depiction of the Chinese ancestor cult fits, in this regard, in the same constellation with Canetti and Kafka: "Without any scruples [the spirits'] fullness is crammed into the fullness of the world. . . . The crowd of spirits is swelled without concern . . . new ones are constantly added to the old ones" (quoted in

Benjamin, "Franz Kafka: On the Tenth Anniversary of His Death," 132
[Benjamin's ellipses]).

11. Kafka owned a copy of Catullus' poetry that had been translated by Max
Brod. Compare, for example:

> O was ist süßer als das Ende aller Pein,
> Wenn ihre Last die Seele abwirft, endlich heim
> Von ausländischer Arbeit abgemattet kommt
> Und schön sich ausstreckt auf dem langersehnten Bett.

From G. Valerius Catullus, *Gedichte*, trans. Max Brod (Munich, 1914), 49
(cited in Binder, *Kafka-Kommentar zu sämtlichen Erzählungen*, 200–201).

12. Cf. Nägele, "Auf der Suche nach dem verlorenen Paradies," 62.

13. Frank's original is "*Ökonomie der Heimkehr.*" Frank's italics are meant to
emphasize "economy's" connection to "home"—through the Greek *oîkos*
[house]. Gracchus is, as Frank puts it, the prototypically "homeless" person
(Frank, *Die unendliche Fahrt,* 19).

14. K. refers to his *"Heimat"* and his *"Heimatstädtchen"* (his "little hometown")
in the first chapter of *The Castle* (*S* 17–8; *C* 8).

15. Frank, *Die unendliche Fahrt,* 18.

16. Odradek's positioning between life and death is also a positioning on a
stairway: "Can it be, then, that he might one day still be rolling down the
stairs, with ends of thread trailing after him, before the feet of my children
and my children's children? He obviously does no harm to anyone; but the
idea that he might outlive me I find almost painful" (*GW* 177).

17. For Kafka's apparent references to the river Styx, across which Charon
brought the dead to Hades, see *NSII* 33–4, 229.

18. Frank, *Die unendliche Fahrt,* 34.

19. Frank, *Die unendliche Fahrt,* 20.

20. Cited in Brod, *Franz Kafka: A Biography,* 75.

21. "Human inadequacy" is Beicken's term (Beicken, *Franz Kafka,* 318); Dietrich Krusche writes of "*Nichtbezogensein*" in "Die kommunikative Funktion der Deformation klassischer Motive: 'Der Jäger Gracchus': Zur
Problematik der Kafka-Interpretation," *Der Deutschunterricht* 25
(1973):140; Hartmut Binder mentions Grachus' lack of human relationship
in "'Der Jäger Gracchus'" (cited in Beicken's summary of the critical debate surrounding Gracchus' guilt [Beicken, *Franz Kafka,* 318]).

22. Because Brod inserted one paragraph from the first-person second fragment (in which Gracchus becomes the first-person narrator of his autobi-
ography) into the third-person first fragment, Beicken mistakenly (and
understandably) sees an authorial intervention where there is none: immediately following Gracchus' excessive denials (igniting the reader's suspicion that Gracchus is protesting too much), Kafka seems to step in
personally and put a stop to such misgivings ("Nobody will read what I
write here"). Because this apparently deliberate "fictional break" (*Fiktions-*

bruch) appears right after we begin to get suspicious of Gracchus' denials, Beicken logically concludes that Kafka wanted to cut short our investigations into Gracchus' guilt and intentionally leave this a mystery (Beicken, *Franz Kafka*, 318). Brod's corrupted cut-and-paste version was collected in Kafka's *Erzählungen* and was not replaced until 1992, by the Fischer critical edition; Brod's version from *Erzählungen* still appears in a widely distributed English translation (*The Complete Stories*, ed. Nahum N. Glatzer [New York, 1983], 226–30).

23. Frank, *Die unendliche Fahrt*, 11, 24.

24. Frank, *Die unendliche Fahrt*, 24.

25. Compare this imaginative error with the brutal, historically traceable ones committed by the European sailors from the "firm of Hagenbeck" in "A Report to an Academy": they capture Red Peter (who had been living happily on the "Gold Coast" of Africa) and bring him back to Europe in a cage (*MO* 188). Gracchus, conversely, never seems to harm anyone along the "coasts we happen to be passing" (*GW* 50).

26. Hartmut Binder describes this encounter, in which Kafka presented the book to Klara Thein, in *Kafka in neuer Sicht*, 127.

    The German title of the *Little Green Book* is *Bei den Indianern am Schingu*, by Karl von den Steinen. This memoir tells the story of a last surviving Indian tribe that still lives as if it were in the "Stone Age" (5). Possible intertextual connections between Steinen's Indians and the "bushman" from "The Hunter Gracchus" are three-fold: both pose in front of the European in the position of launching a spear, without actually launching it; both demonstrate a preference for objects that are elaborately painted ("*bemal[t]*" is the word used in both cases); and both live in the "bush"—in the case of Steinen's Indians, in an "idyllic bush-region" (*GW* 51; *NSI* 312; Steinen, *Bei den Indianern am Schingu*, 62–3, 65, 71).

27. *MO* 28; *DL* 29; *L* 46; *B* 60, trans. rev.; *LF* 416; *BF* 589; *MO* 13; *DL* 12; *MO* 31; *DL* 32.

28. "*Pfand der Hoffnung*" is Walter Benjamin's phrase (Benjamin, "Franz Kafka: On the Tenth Anniversary of His Death," 118; *Benjamin über Kafka*, 16).

29. Comparing the exoticist to the fetishist, Chris Bongie writes: "The fetishist collects, to use Agamben's nice phrase, 'a harem of objects' that provide him with only a momentary satisfaction; to come to rest in any one of these would be to face up to the absence that inhabits it and that the fetishist is intent upon denying" (Bongie, *Exotic Memories*, 77; for further connections between exoticism and fetishism, see *Exotic Memories*, 99–106). On colonialism and fetishism, see Homi Bhabha, "The Other Question: The Stereotype and Colonial Discourse," *Screen* (1983): esp. 25–36.

30. Bongie, *Exotic Memories*, 76. Ali Behdad builds on Bongie and connects the fetishist's experience of absence to melancholia: the exotic traveler "undertakes a project that 'cannot help coming after what it must come before.' The belated traveler thus transforms his or her experience of loss into

a representation of the Orient as a site for melancholia and even mourning" (Behdad, *Belated Travelers*, 92).

31. Frank compares "The Hunter Gracchus" to *Bateau Ivre* in *Die unendliche
    Fahrt*, 30–37. Peter J. Brenner has insightfully argued that "In the Penal
    Colony" demonstrates how colonialism's brutalities, in the end, destroy
    colonialism's own fantasies (Brenner, "Schwierige Reisen," 127–30).

32. Cf. Brenner, "Schwierige Reisen," 129–30.

33. See the final section of chapter five for my reservations—based on the his-
    torical context of Austria-Hungary's imperial swansong—concerning
    Deleuze/Guattari's vision of Kafka as a radical deterritorializer.

34. Frank's concept of a "negative" religiosity applies here to "negative" nos-
    talgia. Just as faithless subjects cannot finally shed their hope in the exis-
    tence of a God, deterritorializing moderns cannot ultimately discard their
    belief in a territory that, in its perfection, would be both a place and a not-
    place (a u-topia) (Frank, *Die unendliche Fahrt*, 34).

35. Kafka's position is not so much deterritorialized as it is "extraterritorial-
    ized." As Kafka writes to Brod in 1921, being extraterritorialized means
    being like a dead man—being spoken of *as if* one were dead: "When you
    speak to [Milena] about me, speak as you would of someone dead. I mean
    as far as my 'externality' is concerned, my 'extraterritoriality' [*Exterritorial-
    ität*]" (*L* 279; *B* 322). "Extraterritoriality" refers here to the concept delin-
    eated by Alfred Ehrenstein (one of the first writers outside of Prague to
    appreciate Kafka's writing) in his essay "Ansichten eines Exterritorialen"
    (Perspectives of an Extraterritorial), *Die Fackel* 323 (May 18, 1911): 1–8.
    See Hannelore Rodlauer, "'Ansichten eines Exterritorialen': Albert Ehren-
    stein und Franz Kafka," in *Expressionismus in Österreich*, ed. Klaus Amann
    and Armin A. Wallas (Vienna, 1994), 225–52, and Spector, *Prague Territories*,
    231–32. For the importance of extraterritorialization in Kafka's "The
    Judgment," see note 34 in chapter five.

36. For evocative readings of this passage, see Maurice Blanchot, "La mort
    contente," in *De Kafka à Kafka* (Paris, 1981), 132–39, and Charles Bern-
    heimer, "On Death and Dying: Kafka's Allegory of Reading," in *Kafka and
    the Contemporary Critical Performance*, 87–90.

37. Neither of these "deaths," however, is as final as it may seem. See my dis-
    cussion in the final section of chapter three regarding Josef K.'s, and other
    Kafka characters', inability to actually die. See also Mark Anderson on the
    officer's undead state at the end of "In the Penal Colony" (Anderson,
    Kafka's Clothes, 188).

38. "Eternal present" is Dorrit Cohn's term (Cohn, "Kafka's Eternal Present:
    Narrative Tense in 'Ein Landarzt' and Other First-Person Stories," *PMLA*
    83 [1968]: 144–150).

39. The German term is *"äußerliche Exotik."* See my first chapter as well as
    Brod's *Prager Kreis*, 111.

40. Corngold, "*The Metamorphosis*: Metamorphosis of the Metaphor," in *Franz
    Kafka: The Necessity of Form*, 47–89 (here, 50). Corngold is reacting to

Günther Anders' *Kafka—Pro und Contra* (Munich, 1951) as well as to Walter Sokel's *The Writer in Extremis: Expressionism in Twentieth-Century Literature* (Stanford, 1959) and *Franz Kafka* (NewYork, 1966).

41. Corngold, *Franz Kafka: The Necessity of Form,* 57.

42. See, in this regard, Homi Bhabha's claim that the fantasy colonial Other (like death in Kafka's scenario) is neither the same nor the not-same; it is, like the psychoanalytic fetish, "between what is always 'in place,' already known, and something that must be anxiously repeated" (Bhabha, "The Other Question," 18).

43. Maurice Blanchot makes a similar point, albeit without introducing the rhetoric of exoticism: "literary immortality is the very movement by which the nausea of survival which is not a survival, death which does not end anything, insinuates itself into the world, a world sapped by crude existence" (Blanchot, "Literature and the Right to Death," in *The Gaze of Orpheus,* trans. Lydia Davis [Barrytown, NY, 1981], 58). See also Charles Bernheimer's elegant psycho-poetical revision of Blanchot (Bernheimer, "On Death and Dying").

Epilogue

1. For more on this interconnection of letters and literature, see Anderson, "Kafka's Unsigned Letters to Milena Jesenská," 242–44.

2. Ludwig Dietz, *Franz Kafka* (Stuttgart, 1990), 104.

3. Jacques Derrida, "Le facteur de la vérité," in *The Post Card: From Socrates to Freud and Beyond* (Chicago, 1987), 413–96 (here, 492–93).

4. See Ken MacMullen's film *Ghost Dance,* in which Derrida, when asked whether he believes in ghosts, mischievously replies, "That's a hard question because, you see, I *am* a ghost" (cited in Maud Ellmann, "The Ghosts of Ulysses," in *James Joyce: The Artist and the Labyrinth,* ed. Augustin Martin [London, 1990], 193).

5. Diamant, "Mein Leben mit Franz Kafka," 179.

6. See Blanchot, "Literature and the Right to Death."

   Pertinent here is also Maud Ellmann's notion that "vivocentrism" is our last accepted form of discrimination. We favor the living over the dead because we—unlike the ancient Greeks—deny their existence (Ellmann, "The Ghosts of Ulysses," 193). A contemporary example of such an uncritical vivocentrism is Peter Hamm's recent intervention in the controversy surrounding Ingeborg Bachmann's literary remains: In a digression from his discussion of Bachmann, Hamm sides with (living) "humanity" over (dead) Kafka—praising Brod for "valu[ing] the good of humanity, which would have lost Kafka's work without him, over the last testament of his friend" (Peter Hamm, "Ingeborg Bachmann," *Die Zeit* 41 [2000]).

7. For background information on the history of the *Scheintod* and the *Herzstich,* see Christoph Daxelmüller "Der Scheintote von Æbelholt: Zum Hintergrund kollektiver Ängste im Mittelalter und in der frühen Neuzeit" and

Franziska Christiansen, "Scheintod und Scheintodängste," both in *Tod und Gesellschaft—Tod im Wandel,* ed. Christoph Daxelmüller (Regensburg, 1996), 75–76 and 77–79.

8. See, among other Poe stories, "The Premature Burial" (1844), in which the narrator, while discussing "Life" and "Death," asks, "Who shall say where the one ends and the other begins?" He continues: "We know that there are diseases in which occur total cessations of all apparent functions of vitality, and yet in which these cessations are merely suspensions" (*The Complete Illustrated Stories and Poems of Edgar Allan Poe* [London, 1988], 354).

9. Malte says curtly to the doctors, as they approach his dead father: "Sie sind wegen des Herzstichs da: bitte" (Rainer Maria Rilke, *Die Aufzeichnungen des Malte Laurids Brigge,* in *Sämtliche Werke* [Munich, 1966], 6:853; translation in *The Notebooks of Malte Laurids Brigge,* trans. Stephen Mitchell [New York, 1990], 157). For a list of those requesting the *Herzstich,* see Beppo Beyerl, "Der Weg alles Irdischen: Einige Geschichten vom Sterben und Begrabenwerden," *Wiener Zeitung,* November 3, 2000.

10. But it is likely that not even this *"Herzstich"* saves K. from the torments of immortality. See the last section of my chapter three.

11. Kafka wrote two versions of his testament: the first one probably from fall/winter 1921 and a second one dated November 29, 1922. The testaments can be found in *EFII,* 365 and 421–22. An English translation of both testaments (from which I cite here) is available in Max Brod's afterword to Kafka's *The Trial* (*T* 264–71). Because I cite more from the second testament in the main text, I will include here only the shorter, first version:

> Everything I leave behind me (in my bookcase, linen-cupboard, and my desk both at home and the office, or anywhere else where anything may have got to and meets your eye), in the way of diaries, manuscripts, letters (my own and others'), sketches, and so on, to be burned entirely and unread; also all writings and sketches which you or others may possess; and ask those others for them in my name. Letters which they do not want to hand over to you, they should at least promise faithfully to burn themselves. (*T* 265–66; *EFII* 365)

12. The German reads: "sollten sie ganz verloren gehn, entspricht dieses meinem eigentlichen Wunsch" (*T* 266; *EFII* 421–22).

13. One might presuppose that Kafka, being Jewish, would never have even considered cremation. But secular Jews such as Kafka and even some reform Jews had been choosing cremation from its legal reinstitution in the late nineteenth century onward. Despite Orthodox Judaism's (like Catholicism's) strong resistance to the new cremation vogue, the Chief Rabbis of England and France (if not of Italy and Württemberg) allowed the ashes of cremated persons to be interred in Jewish cemeteries as early as the 1880s. Some reform rabbis even officiated at cremations (*Encyclopaedia Judaica,* s.v. "cremation"). For Jews critical of organized, institutionalized Judaism—such as Kafka—cremation could

well have been a marker of individuality. As Hans Ulrich Gumbrecht points out, choosing cremation in the 1920s likely signified, for Jews, the "ultimate logical conclusion of 'emancipation' from their cultural roots" (Hans Ulrich Gumbrecht, *In 1926: Living at the Edge of Time* [Cambridge, MA, 1997], 63–64).

14. By 1906 the number of crematoria in Germany had already ballooned to fourteen and the number of cremations to 2,507 (*Encyclopaedia Britannica,* 14th ed., s.v. "cremation").

15. For the arguments from the cremation societies regarding hygiene and land conservation, see Jessica Mitford, *The American Way of Death* (New York, 1978), 161–63, and *Encyclopaedia Britannica,* 14th ed., s.v. "cremation."

16. Cited in Mitford, *The American Way of Death,* 163.

17. See *L* 317; *B* 369; *D* 383; *Ta* 832; *T* 268–69; *EFII* 219.

18. Blanchot turns this paradox luminously: "[The writer] has written because in the depths of language he heard the work of death as it prepared living beings for the truth of their name: he worked for this nothingness and he himself was a nothingness at work. But as one realizes the void, one creates a work, and the work, born of fidelity to death, is in the end no longer capable of dying; and all it brings to the person who was trying to prepare an unstoried death for himself is the mockery of immortality" (Blanchot, "Literature and the Right to Death," 58).

19. According to an 1859 decree from the Austrian Ministry of the Interior, transporting corpses for a period exceeding two hours required an official permit as well as adherence to specific sanitary measures—including the use of doubled coffins (one inside the other). During the summer months, additional regulations obtained: the body needed first to be painstakingly "preserved" (innards removed, cleansed, and replaced), then put inside an inner coffin, which was to be filled with sawdust and chaff and then finally sealed with a coating of tar. An 1874 ordinance from the same Ministry relaxed these stipulations somewhat, insisting only that bodies transported for a week or more be "preserved (embalmed)" (although summer transport called for an earlier embalming). But even for shorter trips and trips in the winter, the body needed to be kept in two coffins, and both coffins were to consist of either hardwood or metal. As before, the inner coffin was to be either sealed with hot tar or, in the case of metal coffins, soldered shut. (According to Brod, who also mentions Kafka's transport to the mortuary, Kafka's coffin was soldered shut [Brod, *Franz Kafka: A Biography,* 209, 212].) For these and other Austrian corpse-transport policies, see Franz Knispel, "Zur Überführung Verstorbener," *Der Österreichische Bestatter* 38 (April 1996): esp. 46–47. For the similar turn-of-the-century German regulations on corpse transport, see "Eisenbahn-wagen für Leichenbeförderung," *Eisenbahntechnische Zeitschrift* 11 (1905): 225. Because eight days passed from Kafka's death to his burial on June 11, it is likely that his body would have been embalmed (see Knispel, "Zur Überführung," 47).

20. Knispel, "Zur Überführung," 47; Hackermüller, *Kafkas letzte Jahre 1917–1924,* 150; Heinz Riedel, telephone interview with Christine Koch, February 7, 2001. Mr. Riedel is resident expert at the Bestattungsmuseum (Funeral Museum) in Vienna. I thank both Mr. Riedel and Ms. Koch for this information, and I also thank Ms. Koch for collecting important data on the techniques of corpse transportation in the 1920s.

21. Riedel, telephone interview; "Eisenbahnwagen für Leichenbeförderung," 223–27.

22. Riedel, telephone interview.

23. Riedel, "Eisenbahnwaggons für Totentransporte," *Der Österreichische Bestatter* 33 (August 1991): 110.

24. The history of transporting corpses by train goes back to 1850 England. Transporting dead dignitaries in special "salon cars"—sometimes dressed up with garlands, fir sprigs, etc.—dates back at least to the deaths of U.S. President James Garfield in 1881 and German Field Marshall Graf Waldersee in 1904. In 1894, the Austrian government went so far as to commission a "Salon-Leichenwagen" (used exclusively for transporting the corpses of celebrities, most notably the murdered Empress Elisabeth in 1898). But only in 1905 did the German firm Uerdingen begin producing *Leichenwagen* for use by ordinary paying customers. See Wolfgang Bahr, *Tote auf Reisen: Ein makabrer Reisebegleiter* (Vienna, 2000), 153; Riedel, "Eisenbahnwaggons für Totentransporte," 108–12; "Eisenbahnwagen für Leichenbeförderung," 223–27.

25. "Eisenbahnwagen für Leichenbeförderung," 225.

26. "Eisenbahnwagen für Leichenbeförderung," 225–26.

27. Brod, *Über Franz Kafka* (Frankfurt a. M., 1966), 212 (not included in the English translation).

28. Brod, "Franz Kafkas Nachlaß," *Die Weltbühne* 20 (July 17, 1924): 106–9.

Works Cited

I list only the works cited in this book, with the exception of a few of the travel books owned by Kafka that I do not explicitly reference (for all of the books owned by Kafka, see Jürgen Born, *Kafkas Bibliothek*). For German- and French-language texts that are widely available in English translation, I generally list the facts of publication for the original but also place the standard translation titles in parentheses; full bibliographical information for most of these translations can be found at the pertinent points in the notes.

1. Primary Sources

Amundsen, Roald. *Eskimoleben: Eindrücke von der Polarfahrt 1903–1907.* Vol. 25 of the *Grüne Bändchen.* Cologne: Hermann & Friedrich Schaffstein, 1912.

"Aus dem Tagebuch einer Reise nach Ostasien," *Die neue Rundschau* 2 (1911): 1403–19.

Baedeker, Karl. *Italien: Handbuch für Reisende.* 15th ed. Leipzig: Karl Baedeker, 1898.

———. *Mittel- und Nord-Deutschland (Westlich bis zum Rhein): Handbuch für Reisende.* 22nd ed. Leipzig: Karl Baedeker, 1887.

———. *Österreich-Ungarn (nebst Cetinje Belgrad Bukarest): Handbuch für Reisende.* 28th ed. Leipzig: Karl Baedeker, 1910.

———. *Palästina und Syrien.* 1st ed. Leipzig: Karl Baedeker, 1875.

———. *Paris und Umgebungen.* 14th ed. Leipzig: Karl Baedeker, 1896.

Baudelaire, Charles. "Anywhere out of this world—N'importe où hors du monde." In *Petits Poèmes en Prose (Le Spleen de Paris)*, 211–13. Paris: Editions Garnier Frères, 1958.

Bayer, M. *Im Kampfe gegen die Hereros: Bilder aus dem Feldzug in Südwest.* Vol. 13 of the *Grüne Bändchen.* Cologne: Hermann & Friedrich Schaffstein, 1911.

Bonsels, Waldemar. *Indienfahrt.* Vol. 3 of *Wanderschaft zwischen Staub und Sternen: Gesamtwerk,* edited by Rose-Marie Bonsels. Munich: Langen Müller, 1980. Originally published in 1916.

Borchgrevink, Carsten. *Festes Land am Südpol: Erlebnisse auf der Expedition nach dem Südpolarland 1898–1900.* Vol. 9 of the *Grüne Bändchen.* Cologne: Hermann & Friedrich Schaffstein, 1911.

Broch, Hermann. *Die Schlafwandler: Eine Romantrilogie* (The sleepwalkers). Zürich: Rhein-Verlag, 1931–32.

Brod, Max. "Franz Kafkas Nachlaß." *Die Weltbühne* 20 (July 17, 1924): 106–109.

———. *Ein tschechisches Dienstmädchen: Roman.* Berlin: Axel Juncker, 1909.

Catullus, G. Valerius. *Gedichte.* Translated by Max Brod. Munich: Georg Müller, 1914.

Cortez, Ferdinand. *Erster Bericht des Ferdinand Cortez an Kaiser Karl V. über die Eroberung von Mexiko.* Vol. 10 of the *Grüne Bändchen.* Cologne: Hermann & Friedrich Schaffstein, 1911.

Diamant, Dora. "Mein Leben mit Franz Kafka." In *"Als Kafka mir entgegenkam . . .": Erinnerungen an Franz Kafka,* edited by Hans-Gerd Koch, 174–85. Berlin: Wagenbach, 1995.

"Eisenbahnwagen für Leichenbeförderung," *Eisenbahntechnische Zeitschrift* 11 (1905): 223–27.

Ehrenstein, Albert. "Ansichten eines Exterritorialen," *Die Fackel* 323 (May 18, 1911): 1–8.

Eliot, T. S. (Thomas Stearns). *The Waste Land.* New York: Boni and Liveright, 1922.

Ellison, Ralph. *Invisible Man.* New York: Vintage, 1972. Originally published in 1947.

Ewers, Hanns Heinz. *Indien und Ich.* Munich: Georg Müller, 1919. Originally published in 1911.

Flaubert, Gustave. *Correspondance 1850–1859.* Vol. 13 of *Oeuvres complètes.* Paris: Club de l'Hônnete Homme, [1971–75].

———. *L'Éducation sentimentale.* Vol. 3 of *Oeuvres complètes.* Paris: Club de l'Hônnete Homme, [1971–75].

———. *Flaubert in Egypt: A Sensibility on Tour.* Translated and edited by Francis Steegmuller. New York: Penguin, 1996.

———. *Par les champs et par les grèves.* In *Oeuvres complètes,* 10:27–274. Paris: Club de l'Hônnete Homme, [1971–75].

———. *Voyage en Orient* (première partie). In *Oeuvres complètes,* 10:431–614. Paris: Club de l'Hônnete Homme, [1971–75].

Fleck, Förster, *Förster Flecks Erzählung von seinen Schicksalen auf dem Zuge Napoleons nach Rußland und von seiner Gefangenschaft 1812–1814.* Vol. 18 of the *Grüne Bändchen.* Cologne: Hermann & Friedrich Schaffstein, 1912.

Fontane, Theodor. *Aus England und Schottland.* Berlin: F. Fontane & Co, 1908. Originally published in two parts in 1854 and 1860.

Gauguin, Paul. *Die Aufzeichnungen von Noa Noa.* Translated by Hans Graber. Wetzlar: Büchse der Pandora, 1982. Originally published as *Noa Noa* in collaboration with Charles Morice in 1901.

Goethe, Johann Wolfgang von. *Die Faustdichtungen.* Munich: Winkler, 1989.

———. *Goethes Briefe: Briefe der Jahre 1786–1805* (Letters from Goethe, 1786–1805). Edited by Karl Robert Mandelkow. Hamburg: Christian Wegner Verlag, 1964.

———. *Italienische Reise* (Italian journey). Edited by Herbert von Einem. Munich: C. H. Beck, 1978. Originally published in 1816–17.

———. *Westöstlicher Diwan* (West-eastern divan). Munich: Wilhelm Golmann, 1958. Originally published in 1819.

———. *Wilhelm Meisters Lehrjahre* (Wilhelm Meister's apprenticeship). Berlin: Aufbau-Verlag, 1970. Originally published in 1795–96.

Hedin, Sven. *Über den Transhimalaja.* Vol. 8 of the *Grüne Bändchen.* Cologne: Hermann & Friedrich Schaffstein, 1911.

Heindl, Robert. *Meine Reise nach den Strafkolonien.* Berlin: Ullstein, 1913.

Henningsen, Nicolaus, ed. *Schaffsteins Grüne Bändchen.* Cologne: Hermann & Friedrich Schaffstein, 1910–70.

Hesse, Hermann. *Aus Indien: Aufzeichnungen, Tagebücher, Gedichte, Betrachtungen und Erzählungen.* Frankfurt a. M.: Suhrkamp, 1982. Originally published in 1913.

Hofmannsthal, Hugo von. "Ein Brief." In *Sämtliche Werke,* 31:45–55, edited by Ellen Ritter. Frankfurt a. M.: Fischer, 1991. Originally published in 1902.

Holitscher, Arthur. *Amerika heute und morgen.* 3rd ed. Berlin: Fischer, 1912.

———. *In England—Ostpreußen—Südösterreich.* Berlin: Fisher, 1915.

———. "Scab." *Die neue Rundschau* 24 (1913): 1267–1280

Hübner, Fritz. "Reise-Impressionismus." *Der Bücherwurm, Eine Monatsschrift für Bücherfreunde* 3/9 (Reiseheft) (July 1913): 263.

Jacques, Norbert. *Heiße Städte: Eine Reise nach Brasilien.* Berlin: Fischer, 1911.

———. *Piraths Insel.* Berlin: Fischer, 1917.

Jung, Carl Gustav, "Wandlungen und Symbole der Libido: Beiträge zur Entwicklungsgeschichte des Denkens" (2. Teil), *Jahrbuch für psychoanalytische und psychopathische Forschungen* 4 (1912): 162–464

Kellermann, Bernhard. *Ein Spaziergang in Japan.* Berlin: Paul Cassirer, 1911.

Kerr, Alfred. "Jagow, Flaubert, Pan." *Pan* 1 (February 1911): 217–23.

Keyserling, Graf Hermann. *Das Reisetagebuch eines Philosophen.* Stuttgart/Berlin: Deutsche Verlag-Anstalt, 1932. Originally published in 1919.

Kleist, Heinrich von. *Über das Marionettentheater. Aufsätze und Anekdoten* (On the marionette theater). Frankfurt a. M.: Insel Verlag, 1987.

Loti, Pierre. *Aziyadé:–1 extrait des notes et lettres d'un lieutenant de la marine anglaise, entré au service de la Turquie, le 10 Mai 1876, tué dans les murs de Kars, le 27 octobre 1877* (Aziyadé). Paris: Calmann Lévy, 1920. Originally published in 1879.

García Márquez, Gabriel. *One Hundred Years of Solitude.* Translated by Gregory Rabassa. New York: Avon, 1971. Originally published as *Cien Años de Soledad* in 1967.

Maistre, Xavier de. *Voyage autour de ma chambre.* Lausanne: privately published, 1794.

Mecklenburg, Adolf Friedrich zu. *Im Hinterlande von Deutsch-Ostafrika.* Vol. 3 of the *Grüne Bändchen.* Cologne: Hermann & Friedrich Schaffstein, 1910.

Mikkelsen, Einar. *Ein arktischer Robinson.* Vol. 17 of *Reisen und Abenteuer.* Leipzig: F.A. Brockhaus, 1922.

Mirbeau, Octave. *Le jardin des supplices* (Torture garden). Paris: Fasquelle, 1957. Originally published in 1899.

Müller, Robert. *Tropen: der Mythos der Reise: Urkunden eines deutschen Ingenieurs.* Paderborn: Igel-Verlag, 1990. Originally published in 1915.

[Napoleon]. *Von Elba bis Belle-Alliance.* Vol. 62 of the *Grüne Bändchen.* Cologne: Hermann & Friedrich Schaffstein, 1915.

Poe, Edgar Allan. "The Premature Burial." In *The Complete Illustrated Stories and Poems of Edgar Allan Poe.* London: Chancellor, 1988. 354–66. Originally published in 1844.

Quincey, Thomas de. "Kant in his Miscellaneous Essays." In *The Works of Thomas de Quincey* 9:439–490. Cambridge: Riverside Press, 1877.

Requadt, F. *Wie wir Ostpreußen befreiten*. Vol. 66 of the *Grüne Bändchen*. Cologne: Hermann & Friedrich Schaffstein, 1915.

Rilke, Rainer Maria. *Die Aufzeichnungen des Malte Laurids Brigge* (The notebooks of Malte Laurids Brigge). In *Sämtliche Werke* 6:707–978. Munich: Insel Verlag, 1966. Originally published in 1910.

Rüttgers, Severin. *Schaffsteins Grüne Bändchen im Schulunterricht und als Klassenlektüre*. Cologne: Hermann & Friedrich Schaffstein, 1930.

Sacher-Masoch, Leopold von. *Venus im Pelz: Mit einer Studie über den Masochismus* (Venus in furs). Frankfurt a. M.: Insel, 1968 [1870].

Sade, Marquis de. *Histoire de Juliette: ou Les prospérités du vice* (Juliette). Paris: Union Générale d'Éditions, 1976.

Schaffstein, Hermann. *Wir Jungen von 1870/71: Erinnerungen aus meinen Kinderjahren*. Vol. 32 of the *Grüne Bändchen*. Cologne: Hermann & Friedrich Schaffstein, 1913.

Stephan, Heinrich von. *Geschichte der Preußischen Post: Nach amtlichen Quellen bis 1858 bearbeitet von Dr. H. v. Stephan. Neubearbeitet und fortgeführt bis 1868 von K. Sautter*. Vol. 1. Berlin: R. Decker, 1928.

Steinen, Karl von den. *Bei den Indianern am Schingu*. Vol. 20 of the *Grüne Bändchen*. Cologne: Hermann & Friedrich Schaffstein, 1912.

Weber, Oskar [Adrian Roesch?]. *Der Bananenkönig: Was der Nachkomme eines verkauften Hessen in Amerika schuf*. Vol. 73 of the *Grüne Bändchen*. Cologne: Hermann & Friedrich Schaffstein, 1918.

———. *Briefe eines Kaffee-Pflanzers: Zwei Jahrzehnte deutscher Arbeit in Zentral-Amerika*. Vol. 50 of the *Grüne Bändchen*. Cologne: Hermann & Friedrich Schaffstein, 1913.

———. *Der Zuckerbaron: Schicksale eines ehemaligen deutschen Offiziers in Südamerika*. Vol. 54 of the *Grüne Bändchen*. Cologne: Hermann & Friedrich Schaffstein, 1914.

Weininger, Otto. *Geschlecht und Charakter: eine prinzipielle Untersuchung* (Sex and character). Vienna: Braumüller, 1903.

Wettstein, K. A. *Durch den brasilianischen Urwald: Erlebnisse bei einer Wegerkundung in den deutschvölkischen Kolonien Süd-Brasiliens*. Vol. 14 of the *Grüne Bändchen*. Cologne: Hermann & Friedrich Schaffstein, 1911; Cologne: Hermann & Friedrich Schaffstein, 1942 (Feldpostausgabe).

Wiederhold, Max. *Der Panamakanal*. Vol. 44 of the *Grüne Bändchen*. Cologne: Hermann & Friedrich Schaffstein, 1913.

Winterstein, Alfred. "Zur Psychologie des Reisens," *Imago. Zeitschrift fuer Anwendung der Psychoanalyse auf die Geisteswissenschaften*. 1. Jahrgang, Heft 1 (March 1912): 489–506.

Wolff, Kurt. *Briefwechsel eines Verlegers*, edited by Bernhard Zeller und Ellen Otten. Frankfurt a. M.: Scheffler, 1966.

Zell, Th. *Majestäten der Wildnis*. Vol. 29 of the *Grüne Bändchen*. Cologne: Hermann & Friedrich Schaffstein, 1912.

2. Secondary Sources on Kafka

Adorno, Theodor. "Aufzeichnungen zu Kafka" (Notes on Kafka). In *Prismen: Kulturkritik und Gesellschaft (Prisms)*. Frankfurt a. M.: Suhrkamp, 1955. 302–42.

Anders, Günther. *Kafka—Pro und Contra*. Munich: Beck, 1951.

Anderson, Mark. "Kafka and Sacher-Masoch." *Journal of the Kafka Society of America* 7 (1983): 4–19.

———. *Kafka's Clothes: Ornament and Aestheticism in the Habsburg Fin de Siècle*. Oxford: Clarendon, 1992.

———. "Kafka's Unsigned Letters to Milena Jesenská." In *Reading Kafka: Prague, Politics, and the Fin de Siècle*, edited by Mark Anderson, 241–56.

———, ed. *Reading Kafka: Prague, Politics and the Fin de Siècle*. New York: Schocken, 1989.

Angress, Ruth Klüger. "Kafka and Sacher-Masoch: A Note on *The Metamorphosis*." *MLN* 85 (1970): 745–46.

Beck, Evelyn Torton. *Kafka and the Yiddish Theater: Its Impact on His Work*. Madison: Univ. of Wisconsin Press, 1971.

Beicken, Peter. *Franz Kafka: Eine kritische Einführung in die Forschung*. Frankfurt a. M.: Athenaion, 1974.

Beilhack, Hans. "Fünfter Abend für Neue Literatur." In *Franz Kafka: Kritik und Rezeption zu seinen Lebzeiten 1912–1924*, edited by Jürgen Born, 121. Frankfurt a. M.: Fischer, 1979. Originally published in 1916.

Beissner, Friedrich. *Der Erzähler Franz Kafka*. Stuttgart: Kohlhammer, 1952.

Benjamin, Walter. *Benjamin über Kafka: Texte, Briefzeugnisse, Aufzeichnungen*, edited by Hermann Schweppenhäuser. Frankfurt a. M.: Suhrkamp, 1992.

———. "Franz Kafka: On the Tenth Anniversary of His Death." In *Illuminations*, translated by Harry Zohn and edited by Hannah Arendt, 111–40. New York: Schocken, 1968.

———. "Some Reflections on Kafka." In *Illuminations*, translated by Harry Zohn and edited by Hannah Arendt, 141–45. New York: Schocken, 1968.

Bernheimer, Charles. *Flaubert and Kafka: Studies in Psychopoetic Structure*. New Haven: Yale Univ. Press, 1982.

———. "On Death and Dying: Kafka's Allegory of Reading." In *Kafka and the Contemporary Critical Performance: Centenary Readings*, edited by Alan Udoff, 87–96.

Binder, Hartmut, "'Der Jäger Gracchus': Zu Kafkas Schaffensweise und poetischer Topographie," *Jahrbuch der deutschen Schillergesellschaft* 15 (1971): 375–440

———, ed. *Kafka-Handbuch in Zwei Bänden*. 2 vols. Stuttgart: Alfred Kröner, 1979.

———. *Kafka-Kommentar zu sämtlichen Erzählungen*. Munich: Winkler, 1975.

———. *Kafka in neuer Sicht: Mimik, Geste und Personengefüge als Darstellungsformen der Autobiographie*. Stuttgart: Metzler, 1976.

———. *Kafka in Paris: historische Spaziergänge mit alten Photographien*. Munich: Langen Müller, 1999.

Blanchot, Maurice. *De Kafka à Kafka*. Paris: Gallimard, 1981.

Blank, Herbert. *In Kafkas Bibliothek: Werke der Weltliteratur und Geschichte in der Edition, wie sie Kafka besaß oder kannte*. Stuttgart: Antiquariat Herbert Blank, 2001.

Bloom, Harold, ed. *Franz Kafka's "The Castle."* New York: Chelsea House, 1988.

Boa, Elizabeth. *Kafka: Gender, Class, and Race in the Letters and Fictions*. Oxford: Clarendon, 1996.

Born, Jürgen, ed. *Franz Kafka: Kritik und Rezeption zu seinen Lebzeiten 1912–1924*. Frankfurt a. M.: Fischer, 1979.

————. *Kafkas Bibliothek: Ein beschreibendes Verzeichnis.* Frankfurt a. M.: Fischer, 1990.

Born, Jürgen and Michael Müller, "Kafkas Briefe an Milena: Ihre Datierung." *Jahrbuch der deutschen Schillergesellschaft* 25 (1981): 509–24.

Brod, Max. "*The Castle;* Its Genesis." In *Franz Kafka Today,* edited by A. Flores and H. Swander, 161–64.

————. "Nachwort zur ersten Ausgabe." Afterword to *Amerika,* by Franz Kafka, edited by Max Brod, 260–62. Frankfurt a. M.: Fischer, 1956. Originally published in 1927.

————. "Nachwort zur ersten Ausgabe." Afterword to *Das Schloß* (*The Castle*), by Franz Kafka, edited by Max Brod, 347–54. Frankfurt a. M.: Fischer, 1968. Originally published in 1926.

————. "Nachwort zur ersten Ausgabe." Afterword to *Der Prozeß* (*The Trial*), by Franz Kafka, edited by Max Brod, 223–29. New York: Schocken, 1979. Originally published in 1925.

————. *Der Prager Kreis.* Stuttgart: Kohlhammer, 1966.

————. *Über Franz Kafka* (Franz Kafka: a biography). Frankfurt a. M.: Fischer, 1966.

————. "Uyttersprot korrigiert Kafka," *Forum* 43/44 (1957): 265.

Buber-Neumann, Margarete. *Milena.* Translated by Ralph Manheim. New York: Seaver Books, 1988.

Canetti, Elias. *Der andere Prozeß: Kafkas Briefe an Felice* (Kafka's other trial: The letters to Felice). Munich: Hanser, 1969.

Černá, Jana. *Kafka's Milena.* Translated by A. G. Brain. Evanston, IL: Northwestern Univ. Press, 1993.

Cersowsky, Peter. *"Mein ganzes Wesen ist auf Literatur gerichtet": Franz Kafka im Kontext der literarischen Dekadenz.* Würzburg: Königshausen & Neumann, 1983.

Citati, Pietro. *Kafka.* Translated by Raymond Rosenthal. New York: Knopf, 1990.

Cohn, Dorrit. "Kafka's Eternal Present: Narrative Tense in 'Ein Landarzt' and Other First-Person Stories." *PMLA* 83 (1968): 144–150.

Corngold, Stanley. "Allotria and Excreta in 'In the Penal Colony.'" *Modernism/Modernity* 8 (2001): 281–293.

————. *The Commentators' Despair: The Interpretation of Kafka's "Metamorphosis."* Port Washington, NY: Kennikat Press, 1973.

————. *Franz Kafka: The Necessity of Form.* Ithaca, NY: Cornell Univ. Press, 1988.

Cournot, Michel. "Toi qui as de si grandes dents . . ." *Le Nouvel Observateur,* April 17, 1972.

Deleuze, Gilles, and Félix Guattari. *Kafka: Pour une littérature mineure* (Kafka: Toward a minor literature). Paris: Les Éditions de Minuit, 1975.

Delfosse, Heinrich P. and Karl Jürgen Skrodzki. *Synoptische Konkordanz zu Franz Kafkas Romanen.* 3 vols. Tübingen: Niemeyer, 1993.

Dietz, Ludwig. *Franz Kafka.* Stuttgart: Metzler, 1990.

Dowden, Stephen. *Kafka's Castle and the Critical Imagination.* Columbia, SC: Camden House, 1995.

Eisner, Pavel. "Franz Kafka and Prague." *Books Abroad* (Summer 1947): 264–70.

————. *Franz Kafka and Prague.* New York: Golden Griffin, 1950.

————. "Franz Kafkas *Prozess* und Prague." *German Life and Letters* 14 (1960): 16–25.

Emrich, Wilhelm. *Franz Kafka* (Franz Kafka: a critical study of his writings). Frankfurt a. M.: Athenäum, 1957.

Flores, A., and H. Swander, eds. *Franz Kafka Today.* Madison: Univ. of Wisconsin Press, 1958.

Gilman, Sander. *Franz Kafka, the Jewish Patient.* New York: Routledge, 1995.

Goebel, Rolf. *Constructing China: Kafka's Orientalist Discourse.* Columbia, SC: Camden House, 1997.

————. "Kafka and Postcolonial Critique: *Der Verschollene,* 'In der Strafkolonie,' 'Beim Bau der chinesischen Mauer.'" In *A Companion to the Works of Franz Kafka,* edited by James Rolleston, 187–212.

Göhler, Helga. *Franz Kafka: "Das Schloß."* Bonn: Bouvier, 1982.

Gray, Ronald. *Kafka's Castle.* Cambridge: Cambridge Univ. Press, 1956.

Haas, Willy. Afterword to *Briefe an Milena,* by Franz Kafka, edited by Willy Haas. Frankfurt a. M.: Fischer, 1952.

Hackermüller, Rotraut. *Kafkas letzte Jahre 1917–1924.* Munich: P. Kirchheim, 1990.

Heller, Erich. "The World of Franz Kafka." In *Twentieth-Century Interpretations of "The Castle",* edited by Peter F. Neumeyer, 57–82.

Hesse, Otto Erich. "Franz Kafka, In der Strafkolonie." In *Franz Kafka: Kritik und Rezeption zu seinen Lebzeiten 1912–1924,* edited by Jürgen Born, 97. Frankfurt a. M.: Fischer, 1979. Originally published in 1921.

Hockaday, Mary. *Kafka, Love, and Courage: The Life of Milena Jesenská.* London: André Deutsch, 1995.

Hughes, Kenneth, ed. *Franz Kafka: An Anthology of Marxist Criticism.* Hanover, NH: Univ. Press of New England, 1981.

Jahn, Wolfgang. *Kafkas Roman "Der Verschollene" ("Amerika").* Stuttgart: Metzler, 1965.

————. "*Der Verschollene (Amerika).*" In *Kafka-Handbuch,* edited by Hartmut Binder, 2:407–20.

Janouch, Gustav. *Gespräche mit Kafka* (Conversations with Kafka). 2nd ed. Frankfurt a. M.: Fischer, 1968.

Kaiser, Hellmuth. "Franz Kafkas Inferno: Eine psychologische Deutung seiner Strafphantasie." *Imago* 17 (1931): 41–103.

Kisch, Guido. "Kafka-Forschung auf Irrwegen." *Zeitschrift für Religions- und Geistesgeschichte* 23 (1971): 339–50.

Kittler, Wolf. "Schreibmaschinen, Sprechmaschinen. Effekte technischer Medien im Werk Franz Kafkas." In *Franz Kafka: Schriftverkehr,* edited by Wolf Kittler and Gerhard Neumann, 75–163.

Kittler, Wolf, and Gerhard Neumann, eds. *Franz Kafka: Schriftverkehr.* Freiburg: Rombach, 1990.

Kobs, Jörgen. *Kafka: Untersuchungen zu Bewußtsein und Sprache seiner Gestalten,* edited by Ursula Brech. Bad Homburg: Athenäum, 1970.

Koelb, Clayton. "'In der Strafkolonie': Kafka and the Scene of Reading." *German Quarterly* 55 (1982): 511–25.

Krusche, Dietrich. "Die kommunikative Funktion der Deformation klassischer Motive: 'Der Jäger Gracchus': Zur Problematik der Kafka-Interpretation," *Der Deutschunterricht* 25 (1973): 128–40.

Kuna, F. M. "Art as Direct Vision: Kafka and Sacher-Masoch." *Journal of European Studies* 2 (1972): 237–46.

Kurz, Gerhard, "Figuren." In *Kafka-Handbuch,* edited by Hartmut Binder, 2:108–30

————, ed. *Der junge Kafka.* Frankfurt a. M.: Suhrkamp, 1984.

————. *Traum-Schrecken: Kafkas literarische Existenzanalyse.* Stuttgart: Metzler, 1980.

Leahy, Caitriona. "Reisen in einem Zimmer, oder: die Wände hochgehen." In *Reisen im Diskurs: Modelle der literarischen Fremderfahrung von den Pilgerberichten bis zur Postmoderne,* edited by Ann Fuchs and Theo Harden, 87–101.

Loose, Gerhard. *Franz Kafka und Amerika.* Frankfurt a. M.: Klostermann, 1968.

Lukács, Georg. "Franz Kafka oder Thomas Mann?" In *Wider den Mißverstandenen Realismus* (The meaning of contemporary realism), 49–96. Hamburg: Claasen, 1958.

Miles, David. "'Pleats, Pockets, Buckles and Buttons': Kafka's New Literalism and the Poetics of the Fragment." In *Probleme der Moderne,* edited by B. Bennett, A. Kaes, and W. J. Lillyman, 331–42. Tübingen: Niemeyer, 1983.

Müller-Seidel, Walter. *Die Deportation der Menschen: Kafkas Erzählung "In der Strafkolonie" im europäischen Kontext.* Stuttgart: Metzler, 1986.

Nagel, Bert. *Kafka und Goethe: Stufen der Wandlung von der Klassik zur Moderne.* Berlin: Schmidt, 1977.

Nägele, Rainer. "Auf der Suche nach dem verlorenen Paradies: Versuch einer Interpretation zu Kafkas 'Der Jäger Gracchus.'" *German Quarterly* 47 (1974): 60–72.

Neider, Charles. *The Frozen Sea: A Study of Franz Kafka.* New York: Oxford Univ. Press, 1948.

Neumann, Gerhard. "Kafka's 'Schloß'-Roman: Das parasitäre Spiel der Zeichen." In *Franz Kafka: Schriftverkehr,* edited by Wolf Kittler and Gerhard Neumann, 199–221.

————. *"Das Urteil": Text, Materialien, Kommentar.* Munich: Carl Hanser, 1981.

Neumeyer, Peter F. "Franz Kafka, Sugar Baron." *Modern Fiction Studies* 17 (Spring 1971): 5–16.

————, ed. *Twentieth-Century Interpretations of "The Castle."* Englewood Cliffs, NJ: Prentice Hall, 1969.

Norris, Margot. *Beasts of the Modern Imagination: Darwin, Nietzsche, Kafka, Ernst, & Lawrence.* Baltimore: Johns Hopkins Univ. Press, 1985.

Northey, Anthony. *Kafka's Relatives: Their Lives and His Writing.* New Haven: Yale Univ. Press, 1991.

————. "Myths and Realities in Kafka Biography." In *The Cambridge Companion to Kafka,* edited by Julian Preece, 189–205.

Pasley, Malcolm. "The Act of Writing and the Genesis of Kafka's Manuscripts." In *Reading Kafka: Prague, Politics and the Fin de Siècle,* edited by Mark Anderson, 201–14.

———. "Kafka als Reisender." In *Was bleibt von Franz Kafka? Positionsbestimmung Kafka-Symposium Wien 1983,* edited by Wendelin Schmidt-Dengler, 1–15. Vienna: Braumüller, 1985.

Peters, Paul. "Witness to the Execution: Kafka and Colonialism." *Monatshefte* 93 (2001): 401–425.

Phillipi, K.-P. *Reflexion und Wirklichkeit: Untersuchungen zu Kafkas Roman "Das Schloß."* Tübingen: Niemeyer, 1966.

Piper, Karen. "The Language of the Machine: Kafka and the Subject of Empire." *Journal of the Kafka Society of America* 20 (1996): 42–54.

Politzer, Heinz. *Franz Kafka, der Künstler.* Frankfurt a. M.: Fischer, 1965. Originally published in English in 1962.

Preece, Julian, ed. *The Cambridge Companion to Kafka.* Cambridge: Cambridge Univ. Press, 2002.

Pütz, Jürgen. *Kafkas* Verschollener—*ein Bildungsroman.* Frankfurt a. M.: Peter Lang, 1983.

Rhine, Marjorie. "'Post'-Modernity in Kafka's *Briefe an Felice.*" *Journal of the Kafka Society of America* 18 (1994): 35–40.

Rickels, Laurence. "Writing as Travel and Travail: *Der Prozeß* and 'In der Strafkolonie.'" *Journal of the Kafka Society of America* 5 (1985): 32–40.

Robert, Marthe. *L'ancien et le nouveau, de Don Quichotte à Franz Kafka* (The old and the new: from Don Quixote to Kafka). Paris: B. Grasset, 1963.

Robertson, Ritchie. *Kafka: Judaism, Politics, Literature.* Oxford: Clarendon, 1985.

———. "*Der Proceß.*" In *Franz Kafka: Romane und Erzählungen,* edited by Michael Müller, 98–145. Stuttgart: Reclam, 1994.

Rodlauer, Hannelore. "'Ansichten eines Exterritorialen': Albert Ehrenstein und Franz Kafka," in *Expressionismus in Österreich,* ed. Klaus Amann and Armin A. Wallas, 225–52. Vienna: Böhlau, 1994.

———. "Kafkas Paris." *Etudes Germaniques* 39 (1984): 140–151.

———. "Kafkas Pariser Tagebuch." Ph.D. diss., Vienna, 1984.

———. "Die Paralleltagebücher Kafka-Brod und das Modell Flaubert." *Arcadia* 20 (1985): 47–60.

Rolleston, James, ed. *A Companion to the Works of Franz Kafka.* Rochester, NY: Camden House, 2002.

———. "Die Romane: Ansätze der Frühzeit." In *Kafka-Handbuch,* edited by Hartmut Binder. 2:402–7.

Schillemeit, Jost. "Mitteilungen und Nicht-Mitteilbares: Zur Chronologie der *Briefe an Milena* und zu Kafkas 'Schreiben' im Jahr 1920." *Jahrbuch des freien deutschen Hochstifts* (1988): 253–303.

Sebald, W. G. "The Undiscover'd Country: The Death Motif in Kafka's *Castle.*" *Journal of European Studies* 2 (1972): 22–34.

Sheppard, Richard. *On Kafka's Castle.* London: Croom Helm, 1973.

Sokel, Walter. "Franz Kafka, *Der Process* (1925)," In *Deutsche Romane des 20. Jahrhunderts,* edited by Paul Michael Lützeler, 110–27. Königstein: Athenäum, 1983.

———. *Franz Kafka.* New York: Columbia Univ. Press, 1966.

————. *Franz Kafka—Tragik und Ironie: Zur Struktur seiner Kunst* (Franz Kafka: tragedy and irony). Munich and Vienna: Langen and Müller, 1964.

Sonnenfeld, Marion. "Die Fragmente 'Amerika' and 'Der Prozeß' als Bildungsromane," *German Quarterly* 35 (1962): 34–46.

Spector, Scott. *Prague Territories: National Conflict and Cultural Innovation in Franz Kafka's Fin de Siècle.* Berkeley: Univ. of California Press, 2000.

Spilka, Mark. *Dickens and Kafka: A Mutual Interpretation.* Bloomington: Indiana Univ. Press, 1963.

Stach, Rainer. *Kafkas erotischer Mythos: Eine ästhetische Konstruktion des Weiblichen.* Frankfurt a. M.: Fischer, 1987.

Stölzl, Christoph. "Prag: Die Verhältnisse um 1900." In *Kafka-Handbuch,* edited by Hartmut Binder, 1:40–100.

Suchoff, David. *Critical Theory and the Novel: Mass Society and Cultural Criticism in Dickens, Melville, and Kafka.* Madison: Univ. of Wisconsin Press, 1994.

Theweleit, Klaus. "Gespensterposten. Briefverkehr, Liebesverkehr, Eisenbahnverkehr. Der Zug ins Jenseits: Orpheus 1913 in Prag." In *buch der könige,* vol. 1 (orpheus ~~und~~ eurydike), 976–1055. Basel: Stroemfeld, 1988.

Thiher, Allen. *Franz Kafka: A Study of the Short Fiction.* Boston: Twayne Publishers, 1990.

————. "The *Nachlaß:* Metaphors of *Gehen* and Ways Toward Science." In *Kafka and the Comtemporary Critical Performance,* edited by Alan Udoff, 256–65.

Tucholsky, Kurt [Peter Panter, pseud.]. "In der Strafkolonie." *Die Weltbühne,* June 3, 1920. Rpt. in *Franz Kafka: Kritik und Rezeption zu seinen Lebzeiten 1912–1924,* edited by Jürgen Born, 93–96. Frankfurt a. M.: Fischer, 1979.

Udoff, Alan, ed. *Kafka and the Contemporary Critical Performance.* Bloomington: Indiana Univ. Press, 1987.

Vogl, Josef. *Ort der Gewalt: Kafkas literarische Ethik.* Munich: Fink, 1990.

Wagenbach, Klaus. *Franz Kafka: Bilder aus seinem Leben.* Berlin: Wagenbach, 1994.

————. *Franz Kafka: Eine Biographie seiner Jugend.* Bern: Francke, 1958.

————, ed. Franz Kafka. *In der Strafkolonie. Eine Geschichte aus dem Jahre 1914. Mit Quellen, Abbildungen, Materialien aus der Arbeiter-Unfall-Versicherungsanstalt, Chronik und Anmerkungen von Klaus Wagenbach.* Berlin: Wagenbach, 1995. Expanded version of original, 1975 edition.

————. *Kafkas Prag: Ein Reiselesebuch* (Kafka's Prague: A travel reader). Berlin: Wagenbach, 1993.

————. "Prague at the Turn of the Century." In *Reading Kafka: Prague, Politics, and the Fin de Siècle,* edited by Mark Anderson, 25–54.

Walser, Martin. *Beschreibung einer Form.* Munich: Hanser, 1961.

Weltsch, Felix. *Religion und Humor im Leben und Werk Franz Kafkas.* Berlin: F. A. Herbig, 1957.

Wilke, Sabine. "'Der Elbogen ruhte auf dem Kissen der Ottomane': Über die sadomasochistischen Wurzeln von Kafkas *Der Process.*" *Journal of the Kafka Society of America* 21 (1997): 67–78.

Winkelman, John. "An Interpretation of Kafka's 'Das Schloß.'" *Monatshefte* 64 (1972): 115–31.

Wirkner, Alfred. *Kafka und die Außenwelt: Quellenstudien zum 'Amerika'-Fragment.* Stuttgart: E. Klett, 1976.

Zilcosky, John. "Franz Kafka, Perverse Traveler: Flaubert, Kafka, and the Travel Writing Tradition." *Journal of the Kafka Society of America* 23 (1997): 80–87

———. "Of Sugar Barons and Banana Kings: Franz Kafka, Imperialism, and Schaffsteins' *Grüne Bändchen.*" *Journal of the Kafka Society of America* 22 (1996): 63–75.

Zischler, Hanns. *Kafka geht ins Kino.* Hamburg: Rowohlt, 1996.

3. Secondary Sources on Travel and General Topics

Abraham, Karl. *Psychoanalytische Studien.* Edited by Johannes Cremerius. 2 vols. Frankfurt a. Main: Fischer, 1971.

Adorno, Theodor, and Max Horkheimer. *Dialektik der Aufklärung: Philosophische Fragmente* (Dialectic of enlightenment). Frankfurt a. M.: Fischer, 1969.

Alloula, Malek. *The Colonial Harem.* Translated by Myrna and Wlad Godzich. Minneapolis: Univ. of Minnesota Press, 1986.

Althusser, Louis. *Lenin and Philosophy.* Translated by Ben Brewster. New York: Monthly Review Press, 1971.

Appadurai, Arjun. *Modernity at Large: Cultural Dimensions of Globalization.* Minneapolis: Univ. of Minnesota Press, 1996.

Auden, W. H., and Elizabeth Mayer. Introduction to *Italian Journey,* by Johann Wolfgang von Goethe, 7–19. Translated by W. H. Auden and Elizabeth Mayer. New York: Penguin, 1970.

Bahr, Wolfgang. *Tote auf Reisen: Ein makabrer Reisebegleiter.* Vienna: NP Buchverlag, 2000.

Barner, Wilfried. "Jüdische Goethe-Verehrung vor 1933." In *Juden in der deutschen Literatur: Ein deutsch-israelisches Symposion,* edited by Stéphane Moses and Albrecht Schöne, 127–51. Frankfurt a. M.: Suhrkamp, 1986.

Barrell, John. *English Literature in History 1730–80: An Equal, Wide Survey.* New York: St. Martin's, 1983.

Barthes, Roland. *Camera Lucida.* Translated by Richard Howard. New York: Hill and Wang, 1981.

———. *Empire of Signs.* Translated by Richard Howard. London: Cape, 1983.

———. *Sade, Fourier, Loyola.* Translated by Richard Miller. New York: Hill and Wang, 1976.

Baudrillard, Jean. *Symbolic Exchange and Death.* Translated by Ian Hamilton Grant. London: Sage, 1993.

Bauman, Zygmunt. *Modernity and Ambivalence.* Ithaca, NY: Cornell Univ. Press, 1991.

Behdad, Ali. *Belated Travelers: Orientalism in the Age of Colonial Dissolution.* Durham, NC: Duke Univ. Press, 1994.

Benjamin, Walter. "Berliner Chronik" (A Berlin chronicle). In *Gesammelte Schriften* 6:465–519, edited by Rolf Tiedemann and Hermann Schweppenhäuser. Frankfurt a. M.: Suhrkamp [1972–89].

————. "Einbahnstraße" (One way street). In *Gesammelte Schriften* 4(1):83–148. Frankfurt a. M.: Suhrkamp, [1972–89].

————. "Das Kunstwerk im Zeitalter seiner technischen Reproduzierbarkeit" (The work of art in the age of mechanical reproduction) (2. Fassung), in *Gesammelte Schriften* 7(1):350–84. Frankfurt a. M.: Suhrkamp, [1972–89].

————. "Über den Begriff der Geschichte" (Theses on the philosophy of history), in *Gesammelte Schriften* 1(2):691–704. Frankfurt a. M.: Suhrkamp, [1972–89].

Berman, Russell. *Enlightenment or Empire: Colonial Discourse in German Culture.* Lincoln: Univ. of Nebraska Press, 1998.

Beyerl, Beppo. "Der Weg alles Irdischen: Einige Geschichten vom Sterben und Begrabenwerden." *Wiener Zeitung,* November 3, 2000.

Bhabha, Homi. *The Location of Culture.* New York: Routledge, 1994.

————. "The Other Question: The Stereotype and Colonial Discourse," *Screen* 24 (November–December 1983): 18–36.

Blanchot, Maurice. "Literature and the Right to Death." In *The Gaze of Orpheus,* translated by Lydia Davis and edited by P. Adams Sitney, 21–62. Barrytown, NY: Station Hill, 1981.

Bongie, Chris. *Exotic Memories: Literature, Colonialism, and the Fin de Siècle.* Stanford: Stanford Univ. Press, 1991.

Bradbury, Malcolm, and James McFarlane, eds. *Modernism: 1890–1930.* Harmondsworth: Penguin, 1976.

Brenner, Peter J. *Der Reisebericht in der deutschen Literatur: Ein Forschungsüberblick als Vorstudie zu einer Gattungsgeschichte.* Tübingen: Niemeyer, 1990.

————, ed. *Der Reisebericht: Die Entwicklung einer Gattung in der deutschen Literatur.* Frankfurt a. M.: Suhrkamp, 1989.

————, "Schwierige Reisen: Wandlungen des Reiseberichts in Deutschland 1918–1945." In *Reisekultur in Deutschland: Von der Weimarer Republik zum "Dritten Reich,"* edited by Peter J. Brenner, 127–76. Tübingen: Niemeyer, 1997.

Bruneau, Jean. *Le "Conte Orientale" de Flaubert.* Paris: Denöel, 1973.

Buch, Hans Christoph. *Die Nähe und die Ferne: Bausteine zu einer Poetik des kolonialen Blicks.* Frankfurt a. M.: Suhrkamp, 1991.

Butler, Judith. *Gender Trouble: Feminism and the Subversion of Identity.* New York: Routledge, 1990.

————. *The Psychic Life of Power: Theories in Subjection.* Stanford: Stanford Univ. Press, 1997.

Buzard, James. *The Beaten Track: European Tourism, Literature, and the Ways to Culture, 1800–1918.* Oxford: Clarendon, 1993.

Canetti, Elias. *Masse und Macht* (Crowds and power). Frankfurt a. M.: Fischer, 1996.

Cersowsky, Peter. *Phantastische Literatur im ersten Viertel des 20. Jahrhunderts.* Munich: Fink, 1983.

Chard, Chloe. "Effeminacy, Pleasure and the Classical Body." In *Femininity and Masculinity in Eighteenth-Century Art and Culture,* edited by Gill Perry and Michael Rossington. Manchester: Manchester Univ. Press, 1994. 142–61.

————. *Pleasure and Guilt on the Grand Tour: Travel Writing and Imaginative Geography, 1600–1830.* Manchester: Manchester Univ. Press, 1999.

Chard, Chloe, and Helen Langdon, eds. *Transports: Travel, Pleasure, and Imaginative Geography, 1600–1830*. New Haven: Yale Univ. Press, 1996.

Christiansen, Franziska. "Scheintod und Scheintodängste." In *Tod und Gesellschaft—Tod im Wandel*, edited by Christoph Daxelmüller, 77–79.

Clifford, James. *The Predicament of Culture: Twentieth-Century Ethnography, Literature, and Art*. Cambridge: Harvard Univ. Press, 1988.

———. "Traveling Cultures." In *Cultural Studies*, edited by Laurence Grossberg, Cary Nelson, and Paula Treichler, 96–116. New York: Routledge, 1992.

Corngold, Stanley. *Complex Pleasure: Forms of Feeling in German Literature*. Stanford: Stanford Univ. Press, 1998.

Cowley, Malcolm. *Exile's Return: A Literary Odyssey of the 1920s*. Harmondsworth: Penguin, 1982.

Culler, Jonathan. *Framing the Sign: Criticism and Its Institutions*. Norman: Univ. of Oklahoma Press, 1988.

Davis, Fred. *Yearning for Yesterday: A Sociology of Nostalgia*. New York: Free Press, 1979.

Daxelmüller, Christoph, ed. *Tod und Gesellschaft—Tod im Wandel*. Regensburg: Schnell & Steiner, 1996.

Deleuze, Gilles. "Coldness and Cruelty." In *Masochism*, 9–138. New York: Zone Books, 1991.

Derrida, Jacques. "Living On / Border Lines." Translated by James Hulbert. In Harold Bloom et al., *Deconstruction and Criticism*, 75–176. New York: Seabury, 1979.

———. *The Post Card: From Socrates to Freud and Beyond*. Translated by Alan Bass. Chicago: Univ. of Chicago Press, 1987.

Downing, Eric. "Dead Woman Walking: Jensen's 'Gradiva.'" Paper presented at the annual meeting of the American Comparative Literature Association, San Juan, Puerto Rico, April 2002.

Dumesnil, René. Introduction to *Voyages,* by Gustave Flaubert. Vol. 1. Edited by René Dumesnil. Paris: Société les Belles Lettres, 1948.

Ellmann, Maud. "The Ghosts of Ulysses." In *James Joyce: The Artist and the Labyrinth*, edited by Augustin Martin, 193–228. London: Ryan, 1990.

Enzensberger, Hans-Magnus. "Eine Theorie des Tourismus." In *Einzelheiten I: Bewusstseins-Industrie*, 179–205. Frankfurt a. M.: Suhrkamp, 1964.

Foucault, Michel. *Histoire de la sexualité*. Vol 1 (The history of sexuality: An introduction). Paris: Gallimard, 1976.

———. *Les Mots et les choses: Une archéologie des sciences humaines* (The order of things: An archaeology of the human sciences). Paris: Gallimard, 1966.

———. *L'ordre du discours* (The discourse on language). Paris: Gallimard, 1971.

Frank, Manfred. *Die unendliche Fahrt: Ein Motiv und sein Text*. Frankfurt a. M.: Suhrkamp, 1979.

Freud, Sigmund. *Bruchstücke einer Hysterie-Analyse*. In *Freud-Studienausgabe*, edited by Alexander Mitscherlich, Angela Richards, and James Strachey, 6:83–186. Frankfurt a. M.: Fischer, [1969–1975]. (*Fragment of an Analysis of a Case of Hysteria*. In *The Standard Edition of the Complete Psychological Works of Sigmund Freud*, edited by James Strachey, 7:1–122. London: Hogarth Press, [1953–74].)

————. *The Complete Letters of Sigmund Freud to Wilhelm Fliess, 1897–1904.* Translated by Jeffrey Moussaieff Masson. Cambridge: Harvard Univ. Press, 1985.

————. *Drei Abhandlungen zur Sexualtheorie* (Three essays on the theory of sexuality). In *Studieausgabe,* 5:37–145 (*Standard Edition,* 7:125–245).

————. *Jenseits des Lustprinzips* (Beyond the pleasure principle). In *Studienausgabe,* 3:213–272 (*Standard Edition,* 18:7–64).

————. *Die Traumdeutung* (The interpretation of dreams). Vol. 2 of *Studienausgabe* (vols. 4–5 of *Standard Edition*).

————. *Das Unbehagen in der Kultur* (Civilization and its discontents). In *Studienausgabe,* 9:191–270 (*Standard Edition,* 21:57–145).

————. "Das Unheimliche" (The uncanny). In *Studienausgabe* 4:241–274 (*Standard Edition,* 17:217–252).

————. *Vorlesungen zur Einführung in die Psychoanalyse* (Introductory lectures on psycho-analysis). In *Studienausgabe,* 1:34–447 (vols. 15–16 of *Standard Edition*).

Friedrichsmeyer, Sara, and Sara Lennox, and Susanne Zantop, eds. *The Imperialist Imagination: German Colonialism and Its Legacy.* Ann Arbor: Univ. of Michigan Press, 1998.

Fuchs, Anne, and Theo Harden, eds. *Reisen im Diskurs: Modelle der literarischen Fremderfahrung von den Pilgerberichten bis zur Postmoderne.* Heidelberg: Carl Winter Universitätsverlag, 1995.

Fussell, Paul. *Abroad: British Literary Traveling Between the Wars.* New York: Oxford Univ. Press, 1980.

Glaser, Hermann. *Literatur des 20. Jahrhunderts in Motiven.* Vol. 1 (1870–1918). Munich: C.H. Beck, 1978.

Goetschel, Willi. *Constituting Critique: Kant's Writing as Critical Praxis.* Translated by Eric Schwab. Durham, NC: Duke Univ. Press, 1994.

Göktürk, Deniz. *Künstler, Cowboys, Ingenieure . . .: Kultur- und mediengeschichtliche Studien zu deutschen Amerika-Texten 1912–1920.* Munich: Fink, 1998.

Goldstücker, Eduard. "Die Prager deutsche Literatur als historisches Phänomen." In *Weltfreunde. Konferenz über die Prager deutsche Literatur 1965,* edited by Eduard Goldstücker, 21–45. Prague: Luchterhand, 1967.

Greverus, Ina-Maria. *Der Territoriale Mensch: Ein literatur-anthropologischer Versuch zum Heimatphänomen.* Frankfurt a. M.: Athenäum, 1972.

Grivel, Charles. "Travel Writing." In *Materialities of Communication,* edited by Hans Ulrich Gumbrecht and K. Ludwig Pfeiffer, 242–57. Stanford: Stanford Univ. Press, 1994.

Gumbrecht, Hans Ulrich. *In 1926: Living at the Edge of Time.* Cambridge: Harvard Univ. Press, 1997.

Hamann Richard, and Jost Hermand. *Impressionismus.* 2d ed. Munich: Nymphenburger Verlagshandlung, 1974.

Hamm, Peter. "Ingeborg Bachman," *Die Zeit* 41 (2000).

Hammond, Theresa Mayer. *American Paradise: German Travel Literature from Duden to Kisch.* Heidelberg: Carl Winter Universitätsverlag, 1980.

Hegel, G. W. F. *Die Phänomenologie des Geistes* (Phenomenology of spirit). Edited by Hans-Friedrich Wessels and Heinrich Clairmont. Hamburg: Meiner, 1988.

Heidegger, Martin. "Bauen Wohnen Denken" (Building dwelling thinking). In *Vorträge und Aufsätze*. Pfullingen: Neske, 1954.

Hénaff, Marcel. *Sade: The Invention of the Libertine Body*. Translated by Xavier Callahan. Minneapolis: Univ. of Minnesota Press, 1999.

Hinrichsen, Alex W. *Baedeker-Katalog: Verzeichnis aller Baedeker-Reiseführer von 1832–1987*. Holzminden: Ursula Hinrichsen Verlag, 1988.

Hobson, J. A. *Imperialism: A Study*. Ann Arbor: Univ. of Michigan Press, 1965. Originally published in 1902.

Kaplan, Caren. *Questions of Travel: Postmodern Discourses of Displacement*. Durham, NC: Duke Univ. Press, 1996.

Kappeler, Susanne. *The Pornography of Representation*. Oxford: Polity Press, 1986.

Kaufmann, Vincent. *Post Scripts: The Writer's Workshop*. Translated by Deborah Treisman. Cambridge: Harvard Univ. Press, 1994.

Kittler, Friedrich. *Aufschreibesysteme 1800/1900* (Discourse networks 1800/1900). Rev. ed. Munich: Fink, 1987.

———. *Grammophon Film Typewriter* (Gramophone, film, typewriter). Berlin: Brinkmann & Böse, 1986.

Klüter, Heinz, ed. *Querschnitt durch die Gartenlaube*. Bern: Scherz, 1963.

Knispel, Franz. "Zur Überführung Verstorbener." *Der Österreichische Bestatter* 38 (April 1996): 44–50.

Knowlson, James. *Damned to Fame: The Life of Samuel Beckett*. New York: Simon & Schuster, 1996.

Kojève, Alexandre. *Introduction to the Reading of Hegel*. Translated by James H. Nichols. New York: Basic Books, 1969.

Koshar, Rudy. *German Travel Cultures*. New York: Berg, 2000.

Kubin, Wolfgang. *Mein Bild in Deinem Auge. Exotismus und Moderne: Deutschland— China im 20. Jahrhundert*. Darmstadt: Wissenschaftliche Buchgesellschaft, 1995.

Kundera, Milan. "Somewhere Beyond," *Cross-Currents* 3 (1984): 61–70.

Lowe, Lisa. *Critical Terrains: French and British Orientalisms*. Ithaca, NY: Cornell Univ. Press, 1991.

Maccagnani, Roberta. "Esotismo-erotismo—Pierre Loti: Dalla maschera erotica alla sovranità Coloniale." In *Letteratura, esotismo, colonialismo*, edited by Anita Licari, Roberta Maccagnani, and Lina Zecchi, 63–99. Bologna: Cappelli, 1978.

MacCannell, Dean. *The Tourist: A New Theory of the Leisure Class*. New York: Schocken, 1976.

Magill, Daniela. *Literarische Reisen in die exotische Fremde: Topoi der Darstellung von Eigen- und Fremdkultur*. Frankfurt a. M.: Peter Lang, 1989.

Maler, Anselm. *Der exotische Roman: bürgerliche Gesellschaftsflucht und Gesellschaftskritik zwischen Romantik und Realismus*. Stuttgart: E. Klett, 1975.

Marx, Karl. *Ökonomisch-philosophische Manuskripte* (Economic and philosophic manuscripts). In *Marx/Engels Gesamtausgabe*, edited by Institut für Marxismus-Leninismus, 1. Abteilung, vol. 2, 187–438. Berlin: Dietz, 1982.

Mitchell, Tim. *Colonising Egypt*. New York: Cambridge Univ. Press, 1988.

Mitford, Jessica. *The American Way of Death*. New York: Simon and Schuster, 1978.

Moses, Stéphane, and Albrecht Schöne, eds. *Juden in der deutschen Literatur.* Frankfurt a. M.: Suhrkamp, 1986.

Nägele, Rainer. "Introduction: Reading Benjamin." In *Benjamin's Ground: New Readings of Walter Benjamin,* edited by Rainer Nägele, 7–18. Detroit: Wayne State Univ. Press, 1988.

Nietzsche, Friedrich. *Jenseits von Gut und Böse: Vorspiel einer Philosophie der Zukunft* (Beyond good and evil: Prelude to a philosophy of the future). In *Kritische Gesamtausgabe,* edited by Giorgio Colli and Mazzino Montinari, 6. Abteilung, vol. 2. Berlin: de Gruyter, 1968.

———. *Zur Genealogie der Moral* (On the genealogy of morals). In *Kritische Gesamtausgabe,* edited by Giorgio Colli and Mazzino Montinari, 6. Abteilung, vol. 2. Berlin: de Gruyter, 1968.

Noyes, John. *The Mastery of Submission: Inventions of Masochism.* Ithaca, NY: Cornell Univ. Press, 1997.

———. "National Identity, Nomadism, and Narration in Gustav Frenssen's *Peter Moor's Journey to Southwest Africa.*" In *The Imperialist Imagination: German Colonialism and Its Legacy,* edited by Sara Friedrichsmeyer, Sara Lennox, and Susanne Zantop, 87–105. Ann Arbor: Univ. of Michigan Press, 1998.

Percy, Walker. *The Message in the Bottle.* New York: Farrar, Strauss, 1975.

Porter, Dennis. "The Perverse Traveler: Flaubert's *Voyage en Orient.*" *L'Esprit Créateur* 29 (1989): 24–36.

Poulantzas, Nicos. *State, Power, Socialism.* Translated by Patrick Camiller. London: NLB, 1978.

Pratt, Mary Louise. *Imperial Eyes: Travel Writing and Transculturation.* New York: Routledge, 1992.

———. "Scratches on the Face of the Country; or, What Mr. Barrow Saw in the Land of the Bushmen." *Critical Inquiry* 12 (Autumn 1985): 119–43.

Rabinow, Paul. "Representations are Social Facts: Modernity and Post-Modernity in Anthropology." In *Writing Culture,* edited by James Clifford and George E. Markus, 234–61. Berkeley: Univ. of California Press, 1986.

Reif, Wolfgang. "Exotismus im Reisebericht des frühen 20. Jahrhunderts." In *Der Reisebericht: Die Entwicklung einer Gattung in der deutschen Literatur,* edited by Peter J. Brenner, 434–62.

———. *Zivilisationsflucht und literarische Wunschräume: Der exotistische Roman im ersten Viertel des 20. Jahrhunderts.* Stuttgart: Metzler, 1975.

Reik, Theodor. *Aus Leiden Freuden: Masochismus und Gesellschaft* (Masochism in modern man). Hamburg: Hoffmann und Campe, 1977. Originally published in 1940.

Richards, I. A. *The Philosophy of Rhetoric.* New York: Oxford Univ. Press, 1936.

Riedel, Heinz, "Eisenbahnwaggons für Totentransporte." *Der Österreichische Bestatter* 33 (August 1991): 108–12.

Rosaldo, Renato. *Culture and Truth: The Remaking of Social Analysis.* Boston: Beacon Press, 1993.

Said, Edward. *Culture and Imperialism.* New York: Knopf, 1993.

———. *Orientalism.* New York: Vintage, 1979.

Saper, Craig. *Artificial Mythologies: A Guide to Cultural Invention.* Minneapolis: Univ. of Minnesota Press, 1997.

Sartre, Jean-Paul. *L'idiot de la famille: Gustave Flaubert de 1821 à 1857.* 2 vols. Paris: Gallimard, 1988.

————. Preface to *The Wretched of the Earth,* by Frantz Fanon, 7–31. Translated by Constance Farrington. New York: Grove Weidenfeld, 1963.

Schivelbusch, Wolfgang. *The Railway Journey: The Industrialization of Time and Space in the 19th Century.* Berkeley: Univ. of California Press, 1986.

Schneider, Cornelia. "Die Bilderbuchproduktion der Verlage Jos. Scholz (Mainz) and Schaffstein (Köln) in den Jahren 1899 bis 1932." Ph.D. diss., Frankfurt a. M., 1984.

Scholdt, Günther. *Der Fall Norbert Jacques: Über Rang und Niedergang eines Erzählers (1880–1954).* Stuttgart: Akademischer Verlag Heinz, 1976.

Schulte-Sasse, Jochen. "Karl Mays Amerika-Exotik und deutsche Wirklichkeit: Zur sozialpsychologischen Funktion von Trivialliteratur im wilhelminischen Deutschland." In *Karl May,* edited by Helmut Schmiedt, 101–29. Frankfurt a. M.: Suhrkamp, 1983.

Siegert, Bernhard. *Relais: Geschicke der Literatur als Epoche der Post, 1751–1913* (Relays: Literature as an epoch of the postal system). Berlin: Brinkmann & Böse, 1993.

Silverman, Kaja. *Male Subjectivity at the Margins.* New York: Routledge, 1992.

Skinner, Quentin. *Foundations of Modern Political Thought.* 2 Vols. New York: Cambridge Univ. Press, 1978.

Sokel, Walter. *The Writer in Extremis: Expressionism in Twentieth-Century Literature.* Stanford, CA: Stanford Univ. Press, 1959.

Spivak, Gayatri, et al. "Discussion [of Stanley Corngold's 'Consternation: the Anthropological Moment in Literature']." In *Literature and Anthropology,* edited by Jonathan Hall and Ackbar Abbas, 189–96. Hong Kong: Hong Kong Univ. Press, 1986.

Spurr, David. *The Rhetoric of Empire: Colonial Discourse in Journalism, Travel Writing, and Imperial Administration.* Durham, NC: Duke Univ. Press, 1993.

Stableford, Brian. Introduction to *Torture Garden,* by Octave Mirbeau. Translated by Michael Richardson. Sawtry, Cambs, England: Dedalus, 1995.

Staples, Brent. "Unearthing a Riot." *New York Times Magazine,* December 19, 1999.

Terdimann, Richard. *Discourse/Counter-Discourse: The Theory and Practice of Symbolic Resistance in Nineteenth-Century France.* Ithaca, NY: Cornell Univ. Press, 1985.

Van Den Abbeele, Georges. "Sightseers: The Tourist as Theorist." *Diacritics* 10 (December 1980): 2–14.

Wilke, Sabine. "The Colonial Pedagogy of Imperial Germany: Hegelian Dialectics, Hermeneutics, and Masochism." In *Competing Imperialisms,* edited by Elizabeth Sauer. Forthcoming.

Wittmann, Rebecca. "Holocaust on Trial: The Frankfurt Auschwitz Trial in Historical Perspective." Ph.D. diss., Univ. of Toronto, 2001.

Wittgenstein, Ludwig. *Tractatus Logico-Philosophicus* (bilingual edition). London: Routledge & Keegan Paul, 1961.

Zantop, Susanne. *Colonial Fantasies: Conquest, Family, and Nation in Precolonial Germany, 1770–1870.* Durham, NC: Duke Univ. Press, 1997.

Kafka's Travels Index